South

of

Superior

South

of

Superior

Ellen Airgood

RIVERHEAD BOOKS

A member of Penguin Group (USA) Inc.

New York

2011

June 2011

RIVERHEAD BOOKS
Published by the Penguin Group
Penguin Group (USA) Inc., 375 Hudson Street, New York,
New York 10014, USA • Penguin Group (Canada), 90 Eglinton Avenue East,
Suite 700, Toronto, Ontario M4P 2Y3, Canada (a division of Pearson Penguin
Canada Inc.) • Penguin Books Ltd, 80 Strand, London WC2R 0RL,
England • Penguin Ireland, 25 St Stephen's Green, Dublin 2, Ireland (a division
of Penguin Books Ltd) • Penguin Group (Australia), 250 Camberwell Road,
Camberwell, Victoria 3124, Australia (a division of Pearson Australia Group
Pty Ltd) • Penguin Books India Pvt Ltd, 11 Community Centre, Panchsheel Park,
New Delhi–110 017, India • Penguin Group (NZ), 67 Apollo Drive, Rosedale,
North Shore 0632, New Zealand (a division of Pearson New Zealand Ltd) •
Penguin Books (South Africa) (Pty) Ltd, 24 Sturdee Avenue,
Rosebank, Johannesburg 2196, South Africa

Penguin Books Ltd, Registered Offices: 80 Strand, London WC2R 0RL, England

Library of Congress Cataloging-in-Publication Data

Airgood, Ellen.
South of superior / Ellen Airgood.
p.   cm.
ISBN 978-1-59448-793-4
1. Self-realization in women—Fiction.   2. Michigan—Fiction.   I. Title.
PS3601.I74S68   2011   2011003673
813'.6—dc22

Printed in the United States of America
1   3   5   7   9   10   8   6   4   2

BOOK DESIGN BY AMANDA DEWEY

This is a work of fiction. Names, characters, places, and incidents either
are the product of the author's imagination or are used fictitiously, and any
resemblance to actual persons, living or dead, businesses, companies,
events, or locales is entirely coincidental.

While the author has made every effort to provide accurate telephone numbers
and Internet addresses at the time of publication, neither the publisher nor
the author assumes any responsibility for errors, or for changes that occur after
publication. Further, the publisher does not have any control over and does not
assume any responsibility for author or third-party websites or their content.

For my father,
Henry Sines Airgood,
who would have been so proud

South

of

Superior

Prologue

The letter from Gladys Hansen was written in blue ink in an angular hand, on one sheet of plain white paper.

Dear Madeline Stone, it began,
I have thought to write to you for quite some while. I didn't because I supposed you wouldn't appreciate it, that you'd think it wasn't my place. I should have gone ahead and written anyhow.

I was sorry to hear of Emmy's passing. I know she was your mother, much more than Jackie Stone ever could've been. It is a hard loss, of someone so close. I expect you are at sea still without her—a year is not really long in the scheme of things. I won't say it was for the best or any of that. It can never feel right to lose someone so dear.

Emmy wrote me now and then, I don't know if you knew. She told me about the cancer, and how you helped her. She always said she wanted there to be some link for you up north, a door open if you wanted it. I should have done better with that.

I am writing now because I need help. My sister, Arbutus,

has taken a bad turn. She's crippled up with the arthritis and since she fell this last time she can hardly get around at all. We are here in Chicago where you are, staying with my nephew Nathan. Moving in with him seemed like the only thing to do, but it is no good. Butte has hardly stirred from her chair since we got here, she says it is too much trouble. This isn't home and if we don't get home I swear she will be dead before many more months are gone.

What I need is someone to come back up north with us, someone to live in, to lift and bathe her and so forth, someone young and strong to help with whatever is needed. At least for a while. I hope you won't take this amiss but I know that you know how to do this. I thought you might come and help us. And I thought that maybe you should see where your people came from. Maybe it's time.

I would pay a small wage, not much I'm afraid, but there would be your room and board included. There is nothing much to buy up home, so if you had a mind to you could live cheap. Let me know your answer soon. If you say no I will have to think of something else. Nathan seems restless now at having us here and I am afraid he will put Arbutus in a home. I cannot stand to think of that. Please do come.

> *Yours truly,*
> *Gladys Hansen*

Madeline had opened the letter as she came in the door from work, and now she stood in the entryway, still wearing her pink waitress dress that smelled faintly of fryer grease, gazing at it in astonishment. This from the woman who had been her grandfather's—what? Lady-friend? Paramour? Lover?—the estranged grandfather who'd abandoned Madeline to her fate more than thirty years ago. She'd only been three years old. Cards had come like clockwork on her birthday and at Christmas, always with a five-dollar bill taped inside, written in this same hand: *Best Wishes from Joe Stone and Gladys Hansen*, the return address a post office box in McAllaster, Michigan. Those cards—answered only by a perfunctory thank you and then only because Emmy insisted—had been the sum total of her relationship with her grandfather.

Emmy had explained it all when Madeline was very small. Gladys was a good friend of Joe Stone's, and ladies often did do things like that, of the two in a couple—sent the cards, remembered the birthdays. Emmy explained also that Madeline's grandfather was just too old and set in his ways to look after a little girl, which was why the two of them were so lucky, to be able to live together in Chicago. The lucky part was true, but the part about Madeline's grandfather was a polite fiction, and she wasn't very old at all when she understood that.

What her grandfather was in reality was a heartless, irresponsible bastard. Of course someone as kindhearted as Emmy would never have said anything so blunt, not to a child. Not even to an adult. They'd disagreed about it when Madeline got old enough— Emmy counseling Madeline to be forgiving, not to harbor such bitterness, Madeline telling Emmy in the sharp way of the young not to be naïve and soft. Eventually—well, after Emmy got so sick— they'd agreed to disagree and left the topic where it belonged, tucked away, not worth discussing. It was only at the end that Emmy brought it up again. *Promise me you'll try to forgive the man*, she'd said. *For your own sake.* Madeline had promised, not meaning it really, just wanting the worried look to leave Emmy's eyes, but in the end her insincerity didn't matter. She'd given her word to the person she loved most on earth, and against her will she began to feel obliged to live up to it. At least to make some stab at living up to it.

Those five-dollar bills Gladys Hansen sent stopped when Madeline turned twenty-one (to her relief—both the cards and money had made her uncomfortable; she still had them all, tucked into a box somewhere, the money unspent), but the cards kept coming, two a year, even after Joe Stone died. Nowadays they were just signed, with no message: *Gladys Hansen*.

And now this. It took a lot of nerve to ask. The idea was preposterous.

Madeline crumpled the letter into a ball and hurled it toward the wastebasket, but of course something so insubstantial—one frail piece of paper—couldn't carry off the gesture. It drifted to the floor a few feet short of its mark. Madeline left it there.

An hour later she was back in the entryway, frowning into the mirror, tugging at her slip. Richard—her boyfriend of three years and fiancé of six months—had said to dress up, they were going someplace fancy, and she had, but she resented the effort. It was a raw night, and she was not in the mood for strappy high heels and the skimpy, clingy red dress Richard had surprised her with on Valentine's Day. She sighed. The dress was ridiculous. She didn't have the figure for it, aside from her bosom, which was undoubtedly what he was thinking of when he chose it. She was a sturdy person, not very tall, top heavy, all-over muscular from her years of waiting table. *A serviceable person*, she thought, standing there in front of the wavy-glassed mirror.

Brown eyes stared back at her bleakly. A serviceable, capable person with a heart like a volcano, one that was spewing out a lava of rage and confusion and grief. Oh, no one would ever guess it. Her customers would never believe her capable of such fury and desolation, the unending baffled confusion she felt as to how to go on living without Emmy. She was like an animal who'd been blinded and maimed, clawing and flailing in a cage. She hid this well, she knew.

She was ever the sensible and steady one, the cheerful, dependable one, the one who made everyone laugh but always kept their orders straight. But beneath the surface, down in the tunnels of the real Madeline, a train wreck had happened. Madeline felt from moment to moment that there was no telling what she might do.

Her gaze caught the crumpled letter from Gladys Hansen. She stared it down for a moment. Let it lie there, damn it. But she couldn't. It was untidy, for one thing. Also it looked helpless. Helpless and reproachful. Madeline bent and picked the letter up, smoothed it out, propped it against the small lamp on the library table next to the door. Then she reached for the old navy peacoat she'd had since the fall she almost went to college—one thing she would not do was be cold all evening—and the doorbell rang and she buzzed Richard in.

1

Madeline left Chicago three weeks later, on a windy night in the middle of April. It hadn't taken long to arrange things, once she'd decided. Almost before she knew it she'd quit her job, packed her belongings, said her goodbyes, taken one last look at everything. Of course she'd be back eventually, but for now she was headed for the middle of nowhere.

The general consensus—and it was a popular topic at Spinelli's, where she'd worked for so many years—was that this was a terrible idea, she'd lost her judgment, and she was going to wake up in Timbuktu feeling very, very sorry. Richard (whom she'd met at Spinelli's, back when he was working on his dissertation and liked to come in with his laptop and sit at the counter drinking coffee for hours) thought that too, with a fury. The size of his anger had surprised Madeline, though it probably shouldn't have.

"Look," she'd told him toward the end of yet another argument about her decision. "Our plans—they're your plans, really."

"They're good plans," he fumed. "And we've practically signed the papers on the house. Why are you making things so complicated? All this upheaval—it's for nothing. You're afraid to actually live your own life, now that you can."

She couldn't tell him that the nearer it came, the idea of the life they were supposed to lead together in that sweet little Victorian a few blocks from campus—him teaching at Northwestern, her in art school finally, on his dime, their friends (his friends?) coming over for casually gourmet dinners that involved lots of talk about books and films and music—made her uneasy. Uneasy and curiously flat. Confined instead of secure, angry instead of happy. But then, she was angry almost all the time now.

Madeline stared at his craggy face, that shank of dark hair that fell over his eye. At first, when he was a doctoral student and she was a waitress who'd once dreamed of being an artist, the differences between them hadn't been so apparent. But that would change. It was already changing. They came from such different worlds.

Richard's parents still lived in his childhood home, six thousand square feet of elegance that required not one but two massive furnaces in the basement to heat it. Emmy, on the other hand, had struggled just to hang on to their not-huge, not-fancy apartment. She'd scrimped and saved to keep it all together, and that was what Madeline was used to. She wasn't sure she could glide across the tracks into Richard's world. Not and still be herself, whoever that was.

She bit her lip, her heart sinking. Then she said. "I'm sorry, but I am going. I have to. I'm not sure when I'll be back."

And suddenly there was nothing more to say. She gave his ring back. She'd been surprised at how relieved she felt when she called the bank to say that they wouldn't be buying the house after all.

Maybe everyone was right, maybe she was crazy. But the thing was, she had nothing to lose. That shouldn't have been so. Chicago was her home—Chicago, Spinelli's, the dear old drafty apartment Emmy'd bought before she ever took Madeline in, the neighborhood that was so familiar Madeline knew every angle and shadow by heart. There was her job, her friends, Richard, all their plans,

everything. But the emptiness inside was more real and more pressing than any of it.

So, she was going five hundred miles north to live with strangers,
taking nothing with her but her beloved cat Marley, a miscellaneous
assortment of bags and boxes containing sturdy, warm clothes and
a lot of books, mainly, and the Buick she'd inherited from Emmy.
The Buick. Emmy's folly. What a heap. She'd bought it, used, when
Madeline was a senior in high school. She'd had ideas of taking little
trips with it after Madeline was in college—up to Madison for an
annual bookkeepers' convention, to Milwaukee to tour the breweries,
to Decatur and Springfield and Hannibal on the trail of Laura Ingalls
Wilder. Small, innocent dreams. None of it had ever happened,
though they did drive up to Lake Winnebago every autumn to see
the fall colors. The rest of the time it sat in storage, gently decaying.

It was only running well enough to make this trip thanks to the
local mechanic who'd always tuned it up for them. Madeline had
been serving Pete Kinney runny eggs on rye toast for as long as she'd
been at Spinelli's, and he'd become a friend over the years. He was
also nearly the only person who didn't think Madeline was crazy
for leaving. He'd told her that he and his late wife had loved going
north, that he envied Madeline the adventure. So that's the line she
began to take with people: this was to be an adventure. And it was
to maybe fix what was broken in her, if anything could, but that fact
she kept to herself.

On the day of her departure, Madeline left Chicago after midnight, hoping to avoid traffic. She drove slowly—the car was old
and she was an inexperienced driver—but finally got through Green
Bay. After that the cities and traffic fell away, the towns got smaller
and shabbier and farther apart, and near dawn she crossed from
Wisconsin into Michigan and was on a narrow two-lane highway
that threaded through pines and cedars.

Lake Michigan crashed on shore to her right, acting wilder than it did in Chicago. She rolled down her window and sucked in the blustery air, and a shot of glee coursed through her, her excitement as involuntary as hunger. For better or worse, she was here. Before long her route curved north, away from Lake Michigan and toward Lake Superior, through more expanses of trees and swamps and scattered towns so small you hardly had time to notice you'd come into one before you were out again. She stopped often, as much to satisfy her curiosity as for the coffee, and her progress was slow, but she told herself that was all right. She could almost hear Emmy telling her to enjoy the journey, not to think ahead too much to its end.

At eleven fifteen she cruised through Crosscut—big enough to have a school and two gas stations and an auto supply store; not big enough for a McDonald's or a Pamida, which seemed to be the north's miniature version of Walmart—and turned north for the last leg of her journey. By noon she was approaching McAllaster, where Gladys Hansen and her sister Arbutus were waiting. It was just a dot on the map at the edge of Lake Superior, a tiny village settled for some reason that by now must be defunct—fur trading? fishing? lumber?—at a scoop in the shoreline called Desolation Bay. It was the edge of the earth. And her birthplace, though she remembered nothing of it. Jackie Stone had left when Madeline was a baby. It had never been anything but a hazy idea to her.

Suddenly, it was real. She came around a bend and over a small rise, and the lake and town appeared below her. It was as if the road had been unfurling for all these miles for just this purpose: to bring her to this spot.

The town sat at the base of a steep hill at the edge of the water, a lonely collection of buildings she could take in all in one glance from this distance. Huddled under the sleet that had been falling for hours, it looked stark and desolate. And beautiful. There was still snow on the ground—had been, for the last twenty miles—and small icebergs bobbed near shore, waves lashing over them. Madeline had read that Lake Superior was as big as the State of South Carolina. It looked like an ocean. Without it, McAllaster might have been any of the small, drab hamlets she'd driven through today. With it—and from this vantage point high above—the effect was somehow thrilling.

Madeline slowed to a stop and sat motionless at the wheel, her hands still carefully placed at the ten and two o'clock positions, staring. Even in the driving rain the lake glittered and shone with movement, with the mystery of its whole huge self. It dawned on her that everyone's cautions had been correct, even if for the wrong reasons. This was a foreign, otherworldly place, complete with magic and perils and tests.

Madeline spent a long moment gazing at the town. She understood in a way she hadn't before that if she drove down that hill, her life would change forever. Was it really too late to forget this idea? She shifted the car back into gear: of course it was. She had plenty of faults but being a coward wasn't one of them. She would not make herself ridiculous by turning back now, no matter what her misgivings. She cruised down the hill and pulled up in front of a grand old empty relic of a building—faded lettering above the second-floor windows proclaimed it "The Hotel Leppinen" but Madeline doubted anyone had stayed there in fifty years—and looked at Gladys Hansen's directions.

Pass the Hotel on Main, the note said. *Go left on Edsel two blocks, left again on Lake, and right on Bessel. Go just past the big hemlock that's cracking the sidewalk. We are the third house from the corner, number 26.* Madeline had read this a dozen times before she left. It hadn't seemed quite real. But now she was at the hotel and could see the sign for Edsel and there was no going back.

She started the Buick again. From high on the hill, the town had appeared mythical, a symbol of man's insignificance in the great scope of nature. Up close it was far more prosaic. She saw a hardware store, a grocery, a gas station, a bank, a bar, a few parked cars and pickups, and not one person. A dog trotted down the center of the street, as purposeful as a pedestrian out on errands. She turned left on Edsel and felt foolish for flicking on her blinker.

Number 26 Bessel was a small, elderly house covered in pebbly brown shingles. Lace curtains hung in the two windows that were centered on either side of the front door. Daffodils bloomed at the base of the steps and marched in a narrow row around the house's perimeter, and patches of grimy snow lay in shady places, but otherwise the yard was bare. It was a little forbidding—so spare and plain. Madeline sat very still, listening to the roar of the lake, the rain streaming on the car's roof, the sharp, solitary scream of a gull. This was a wide, wild quiet, so spacious it seemed endless, and she wondered how it might change a person.

"Are you going to sit there all day noodling, or are you getting out?" Gladys Hansen said, loud enough to be heard through the window, tapping on the glass.

"I'm coming—" But Gladys was already brisking away. Marley made an inquisitive mew and Madeline rubbed his ears. "We'll be fine," she said, hoping. She scooped him from the passenger's seat and followed in Gladys's wake. Details loomed up: the cement walk was cracked, the front door—which had already clacked shut behind Gladys—was red (this surprised her), the trim needed painting, the streaming rain fell straight off the eaves into the flower beds. The daffodils poking up through a scrim of snow and ice were getting battered, which seemed like a shame—and then Gladys was opening the door again and Madeline was going in.

2

Madeline stepped into a parlor that smelled faintly of moth-balls and looked frozen in time somewhere around 1950. "Thought you'd decided to set up camp out there," Gladys said, heading toward the back of the house. Madeline followed, uncertain this was the right thing to do but unable to think of an alternative.

"I'm tired, I guess," she said to Gladys's back. "It was a long drive."

"Nathan drove like a bat out of Hell in that fancy vehicle of his last weekend. I thought we'd all perish. I watched the speedometer, he had it up over eighty-five most of the way. He got us back here even faster than he took us down in the first place." Gladys gave Madeline a brief glance over her shoulder and Madeline thought her eyes were twinkling a little, but she couldn't be sure. "Arbutus has asked me fifteen times already when I thought you'd be here. You'd best come set her mind at ease."

They crossed into a kitchen that was broilingly warm. Arbutus was sitting at the table, her walker close by. Her face lit up. "Madeline! You're here. I'm so glad."

"Me too." Madeline went and gave Arbutus a hug and her trepidation eased some. Even if everything else was a bust, Arbutus was a good, legitimate reason to have come. She smiled to herself. God forbid she should ever do something for no particular reason at all, or a selfish reason, or a frivolous one. "How are you feeling?" she asked. "How was your trip last weekend?"

"I'm fine, dear. It's good to be home. I can't tell you how glad I am—"

"Do you want coffee?" Gladys broke in.

After a tiny pause Madeline said, "I'd love some." She was a guest here, she reminded herself. She'd just come. It was ridiculous to be so irritable that the least little thing, a tiny rudeness, made her want to lash out in frustration. She was tired, that was all. It had been a stressful three weeks getting ready, a big change. And it was going to *be* a change, *she* was going to change, she was no longer going to constantly feel like a wire stretched tight, about to snap.

Gladys poured the coffee and Madeline studied the room, stroking Marley to reassure him. The metal coffeepot had come off the back of a huge white porcelain range which had a stovepipe running up from its top—a woodstove. The floor was linoleum in a pattern of brown and green squares, and the table was blue Formica with stainless-steel legs. A kerosene lamp sat in its center, along with a ceramic salt and pepper set shaped like a hen and rooster. The cupboards were covered with coffee-colored paint and the counters were narrow, with a big porcelain sink built into them. The room had lived-in warmth that Madeline liked. She took the mug Gladys offered and ventured a smile, about to say so. "Sit down, why don't you," Gladys said, and it sounded more like an order than an invitation. Madeline sat, stifling her irritation.

Gladys got coffee for Arbutus too, rinsing out the dregs from her last cup, adding a dash of salt and cream and stirring them in, bringing the cup to the table and wrapping her sister's hand around it. Madeline had a flash of connection with Gladys in that moment. So many times in that last year she'd been careful to make sure Emmy's hands were steady on her mug of tea.

She sipped at the coffee, intending to visit, but the bone-deep warmth of the kitchen, the smell of the wood heat (it was something like ironing, and Emmy had ironed when Madeline was small, and the smell swept her back to that long-past time), the sisters' voices washing over her, was so soothing that she nodded off almost to sleep and took in their conversation only hazily.

"Cold today," Arbutus said.

"Down around twenty last night, I expect," Gladys answered.

". . . that low, you think?"

". . . call on Emil to get us some more wood in."

"Yes."

It *was* like a fairy tale: the cold air and icy rain, the pounding lake, the acres of forest that had closed in behind her, the aged sisters in their kitchen, the boiled coffee and cook woodstove, her deep sleepiness.

"You may as well go along to bed for a nap," Gladys said from far away at some point. Madeline began to apologize.

"Don't be silly, you've driven all night," Gladys said, frowning.

"You're tired, dear. Go on and rest." Arbutus beamed, and Madeline could not help but smile back. She was so very weary. It was as if years of tiredness had caught up with her all at once. She let Gladys steer her up narrow stairs to a small bedroom with faded wallpaper where there was an iron-framed bed with scratchy wool blankets and soft flannel sheets. She dropped into it and slept with abandon.

She woke up in time to eat dinner, feeling guilty and apologetic throughout, but nearly dozed off again in her chair afterward. Gladys refused her help with the dishes and sent her back upstairs to bed. Madeline considered protesting, but she didn't have it in her. The drive had done her in.

She woke up once to find the room black and the house deeply quiet. She felt her way to the stairs, made her way to the bathroom, peered at her wristwatch—three a.m.—and when she was finished made a detour to the parlor window. The rain was still streaming down, her car sat out front like a faithful dog, the dark street was empty, and she could still hear, faintly, the pounding surf of Lake Superior. Out of nowhere the gleeful feeling shot through her again. She was *here*.

In the morning she found Gladys and Arbutus—and Marley—in the kitchen again. The cookstove was shoveling out heat and the coffee was boiling. "We opened the stair door hoping you'd smell the coffee and get up," Gladys said, and Madeline heard criticism in her voice.

"I'm sorry I slept so long. Tell me what you need me to do, I'll get started."

"Nonsense," Gladys said, her frown deepening. "You've just woken up."

"Sit." Arbutus patted at a chair. "Have coffee."

"And toast. There's blueberry jam I made."

"*Wild* blueberry," Arbutus confirmed.

Each day began in more or less the same way except that Madeline never let Arbutus beat her out of bed again. She'd open her eyes from a deep sleep, fish around on the covers for Marley (never to find him, he'd adopted the space beside the kitchen range as his own), smell a whiff of coffee, and climb down the stairs. She'd join Gladys in the kitchen and visit—thin, stilted conversations that touched on nothing of much consequence—until they heard Arbutus stirring (it turned out Gladys was the true early riser of the two;

Arbutus had just been excited that first morning). Then she'd help Arbutus get up and around and situated, and try to find enough to do to fill her days.

That was a problem she hadn't foreseen. Gladys relinquished no control of anything except the most basic aspects of helping Arbutus. She wanted no interference in her routine, allowed little help with the cooking or cleaning or dishes, had no big projects to tackle that might have filled some of Madeline's hours. That hadn't occurred to her as a potential issue, back in Chicago. She'd just latched on to the decision and ran with it.

Why? she had to wonder now. But there had been genuine kindness in Gladys's letter and Madeline had grasped at that. At last, someone who understood. Where had *that* woman gone, the one who wrote, *I expect you are at sea still without her—a year is not really long in the scheme of things. I won't say it was for the best or any of that. It can never feel right to lose someone so dear.* More than a year after Emmy's death Madeline was absolutely not all right, and no one seemed to see that. She was supposed to be over it, moving on, reshaping her life, which after all had been put on hold to take care of a dying woman. But that wasn't how Madeline felt. Her life had not been on hold, for one thing, and it certainly wasn't racing forward now.

She was lost and enraged and she wasn't even completely sure why. People died, that was a fact of life. Inescapable. Madeline was not ordinarily someone who kicked against the inescapable. And there had been years and years to get used to the idea while they battled the cancer, lived with it, rejoiced at the remissions, got knocked down again by the renewed onslaughts. So she should have been ready for the end when it finally came. But she hadn't been of course and now she couldn't seem to get back on track. Her despair was like a virus that had infected her entire system, destroyed her at the core.

She'd come north partly because Gladys Hansen maybe understood that. And partly to be with Arbutus, who was not like Emmy in age or background or interests, but seemed exactly like her in spirit. Good. Merry. Wise. There was no right word for it that Madeline could find except one she'd forgotten. A Jewish friend had used it to describe Emmy at her funeral. One of the pillars of the world that God put on earth to live among us and help us cope and see the point of things, was what it meant. Madeline had understood it was a singular compliment and wanted to remember the word always. She'd even asked her friend to write it down, but was in such a haze of grief that she misplaced the scrap of paper almost immediately. So she'd lost the word but not the idea, and she thought it fit Arbutus too, the moment she met her.

She'd gone across town to meet Gladys Hansen and her sister after the letter came because it seemed ridiculously churlish not to, had gone filled with dread and curiosity and not one shred of interest in doing what Gladys asked. But then she met Arbutus and everything changed. It was as if Arbutus was a beloved grandmother she'd known all her life and would do anything for. There was a deep sweetness about her, an ineffable specialness, a rareness of character you'd be a fool not to latch on to.

Madeline had arrived at Nathan's apartment to find the door unlocked (in Chicago!) and Arbutus in the bathroom, struggling to get herself into a fresh pair of Depends. It turned out that Gladys had gone to the corner market and was later than she meant to be getting back.

"I'm sure this isn't what you expected," Arbutus said once Madeline made her tentative way down the hall. She had a rueful smile on her face—so pretty still—and despite the embarrassing situation her eyes were bright behind her gold-rimmed glasses.

"I didn't expect anything," Madeline said, all the defensive prickliness she had at the ready dissolved.

"Well, that's the best way, isn't it? Really it's the only way."

Right then Madeline decided: she would go north with them, to the end of the earth, to stay for an undetermined length of time and almost no money. It wasn't a decision, even—it was just inevitable. And besides, what else was there to do? Life had trudged on since Emmy died but there was no meaning in it. She had to do something different, maybe *any*thing different. On her own she had not been able to figure out how to go on. How could she ignore it when it seemed as if maybe she'd met another of those rare people, a pillar of the world? And of course she couldn't completely ignore the suggestion that it was time to see where Joe and Jackie Stone had come from.

So she'd come, but she hadn't penciled *boring* into her idea of how it would be. There were simply no distractions. No shopping, no movies, no museums, no events, no nothing. There was barely even any TV because Gladys was too cheap—or more likely too poor, Madeline corrected herself with chagrin—to hook up to cable or buy a satellite dish, and only two stations came in, usually fuzzily, with the antenna.

Madeline had never thought of herself as someone who required entertainment. It wasn't like she'd been out on the town all those years when she was taking care of Emmy, so what was the difference, really? Maybe most of all it was a lack of possibility. She had only the diversions she could manufacture herself, and no hope of any others. She couldn't even watch *other* people being entertained.

She loved to read, but there were limits. Plus she'd already run through half of one of the boxes of books she'd brought with her, which gave her an uneasy feeling. She had the impulse to hoard what was left. There was no library, no bookstore, no borrowing from a friend. Gladys's shelves held only the Bible and half a dozen Reader's Digest Condensed Books from the 1960s, and Arbutus read only romances. These were brought to her by friends from the library in Crosscut, and Madeline didn't see herself getting *there* on any regular basis. She'd already figured out that the round-trip would cost at least ten dollars in gas, which was not nothing, now that she had no real income, just the tiny wage from Gladys and a small savings account from Emmy's insurance policy set aside for emergencies. Besides which, it was obvious the Buick only had so many miles left in it. So, no frivolous driving.

McAllaster did have a small antique store that was closed in the winter; when she peered in the window she could make out a shelf of paperbacks toward the back. It was obvious even from the street that they were worn-out old mysteries and romances and celebrity bios and true crime thrillers, but still she longed to get at them, just so she wouldn't feel so deprived.

She loved to walk, but there were limits to that, too. Besides which, the weather was dismal, day after day of sleet and scattered snow showers and drizzling rain and endless wind. Chicago wasn't exactly balmy, but it was a playground compared to this. She kept going out doggedly, marching up and down the same few streets of town or slogging along the beach, willing to be amazed by the lake no matter what, but if she didn't get pneumonia pretty soon it was going to be a miracle.

She rarely saw anyone else on the beach, and hardly anyone in town, unless they were in their cars or popping in and out of the handful of businesses. There were practically as many dogs as people out and about. They wandered freely, trotting with great purpose to wherever their dog business took them, and Madeline was beginning to wish they'd invite her along. She was getting to know them: a mischievous-looking spaniel, a lumbering chocolate Lab, a beagle, a retriever, a couple of unclassifiable mutts.

There were a few hints that she hadn't somehow wandered back in time to 1950—mainly the huge new homes lining the beach and the ridge above town, summer places undoubtedly—but not many. She had never been out of the United States, never even out of the Midwest, but McAllaster seemed to her like a small Cornish, or perhaps Welsh, village on the sea. There was more loneliness and less charm to this than she would have imagined from the novels she'd read.

Her only job was taking care of Arbutus, and that had turned out to be an understudy position. So what else was left? She had an edgy, dissatisfied sense of waiting. But what did she expect to happen? What *could* happen? It was a town of eight hundred or so, and half—more than half?—of these people were over the age of sixty. Arbutus had told her that the grade school only had forty children in it. The high schoolers were bussed to Crosscut. The parents of these few kids had to be busy working and raising their families. So who, exactly, was she expecting to run into, and what exactly was likely to happen?

Occasionally she recalled her sense of being on the brink of adventure, up on the hill that first day. Richard had been right. She had been—naïve.

3

Madeline was forever reading a book or taking a walk. Gladys supposed she couldn't blame her. What else was there to do for a person accustomed to the city? Arbutus didn't need watching every second and Madeline did finish her chores first. She was a good worker and that didn't surprise Gladys. Madeline might've been Jackie's daughter, but she was Joe's granddaughter, too. Still, she would've liked Madeline to be there when she got back from the market. It would've been nice to have someone to grouch to. Arbutus was napping, and Gladys didn't like to bother her with worrisome things anyway.

Gladys hauled in the last of her groceries and sat down at the table with a plunk. Everything of course was just the same as ever. The floor in its pattern of squares, the table she and Frank had bought new a million years ago, the kerosene lamp that had been her grandmother's, the salt and pepper set she'd been so proud of way back when. It had all been more or less this way for ages, and what was wrong with that?

But something did seem wrong with it lately. Gladys blew out a dissatisfied puff of air. Brooding was no good. She began stowing the groceries away but the more she thought about what her friend

Mabel had told her, the madder she got, and before long she was flinging things around. *Bang!* went a can of baked beans, *Crash!* a box of oatmeal.

"What's wrong?"

Madeline, back at last. "Do you know what those people have done?" Gladys demanded.

"What people?"

Gladys slammed a box of bran flakes down on the counter. "I don't know what things are coming to. These new people come here and think they can just change things, just do whatever it is they want, it's terrible!"

"What happened?"

"I stopped at Mabel's for coffee on my way home, and you would not believe what she told me, it's the last straw. The more I think about it, the more disgusted I get. They've done a nice job with that store, I can't say they haven't, but they've overstepped their bounds, now. Besides which, their prices are too high and half the things they have in there no one wants. *Pesto* and *hummus*," Gladys sneered. "What for?"

"What happened?" Madeline asked again. It was clear she didn't think anything *could* have happened in the few blocks between 26 Bessel and the grocery store. Little did she know.

"They've cut people off their credit."

"Ah."

"They've cut off Emil Sainio, for one, and Randi Hopkins, and Mary Feather."

"I'm sorry. Do they not have money to pay?"

"Money to pay!" That was hardly the point of anything. Did this girl know nothing? When had the last owners, Everett and Nancy, ever worried about money to pay? They'd run that store for thirty years without seeing fit to change the way things were done, and they'd survived, hadn't they? Just barely. But just barely was all you could expect in a place like this, or all you *should* expect. You couldn't get blood out of turnips. The Bensons might be just trying to make a living, but they wanted too much. They wanted it at the expense of the way things had always been done, and Gladys wasn't going to go along with that. She began shoving groceries back into sacks.

"What are you doing?"

"I'm returning these things." Gladys felt deeply irked at Madeline's lack of ire and banged a can of tomato puree into a bag, then followed it with a tin of smoked oysters. That gave her a pang; she loved oysters. A box of noodles went in next, then a package of frozen peas. She hesitated at the baggie of the pricey cardamom seed she flavored her rolls and breads with—she was out and that was like being out of coffee, unthinkable—but then flung it in too.

"So who are these people, the ones they've cut off?" Madeline asked, taking things out of the bags and putting them back in more neatly. "Are they friends of yours?"

"They're just people. What are they supposed to do? Mary Feather's older than dirt and they just tell her, sorry, we can't help you any longer? It's not right."

"Why'd they cut them off?"

Gladys didn't answer. Instead she opened every cupboard door and then the icebox, making sure she'd gotten everything.

"Did they just stop giving credit in general? I know some places have a policy—"

"No! No, it's not everybody, it's just a few."

"So it's just some people, people they don't like."

"It's nothing to do with liking." Gladys clamped her lips shut.

"What is it, then?"

"Is that all you can think of, nitpicky questions?"

Madeline raised her eyebrows. "I only asked a simple question."

Gladys slapped a bag of kidney beans onto the counter. Then she said, "It's people who haven't paid on time, if you must know. People who—tend not to."

"Oh."

"Yes." Gladys's shoulders slumped and she sat in the closest chair and plucked up the rooster pepper shaker. She frowned at it. "I got this from the grocery in 1953. Jack and Irene Whistle had the store then. They gave out Green Stamps, and you could get things with them. I got that set of nested mixing bowls in the cupboard too, the yellow Pyrex."

"Those are nice."

"One year when Frank was out of work, Jack and Irene didn't charge me a penny. Frank was my husband, he passed on in seventy-one, you know, his heart." Madeline made a sympathetic face and Gladys sighed. "How time flies. I never got anything extra, just flour and sugar and coffee, a little meat and cheese. They let me pay it off when I could. Mary Feather brought us fish all that summer." She rubbed the rooster's painted red comb. It needed washing. "That was how things were always done, when I was a girl. Nobody had enough to make it through the winter. Everybody ran up their bill. They had to. It's not so different now. Not for some people. Not for the *real* people."

"Who are the real people?" Madeline asked quietly.

"I didn't come here with a retirement, you know," Gladys said, feeling querulous even though there had been nothing but under-standing in Madeline's voice. "I've been here my whole life."

"I know," Madeline said.

Gladys frowned and ran her thumb over the rooster's comb again. It was hard to say who the "real" people were. She didn't have anything against most of the new people, not the retirees or the summer people or tourists or even the snowmobilers, not on a case-by-case basis, except that they tended to expect too much, to *assume* too much. But they paid their taxes and kept their lawns mowed and volunteered at the school and spent money in the local stores and had as much right to be here as Gladys did, she realized that. And McAllaster had always been a tourist town, a resort town; her own parents had made a living off that fact.

But things were changing fast, now. Too fast. Half a dozen new summer places got built on the beach every year, and no one was content with a regular house, everyone had to have a mansion. At this rate she wouldn't be able to afford the taxes on the house she'd lived in for more than fifty years, and any of the young kids who'd grown up here and wanted to stay, forget it. There was almost nothing they could afford to rent, certainly nothing they could afford to buy. And worse than that was that *people* were changing, the rules of life were changing. Money to pay, indeed. Fury began to roil in her gut again.

"What are you going to do?" Madeline asked after a moment.

"Take these groceries back for starters. I mean to let them know how I feel."

It only took a minute to load the things in her car. She climbed in the driver's seat and waited, but Madeline hesitated. "Coming?" Gladys asked, flicking the visor down.

"Arbutus will be awake soon."

"She'd be with me in a heartbeat if she knew about this."

"I don't really think—"

"Oh, *fizzle*." Gladys clicked on the ignition and pulled off in a splash of gravel.

Madeline felt gutless in the wake of her leaving. She checked on Arbutus (still sleeping), and set off for another walk, down Bessel

Street in the opposite direction of Gladys. What did it matter if she hadn't taken a stand on this, she told herself, striding along the uneven sidewalk. How false it would have been to seem decisive. She didn't know these people. Boy oh boy, did she not know these people. She'd been here two weeks, and every day she felt more like a square peg in a round hole. Probably this move had been a mistake. But she was here and Arbutus needed her, so here she would stay.

She marched past the rows of houses that had been put up by the mill at the height of the lumber boom, according to Arbutus. She liked the way the small old houses, built all the same, had been weathered and used into individuality. It said something about the triumph of the human spirit, only "triumph" was too grand a word for it—it was nothing sweeping or orchestral. The houses had been built poor and they were still poor, but each one had its own personality. Madeline respected that.

It was a chilly day, and sunny at last. As usual she was nearly the only one out walking. Sometimes she saw a tall woman with the beagle on a leash, an ancient-looking man with a cane and a sparkly grin, an old lady trundling slowly along with a walker. These people usually smiled at her, but no one ever said anything, and she didn't, either. She felt shy.

She always saw a car or two, or a few rumbling pickups, but there was never any actual *traffic*. There were always vehicles on the streets, people going in and out of the bank and the stores, but so few of them that it still disconcerted her, a little. If she'd stood in the middle of the street and screamed, there might only have been ten or twenty people available at any given time to come running.

She had never been anywhere so empty, or so silent. After that first exhausted night, the silence had actually kept her awake. It took awhile to figure out what made her feel so uneasy, what was missing. It was the accustomed constant background sound of traffic, horns, sirens, voices drifting up from the sidewalks at all hours of the day and night. Here there was just—nothing, pretty much. Wind. Waves. Gulls. If she stood outside at noon, she could hear the bells of two different churches tolling from opposite ends of the town. On pea-soup days, a foghorn blasted, mournful and patient. At nine every night an air siren blew, and she always saw children running for home just afterward. That was it.

The effect of the stillness was primeval, like the woods and swamps and the lake. She had fallen in love with the lake. The feeling it gave her—boundlessness. Hope, maybe. Awe. It was the best thing about McAllaster so far, aside from Arbutus. She wanted to paint it. She was actually trying to paint it, and it had been how many years since she'd allowed a thought like that in her head? But today even the lake couldn't distract her. Before long she turned right and then right again.

It was too late by the time she got to Benson's SuperValu, either to support Gladys in her cause or to slow her down. She pulled the double glass door open just as Gladys marched out. She swept along, giving Madeline a regal nod as she passed, and Madeline was left alone to face the woman at the register. A badge pinned to her shirt said "Terry Benson."

Terry Benson had been popular in high school, Madeline thought. She had been popular and pretty and had worn her honey-colored hair feathered or curled or layered or waved, whatever the current style had been, and she had believed—still did believe—very much in her looks. She was still pretty, in a widened way, with a broad but shapely rear end and a prominent bosom. She stood with a hand on one hip and glared at the groceries Gladys had dumped on the conveyor belt. "You're the one staying with Mrs. Hansen, aren't you?" she asked when Madeline walked up.

"That's right."

"Do you plan on paying for this? Because we don't take returns. Not on food. What is she thinking?"

"Nothing's been opened," Madeline pointed out, still not sure of her stand in this little war, but wanting to help Gladys if she could.

"She took it out of the store, I'm not putting it back on the shelves, what would my customers think?"

"Can't you just—"

"I won't take those groceries back. I can't! People can't get the idea they can take food home and then change their minds."

From outside, the horn of Gladys's jaunty little red car beeped and Madeline glanced at her, sitting so erect behind the wheel. Proud, stubborn, cranky, and—fragile, somehow. Madeline took a breath. She reached for her wallet, thinking the total couldn't come to more than sixty dollars or so, she probably had that much. But before she could pull out any money Gladys tooted the horn again. Her expression was calm. Behind her, over the low rooftops of the stores across the street, Lake Superior crashed to shore in huge, white-capped waves. There was something magic in that endless turn of water, something oceanic and wild and old, something that would outlast the petty arguments of customers and cashiers. Out of nowhere a conviction rose in Madeline, inconvenient and romantic and maybe mistaken, but a conviction nonetheless.

She turned away from the window. What she saw: a fluorescent-lit store bright with packaging, clean, neat, and somehow feature-less. She saw a very conventional woman with an understandable gripe that she nonetheless did not sympathize with. It was not so much that Terry Benson was wrong. It was just that these other things—Gladys's staunchness, the endless roll of the lake—felt so right, so rare, and so much more interesting.

"Well? Are you paying or not?"

"Not," Madeline said, giving the woman a flicker of apologetic smile. She glanced at the man who'd come to stand next in line. Already she'd be getting a bad reputation in this tiny town. Arguing with the proprietor, refusing to pay a bill. But the man—about her age, dark-haired and brown-eyed with a little goatee—gave her a conspiratorial wink and Madeline felt herself smile in return.

"I'll be sending a bill," Terry snapped.

Madeline nodded and went to get in the car with Gladys. Her heart was pounding and she put her hands—which had turned ice cold—up to her flushed cheeks to cool them. The man who'd winked at her came out of the store and Madeline watched him walk off down the street with a very slight limp.

Gladys was triumphant on the return trip to the house. "Pompous so-and-sos. Foolish little name tag, who does she think she's kidding, she's not in the city. Cutting off Mary Feather, I never heard the like. I hope you didn't give her an ounce of satisfaction."

"No," Madeline said.

"That woman had better cut back on the bread and cookies, she wants to keep what's left of her figure. Maybe she better start walking to work instead of driving, I never saw such people for driving. Four blocks from the store they live, and here they come by the house every morning in the car, and she comes back to run the kids to school every day to boot. It wouldn't hurt those kids to walk to school, we always did." She flicked on her turn signal and made a right onto Bessel Street with no apparent sense of irony. Madeline cut a sideways glance at her.

Gladys gave a little shrug. "I had the groceries, that's my excuse." She pulled in the drive at 26 Bessel, and then she shocked Madeline by patting her hand. "Sometimes you have to take a stand, that's all. Now. You go look in on Arbutus, I'm going down to the gas station for milk, we're out."

Madeline expected her to drive away but instead Gladys got out and set off down the walk at a brisk pace, her feet churning like two small engines.

4

Madeline came downstairs the next morning, poured her coffee, sat down across from Gladys, and said, "So. I've been wondering, which house in town was Joe Stone's?"

It was impossible for her to say "my grandfather's." She really couldn't think about him without a wave of dislike washing over her, but she was here and ought to learn at least a little about him. She assumed Gladys would be a little more forthcoming after yesterday. They'd had that bonding moment in the car. But Gladys gave her an unreadable look. "None of them."

"Really." Madeline was unable to keep the irritation out of her voice. "That doesn't make any sense."

"And how would you know what makes sense and what doesn't?"

Just like that, Madeline saw red. It wasn't like her, or rather, wasn't like who she'd always been until recently, but she gave in to it. "Whose fault do you think that is? Mine, or your old sweetheart, Joe's?" She scraped her chair away from the table and exited through the kitchen door, managing not to slam it behind her.

She went to the water and along the shore for half a mile before the cold seeped into her bones and sent her back to town. She dawdled in front of the old closed-up hotel for a while, gazing at the little peaked-roof attic windows, wishing she could be up there taking in the view, which would surely be long and wide and comforting, because after all what were these petty human squabbles but so much dust in the wind? Why did she care so much about Joe Stone when she'd had all the love any child could need from Emmy? There was no real answer except that it was simple human nature.

When she returned to 26 Bessel, Gladys had transformed the kitchen into a food factory and Arbutus was sitting at the table in her bathrobe. She beamed at Madeline and Madeline smiled back. She resolved to be pleasant to Gladys for Arbutus's sake.

"You're up early," she said, straightening the collar of Arbutus's robe. Arbutus looked rumpled somehow, as if her journey out of bed had been rocky.

"I smelled the cooking. Glad came in and helped me."

"Okay, but be careful. I don't want any accidents. I'm sorry I wasn't here."

Arbutus's eyes seemed full of understanding. Probably Gladys had told her about their little scuffle. "We can manage getting me around on our own now and then."

Madeline decided not to argue, but she knew she should have been there. "What's all this?" she asked, nodding at the table spread with mixing bowls and cake pans and cookie sheets, eggs and milk and flour, canned tomatoes, onions, a whole chicken and a bag of ground beef that appeared to be frozen solid.

"I'm low on sugar." Gladys glanced at her, seeming to gauge her mood. "And I need more eggs. Also ketchup. And pimientos."

"It's a little early in the day for pimientos, don't you think?" Madeline went to get a second cup of coffee, squatted down to scratch Marley's head, then stood near the stove to dry the chill out of her bones.

Arbutus had watched their exchange and her eyes were sparkling. She seemed to find life very amusing. Well, probably it was amusing if you could just look at it from the right angle and maybe Madeline could learn that skill while she was here. It was Arbutus, after all, who had clinched this deal. Madeline tried to think of that word again, the one that meant one of the pillars of the world. She couldn't, but it didn't matter. Arbutus was there, right before her, seeming to hold some vital knowledge about life that Madeline hoped to learn.

"They're for the meat loaf," Gladys said, bringing her back to the pimientos. "I need you to go to the store."

"After yesterday?"

"Not that store, don't be foolish. No, you'll have to run down to Crosscut."

Madeline gave Gladys a look over the rim of her coffee cup. Crosscut was thirty-two miles away! And it was grim: empty storefronts, dilapidated houses, a pall of poverty. "Come on. You can't go to Crosscut every time you want a bottle of ketchup."

Gladys's eyes snapped up from her recipe and she surveyed Madeline over the top of her glasses. "Watch me."

Madeline couldn't help feeling that stab of admiration for Gladys again. She slid Gladys's shopping list around in front of her and perused it: *1 doz. large brown eggs, 5 lb. sugar, lg. bott. ketchup, 3 jars pimientos, 10 lb. flour (Gold Medal, no off-brands!), 5 lb. hamburger, 2 gall. whole milk, 4 lbs. butter, half doz. green peppers (if decent, not soft), 2 hds. cabbage, 2 bags carrots and celery, whole cardamom*—it went on and on. "This is a lot of food. What are you up to, anyway?"

"Cooking."

"You expect the three of us to eat all this?"

"It's not for us."

"No?"

"We'll take a pan of meat loaf and some molasses cookies to Mary Feather, she loves those I know, and something for Randi Hopkins, she's got that child to think of, and Emil of course. Although the only thing he'd really want is a pint of Old Grand-Dad and I'm not getting that." Gladys flashed a rare sunny smile, and Madeline could see that she was truly happy. Because she had a plan, maybe. Because she was *doing* something. "If you leave right now, you could be back in time for me to get done by afternoon."

So, a journey of more than sixty miles round-trip for some flour and ketchup. It might have been more sensible to say no, but Madeline didn't.

Gladys went to the parlor and stood beside her desk, holding her wallet, fingering slowly through the bills, and suddenly Madeline understood something she hadn't considered before. Gladys maybe couldn't afford this feeding of the needy. Maybe she couldn't even afford to feed Madeline.

In a moment Gladys came back. "I think this will be enough. If not—"

"I've got a little cash on me."

Gladys nodded stiffly and cleared her throat. "You asked about your grandfather. Where he lived. He didn't live up here until later. He was from Crosscut, really."

Madeline's birth certificate said she'd been born in McAllaster, Michigan, on the fourth of November, 1974, to Jackie Lee Stone, father unknown. "But then how was I born here, why was Jackie—"

"He lived at 512 Pine Street," Gladys went on doggedly. "Since you're going down there I thought you might want to know."

Madeline studied Gladys. She'd said all she meant to for now, that was clear. "Okay. Thanks for telling me."

"I'll reimburse you if I'm short of cash on the groceries. And hurry, I don't want to wait all day."

———

The miles themselves defeated the idea of hurry. The sun had come out, the sky was blue, the swamps were watery and mossy, ringed with pines. Endless, endless miles of that. How long would it take to find anyone who wandered off and got lost? Days? Weeks? Never? The road wound its lonesome, resolute way south, and it seemed as if the rest of the world might not exist. Between McAllaster and Crosscut there were only a few settlements and crossroads. Madeline passed Wolf and Halfway, both of them hardly more than a handful of shacks, though at Halfway there was a bar and a general store with one gas pump out front. Here and there a dirt track wound off into the woods to who knew where.

The swampy forests, the bright, sharp air, the smell and feeling of it all—it smelled like freedom, like something wild and elemental that she'd never known before. Then she passed a decrepit cabin with a yard strewn with garbage and it was impossible to imagine the life lived there as anything but hopeless.

It's was all mixed up, beautiful and bleak, both. Finally she emerged from the swamp and came up on the town. The first thing she saw was a sign that said "Prison Area—Do Not Pick Up Hitchhikers." Next she passed a glass case with a smashed-up snowmobile in it. A banner over the top said, "Ojibwa County Snowtrails Wants You to Drink Responsibly!" Across the road from that was the Crosscut State Correctional Facility, where double wire-mesh fences twenty feet high and topped with cyclones of barbed wire surrounded a swampy meadow. She crossed a railroad track where a train sat with its cars loaded with timber, and then passed an enormous, listing hulk of a building with boarded-up windows that had "Crazy L Saloon" painted in faded letters across one wall.

She found the grocery store (there was only one), and spent all of Gladys's money plus a little of her own. Then she went in search of her grandfather's house.

Number 512 Pine was two stories of unpainted clapboard with no porch or shutters to soften it, not even a step up to the front door. An upstairs window had a long crack in the glass and the curtains looked like old bedsheets. There were half a dozen kids' bikes in the yard, a dented pickup in the drive, a big, skinny dog chained to a stake beneath a tree. It leapt up and barked at her furiously when she made a tentative move to get out of the car. The front door opened and a lumpy woman with an aura of rage leaned out and screamed at the dog to shut up.

After an uneasy moment Madeline put the car in drive and headed back to McAllaster.

Gladys helped pack up Madeline's car with casserole dishes and plates of cookies and loaves of bread wrapped in tinfoil late that afternoon, and then gave her directions.

"You'd better hurry, it looks like rain, those clouds came out of nowhere. Go to Randi Hopkins's place first, she's right in town, I made you a map." Gladys produced a sheet of paper she'd worked on while Madeline was gone and laid it out on the hood of the Buick. She pointed at an *x* that marked the first place she wanted Madeline to stop. "Then after that, go to Emil's, you can't miss his place. See?" Madeline nodded, uncertainly it seemed to Gladys, but nothing could be simpler than this, there were only so many roads to choose from, surely she could figure it out. "Mary's place is a little trickier but you'll be all right. The road'll get bad in a downpour, though."

"Wait a minute, you're not sending me off on my own to do this."

"Piffle. You'll be fine. Just remember, for Mary's, you've got to look for a big boulder and then the old Studebaker sitting in the woods—that was Jim Dollar's truck, it quit out there one day back in 1962 and he just left it. I put it all on the map. Take the first left after that and go about two more miles."

"No way. I don't know these people, I've never even met them. I'll *drive* but I'm not going to deliver."

"Nonsense."

"Gladys—"

"I can't go. It'd seem like charity and that's not what this is. This is just a case of I made too much meat loaf and we can't eat it all, so you're dropping some by and they're helping me out, taking it off my hands. If I'm there it'll be awkward. Plus it'll take forever. Introductions, chitchat, gossip. Coffee. Or in Emil's case, whiskey." Gladys grinned as Madeline frowned even more stubbornly.

"I'm really not comfortable with this," she said in such a stodgy way that Gladys wanted to pinch her.

"Oh, fiddle. You waited on tables at a busy place in Chicago for how many years, and you can't drop off a few casseroles in McAllaster? Get going, you'll be fine."

Just then Arbutus called, "Glad," from the kitchen door, her voice a little feeble, and Gladys seized upon this. "Arbutus needs me. Don't get lost." With that, she strode up the walk. She knew that Madeline was glaring, but she didn't hesitate. She was counting on having known Joe well enough to know what his granddaughter would do. Blood would tell. Maybe. Pretty soon she heard the car start up and pull away and Gladys smiled, pleased for reasons she didn't articulate to herself.

No one was home at Randi Hopkins's house, and Madeline was certain she had the right place. It was a shabby house painted mustard yellow, with colorful plastic toys strewn around the yard, and Gladys had said Randi had a child. Plus she had written "Ugly yellow house" on the map. Madeline left the box of food inside the front door after she found it unlocked and hurried back down the walk feeling guilty, of what she didn't know. Emil Sainio's trailer seemed empty too. She knocked several times without getting an answer, but she couldn't work up the nerve to try the door—it would open so instantly into the man's entire life—so she left his box on the step, hoping for the best. She got back in the car feeling more carefree. Maybe no one would be home at all and she'd be back at 26 Bessel drinking coffee with Arbutus within the half hour.

Mary Feather opened her door when she heard a car pull up. She leaned in the doorway, bracing herself with her hands, her body angled forward by a hump in her back but her feet planted solid on the threshold. She wore denim overalls, rubber galoshes, a woolly cardigan over a long-sleeved undershirt. Her white hair fell in braids along an angular face, and her eyes were bright, snapping blue. A black-and-white terrier squeezed past her and raced down the steps.

"Jack!" she cried in a gravely voice. The woman who'd gotten out of the car stopped as Jack jumped in ecstatic circles around her knees.

"Jack, get down, get back here," Mary rasped, her voice even gruffer than usual. She'd had a start, her eyes playing tricks on her, seeing the face of a woman who'd been dead and in the ground for a long, long time. *Ada Stone*, she'd thought for one shocked moment. "Jack," she rasped again, and after a few more leaps he trotted back to her.

Her visitor made her way forward, her arms full of boxes. "Hi, I'm Madeline Stone, I'm staying with Gladys Hansen?"

"I thought so." Mary turned herself around to go in the door but the girl didn't follow. "Come on, then!" Mary barked and heard the plank steps creak behind her.

Mary had cobbled her place together and knew what it must look like to her visitor: a couple of wooden boxes up on wheels. Which it was. Virgil Higley of Higley Logging had given her two old tool cribs when he was finished with them and she'd bolted them together and cut a doorway in between. The place suited her. Real small, so it heated up good. The girl would find out, if she stayed north long enough. You only needed what you needed, nothing more. The woodstove was burning hot in the first room and it was warm as toast. A cracked leather armchair was pulled up close by it, and six chickens sat in beds of straw in a long wire hutch on the floor, clucking softly. Jack gave them a calculating look and Mary growled, "Jack." Jack sighed and trotted past.

The second room held a cookstove, a pegboard hung with pots and pans, a countertop and cupboards and a sink without spigots, a gas refrigerator, a footstool, a couple of old easy chairs. There was a bunk along one wall, covered with a quilt and bolstered with pillows, a metal wardrobe, shelves of food and books, an old card table with a puzzle spread across it, and finally another wire cage, Jack's. Mary shooed him into it.

"He's still got his puppy ways. Got to be able to get some peace now and then. John Fitzgerald brought him to me, you know John?"

Madeline Stone shook her head.

"Lives in town, you'll meet him. A great knurl of a man, built like a stump. Runs the hardware. Anyway, John brought Jack to me and I told him I didn't want a dog but he wouldn't take no. Somebody dropped him off, looks like, left him to die or find a home. No collar, no tags, skinny, running loose. Maybe he just run off and got lost, I don't know, but either way, John couldn't find nobody to take him, so here he is." Mary sat in the chair beside Jack's cage and scratched his head through the wire. "Sit down, it don't matter where."

Madeline set her load of boxes on the table and eased into the other chair. Mary took note of her unease. Well, what could you expect? She was from the city and she looked it—not fancy, but smooth. Smooth skin, smooth hands, a real modern short haircut showing, now that she'd plucked off the cap she'd been wearing. (It was the hat that made her look so like that face out of the past, Mary decided. She couldn't recall if she'd ever seen Ada minus her hat. And the girl was bosomy too, like Ada had been. Bosomy and solid. She could do some work if she had to, not like some of these girls who looked as if a stiff breeze would blow them away.) She had on very clean blue jeans with a cream-colored sweater knitted in intricate cables, and shiny, smooth-soled leather shoes. Those would be useless if she ended up having to walk out of the woods. Mary wondered what she'd have to say for herself.

"Gladys sent some things for you," Madeline said, then cleared her throat. Polite. Uncomfortable. She wouldn't have lasted ten minutes around Joe. Though maybe that was wrong. Probably was. Mary knew this girl had looked after the woman who'd raised her for years and years when she was real sick, so she was no coward. And she had turned up here, staying with Gladys to boot, so she had some spark to her. "Gladys made too much meat loaf," Madeline was saying. "And cookies, and bread."

"Did she now? Well, that was nice of her. You tell her she don't have to."

"Oh, it's just extra—"

"Ha. Extra all done up in its own pan, eh? Well, you tell her I'm grateful, and I'll get her pan back to her directly, next time I'm in town. I'll be bringing the maple syrup in, might be some people

about if the weather ever clears. Ought to be some travelers showing up by Memorial Day anyway."

"Do you make the syrup?"

"Got near to fifty gallons this year." Mary heaved herself up out
of her chair and went to the cupboard and pulled out a jug. She
poured a dollop of golden brown syrup as thick as molasses into a
teaspoon and held it out.

Madeline took the spoon and hesitated. Mary gave her a sar-
donic look and Madeline popped the spoon in her mouth. "Wow,"
she said, then licked the spoon. "That's amazing. It's so good."

"Damn good." Mary took the spoon back. "I sell out every year,
got people asking after it's gone, but now they want to get rid of me."

"Who does?"

"Folks at the grocery. They don't like me peddling my stuff. Cuts
into their trade."

"Oh."

"You don't believe me but it's true. Gladys tell you they cut me
off my credit?"

Madeline nodded.

"They don't want my fish no more, either. I been supplying that
grocery with all I could get for fifty years. Smoked, fresh, you name
it. Now they don't want it. Don't want the fish or the syrup or the
berries I get in the summer. It ain't hygienic, they said, and I'm not
licensed. Damn right I'm not licensed, I never had to be. Says right
on my deed I got the right to farm my property, I can show you. They
don't want me to set up and sell it myself, either, no more than they
do the fruit man, and he's been coming here since sixty-six. Bah."
She made a gesture of disgust and changed the subject.

It was good to have company. Mary showed Madeline all over
her place that afternoon—the sugar shack and maple grove, the
smokehouse, the root cellar and woodshed, the pump in the yard for

water and further back the outhouse, the little old camping trailer she'd bought for a good deal years ago now but then never done anything with. "This here was my house," she told Madeline, waving at a burned-out structure.

"Oh—what happened?"

"Chimney fire. Been meaning to rebuild. But Higley give me them old tool cribs and I'm okay there."

"When did it happen?"

"Been fifteen years ago or so now, I guess. Time gets by."

Madeline nodded.

They walked across the yard to a small barn and pasture in which stood one cow and a handful of sheep. "I got forty acres," Mary said. "I cut my wood from the property, got all the heat you could ask for. Well, folks help me now I've got older, but still, this place keeps me going. I got all I need."

Mary felt compelled somehow to show Madeline everything—her old truck stowed in its tiny shed, the earrings she made of beads and porcupine quills, the boxes of paperbacks people brought her out to read, the wool she had clipped from the sheep and not yet spun into yarn. She even showed Madeline the family plaid, for she was a Scotswoman, the great-great-granddaughter of one of the earliest white settlers in the Upper Peninsula, or the U.P. as everyone in Michigan called it.

"Was this his place then?" Madeline asked and Mary frowned with impatience—of course it wasn't!—forgetting in a way that Madeline hadn't grown up here and had no reason to know one way or the other.

"I bought it myself, years ago. Saved my money hard to get it. Always did like it up here near the big lake. I was born down in Crosscut. My mother run a hotel there when I was young." *Same as Glad and Butte's ma and dad did here*, she had been about to say, but got distracted by the look on Madeline's face.

"I was there today, in Crosscut. I saw my grandfather's house. It was pretty awful."

Pretty nice, is what Mary would've said. Gas heat, indoor toilet, two bedrooms upstairs if she recalled right, a good many closets and cupboards, which is something she felt the lack of. But of course to this girl it mightn't look like much. "I know the house. I knew Joe."

Madeline looked startled, alarmed even. "You did?"

"Of course I did. He played a mean fiddle. Always played at the fiddle jamboree they hold in Crosscut every summer, you should have heard him."

"I didn't know that."

"Yup. Nobody could play 'Sally Barton' like your granddad."

Madeline nodded, seeming speechless.

"You play?"

"What? Me? Oh, no. I don't play anything."

"I'll bet you can draw."

"*What?*"

"Joe was a dab hand at drawing. Used to do these little cartoons at the jamboree. You paid him a dollar, he give you a drawing of yourself. Did it in about two minutes flat, I never saw the like."

"Oh," Madeline said, looking shaken. Mary would've bet the farm the girl was good with a drawing pencil.

"You look a mite like him. But more like his ma—your great-grandma, I mean."

"*Oh.*"

"You got her eyes, and that same dark hair, though she always wore a cap, I can't recall if I ever saw her without it. You got her build, too—" Mary made a shape with her hands in the air.

"Square," Madeline said glumly and a smile flickered over Mary's face.

"Sturdy," she said. "Real pretty, in her own way."

There was a long moment of silence and then Madeline said, very softly, "What was her name?"

Mary frowned. Didn't this girl know anything? "Ada. Ada Stone. You give me a start when you got here. I always liked her real well, so I remember."

"I—I didn't know. I don't know anything about them. Joe Stone didn't want me. The authorities tracked him down but he said no."

"Oh well, a man. It don't surprise me. Course he probably could've found somebody to help out, if he tried. Jackie's ma took off on him when Jackie was pretty young, and Ada would've passed on by the time you came along. I expect he was too proud to go asking."

Madeline bit her lip, and then she said, like she was admitting to something she might rather not've, "I looked in Gladys's phone book. It said it covers this whole area, three counties. There weren't any Stones. I just thought maybe—you know."

Mary nodded. There wouldn't be any Stones in the book, she could've told the girl that. She studied Madeline, sizing her up, considering saying something more, but in the end she didn't. It wasn't her place. If Gladys and Arbutus hadn't told Madeline about her family, it wasn't up to her to butt in.

Madeline saw in her rearview mirror that Mary watched until she was out sight. The rain beat down, smoke drifted from the chimney. Jack danced at her ankles but she seemed unaware of him. Her loneliness and independence seemed absolute. Maybe they went hand in hand.

Madeline bumped down the narrow two-track, peering through the increasing rain. She turned the windshield wipers on high, but before she'd gone a quarter mile the driver's-side blade peeled away from its clip and fell along the road. She stopped and searched in the weeds, the rain pelting on her back, until she found the pieces. The rubber had rotted and there was nothing left but two cracked, broken halves.

She tossed the chunks aside. She started the car up again but stopped right away. The metal of the blades was screeching against the windshield, scratching the glass. She sat and thought, then climbed out and kneeled in the mud to search on the floor under the seats until she found an old, long-cuffed knit glove, each finger a different garish color, a many-years-old and not very well-liked gift from someone or other. Wet and cold and muddy now, she leaned grimly over the windshield to fit it over the naked blade and made her way back to 26 Bessel, the glove waving gaily.

"Lonely!" Gladys scoffed when Madeline got back. "Mary Feather doesn't want a thing or soul on earth but what she's got, she's not lonely."

Madeline didn't say what she really thought: *Everybody's lonely, who are you kidding?*

She might have said it to Emmy and she wished for her with a sudden intensity. Emmy with her gray braids and pretty smile, her blue felt hat with the yellow daisy on it, her Birkenstocks and cotton smocks, her fresh vegetables and herb tea and never a cigarette ever. How could she die of cancer and how could Madeline live without her? *Oh Emmy.* Her grief sliced as sharp as when it was new. It unnerved her, that Mary Feather had known her grandfather, spoke of him so easily, revealed these things—the fiddle, the drawing (and she couldn't even think about the fact that they had this in common)—as if they were nothing more than comments on the weather. Unnerved her to think that she looked like him but more like his mother. In her heart she went running for safe harbor, for Emmy.

"Mary knew my grandfather," she blurted out, and was instantly angry at herself, and yet could not stop. "She said he played the fiddle. And that he liked to draw."

"He did," Gladys said coolly. "He was good."

Madeline waited for her to say something more but she didn't. So Madeline said, "Well. Goodnight." She didn't care if she seemed abrupt. No one here cared that Joe Stone had not had the decency to look after his own granddaughter, had refused to even really acknowledge her existence. And that was fine because she'd been better off without him. Clearly his had been a bleak, mean life lived in a bleak, mean town, and there was nothing to be gained by considering it. She headed for the stairs.

5

Paul Garceau stood in the general store in Halfway, sipping a cup of coffee. He didn't have time for the stop, really—there was never enough time for things—but he liked Lily Martin, who owned the place. She cheered him up. She wasn't trying to. It was just that she never complained, and she could have. The store had to be nearly profitless, the building was desperate for repairs, and most of the merchandise was old. But Lily took life as it came, never seeming to wish things were different.

Paul found this humbling, and tonic. It reminded him that his own problems were probably not that bad, and if they were, he'd survive them. So despite his chronic shortage of time, he sometimes stopped for coffee on his way from one job to another. Besides which, as far as stops went between Crosscut and McAllaster, this was it—this or the bar next door. Halfway was just a wide spot in the road, a place where the trains used to take on water and where mail and supplies had been dropped off for the lumber camps, back in the day. All that was left of it was Lily's store and the Trackside Tavern, two desolate establishments that most of the tourists flew right past on their way up to the Gitche Gumee, the Big Water.

Paul glanced at the clock that hung behind the register. He had

maybe five minutes before he had to hit the road and make the fifteen miles up to McAllaster himself. He was listening to Lily at the
same time as he considered how fast he could push the Fairlane and
gain a minute, maybe.

"I asked Roscoe to pick me some of those flavored creamers
when he was over at the Soo yesterday," she was saying. "The Soo"
was shorthand for Sault Ste. Marie, ninety miles away and the
nearest city of any size. "The tourists like 'em and I got hooked on
the Irish cream myself. He forgot, so I guess I get a lesson in self-
denial." She laughed as she said this.

It was such a small thing to want. And it was something he
could fix. That was rare, these days. "I'll order some for you on my
next load. I'll drop them off on Friday."

"Oh, don't bother yourself, it's nothing."

"You'll use them if I bring them?"

"Can't stay away from 'em when they're around."

"Okay. Consider it done. And now, sorry to say, I'd better run.
Thanks for the coffee. I needed a break between jobs today."

"I'll bet. That place has got to get you down."

"It's a job." Paul worked in the prison cafeteria in Crosscut five
days a week, five a.m. to eleven. Today had been bad. Maybe the
full moon, who knew, but the prisoners were at their worst, yelling
and scuffling and banging their trays, starting fights, throwing food
around. He hated the job but it was a necessity.

Paul heard the door open and took that as his cue. Time to really
go. He dug in his pocket for change, which Lily waved away. "I'm
not charging you for that slop. That coffee's been sitting there since
Emil left."

"No, it was good. I like it strong," Paul said, putting a couple
of dollars on the counter. He turned to leave and bumped into the
woman who'd stood up to Terry Benson in the SuperValu the other

day—Madeline Stone, he knew her name was. Just as he was about to say something, the door opened again and Randi Hopkins rushed in.

"*Paul*. Thank God you're here, I can't find Greyson."

"What do you mean?" He wasn't too worried. Greyson was a smart kid, five years old and acting like fifty half the time, but anyway about ten times as levelheaded as his mother. She'd had Greyson when she was seventeen and dropped out of school before she graduated. Nowadays she worked nights at the Tip Top Tavern, enlisting whoever she could find to look after Greyson while she was there, and roaming restlessly around McAllaster and Crosscut and everywhere in between the rest of the time. But what she lacked in maturity she made up for in spark and personality. She was one of those people you couldn't help but like.

She wore her red hair down her back in a hundred little braids threaded with beads and bells that clacked and jingled every time she moved, and today she had on a low-cut peasant blouse and blue jeans covered with patches. She looked good, despite having lost track of Greyson, and it was impossible to believe he wouldn't turn up someplace completely mundane, unharmed and unalarmed.

"We were just over at the Trackside, I stopped by to say hey to Roscoe and Annie. Grey was playing with their Andrea right behind me on the floor, and then I turned around and he was gone. Oh my God, Paul, where is he?"

"Slow down, take a breath. How long's he been gone?"

"I don't know. I don't *know*. I noticed it was too quiet, you know? I looked everywhere, we looked everywhere, Roscoe checked all over the buildings and Annie and me went calling and calling and he's just nowhere. Paul, what if he's hurt?"

"I'm sure he's okay. Maybe he's just playing a game, doesn't realize how he'll scare you," Paul said, but despite himself he felt a niggle of concern.

Gladys Hansen came in just then. "My word, Madeline, *what* is taking so long? Arbutus is all stove up from sitting in the car, we've got to get home. This was supposed to be a simple trip to Crosscut, all I wanted to do was go pay my taxes. You'd think—"

"Greyson's gone missing," Paul said, cutting in.

"*Missing*. How?"

"We don't know. Wandered off, maybe. Or maybe he's just playing around."

Gladys pursed her lips and flicked a look at Randi that was easy to read. Of course Randi had let her child vanish, she couldn't do anything else, no use beating your head against a wall about it. Things were what they were, Gladys Hansen knew that.

Madeline Stone, meanwhile, looked pale. "I've just got to pay for the gas I pumped," she said. "We'll get Arbutus right home."

Gladys stared at her. "There's a child missing, for Lord's sake, we're not just getting in the car and driving home, where is your brain?"

"No, Gladys, I can't—"

"I'll get Butte, and we'll wait with you at the tavern, Randi. If that's the last place you saw him, it's where he'll turn up." Gladys took Randi in tow and headed out the door. Paul expected Madeline to follow but she didn't. She just stood there looking ill.

"What a mess," he said, trying to think what to do.

Lily had been on the phone. "I called John Fitzgerald, had him get the word out in town. He's on his way, and he sent a call out on the pager."

Paul ran a hand through his hair. Mostly he felt annoyed. Greyson was fine. This was a wild-goose chase and he was going to be late, he should just leave the hunt to the search crew. But that impulse left him with a mild, hopeless distaste for himself. "Where is that kid? I can't believe he'd wander off, and surely Randi would've noticed if somebody came in and took him."

"There hasn't been anybody around today out of the ordinary. Emil was my only customer, besides you. He came in an hour or more ago."

"Maybe I'll look outside, see if I can see anything Roscoe didn't."

Lily nodded. "I'll stay by the phone. Just in case."

Madeline hadn't said a word; she seemed extremely rattled. "You want to come with me?" Paul asked. "Two heads are better than one, maybe."

She bit her lip, then said, "All right."

"So I heard you're from Chicago," he said as she followed him across the yard. He felt very conscious of his limp. He had resigned himself to it, long ago, but he always assumed people wondered about it when they first met him. Madeline Stone seemed off in another world, however. He started to think she wouldn't answer but after a moment she said, "Yes."

"Nice to see the old girls home. They can't have liked it down there much."

"No."

"It's a different world down there, that's for sure."

"That's true."

Paul gave up on the chitchat. They walked across a meadow of grasses that whispered in the breeze, looking for any trace of Greyson. "I think he's okay, you know," he said eventually. "He's pretty levelheaded." Her mouth twisted into a wry smile but she didn't reply, just kept scanning the waving grasses. "I don't think he'd wander into the swamp. He's not the type of kid to wander off at all. He sticks to his mom. Looks after her, sort of."

"And he's what, five?"

There was bitterness in her voice, but he didn't blame her. Like almost everyone in town, Paul knew the basic outlines of her story.

He wondered how she'd do here. He remembered first coming to McAllaster himself. It had never been in his plans.

Nine years ago he'd set off on an epic journey to Nova Scotia from his home downstate, intent on escaping all reminders of his ruined marriage, and got exactly three hundred and eighteen miles into the trip when the transmission in his truck failed and left him stranded in Crosscut for three weeks waiting for parts. The mechanic there rented him a loaner car, and there'd been nothing much to do but drive around sightseeing. Paul had ended up in McAllaster one day, and got the idea of staying.

He'd come across a little pizzeria for sale cheap (the owner was desperate to get out), and buying it had suddenly seemed like the right thing to do. The truth was, investing in property seemed a lot smarter than blowing his money on travel, and he was already a little bored with the trip. It was in his nature to work, not fool around. Serving pizzas was something he knew he could do, something he thought he could make a living at, and McAllaster had seemed remote enough to satisfy his urge to leave the life he'd been leading far behind. All of which had turned out to be more or less true.

Madeline made a small noise of surprise and stumbled on a hummock hidden in the grass and Paul reached out to steady her. "I thought I saw something," she said. "Over there. But it's just a tree stump." Paul nodded, seeing the stump she meant, which could look a lot like a huddled-up boy if that's what you were looking for.

He and Madeline moved slowly along the edge of the swamp, watching, listening. There was nothing to hear but the rustle of grass and the occasional call of a raven. They made a wide loop around the buildings and came back where they'd started just as the search crew began to arrive from town.

———

Madeline retreated to the tavern. The hand-painted sign above the door said "The Trackside," and she wondered if trains ever went by anymore, the cars loaded with lumber like the ones she'd seen in Crosscut. Could Greyson somehow have gotten on one? It seemed impossible. She crossed the room and sat beside Arbutus on a wooden chair. The place was no frills. Most of the light filtering in came from the few windows set high on one wall, and the air smelled of old fryer grease and smoke.

Randi was wringing her hands, saying over and over that Greyson must be hurt, or dead, lost in the swamp, drowned. Madeline yearned to shake her, to make her be quiet. Oh God, would this day never end, and where was this child?

Arbutus of course was kind to Randi. "Try and stop, dear, you're upsetting yourself. It really isn't very likely that he's come to any harm. He's such a smart boy. I think we'll find he's all right." She looked very tired, and Madeline could see by the way she shifted in the chair every few moments that she was hurting. Madeline yearned to take her home—as much to escape the grim bar and distressing situation as to help Arbutus, she admitted that to herself—but doubted Arbutus would go.

But oh God, Madeline needed out. She had only been three when Jackie left her in a church basement soup kitchen, never to return. Only three, but she had never forgotten the terror. It was as frightened and alone as she'd ever been.

"*Think*, Randi," Gladys said. "Stop caterwauling and think. Was there anyone here that he might've wandered off with?"

"No! He's not going to wander off, he just isn't."

No one responded to this, because clearly he had done exactly that.

They all looked up when the door opened. Paul came in and shook his head at the unspoken question in the room, looking more worried now than he had before. "No sign. Randi, sweetheart, are you sure there's nothing you can think of that was different about today? What were you doing down here, anyway?"

"Nothing! I didn't have anything else to do so I came down to see Roscoe and Annie. I was mad because they cut off my credit at the grocery, I didn't want to sit at the bar there in town and have one of the Bensons come in, I'd have probably lit into them. I mean, I have a kid to support, who do they think they are? So I came down here. Roscoe's my cousin, you know. I knew they wouldn't let us starve."

"Are you out of food at home?" Paul asked, and Madeline was impressed at how matter-of-fact he was about it, like a doctor asking about some humiliating symptom, impersonal and yet kind.

Randi shrugged. "We had that meat loaf and stuff Gladys sent, and it was real good, but it's gone now. I'm just kind of sick of peanut butter on bread."

"Lily said Emil Sainio's the only one that came through today. She said he got some gas, bought a couple of things, more than an hour ago now. I wonder—"

"Emil Sainio is not going to kidnap Greyson!" Gladys snapped. "You're wasting time. You've watched too much TV. How about actually *doing* something?"

Madeline wondered how Paul kept from bristling at Gladys. He even sort of smiled at her. "I know. But we've covered everything we think could have happened. So now we've got to look at what couldn't, right?"

Gladys grudgingly nodded.

"So. What if Greyson stowed away with Emil, rode back up the highway with him, and Emil didn't know it?"

"He's not going to do something like that," Randi cried. "Why would he? He never wanders off from me, never. He's real good." Tears brimmed in her eyes.

This was almost unbearable to Madeline. Of course the boy was good, he had to be, he was busy looking after his mother, who seemed about as reliable as the weather, but let *him* do something unpredictable for once—Madeline wanted to cram the fact that all this was her own fault down Randi's throat. Why act upset *now*? Why not pay attention in the first place? Her stomach churned with anger.

"I'll stay here with you while Paul goes and checks, Randi," Gladys said. "Madeline, you take Arbutus home and then come back and fetch me."

"No," Arbutus said. "I'll stay too. I'm fine."

Gladys began to argue but Arbutus set her chin. "I'm staying and there's no use in arguing about it so you might as well not even start."

But Madeline had to escape. "I'll go with you." Paul looked surprised but didn't object, and she followed him to his car. It was big and old, muted red with shiny chrome.

Paul opened the passenger door and Madeline was startled but oddly touched. He checked she was well settled in before closing it with a firm assurance that surprised her again. She ran a hand over the upholstery—red vinyl with white piping trim.

"Genu-ine imitation leather," Paul said, sliding into the driver's seat.

"It's nice. What year is it?"

"It's a 1963 Ford Fairlane. Most of them rusted to pieces, I was lucky to find her." He turned on the ignition and country music blared out the speakers. He switched the radio off. "It's the only station I can get, so I play it really loud, hoping it'll make me like it better."

"That makes all kinds of sense."

Paul smiled. A few miles down the road he said, "You're pretty upset."

She kept her expression neutral with difficulty. "It's scary, a kid getting lost."

"I know, but I don't think he is. Lost, I mean. He's just not one to wander off."

"Mmm," Madeline said, thinking, *Wake up. Anything could've happened.*

"I really do think he's okay."

"I hope you're right." She stared out the window, not trusting herself to say anything else. They rode on in silence.

Greyson Hopkins had it pretty much figured out. He had to help his mom, who was worried about a bunch of stuff. The main thing was food—the mean people at the store said she couldn't have any more. Old Mrs. Hansen had sent that box—the cookies in it were super good, which was kind of funny because she was such a cranky lady—but that didn't last forever, so now they were going to starve. Greyson wasn't going to let that happen. He'd been thinking and thinking how to fix it and he hadn't been able to come up with anything. He'd gotten bored playing with Andrea—she was just a baby, only two—and went outside to sit on the steps and think some more.

Then Emil pulled up and went in the store and Greyson had a brilliant idea. He'd go home with Emil, and Emil would help him catch some food. Like rabbits, or birds. Maybe a whole deer. Emil was a hunter, he hunted all year round, everybody knew that. Emil was an old man, too—ancient, practically—so he would know everything. Plus he didn't have much of anything. He lived in a little tiny camping trailer from the olden days and drove a rusty old truck that was from the olden days too, and he was funny. Odd, kind of. Not *bad* odd, not scary, just different from most regular people. He was the kind of person who would *have* to hunt to get himself food, so he would for sure be really good at it.

But what if he didn't feel like teaching Greyson hunting stuff? What if he thought he was too little to use a gun or something?

Greyson decided the best thing to do would be to stow away in the back of Emil's truck, and then just show up at his door. It'd be hard for Emil to say no. And then pretty soon, after they hunted something down, he'd be going home with a bunch of food and his mom wouldn't be complaining to everyone about how unfair and terrible everything was.

That was basically how things worked out. Emil drove home and went into his trailer and Greyson followed him up the steps a minute later. Emil was surprised to find him there, but he didn't worry about it. He knew Greyson, knew Randi, had known Randi's mother and grandmother too. It didn't dawn on him to puzzle out how Greyson had managed to get to his place, which was a good couple of miles out of town, or to wonder what had prompted this sudden interest. The boy wanted to learn to hunt. That was just natural. Emil wasn't a great one for questioning the events that life laid out before him. He whistled up his beagle, Sal, pulled his knitted chook down over his ears, loaded his gun, and slammed the trailer door shut behind them.

They were just coming back—empty-handed—when Paul Garceau pulled up in his big old boat. It was quite the day for visitors.

"Hey, Emil," Paul said, easing out of the car, careful with that bad leg of his like always. "I see Greyson's here."

"Yup. We just been out scouting around for rabbits, but we didn't find nothing."

"We're going tomorrow, too," Greyson said. "I'm going to learn how to shoot a gun."

"Well, now, slow down there, boy. I said *maybe* we'd do a little target practice."

Greyson grimaced. "We *have* to. I have to catch some food for my mom and me."

A woman had climbed out of the car to stand beside Paul and the two of them glanced at each other. Well, now, Emil thought to himself, squinting. *If that ain't Joe Stone's granddaughter come back to town finally, I'll eat my hat. Looks just like her great-grandma.*

Paul ran a hand through his hair and then he said, "The thing is, Greyson, your mom's pretty worried. She didn't know where you got off to."

Emil turned to gaze at Greyson, realizing for the first time that the kid had got himself up here without anyone's leave.

Greyson looked startled, and then worried. He bit his lip. "Oh."

"How about we go back to the Trackside and we can get this sorted out?"

"Okay, Mr. Garceau," Greyson said. He looked up at Emil. "Thank you for taking me out hunting, Mr. Sainio."

Emil was surprised to hear himself referred to as Mr. Sainio, but he nodded and said sure, they'd go again sometime, but he'd better get his ma's permission first.

Madeline and Paul and Greyson climbed back into the car, Greyson wedged on the shifter between the seats. Madeline was so relieved she felt shaky. The boy was found, he wasn't hurt, he was going back to his mother, who—useless as she might seem—he obviously loved.

Madeline listened as Greyson explained what his plan had been. His thin face was intelligent, intense. He looked right at her as he talked, leaning forward a little and twisting his head at an awkward angle to do so, intent on his story. Madeline found herself nodding—*Yes, I see how it was.* He sighed with frustration about not getting any rabbits, and there was nothing cute about it, nothing to make her think, Isn't it sweet how children think? No, she just sympathized.

She listened and wished—what? That his life was different, that his mother was different. But then he wouldn't be himself, would he? a little voice in her head inquired. He wouldn't be just exactly this boy with the lively green eyes in the seat beside you.

6

One sunny afternoon in May, the first day that really felt like spring, Madeline knelt on the lawn outside the open kitchen window, sprinkling fertilizer around the tulips. "Look at this!" she heard Gladys say. "The nerve! Like I'm some kind of deadbeat."

Arbutus murmured something.

"I'm not paying it. I returned those groceries. And I'll take my own sweet time on the rest that's due, too. Let them wait, they can afford it. You see that new truck they're driving?"

Arbutus answered but Madeline couldn't make out what she said.

"I won't!" Gladys declared.

"We'll have to pay somehow, else there'll be trouble."

"Let them sue. Look at this—" Gladys's voice became mincing. "'*Please pay.*'"

"What do you want it to say?"

"Nothing! It'd be better if they'd just sent the bill and said nothing, no snotty comment needed, thank you very much."

"There's no sense getting all worked up."

"I was *born* here. Who are they?"

"They're the folks who own the store you took the groceries

from," Arbutus said in a dry tone that surprised Madeline a little. "Why are you so angry? They don't owe us anything."

"Well. Be that as it may. I know what you're thinking and we're not selling, that's final."

"It would make everything easier."

"No, it's not necessary. We'll get by."

"How?"

There was a pensive silence. Madeline dug in the dirt again, unhappy to be eavesdropping but unable to stop.

"Maybe we ought to count ourselves lucky there's someone who wants to buy. Nathan would like me to sell, you know," Arbutus ventured.

Madeline hoped they didn't mean Gladys's house or Butte's either, which was just a few blocks away.

"Nathan." Gladys's voice dripped acid. "I'll just bet he would. Like to get his hands on the money, that's what, so he could fritter it away on investing. You know what I think? I think he's desperate. You see it on the television all the time, people who've got in too deep, made bad investments, lost everything."

There was a brief silence. Then Arbutus said, in a voice that was firm and also a little angry, "Maybe so. And maybe I'd like to help him if that's the case."

"Help him! When has he helped you?"

"That's not fair. He moved us into his place when I got so bad, then brought us back when we asked."

"I had to hound him, Butte. I practically had to threaten him."

"That's not true! He didn't think it was a good idea, us coming back up here, even with help. And he still did it in the end, didn't he?"

Gladys made a strangled noise. "You spoiled that boy, Arbutus. I hate to criticize, but it's a fact. It's the only thing you ever did wrong in your life, I think."

"Except for marry his father." The annoyance had left Arbutus's voice. She sounded rueful but not overly concerned about such a grave error.

"Well," Gladys said. "That's hardly the point. The point is, we're not selling."

"What do you think of putting my house on the market, then? You know, Matilda's son got close to a hundred thousand for her place, and it's not that much bigger than mine."

"It was the *view*, Butte, the location. The water, the water, that's all anyone can think about. You don't have that. Besides, you need your house, you love it. You'll get back there someday. This summer even. You're doing better."

"I need to pay my way is what I need."

"We'll get by," Gladys said again.

Arbutus didn't answer and they both must have left the room because Madeline didn't hear any more conversation. She emptied the box of bone meal and went inside to see if Gladys had any more tucked away.

The house was quiet, the kitchen deserted. A stack of mail sat on the table. All bills. The groceries Gladys returned had come to $75.13, but Madeline was shocked to see that she owed the Bensons over five hundred. She slowly fingered through the rest. There were past due notices for everything. Fuel oil, electricity, the phone. In each envelope a pink slip was enclosed, threatening a shutoff. Even the gas station wanted fifty dollars, but the really impressive things were the bills from the hospital and rehab center where Arbutus had gone after her last fall, before Nathan took them to Chicago.

She owed over sixty thousand dollars. Medicare must not have paid for everything, and Madeline wondered why she wasn't covered by Medicaid. Maybe because of whatever they'd referred to selling. Madeline saw that Gladys had been paying everyone a little—ten dollars here, twenty there. She looked again at the grocery bill. How it had gotten so high without them cutting Gladys off like they had Mary and Emil and Randi?

"What are you doing?" Gladys demanded, appearing from the parlor.

"I'm—nothing." Gladys snatched the bills from Madeline's hand and Madeline met her gaze uneasily. "The bone meal's gone. There wasn't enough to finish."

"Well, go get more, it doesn't take a rocket scientist."

"All right. Where do I go?"

Gladys's expression was withering. "To the hardware, where else?" She was clearly furious. "Looking at a person's mail. I should have known better than to leave it lying around."

"I'm sorry—"

"Sorry doesn't do any good. Just go get the fertilizer. I'll get you the money." Gladys stalked to her desk in the hall and took her wallet from her purse. She turned her back, but Madeline knew how carefully she must be counting money that really did not exist. She came back with a worn five-dollar bill and Madeline took it from her, not wanting to but knowing Gladys would insist.

"Take your car. There's something I want you to pick up for me while you're down there. And I'm telling you right now, not one word to my sister. You can keep your busybody ways to yourself."

Some kindness or patience that Emmy had drilled into her—and her own guilt—made Madeline keep her mouth shut.

Gladys held out a key—a skeleton key no less—on a narrow leather strap. "There's something I want out of the hotel. This is for the back door. Pull in the alley and park there. You're going to go into the kitchen. Go straight through to the front hall. I want the kicksled, it's right next to the door, you can't miss it. It's awkward and it's heavy, but I think you can handle it. You've got a big trunk on that car of yours, it ought to fit. And be careful, it's an antique. Wrap some sheets around it, take them off the furniture."

"Why—"

"Just please don't ask me any questions."

Madeline counted to five and then said, "Am I allowed to ask what hotel it is I'm going to?"

"Our hotel, of course. On the main street. The Hotel Leppinen."

Madeline didn't bother to stay annoyed at Gladys, not with the key to the building she'd admired so often in her hand. As soon as she got the bone meal at the hardware, she hurried back across the street. She'd already parked in the alley, as Gladys instructed, so now she made her way around the side of the hotel, past a dense thicket of lilacs and through a tiny orchard of gnarled apple trees, up three steps to the back entry. She fitted the key into the lock and pushed the door open.

She stepped inside and drew in a wondering breath. Ten-foot ceilings, hardwood floors, walls wainscoted in dark paneling, massive counters of the same dark wood. The hanging cupboards were fronted with leaded glass and showed orderly stacks of thick white china cups and plates. Lightbulbs hung overhead from their cloth-covered wires, and Madeline saw they were operated by push buttons instead of flip switches. She pushed a button and looked up at the dangling bulbs, but nothing happened. Maybe the electricity wasn't on. The room was dusty and cool, but did not feel abandoned. Frozen, more like. Waiting.

She walked across the kitchen and through a double swinging door and was behind the registration desk, another massive construction of wood and glass. An enormous, ornate cash register sat on top, and Madeline could not resist reaching out to push the "No

Sale" key. The drawer sprang open with a brisk *ching* that startled her. She eased it shut again and moved around the desk into the front room. Furniture sat covered with sheets, and a rug lay rolled against the far wall. A pendulum clock sat on a shelf, and Madeline could almost hear the unflappable, eternal ticktock it would make if it was wound. There was no clutter or disorder, no sense of a place packed up into permanent storage. It was more as if someone had closed down in the fall and would soon be bustling in to open for another season.

She yearned to pull the sheets off everything, unroll the rug, pull open the drawers of every cabinet and counter, but instead she made herself go to the front hall to find the kicksled. Once she saw it—a sort of wooden chair on runners—and lugged it out the back door, stole a couple of sheets from a china cabinet and a settee and swaddled it into the trunk, she couldn't make herself drive straight to Bessel Street.

Instead she went back inside. She wandered through every room, climbed every flight of stairs, peered in every closet. She'd stepped back in time. The woodwork and hardware and floors and wallpaper—everything spoke of another era, not so much simpler as more definite, more solid. The place had been built beautifully, but was without ostentation. Each of the twelve guest rooms was furnished with just a bed and dresser and chair. The beds had black metal frames, each with a blue-striped ticking mattress stripped bare, the blankets and pillow stowed in a plastic bag at the foot. Every pine dresser had a china bowl and pitcher, every dangling bulb a frosted glass shade. The blinds were pulled at every window, waiting to be opened and let the light in.

Madeline creaked along the hallways and with every step her enchantment grew. The final set of stairs led to the attic, and she made her way up, determined to look out the dormered windows she'd seen from the street. At the top of the stairs she pushed a small door open to reveal a large room with rectangles of sunlight falling across the floor—no blinds in these highest windows. There were a few pieces of furniture in a corner, but nothing else. Just a big, empty room. A perfect place for painting. Plenty of light and space, few distractions. She went to the closest north-facing window, and Lake Superior was laid out before her in all its vastness.

Madeline was, suddenly and unequivocally, filled with yearning. This place should be open, running, welcoming visitors, showing itself off, reinstated in its rightful place as queen of the street. Why had Gladys and Arbutus ever closed? The hotel was so beautiful and so ready to work. Maybe it was just too much for them, but if they found someone to help—what a place. If it was open, Madeline could hang out up here, painting, while the business of the hotel clattered away below her.

For the first time since Emmy died—and before that, before the last battles of the illness had worn them down, before all the years of work and worry and tending to practicalities—Madeline felt a charge of possibility run all the way through her.

A car door slammed on the street below with a muted thump and jolted her back to the moment.

All this dreaminess was brought on by the building—so romantic and lovely, perched in this beautiful spot, so full of potential. She was a sucker for architecture, she always had been—and *light*, she loved the light on the big lake. And she'd always been insanely sensitive to the spirit of a place. For whatever reason, this hotel called to her at some deep level, called to a self she'd packed up and put away a long time ago, a self who was going to be an artist, have adventures, live in a garret in Paris maybe, or a remote shack in Alaska.

All those ideas had been nothing but unformed, youthful dreams.

Still, she *could* do something new and different now, if she wanted to. Wasn't that why she was here in the first place? She shouldn't forget that. She should find a way—a reasonable way of course—to keep those old dreams alive. She should keep drawing, for sure. After one last look out the window, Madeline headed back to the car.

A *few mornings later* the burner on the gas stove didn't light when Gladys turned the knob. After peering into the oven to check the pilot, she sent Madeline out to check the tank.

Madeline came back in. "It says it's empty."

"That can't be."

"That's what it says."

Gladys glanced over her shoulder, thinking of Arbutus, not wanting her to hear from where she sat in the parlor watching the television. "Let me see."

She went outside and peered at the gauge and tapped it, hard, but the reading didn't change. She picked up a branch and whacked at the belly of the tank and sure enough, it sounded hollow. She dropped the branch. "Damn it, I just filled the thing." She bit her lip, chagrined at herself for cursing.

Madeline came up behind her. "Are you sure?"

"Of course I'm sure." But even as she said it she knew she was wrong. When she let herself think about it, Gladys knew that the tank hadn't been filled in months. Time just went so fast, was all, and money went almost nowhere. She took a deep breath, exhaled in a gust. "We'll have to get more, that's all."

Of course it wasn't that easy and Madeline would know it. She'd snooped at the bills and probably had seen the one from the gas company stamped "Delinquent." The stamp went on to say, *"Please*

note that we can no longer refill any tanks for delinquent accounts."
One good thing, if they'd had a rubber stamp made up to say all that,
she couldn't be the only one with money troubles. Which wasn't
much consolation.

Gladys felt like flinging herself on the ground and having a
good old-fashioned tantrum. It was a shame and a waste, but she
was going to have to sell the kicksled, Grandma's *potkukelkka* she
brought all the way from Finland, to raise the money to pay the bill.
She'd find some way to explain it to Arbutus later. It was just a thing,
after all. A thing that had been sitting in the front hall of the hotel
for years, not doing anybody any good. And the antiques man from
over in the Soo had offered her a big price for it a decade ago, before
she'd closed the place up for good. She'd scoffed at him, told him
she was poor but not so poor she'd go selling off family heirlooms.
Well. How the mighty had fallen.

She'd just about made up her mind to sell it even before the gas
tank turned up empty. The jolt of fury she'd felt when she caught
Madeline inspecting her bills finally gave her the courage—or
foolhardiness?—to take the first step in doing this terrible, terrible
thing. Only it wasn't so terrible. It was just necessary. Now that first
step was taken, it wouldn't be so hard to take the next one. That
was the way of life. She'd call the man if she could get a minute
alone. She knew he was still in business at the same place. She
allowed herself to wonder if it had been a mistake, after all, to close.
It would have been a trickle of money coming in, at least. But the
expense of it all—the heat, the electric, fixing the roof, a hundred
other things the old behemoth needed.

"What are we going to do?" Madeline asked.

That startled Gladys back to the present. Of course Madeline
wouldn't know anything about trouble like this. She'd grown up
coddled and modern in Chicago, a world away from the life Gladys

led, or Joe Stone, or even Jackie, come to that, though it was not
Gladys's habit to give Jackie the benefit of any doubt.

"*We're* not going to do anything. I'll take care of the gas company.
You go bring in some wood for the cookstove, I can't think why you
let it get so low by the door."

Madeline gave her an exasperated look but headed for the
woodpile beside the shed without saying anything. That stack was
low too, Gladys noticed, narrowing her eyes. It hadn't concerned
her much before—summer was coming—but now its meagerness
seemed ominous. She stood chewing her bottom lip a moment
before she bent and picked up two small pieces near the door.

"Arbutus!" she called out once she had a fire snapping. "Come
get your coffee." She gave Madeline a severe look: *not one word*.

"Glad, it's too hot for a fire," Arbutus complained when she
came in.

"Nonsense. Nothing like a fire for baking, I'm making bread
today. *Hiivaleipä*, like Mother used to make, if we've got the barley.
You'll like that."

Arbutus sighed and pulled at the neckband of her blouse, fan-
ning herself.

After breakfast, Madeline went to Emil's to find out about getting more wood. "And stop by the fruit man on your way back, I
want some apples," Gladys said.

Emil's place sat atop the hill that plunged into town, along a dirt
road that seemed to lead into the depths of nowhere. When Madeline got out of the car, she stopped a moment to take in his million-
dollar view, which she hadn't bothered to do the other two times
she'd been there. Tiny McAllaster sat nestled below; the forest and
bogs stretched far in either direction; Lake Superior churned in all

its stunning immensity to the north. Then Emil came around the corner and Madeline headed toward him.

Emil was built small and wiry—it was hard to guess his age but she thought seventy or even eighty—and he looked as tough as an old strap of leather. He wore a red and black plaid shirt buttoned up to his chin, rubber boots tied up tight to his knees, and despite the mildness of the day, a lumpy knitted cap. His expression was watchful, a little amused, and Madeline had the uncomfortable sense that he was reading her mind. He carried a gun, the barrel easing toward the ground. A beagle trotted after him and came up to her to have its ears rubbed. Emil lifted his chin in greeting.

"I'm Madeline Stone," she began.

"You came with Paul Garceau to pick up the kid. And you're Joe Stone's granddaughter, that right?"

"Ah—yes."

Emil nodded. "Thought so. You look like your great-grandma."

"So I've heard." Madeline said this calmly—coolly, almost—but she felt a thrill of curiosity that she immediately stomped out, like a tiny grass fire that could be controlled if she was fast enough and vigilant.

"You drop that food off on my step awhile back?"

"Gladys sent it out for you, extra she made, she thought you might like it."

"Meat loaf was a mite spicy, you ask me. I don't like them red things in it."

"Pimientos?"

"I don't know, red things. They give it a funny flavor. I fed it to Sal, she ate it up, she ain't fussy. The cookies was tasty, though. I don't suppose she sent any more?"

"No. Actually she needs a favor."

"That so? Glad, she don't ask for nothing easy."

Madeline wondered if he meant Gladys didn't easily ask for anything, or that she never asked for anything simple, thinking both
were probably true. "She needs some wood."

"She run out of what I brang her last fall already? That was
more'n five face cords, I thought they was heating with fuel oil, just
using a little wood here and there."

"It's almost gone."

Emil sighed. "Come on in," he said, walked over to his trailer
and up the steps.

The trailer reeked of sour clothes and dirty dishes and urine,
spilt whiskey and wet dog and skinned raccoon—a pile of skins was
draped on a chair just inside the door. There were boxes piled everywhere, overflowing with rags, oily smelling parts, magazines and
papers, empty bottles, chain saws in various states of dismantlement.

Emil tipped the skins off the chair and waved her into it, then
hiked another chair up close and settled down, pushing Sal aside
with a boot. He crossed his legs tidily, the right knee cocked over
the left. He tapped his toe up and down in the air, thoughtful and
almost dainty. "Butte, she get cold easy now, that the problem?"

Madeline made a noncommittal sound and then challenged into
truth by his look she said, "They're out of propane."

Emil scratched his cheek with a black-nailed finger. "They sold
that car of Butte's here a month or more ago, couldn'ta got much
for it, it was old. Wouldn't be surprised they put Butte's house up
next, eh?"

She nodded. Maybe they would, no matter what Gladys said.
Arbutus was quiet but she was determined, and once she got an
idea about something Madeline thought she was not likely to let
go of it easily. The house was a few blocks away from Gladys's,
on Mill Street. Madeline had gone there to tend the flower beds.

Butte's flowers were much more rambunctious and disordered than Gladys's, much prettier really, and more numerous, though her yard was a fraction of the size. Her place was sweet but minuscule, no more than twenty feet by forty, with no garage or shed, even, and Madeline wasn't sure it would bring what she owed if they did decide to sell.

"They ain't got much, really, but what they do got is going fast. Them bills from the hospital is eating it all up."

Madeline nodded again.

Emil tapped his fingers on his ankle. "This ain't a good time for it," he said at last. "All mud out in the woods with this rain. Hard to get back in where I usually go. Plus the State's keeping a sharp eye out, setting up a sale. Hell, they'll ruin more'n I could ever take if I kept at it steady all year. Knock it over, leave it to rot, God help you, you go in and take a piece. But I'll get 'em some wood."

"Thank you."

"You tell Gladys she can pay me when she's got the money around, no sooner. And send me out some more of them cookies. That's the interest on the loan." He cackled and clumped his right foot to the floor, startling Sal.

"I'll tell her." Madeline stood to leave and then she said, fast before she could think better of it, "So, did you know my grandfather?"

"*Know* him? Slept two to a bunk with him coupla winters in lumber camp down at Wolf, it was that damn cold. Tipped down a few at the Trackside with him now and again too, long time ago. Yeah, I knew him."

Madeline waited, but Emil didn't offer anything else, so she walked to the door, relieved in a way.

"Don't forget them cookies," he said.

She forgot the apples. "I'll go back," she told Gladys when she realized.

"I suppose you'll have to. I thought of a few other things. Make sure you tell Albert it's for me. It makes a difference, don't think it doesn't."

"I'm sure it does."

"Get a rutabeg if he has any. I've got such a taste for them browned in butter, Mother fixed them that way. Get some asparagus too, Butte loves asparagus."

"Okay."

"Get a gallon of milk at the gas station, unless you want to run to Crosscut."

"No, I'll get some."

"Get carrots. And make sure the spuds are firm. And check the onions, he might have Vidalias. Don't let him sell you any of last winter's yellows, their texture'll be no good. And look at the apples, if he got any. Make sure there's no brown spots, and make *sure* they're tart. I don't want any sweet apples."

"I've purchased an apple before, Gladys, I think I can handle it."

"I want what I want, that's all."

"Don't we all."

Before Madeline got halfway down the walk Gladys opened the screen and called out, "Make sure you stop by Mary's stand, see if she needs help with anything."

Madeline waved without turning and got in her car, which still sported its gloved wiper. Also it was developing a knock she couldn't account for and the tailpipe was crumbling, eaten away by rust. She backed out onto Bessel Street, but there was a strange lurchiness in the car's bearing, so she stopped to investigate and found the rear tire on the passenger's side flat. This she was not prepared for. She thought wistfully of her old familiar car guru. She needed a new Pete Kinney. Was there even a mechanic in this town? She supposed there must be, and supposed too that really any self-respecting McAllaster-ite would know how to change her own tire. She sighed and considered her options and then pulled the Buick carefully back into the drive.

After a moment's more consideration she headed down the street on foot rather than taking Gladys's car. It was a beautiful day, and what else was she doing? It'd give her half an hour of privacy anyway. The house was just so small. It seemed strange and unfriendly to sit in her room during the day, so she rarely did. Only if she was sketching. But the truth was that as much as she loved Arbutus and held a cautious regard for Gladys, sometimes Madeline felt like she'd scream if she spent one more hour at the kitchen table with yet another cup of coffee.

A thought she'd been having for days came into her mind as she walked: *You could sneak back into the hotel.* She stomped the thought out, another little grass fire that could be controlled. But the idea was so attractive, before long its spark had flamed up again and she was talking herself into it. She'd forgotten to give the key back that first day, and Gladys had neglected to ask for it. Madeline found it now in her pocket, and her fingers wrapped around it just for the pleasure of holding it. There was no harm in going in. Gladys wouldn't mind. Madeline wouldn't be hurting anything. It would be a very tiny and completely harmless adventure that would take nothing from anyone.

Madeline gave herself twenty minutes in the hotel—up in the attic, staring out at the lake—because anything more than that and Gladys would start to wonder what had become of her. When her time was up she clattered back down the stairs and out the door, taking care to look relaxed and confident, so that if anyone noticed her they'd assume she'd been there on some errand for Gladys.

7

The fruit man's stand was just three long tables with a canvas awning pulled over them, behind which sat a battered white delivery van with the doors slid open. The fruit man himself was tall and lanky, brown from standing out in the sun. He looked tired and worn, as if he had worked too many hours for too many years. But he also looked kind.

He handled the produce fast but gently with big hands that never stopped moving, and he chewed on a stub of unlit cigar as he talked, keeping up a steady stream of conversation with his customers. As quickly as he could sell cartons of tomatoes and bags of onions and bunches of celery and little crates of plums and apples and apricots, he had his helper bring out more from the back of the truck.

His helper was his opposite—short, bandy-legged like a jockey, with a shock of white hair and rheumy blue eyes. He wore hard-soled brown oxfords with a pattern tooled into the toes, brown polyester pants, a silky blue windbreaker. He grumbled over his chores but he didn't seem really to mind them. He hurried as best he could on his crooked legs, saying, "Yeah, yeah," to his boss's orders in a put-upon way that seemed merely habit, flashing a seedy grin at the ladies.

Madeline waited her turn as half a dozen women ahead of her squeezed tomatoes and thunked melons. They must have all simultaneously been watching the television and had seen that the fruit man's line was short.

Apparently there was a webcam mounted on one of the buildings nearby that made a sweep of the main street and the water's edge, panning a nearly changeless landscape day and night. This played nonstop on the local cable channel. Madeline had laughed out loud when she stopped at Mabel Brink's house one day to return a dish Gladys had borrowed and found her watching the static scene with great absorption. Mabel had said she wanted to see how busy it was at the bank before she bothered to drive downtown, a distance of three blocks. So now Madeline waited her turn, struggling to hide how funny she found this because the ladies mightn't have been amused.

The produce looked good and the prices seemed fair, and she thought it was no wonder the grocery didn't want the fruit man coming to town, although she doubted the Bensons would consider him significant competition. Even if he did cut into their business, she didn't suppose they would do anything to stop him. Wasn't competition the gospel of the free market, and weren't they more patriotic than the president himself with their two oversized flags flapping at the front of the store?

"Well now, young lady, what can I do for you?" Albert asked when it was her turn. She explained what Gladys wanted.

"Ah, Gladys." The way he said it made her grin When they'd assembled everything, he said, "Where's your car, I'll send Gus to carry for you."

"*Me* carry? *You* carry, I'm getting too old for this game," Gus said.

"Oh, that's all right, I walked."

"Walk, when you have all this?" Albert shook his head, chewing on the cigar harder. "Naw, that ain't no good, it's too much to lug all that way."

"I'm fine, don't worry. I'll make a couple of trips. It's a nice day."

"Naw, now listen. You just leave it and I'll drop it off on my way out of town."

She protested, but he was immovable. Finally she gave in, and his smile was delighted and boylike. "Here, take an apricot," he said, handing her a big, deeply golden one from a pint basket that the woman next in line had been about to buy.

Madeline stopped by Mary's stand next, but Mary was deep in conversation with a young couple who looked like tourists, so Madeline ambled along Main Street, apricot juice dripping down her chin, looking in shop windows. In the first block there was Taylor's Two Scoops and McAllaster Crafts, neither of which had opened for the season yet; Second Time Around Consignments (only open three days a week); and The Butcher Block Café. The next block was mostly consumed by the hotel—which sat on three lots, at least—and Benson's SuperValu, next to which sat a tiny bakery called Maki's Pasties, also not yet open. The third block had the Tip Top Tavern and a small engine repair shop that didn't have any obvious name. She turned the corner there.

She passed the Village office and the newspaper office and then saw a hand-printed "Help Wanted" sign in the window of the next business, which was Paul Garceau's pizzeria. Gladys and Arbutus had told her that he owned the place. She stuffed the apricot pit in her pocket, suddenly interested. She'd only been thinking of saying hello—she hadn't seen Paul since that day they'd returned Greyson to Randi, but she'd thought about him a few times, thought maybe he was someone who could be a friend—but what about a job? Maybe a job was exactly what she needed.

Paul's building looked like an old house, long and low-slung, white clapboard with red shutters. It was sweet—appealing with its quaint shutters—but the location seemed unfortunate to Madeline, sitting on this uninspiring side street. Though maybe location didn't matter so much in such a small town, maybe all that mattered was being the only pizzeria. She pulled open the door.

Inside it smelled of hot bread and pizza sauce. A chalkboard behind the counter described the menu options, and in the lower corner a quotation was written in blue chalk: *There are no facts, only interpretations. F. Nietzsche.* She grinned. She'd told a customer at Spinelli's almost the same thing one time, not realizing it was an official kernel of philosophy, and had been surprised how angry the woman got. Her eyes traveled on. There were three wooden booths along each wall, the tables covered with red-checked cloths. The floor was a checkerboard of white and black tile and the walls were crowded with framed photos and pictures. Music drifted out of the kitchen, something bluesy.

A bell had jingled when she opened the door and after a moment Paul came out from the kitchen. He wore chinos, a white T-shirt and half apron, silver-rimmed spectacles. She didn't remember those from before.

"Madeline Stone," he said, sounding really pleased. "Hello. What brings you in? Hungry? Thirsty?"

Madeline felt flustered. She only wanted to ask about the job now that she knew there was one. It was true that Arbutus needed her, especially at the crucial moments, but she didn't want to be watched like a hawk from sunup to sundown and even her sweet nature was showing signs of strain. For her own part, Madeline was getting more than a little restless, and more and more worried about money. She was already dipping into her savings to pay the few bills she had, and that made her nervous. "I wondered about your sign," she said, hearing how abrupt it sounded after the words were out.

"Ah." Paul ran his hand through his hair. "Aren't you working for Gladys and Arbutus?"

"Well—yes. But it's not exactly filling all my hours."

"Ah," he said again, and Madeline started to regret having said anything.

"If you've already hired someone—" she began, but he stopped her.

"You took me by surprise, is all. Usually the Russian girls who come for the summer to clean rooms at the big motel come looking, but I put the sign up early this year, so you're the first."

"You get Russians up here to work?"

"Oh, sure. It's an adventure, and good money—to them. But it's not much, I have to tell you. And it's a lot of work."

"I know that."

He squinted at her. "It'd be part-time, at least to start—I hire a few part-timers—and only until fall."

"That'd be perfect."

"I need someone who can do whatever. Wait tables, chop vegetables, grate cheese, sweep the floors, wash dishes. It's no sinecure."

"I was a waitress in Chicago," Madeline said, annoyed. He seemed to have sized her up somehow and found her lacking, or unlikely. "This is the only kind of work I've ever really done. I know what it's like, trust me."

"Sorry. I just would hate to get you in here under false pretenses. If you're really interested, I'll show you around."

Half an hour later she was employed, four days a week from noon to five. It wasn't the busiest shift, he said, but she thought it was the best time of the day to be away from the house. She was almost back there when it occurred to her that probably she should have asked Gladys and Arbutus how they felt about this before she plunged in. Her victorious feeling faded a little. But she needed this job. Gladys and Arbutus would understand. They'd have to.

"How nice for you," Arbutus beamed when Madeline got home—not only empty-handed but also much later than Gladys had expected, how was she supposed to get the *ruskettunut lanttu* ready for dinner when she didn't even have the rutabagas yet?—and told them her news. "You'll meet people, get out of the house."

"Plenty of ways to get out of the house without taking a job. What about Butte?"

"Oh, pshaw. I'm all right."

"She's here to work for us, not go gallivanting around town."

"I'm fine. You're here, and if something goes wrong she's not far away. Goodness, what a worrier you've turned into."

Gladys did worry. She couldn't sleep through the night, as often as not. After tossing and turning she'd go sit at the kitchen table at two and three in the morning, holding Madeline's cat on her lap, stroking his fur—this was more comforting than she ever would have dreamed—staring at nothing.

How to solve this fix they were in? For a while now she'd been selling things on eBay with Mabel Brink's help, a fact she'd wanted to keep to herself but which Madeline had found out. She felt a little lift of pride, remembering how astounded Madeline had been when she stopped in at Mabel's one afternoon and caught them scanning photos of an old silver alarm clock into Mabel's computer. Gladys wanted forty dollars for it, if some fool would pay so much for something that hadn't cost five new in 1956. She had twelve of them, all exactly alike. Madeline had been amazed at the two of them, so handy with the digital camera and scanner, but why shouldn't they know how to do these things? They were old but they weren't dead yet. A now familiar feeling of urgency gripped Gladys, though. She wasn't dead but she was eighty-five. She wouldn't go on forever.

"You might as well help me mail the packages, now that you know," Gladys had said to Madeline after she found out about eBay. Arbutus wasn't to know a thing about it, period, just as she was not to know anything about the kicksled, which Gladys hadn't yet dealt with. It was still lodged in the trunk of that disreputable car of Madeline's that was now sitting like an abandoned wreck in the drive. Madeline had agreed to keep quiet, but reluctantly. She didn't seem to think Gladys should keep so many secrets. Well, she was young, she didn't know there was a lot in life you'd do just as well to keep to yourself.

The fact was that the eBay money was a drop in the bucket compared to what they needed. It helped, but it wasn't enough and never would be no matter what she dragged out of storage and sold. Frank's autograph collection had been one of the first things to go. The Hummel figurines he'd given Gladys in their more prosperous years went next. Right now she had up for auction a 1963 Raleigh bicycle, a six-point antler rack (imagine someone paying good money for that, couldn't go out and get their own), a crate of glass soda bottles from the fifties, and two wool sweaters Mabel Brink had knitted coon's ages ago. Just last night Gladys had Madeline help her wrap up her sterling silver flatware set in its mahogany box. That had been a wedding gift. "Doesn't it hurt to let it go?" Madeline had asked.

"Bah. Someone else may as well have the use of it, it doesn't matter."

This was half true. It did matter, but it also didn't. There was something freeing in letting the old stuff go. It felt a little like a new beginning, although why she should think about such things at her age Gladys really could not imagine.

At any rate, some money came in, but it went out again just as fast. Everyone got something, except for the SuperValu. Gladys refused to budge on that despite the increasing insistence of the Bensons' requests. The reminders came in the mail with the balance due circled in red, and each time there were more exclamation points after the request to *Please Pay!* Gladys tossed every one of these into the garbage.

The only solution was to sell the hotel. No matter what she'd said to Arbutus, no matter how the idea broke her heart, in the end there would be no other way. The kicksled and all the rest of the old things were just the tip of the iceberg.

Albert knocked on the kitchen door just then, a box of produce balanced on his hip, and Gladys was glad of the distraction. With a frown she wasn't even aware of, she snatched the box from his hands and shooed him and Gus into the kitchen for coffee. She noticed as she took the sugar bowl off the side counter that Madeline hadn't taken the bills to the post office like she'd promised. Gladys sighed in vexation. Two of those bills were already close to being late, and now there was no chance they'd go out until tomorrow. She'd have to remind Madeline in the morning, or else do it herself.

Gladys knew very well that Madeline was not like her mother. Jackie had been careless and selfish and immature from the day she was born, and obviously Madeline didn't fit that bill. But still, every now and then Gladys felt a deep stab of uncertainty at what she'd done, pleading with Madeline to come help them, bringing her into their home. Why had she done it, why had she not left well enough alone?

We needed the help, she told herself. *There was no one else.*

But that wasn't really the reason. Not the whole reason anyway.

The real reason was that Gladys was getting old. She felt the truth of that when Arbutus got so bad and there was nothing Gladys could do about it. They'd ended up marooned in Nathan's apartment, helpless to decide their own fate. That was when she really understood, one day she'd be dead and gone. In the meantime, she had to live with herself.

She couldn't stand to think of leaving things so unresolved. The burden of guilt and regret sat heavier and heavier on her shoulders. She had failed when Madeline was a child, failed to ever soften Joe's heart, and that was wrong. He'd been wrong and she'd been powerless to change it. That was why she'd asked Madeline to come here. To make things right. Or at least more right. So far she wasn't doing a very good job of it.

8

Madeline reported at Garceau's for her first shift a little before noon the next day, and realized as she arrived that she'd forgotten the mail again. She'd grabbed it off the counter on her way out but forgot to drop it at the post office. That was so unlike her that she actually stopped in her tracks. But it was too late to fix now, the bills would just have to wait.

Paul let her in the front door. "I just got here myself. Give me a minute."

Madeline nodded, but he was already gone. Her eyes wandered to the chalkboard. The Nietzsche quote had been erased. She studied the setup behind the counter while she waited for him to reappear. There was a juicer, a Bunn, an ice machine, a milk shake maker, an ice cream freezer—a little bit of everything. She was peering into the ice cream case when she heard music come on in the kitchen—something Latin and salsa-y—and then Paul came back out. He went straight to the chalkboard and wrote, *That which doesn't kill us makes us stronger. F. Nietzsche.*

"Having a rough day?" Madeline asked, meaning to be funny. Paul gave her an inscrutable look and didn't answer. She bit her lip.

He wiped the chalk dust from his hands. "Okay, then. Here we go."

When he'd shown her the basics—the equipment, the kitchen, the register—and turned the sign to "Open," he offered her a cup of coffee and sat down in the nearest booth.

"So, you always open at noon?" Madeline asked, sliding in across from him.

"Yeah. I work down at the prison in Crosscut until eleven, so I can't really get here any earlier."

"You have this place *and* you work at the prison?" Gladys and Arbutus hadn't told her this, only that he owned the pizzeria.

"I'm off there on weekends, so it works out."

"But that's, what? Ninety hours a week, at least, between the two? *And* commuting? You must be exhausted."

Just for a moment she saw in his face that it was true. But he shrugged and said, "It's not bad. I don't open up here on Mondays, so that's a day off. Half a day. Gives me a chance to do other things. Pay bills, do laundry."

"That's crazy."

"It's what I signed up for."

Madeline studied him over the rim of her coffee cup, thinking that this attitude was at least in part a front. "You'll kill yourself, nobody can keep that up."

Paul gazed at her, his brows slightly lifted.

"Sorry. None of my business."

He nodded.

"What do you do at the prison?"

"Cook."

"Do you like it?"

"It's a paycheck." He seemed to not like how this had sounded and added, "It's all right. Somebody has to do it."

"Have you been there a long time?"

"Six years."

"How long have you had this place? You know, I always think of pizza guys being Italian, but Garceau sounds French. I guess here it doesn't matter, right? I mean, not so many Italians to go around, and who doesn't like pizza?"

"Garceau is French. Acadian, actually. I've been here nine years. And pizza was just something I fell into. The guy who was in here before me tried it but gave up. I thought I'd have better luck."

"Oh," Madeline said, nodding and smiling. "And have you?"

"Sure." Paul took a long swallow of coffee.

Madeline stayed quiet then, which was awkward, but everything she'd said so far had been worse.

After a moment Paul said, "You'll need a T-shirt, they're in the case beside the register. Take whatever color you want, it doesn't matter. What I'm thinking is, you can get here a little before me, get things set up, open the door. Then when I get here we can start serving." He glanced at the clock. "Speaking of which, it's time I got going in the kitchen. So, what'd I leave out?"

Madeline shook her head. "I don't know yet. Probably a lot, I'll tell you later."

"Sounds fair. So I'll just throw you in and we'll either sink or swim. That okay?"

Madeline was about to say that was fine when the doorbells jingled and Randi Hopkins came in. Despite the cool day she was wearing a short, vividly green dress with satiny spaghetti straps. Madeline felt her lips compress in a prissy disapproval that made her roll her eyes at herself—since when did she censure clothing? The dress showed off Randi's shoulders, which were perfect somehow, neither too bony nor too fat.

"Hey, Paul," Randi said in her husky voice. "You open?"

"Just." Paul stood up, smiling and heading toward her. "How's everything? How's Greyson?"

Randi laughed. Shook her braids so the beads and bells clacked and jingled. "He's *good*. He's a doll. Thanks for looking after him Monday, he sure does like you. It's Mr. Garceau this and Mr. Garceau that every other minute. He kills me."

"Glad he had a good time. Where is he?"

"He's down at Halfway with Roscoe and Annie, he just loves Andrea. He's so cute with her, you'd think he was her big brother or something. Such a little old man."

A thoughtful look flickered across Paul's face. "That he is."

"So, when are you ever finally going to quit that nasty job down at the prison?" Randi asked after a moment.

"Never, I guess. Those poor guys have to have someone who can cook for them."

Randi's eyes drifted over to Madeline and Paul said, "I'm just showing Madeline around. She's going to be working here this summer."

"Oh. Well, that's cool." Randi sounded anything but enthused and Madeline thought, *You've got a thing for him.* Then she thought if that was so it might show the girl had at least some sense, because all in all, Paul Garceau seemed like a decent person.

After a week Madeline felt like she was getting the hang of the place. Paul even left her alone for ten or fifteen minutes sometimes, if he had an errand to run. The doorbells jangled one afternoon and Madeline looked up from juicing lemons to see Randi coming in with Greyson. His red hair was tousled and his freckled, narrow face was as intense as Madeline remembered.

"Hello, Madeline!" he said.

"Grey! You know better. You have to say, 'Miss Stone.'"

"Oh, no," Madeline said. "He can't do that, I won't know who he's talking to."

"Well, but I like him to be polite. He does a real good job of it, don't you, Grey?"

Madeline wondered if she could ever get used to that voice—husky and sexy no matter what Randi said. Randi leaned against the counter and plucked a lemon from Madeline's bowl. "So you're helping Gladys and Arbutus. That is so cool."

"I like them." Madeline squeezed another lemon, her eye on the one in Randi's hand. It was silly, it was only a lemon, but she wanted it back where it belonged.

"It is so cool of Gladys to, like, send me leftovers. She is such a good cook, tell her thank you again for me. I sort of forgot in the Trackside that day, I was so upset." Randi rolled the lemon on the counter under her palm. Madeline wanted to snatch it from her and say, *Tell her yourself, you thoughtless girl, and you don't really think they're leftovers, do you?* But she didn't. She said, "All right."

Randi put the lemon back in the bowl finally and ordered a lemonade, then scooped Greyson up so they could drink it together. After a few sips she said, "So, where's Paul, is he in the kitchen?" Madeline was a little ashamed of herself for feeling a stab of satisfaction at being able to say, no, he wasn't, he'd gone to the bank. Randi shrugged and said "Oh" in a way that was hard to read. Madeline wondered at her own curiosity—were Randi and Paul a couple, did Randi have a crush on him?—but supposed it was only human nature. She watched them leave, Greyson waving from his perch on Randi's hip, then ran a bucket of hot water to clean up the juicer.

For Pete's sake, she sighed to herself, and smiled sadly. (That had been one of Emmy's catchphrases, Emmy who never swore ever.) She made a mental apology to Emmy for wanting to wring Randi's neck. She'd promised to be more forgiving, but so far it wasn't going so well.

The doorbells tinkled again a moment later.

"Hey!" Randi said, popping her head back in. "Are you, like, really super busy?"

"Ah—not right at the moment."

Randi came fully inside, tugging Greyson behind her. "Can I ask you, like, a really, really big favor?"

"Umm. Well. You can ask."

"Could you look after Greyson for a tiny minute? Like for maybe half an hour?"

"I—"

"I promise, he is totally no trouble." Randi turned her son toward her and tugged his T-shirt straight. "You be a good boy for Madeline," she told him and he nodded.

"Hey, I don't—"

"Paul won't mind, I promise, he is *such* a sweetie. I've just got to do, like, *one* thing, and then I'll be back. Forty minutes, tops." She gave Madeline an enormous smile. "Thank you *so much*. You are a sweetheart, I totally owe you. And I will be *right back*, I promise." Then she said, "Mama loves you, sweet pea," to Greyson and gave him a little wave. He waved back, and she grinned with delight. "He kills me," she said, and vanished out the door.

When Paul came back, he turned a CD on low in his kitchen and the Latin, salsa-y music drifted out. He always acted cheerful enough, but nonetheless there were times when she thought he was sad, or thoughtful, and she associated this music with that now. She wondered what he was thinking about.

"What do I do?" she whispered to him across the pass-through when he'd put his apron on. Greyson sat at a table with a place mat and crayons, coloring.

Paul was dicing onions, pushing every now and then with the back of his wrist at the glasses that made him look scholarly and a bit owlish.

"I don't know," he whispered back, seeming to be mocking her a little.

"No, really."

He glanced at Greyson, smiled at him, went back to chopping. "She'll show up sooner or later."

"Oh, that's reassuring. And if she doesn't?"

"Take him home with you if she's not back when you're done."

"*What?*"

"You can't leave him here, I'm sorry."

Madeline gave him a dirty look. "He's absolutely no trouble, I promise."

"I know, he really isn't. But no one's coming on after you tonight, and I have too much going on to be responsible." He waved his knife, indicating the tables, the kitchen, the oven, everything. "Otherwise, I'd say let him stay."

Madeline fidgeted a moment, but couldn't think of anything to do but go on being slightly disagreeable and put upon. "Well, where is she? She said forty minutes."

Paul shrugged. "Welcome to McAllaster."

"Does she, like, just *do* this?"

"She does."

"That's crazy."

"Not really. It's working for her, isn't it? She got me the other day, same way she got you. Not that I minded. He really is a good kid."

Greyson had looked up and was watching them with sharp, unwavering intelligence. Madeline gave him a big smile. He gazed at her for a moment without returning the smile before he went back to his coloring.

"Oh, God."

"Really, you might as well take him home with you, your old ladies will get a kick out of him. I'll tell Randi where you are."

"She drops him off with whoever'll take him. That's great. I'm surprised social services doesn't get after her."

He paused to look at her, then looked back down at his chopping. She could tell her comment had irritated him. "Greyson's fine. Randi'll be back, don't worry. She's just young. Too young to have a kid, maybe, but there you go. It's a done deal, might as well cope with it."

"I don't want to cope with it, it's not my problem. I don't want—" A kid. The responsibility. Anything to do with Randi Hopkins, who rings way too many bells. Madeline didn't say any of this, one, because it didn't reflect well on her and, two, because Greyson was looking at her again, and she knew that he knew what she was thinking.

"Nice," Paul said.

"She's very irresponsible."

Paul never looked up from his chopping. "Not really. She loves Grey. And you're hardly an ax murderer."

"I could be. She doesn't know."

"You're looking after Arbutus, for God's sake. You *radiate* safeness."

"Well, it still seems wrong to me," Madeline said, annoyed.

"Cheer up," he said, impersonally. "Take him home with you, give the old ladies a treat. Randi will be around to pick him up, I promise. And if you really can't, well, he can stay here. I'll figure it out."

At five o'clock Greyson and Madeline walked home, from Avenue C to Main, then down Edsel to Lake to Bessel. Somewhere across town a dog barked. Madeline could hear the lake crashing into shore. A seagull keened. It was sneaking up on her, but this remote outpost was starting to seem normal to her. She remembered how it looked from on top of the hill that first morning: a tiny clearing in a vast wilderness of trees, Lake Superior spread out before it like the sea. Without that oceanlike horizon she'd feel claustrophobic, climb the walls. But with it—despite her frequent loneliness and boredom—she had a sense of having been set free.

"Hey, Miss Stone, guess what?"

"Call me Madeline. But what?" She was taking small steps to match Greyson's and holding his hand at the street crossings, but she realized she hadn't been paying much attention to him really. She wondered at his equanimity.

"Did you know that gravity holds people down onto the earth and it's also the same thing roads are made of?"

"Is that so?"

"Yes, it is. I learned about it on television. The holding-people-down part. The road part I figured out for myself."

Gravity, gravel. Well, he was close. "I see. That's very smart of you."

"Yes. I am pretty smart, people say so."

They walked along quietly for a little while. Madeline tried to figure out something intelligent to say. "So what's your favorite food?" she finally asked.

"Mr. Garceau's meat lover's pizzas, those are the best."

"Do you eat there a lot?"

"Yes. Whenever my mom has enough tips, we go. She loves to eat at Mr. Garceau's. She works at the bar, you know."

"I did know that. Does she like it?"

"It's okay. She says when guys hit on her it's annoying, but it's not too bad unless they're really drunk." Greyson hopped over a crack in the sidewalk, then looked up at Madeline with an expression that was both sunny and knowing.

"Oh," she said. "Well, I suppose."

"Yep. She says, 'What the Hell are you gonna do?' Oops! I'm not supposed to say Hell, she says so."

"Better not, then," Madeline said, feeling sad.

"Okay. Don't tell, okay?"

"Okay."

"She has to come home late and she smells all smoky and sleeps in until noon, I don't like that part. It makes her tired, working there."

"Yes, I imagine so."

"She's a nice person, my mom."

Madeline squeezed his hand. "She must be, you're such a nice kid," she said, and he smiled somewhat smugly.

Gladys and Arbutus were as pleased as punch when Madeline brought Greyson in. They fawned over him and fed him cupcakes and milk and Gladys played hangman with him. "Blue moon" was one of her mystery phrases. "Power Ranger" was one of Greyson's. Gladys ended up hung on that one.

Randi didn't show up until after dinner. There was a quick tap at the kitchen door and then it opened. "Okay if I barge in?" she said, and did without waiting for an answer.

Greyson bolted across the room and jumped into her arms. "Hey, little man!" she cried and gave him a squeeze and a shower of smacky kisses that made him giggle.

Madeline stood with her arms crossed, watching.

"Thank you *so* much," Randi said. "You're a peach to look after Grey."

"It's after seven."

"Oh, I know, time just disappears, doesn't it?"

"Apparently it does. You said forty minutes."

A puzzled look flashed across Randi's face, a look that wondered why Madeline was being so churlish, especially in front of her little boy. Hadn't she enjoyed him, did he deserve to be made to feel like a burden?

"He wasn't a bit of trouble," Gladys declared. Arbutus chimed in, "No dear, not a bit. You bring Greyson by any time, we're always glad to see him."

"He was fine," Madeline said. "He was great. But you're very late."

"Oh, gosh, I got sidetracked. You know how it is."

Madeline gave her a fake, angry smile because she didn't. She did not approve and she didn't mind if she showed it. She assumed she and Gladys would be in solid agreement for once. "That certainly is one feckless girl," she said after they'd gone.

"Randi?"

"Yes, Randi, who do you think? She just left her child with me for the day, a complete stranger."

"Greyson is a dear boy, and you're hardly a total stranger."

"*I* think I am, and besides, that's not the point."

"It didn't hurt you a bit to look after that child, he's no trouble."

"That is *not* the point. *He's* no trouble, she is. Big trouble."

"Randi's young, that I will grant you. But she's not a bad girl."

Real anger boiled inside Madeline. "How can you say that? She treats him like—like a spare jacket or something. He's an *after-*thought. Why do you stand up for her?" She banged a dirty pot into the sink.

"She's a child," Gladys said, her eyes skimming the newspaper she had open.

"That's no excuse."

"It's the best excuse she's got." Gladys clucked at Marley, and he—the traitor—hopped into her lap.

"That is completely lame. Her behavior is inexcusable. She's an unfit mother, he should be taken away from her."

"Glad to know you've got everything all figured out," Gladys said, her tone dry and her eyes still skimming the paper.

"Oh—for*get* it," Madeline snapped, disgusted with Gladys, and Arbutus, too. She'd seemed nothing but pleased to see Greyson, absolutely unconcerned that his mother was hours late to get him. Didn't either of them wonder how that made him feel? She finished the dishes in angry silence and decided to finally tackle the flat on her car.

It took her half an hour to wrangle the kicksled out of the way so she could get at the jack, and then get the jack set to her satisfaction, another ten minutes to find the lug wrench and get the first nut loosened. She kept having to reread the owner's manual, which was—miraculously, really—stowed in the glove box. No matter how frustrating it was, it beat reviewing what a wonderful mother Randi Hopkins was. She gave the next lug nut a fierce wrench and it loosened. She got through the other three that same way: *I do not*, wrench! *like*, wrench! *Randi Hopkins*, wrench!

All done. She stepped back, inspecting her progress. What next? She was on her stomach trying to attach the doohickey to the jack when a great feeling of peace washed over her. Who needed therapy when you had a crappy old car to contend with?

Gladys watched Madeline out the parlor window. When she rolled over on her back and grinned at the sky, Gladys thought, *At least she worked that out of her system. For the moment.* How like she was to Joe in some ways. Quick-tempered, judgmental, so sure of being in the right, so slow to forgive. Stubborn and guarded, not one to wear her feelings on her sleeve. But she seemed to have a good heart like Joe too. Not that Madeline would ever believe that about him.

Gladys knew she'd started things off wrong with Madeline, snapping at her when she asked which house in McAllaster had belonged to Joe. She wasn't sure why she'd done that. Maybe because Madeline already had her mind made up about him. Maybe because her tone that morning had reminded her of Jackie, however unfairly. Too familiar somehow. Chummy ahead of real friendship, charming you out of something. Probably mostly because Gladys felt guilty. For years she had told herself there was no reason why she should, but it was a feeling that would not go away.

Gladys let the lace curtain fall back across the window. She stood frowning for a moment, then headed to the kitchen for a bucket of hot soapy water and some glass cleaner. Enough brooding. Brooding never did any good.

9

"What *jackasses*," Gladys cried after she'd returned from a walk to the post office and was opening the mail one morning the next week.

"What is it?" Madeline asked, looking up from a crossword.

Gladys flapped the papers in the air. "The nerve!" She inhaled a wavering breath. "Those *people*. I should have *known*." She began to pace around the kitchen.

"What are you talking about?"

"They can't get away with this. Why, I ought to—" She slammed a fist down on the table. "Bullies, that's what they are. They think they can have anything they want, any way they want." She was trembling with anger.

"Gladys, stop. Please sit down."

"I don't want to sit down. I will not stand for this kind of—*malarkey*."

"You're going to make yourself ill. Stop a minute and breathe." Madeline had stood up and now prodded Gladys toward a chair.

Gladys sat, making sharp, furious exhales. Madeline went and got her a glass of water. When she'd drunk a little of it, Madeline pulled up a chair and tugged at the letter Gladys still had clenched in her hand. When she finally wrested it free she saw that it said that due to nonpayment of accounts due, Alex and Terry Benson of Benson's SuperValu were pursuing a case in court, to be heard at the courthouse in Crosscut on August the sixteenth.

"Oh, Gladys. This is bad. I've got a little money, I can lend it to you. Maybe I'll drop the insurance off the car, save something there. I practically can't drive it anyway."

"I am *not* paying that bill!"

"But you have to. I mean, you did use the groceries, right? Aside from the ones you took back that day? If you don't pay, they'll get a judgment against you."

"I don't care. I wouldn't pay that bill now if they dragged me to China on the end of a rope."

"But, Gladys—"

"I mean what I say. *I will not pay*."

Madeline sat back. Gladys pressed her lips into a thin line. They glared at each other for a long moment. "What about Arbutus?" Madeline asked at last. "How'll she feel? You tell me you don't want her upset with money worries or anything else, you're sneaking around to sell off your prized possessions, but you're going to fight a battle you can't win in court?"

Gladys brushed invisible specks of lint off her slacks, and said again, "I will not pay that bill. Not like this. Not their way. I won't go crawling. I'll see them in court."

Paul thought the situation was funny when Madeline told him about it the next day. She was doing an extra shift because one of the Russian girls he'd hired claimed she was so ill she couldn't get out of bed, but Paul said it probably had more to do with a party he'd heard went on the night before. "So she's history," he'd said on the phone when he called Madeline to see if she could come in.

"You're firing her? What if she's really sick?"

"She's not sick," he'd said, as if that answered the question completely.

"But it's not funny at all," she said now, snapping an order up on the wheel. "Arbutus will hate it, all the fuss, people talking. Gladys'll get listed in the paper for God's sake, don't you ever read the court news?"

"Everybody reads the court news. Major entertainment."

"My point exactly."

Paul slid a deep-dish Mediterranean onto the shelf and Madeline delivered it. After that they were too busy to talk. The stream of tourists coming through was getting larger; McAllaster was a different town than the one she'd pulled into a month before.

She returned to the subject of Gladys and the SuperValu in the late afternoon lull. "I can't believe she's going through with this." She shucked off her sneakers and flexed her feet. Paul sprawled in the booth opposite her.

"I'll send a calzone down with you to the prison, hide a file in it."

"Stop."

"If Channel Four news comes, mention Garceau's."

"Be serious."

"We could use the publicity. I'll be glad to come out in support of this brave old Finlander who's fighting for her right to free groceries."

"*Paul.*" She swatted at him across the table.

He grinned. "Well, isn't that what she's after?"

Madeline sighed and shoved her feet back into her sneakers. "It really isn't funny, you know."

"But it is. Everyone gets so excited. Every little thing is an inferno."

"I thought you'd be on my side."

"I am on your side."

"Right." She gave him a look.

"Of course I am. Otherwise, would I offer to ruin a perfectly good calzone with a file, and compromise my reputation as a law-abiding citizen to boot?"

"Stop it, I'm worried."

He tipped his head slightly and his glasses glinted in the sun coming through the side window. He ran a hand through his hair. "So do something about it."

"Like what? You know Gladys."

"Go and explain to the Bensons, maybe. I don't like them much but they're not monsters. Maybe they don't really know the situation, maybe they just need to be asked. Sometimes that's all people want, to be made to feel correct, you know? You're right, I'm wrong, forgive me my trespasses." He had his hands together as if in prayer or placation, and he was smiling, but there was sympathy in his face, she thought.

"I don't think so."

Paul shrugged.

Madeline considered his suggestion through the last hour of her shift. Maybe he was right, after all. It was the simplest solution, and maybe for that reason alone it would work.

"*I'll drop the case* when the entire bill is paid in full, including what she returned that day, no sooner," Terry Benson said. "That is, unless she's willing to negotiate."

"What does that mean?"

Terry shrugged.

"I'm sure you'll get paid," Madeline lied, because of course Gladys was as good as her word. "But taking her to court—come on. She's trying to take care of her sister and she's having trouble keeping up. You should see what they charge for a day in rehab. Stuff like this happens and things fall apart." Look at what she and Emmy had gone through, trying to keep things together. Sometimes it was almost impossible.

"That is *not* my problem. Do you have any idea how many unpaid accounts there are? I can't afford it!"

A man in a striped shirt joined her at the register. Her husband, Alex. "I can afford it," he said. (But Madeline wondered. How like a man, especially this sort of man, to claim a wealth he didn't actually possess.) "I'm just not going to. Half these people up here expect a free handout and I'm not going to provide it, not for Gladys Hansen or that old drunk Emil, or anyone. And Randi's got plenty of ways to make a buck from what I hear. You might as well not come begging for *any* of them."

Madeline wanted to dive across the counter and strangle him. When she managed to speak, her voice was uneven. "You know what? I think you're pathetic. You're a pathetic, self-righteous *loser*. You may be in the right legally, but you are just wrong out here in the world where I live. To Hell with you."

She turned and stalked out. Her heart was racing and she felt her pulse everywhere, in her throat and wrists and legs. *God*, she hated smug people. What business was it of his if Emil drank? At least Emil wasn't an uptight, supercilious pig! Besides that, Alex Benson drank plenty himself and lost at cards too, from what she'd heard working at Garceau's. And he should be careful what he insinuated about Randi's habits, given his own reputation for trying to feel up the female employees. Why, Verna Callihan had quit over it not a month ago, Madeline thought with indignation, though she had only heard this secondhand and had never met Verna.

She marched back to her car and slammed the door, then sat panting in fury. One good thing, Gladys would've been proud of her for telling them off. But of course she wasn't going to tell Gladys. Gladys would kill her if she knew Madeline had not only presumed to go peacekeeping, but also failed at it.

Humiliation started to seep in. What had she been thinking, to put herself in such a stupid position? Of course the Bensons weren't going to say, Okay, we'll back off since you've asked so nicely. That had just been a really bad idea of Paul's. Why had she listened?

Madeline huffed in aggravation and closed her eyes, wishing she could hit rewind and undo the last half hour. Eventually she felt a breeze pat her cheek through the open window, heard the lake sloshing into shore, the gulls keening. She opened her eyes and gazed at the Hotel Leppinen. She longed to climb up to the attic, get out her sketchbook, and draw until she forgot this humiliation. The idea was so appealing. The key to the back door was sitting in the ashtray of her car, where she'd put it after that second time she used it. She told herself that when Gladys did ask for the key, it would be most natural if it was there. It would seem as if she'd never used it without permission at all, seem as if it had sat in the car ever since the first errand. It would seem that way to herself as well as to Gladys. That was human nature, right? To justify things, to believe its own half-truths and evasions? And what harm could there be in going in? None. Gladys wouldn't even care. Probably.

Madeline had been up in the attic for nearly half an hour when something clicked into place in her head. Scattered phrases replayed themselves:

Maybe we ought to count ourselves lucky that someone wants to buy.

They're bullies, that's what, they think they can have whatever they want, whenever they want it.

That is, unless she's willing to negotiate.

The Bensons wanted the hotel. It had to be. Frowning, Madeline put her pencil down. It was a horrible thought. She tried to go back to the drawing—Mary Feather in the doorway of her place—but she couldn't. Before long she had trotted down the stairs and was back in the Buick. She had to go ask Gladys straight out.

Madeline turned the key in the ignition, but the car didn't start. It was just—dead. She didn't believe it at first. But after twenty minutes of fiddling, she faced the inevitable. The Buick was staying here, and she was walking home, and no telling how long it would take to fix or what it would cost.

Gladys sat beside Arbutus on Butte's bedroom floor, reading a story out loud. It was one of Butte's sillier romances, but what did she care, as long as it passed the time and kept their minds occupied. She glanced at her watch as she turned a page. *Where* was Madeline? Even if she'd had to work a little late she should have been back by now.

Arbutus had been doing so well lately, they'd gotten lax about her always having help in and out of bed, and sure enough, while Gladys was in the kitchen doing dishes, Arbutus had woken up from a nap and gotten up on her own. Gladys had heard a thump and a yelp and had gone running, her hands dripping dish suds.

Butte had slid to the floor slowly, bolstered by the bed, and at first they thought they could get her up and wouldn't even have to tell anybody. But after fifteen minutes, it became clear that Arbutus wasn't going anywhere without someone stronger to help. Gladys had tucked a blanket around her, propped a pillow behind her back, and sat down beside her. They'd been there for nearly an hour now. The fit of giggles they'd had when they realized their predicament was long over. The last of the fun had seeped out entirely when Arbutus admitted she had to pee desperately.

At last, the screen door banged. Gladys scrambled up to hurry Madeline along. It wasn't Madeline, though. It was Randi, wondering if she could drop Greyson off for a bit. Gladys led her to Arbutus's room and together they got Arbutus up on her feet.

That was how Madeline found them when she got home—Randi holding Arbutus, angling her back toward the bed, laughing and teasing, telling Arbutus she had to stop living so wild. Greyson was standing by, patting the mattress solicitously, and Gladys was hovering, looking tense and gray. "Don't worry, Gladys," Randi said as she eased Arbutus onto the mattress. "I'm strong, I won't drop her. And she's strong too, she's got a good grip on me. Right, Butte? The two of us, we're survivors, aren't we?"

Madeline watched in confusion for a moment, feeling something suspiciously like jealousy, and then she hurried forward to help.

10

Madeline wore Gladys's nerves out, asking Arbutus if she was all right. Finally, after Butte ate a good dinner and watched her favorite television program, Madeline seemed to believe her. She was still wound up, though. She kept saying she should have been there, then this wouldn't have happened.

"Quit fretting," Gladys told her after Arbutus was back in bed for the night. "It might've happened anytime, and she's perfectly fine, not even a bruise. You can't be here every living minute. Now, are you going to help me with these packages?"

Madeline started writing address labels, but she kept glancing at Gladys. Finally she cleared her throat and spit out what was on her mind. "I have to ask you something. Why didn't the Bensons cut off your credit? When they did everyone else?"

Gladys's first reaction was to clam up, refuse to discuss it. But that was suddenly too much effort. She said *huh* in a mirthless way. "They want something from us."

"What?"

"The hotel."

Madeline nodded and Gladys wondered at her lack of surprise. "But what will they do with it?" she asked, very intent.

"They'll tear it down, they've already said so. They want to expand the store and put in a parking lot."

"That's a terrible idea. You can't let them."

Gladys was touched by Madeline's dismay, but startled too. What on earth had gotten into her? Probably she was still worked up over Butte's tumble. But Butte's tumble was right at the heart of the matter: they could not go on this way. "I don't have much choice. That's the truth of it, no matter how I fuss." Gladys fiddled with a package, frowning. "Eventually this loot will run out. And I'm just scraping along. All my big talk is just that: talk. I swore up and down I wouldn't sell, wouldn't this, wouldn't that, but—" She shrugged. "I don't see what else to do. Look at what happened today. If Butte gets hurt, really hurt I mean, we're finished here."

"Oh, Gladys." Madeline looked truly upset, which was decent of her.

Gladys took a breath and then she said, "I went down to Cross-cut the other day when you thought I was just at Mabel's. Went to see if I could get a loan against my house. They turned me down. Said I was too old, and no income."

"Oh, Gladys. I'm sorry."

"I didn't want Butte to know. Or you, either. The fact is I don't see what else to do but let the hotel go. It makes sense."

She picked up an old metal sign advertising tinned Moroccan anchovies. It was going to a woman in McKeesport, Pennsylvania, who had paid thirty-eight dollars for it. Gladys remembered the days when they used to sell anchovies at the hotel. They'd sold all kinds of things, anything to bring a nickel in. Cigarettes, peppermints, matches, woolen socks, chocolate bars, newspapers. To her the sign was as real as anything, as common as a can opener (but not unloved for that), a tiny gear in the business she once ran, but to some stranger halfway across the country, it was an antique, a curiosity.

"That's where you get all this stuff, isn't it? From the hotel?"

"Most of it. I sold all those alarm clocks, you know, but I didn't get as much as I wanted." She shrugged. "The place is full of junk. Might as well clean it out."

"It's not junk."

Gladys made a face.

"Mary Feather told me that your parents ran it."

"Yes, and my grandparents before them. They built it. Eighteen hundred and eighty-six they put in the cornerstone, it's cut into the cement, you can see." Gladys began to tidy the wrapping paper, blinking tears away, furious at herself.

"So you ran it too?"

"Frank and I did. Hansen's General, we tried to call it, but that never took. The Hotel Leppinen it was and always remained."

"I love the place, you know. I have to tell you, I've even—" Madeline broke off, picking up the rooster pepper shaker and rubbing its red comb with her thumb. Gladys had done that a million times herself. Something about the dull glossy red of that comb, you just wanted to touch it. Madeline probably expected to be snapped at for prying into this business of theirs. Gladys knew herself. She had a sharp tongue. It was just her way. Some people were sweet, like Arbutus, and some were sour. It didn't mean she didn't have feelings. It just meant she didn't—couldn't—indulge them. But now she smiled wistfully.

"I love it too. I guess that's why I've hung on so long."

"Did you close it when Frank died?" Madeline asked. She had set the rooster down and had her chin on her hand and looked all dreamy-eyed. As if this was a wonderful make-believe story.

"Heavens no, I had to make a living, didn't I? Mostly I ran it myself anyway, Frank was working in the woods. Oh, Arbutus came and lived with us for a spell, after Nathan's father died, but that was just for a while, before she married her second husband, Harvey Hill. It was when my Frank Junior was small. Those boys were the best of friends, back then. Hard to believe how greedy Nathan got as he grew up."

"Frank Junior?" she said, sitting up straight, the dreaminess gone.

"My son. He was killed. In Vietnam."

"Oh, God. Gladys, I don't know what to say. I had no idea—I'm so sorry."

Gladys could not bear to talk about it. "It was a long time ago." She picked a package up, resmoothed the tape carefully. At last she could look at Madeline again. "I closed the hotel not too long after your grandfather died. I just lost heart, I guess. It seemed like it'd got to be too much for me. The roof sprang a leak and that was the last straw. I patched up the hole but I couldn't see repairing the damage." She shook her head. "I decided to cut my losses. I thought it might be nice for once in my life to not be so tied down and I wasn't making enough to shake a stick at anyway. I thought I might as well let myself have a little freedom." She made the scissors cut the empty air. "But now where do I go? Nowhere."

"Do you ever think of reopening?"

"Not a chance. Things have changed too much. Back in my day, and my mother's, the tourists weren't so fussy. They'd share the bathroom at the end of the hall and didn't need anything in the rooms but a bed and a dresser. It's different now. Of course, every generation says that. I put an electric sign in the window that said 'Rooms to Let,' and my mother was fit to be tied. She thought it was tacky."

"'*Rooms to Let*,'" Madeline repeated, as if that was the most wonderful thing ever.

"I was thinking I'd put it on eBay, I'll bet it brings quite a bit."

"Oh, no, you can't sell it! Please don't."

"There's no reason not to."

"Of course there is!"

"And what would that be?" Gladys asked, giving Madeline the skeptical look she deserved for all this folderol.

"Well—I—it's your history, you just said so. And you might want to reopen. If you had help, say."

Gladys aimed the scissors at Madeline and shook them a little to make her point. "No. There's too much that needs doing. I don't know what it would take to fix the water damage. More than I've got. Besides which the place needs cleaning like you can't imagine, and the plumbing needs work, and the outside painted. I looked into that, it'll cost a fortune. A real fortune. Then there's the roof, and the heat, and the wiring, and a dozen other things. What it would all cost boggles the imagination."

"But it's so beautiful. You can just *feel* it wanting to reopen and run again. It's such a shame that it just sits there."

Gladys gave Madeline a long, quelling look and shook the scissors at her again. "A shame? What it is, is old and out of fashion and expensive as Hades to keep open. And that's *after* repairs."

"I suppose," Madeline said, looking crestfallen, as if Gladys had blasted some cherished dream of hers out of the sky. "I guess you'd know."

Gladys felt a little sorry then for being so severe. She had the same romantic notions about the place as Madeline, or she wouldn't have hung on to it all these years. "It would never bring in much and people want that nowadays, no one's content with just a living," she said more gently. "It's a grand old building, but it's too much for us. I'm tired of fighting it. I'm afraid the decision is made."

"But, Gladys, how can it be that simple? That final? There must be some way—"

"It's got to be done," Gladys cut her off. "And the Bensons seem very serious about their offer."

"If it was *anyone* but them," Madeline said. She seemed so worked up. Gladys could only think it was nerves. The best thing to do about nerves was to ignore them.

"One good thing, I suppose they'll let the grocery bill go," she said.

"Gladys."

"So it goes."

"But you've held out this long. What about your history?"

"Madeline, stop," Gladys said, abruptly tired of the girl's naïveté. "I haven't a choice. I've been nickel-and-diming my way along for months now, and it isn't working. The summer taxes will be due in September. More money I haven't got. I only just got the winter taxes paid, and then they were late. And history?" She swept a pile of paper scraps into the garbage can that sat at her feet. "History doesn't pay the bills. History won't feed us or keep us warm. It's just something that's over and done with."

Madeline seemed to have deflated in front of her. Again Gladys felt an unexpected stab of sympathy. "Do you want to take a walk?" she asked. She knew how Madeline liked walking. Gladys liked walking too. Funny that they'd not done any of it together.

"Isn't it awfully late? And what about Arbutus?"

"Sound asleep," Gladys declared. "And late? What's late? I'm an old lady, I don't sleep anyway. And you're a young one, full of vim and vigor."

A reluctant smile spread across Madeline's face.

Main Street was empty except for a dozen cars and trucks parked around the bar. The windows were open and Madeline heard the jukebox playing, the clink of glasses and silver, the jumble of voices, an occasional shout. Gladys was reminiscing about the old days and Madeline was half-listening.

"We made all our own rugs, every one, out of rags. Flannel shirts and dungarees and bedsheets that were beyond mending. Those things'll survive the next ice age. Lord, the *work* of it. *Bang!* that shuttle on the loom would go all evening long. My grandma could never sit without working. The loom's in the shed out back of the hotel. Dismantled, but all there. And the kicksled, why, I used to use it myself."

"What is it, anyway?"

"It's for the winter, to get around in the ice and the snow, do your errands. See, look." Gladys stopped on the sidewalk and demonstrated, grabbing at an invisible waist-high handle with both hands, making a kicking motion with one foot. "You pushed yourself along, carried your parcels on the seat. See?"

Madeline nodded. For a moment she saw it all—ice, snow, the wooden kicksled, a tiny, robust woman in warm woolen clothes out doing her errands. "Handy."

"A man with an antique store offered us a lot of money for it, but we said no."

"Of course you did."

"Now I don't know what to do. I had made up my mind to sell it, but maybe I oughtn't. Maybe once the hotel's sold I'll wish I'd kept it. But once we're dead and gone, where'll it go?"

"You'll find somewhere. A museum, maybe? Or even Randi." In her sadness Madeline was feeling beneficent and unjudging.

"Not Randi. She'd probably just hock it for the cash. Or worse."

Madeline blinked. "Well, you shouldn't sell it, you'd never forgive yourself."

"Probably not." Gladys began walking again.

"The hotel is really wonderful," Madeline said as they headed up the street, the clatter of the tavern growing fainter. "It's—I've—" She meant to confess to Gladys, both her unlikely daydreams and her unauthorized prowls through the place, but somehow she couldn't. The time wasn't right.

"Hard to believe it's come to this. But I don't know what else to do."

Their feet scuffed on the pavement. After a while Madeline said (not sure why she did, but led into it by their unaccustomed camaraderie, the dark, the quiet), "I went to Pine Street that day. You know, that day you told me where he—Joe—lived."

Gladys nodded. "I supposed you did."

"It was awful."

"Lots of poor people down in Crosscut. Real poor. Joe sold that house."

Madeline waited for Gladys to add more and when she didn't, she said, "I don't know how to ask you about him."

There was only the sound of their shoes on the sidewalk until at last Gladys said, "And I don't know how to tell you. He wasn't a bad man."

Objection rose in Madeline, from her marrow. "But I was his granddaughter." She felt so much about it still, after all this time, after all that Emmy had given her, and wished she didn't. She couldn't seem to stem the tide of protest, though. (And maybe the protest was in a way impersonal. It wasn't so much that this abandonment had happened to her; it was that it had happened at all. It was a philosophical question. Maybe one she should ask Paul, who seemed to be posting each one of Nietzsche's seemingly endless aphorisms on his chalkboard a day at a time. Today it had been, *He who has a why to live can bear almost any how.*) "I was only three. What kind of a person can do that, just—refuse someone? A child."

Gladys kept her eyes on her shoes. "People do what they have to. It's different up here. Hard. People don't know, out in the rest of the world, what it's like."

"But he didn't even consider it."

"He couldn't consider it," Gladys said softly. "He just didn't have it in him."

Unexpectedly, tears filled Madeline's eyes. This was so final, so damning in one way but exonerating in another. Maybe it was the only real answer, and if so, then her search for meaning in the situation would be over. And then what?

Gladys went on. "I met him at the fiddle jamboree. Well, met— it's not like we didn't know each other. But we started sparking at the jamboree. It was July of 1977. My Frank had been gone for years, and Joe—He sure could play. And a man playing a fiddle the way he did?" Gladys put a hand to her heart. "Oh my."

Despite herself, Madeline smiled.

"He was always good to me," Gladys said simply.

Madeline realized, really realized for the first time: Gladys had loved him. She was both touched and infuriated. "So why wasn't he good to me?"

Gladys shook her head, seeming either not to know or not to know how to say.

"He abandoned me. He and Jackie both did. She at least was young and all screwed up. He was old enough to know better. And no one cares."

"It's not a matter of caring. It's a matter of the way things are. It's over and done. Here you are, you're fine. And I'd think you were better off as you were."

The truth of this was undeniable, even though it resolved nothing.

They came to a stop in front of McAllaster Crafts, which had opened the weekend before. Even though it was well after midnight there was a woman inside. She was heavyset, with long black hair that cascaded down her back. Madeline had seen her riding an old bicycle around town, or driving a rusting truck sometimes. She worked at a table by the glow of a lamp, weaving reeds around a frame to make a basket. They watched as she picked the half-made basket up and turned it in one hand to check its balance, then bent over the work again. After a moment, they continued on.

The woman lingered in Madeline's mind. She was making art, of course that had caught her attention, but it was something else too. The innocence of it, maybe, the lack of expectation. She was so engrossed in her work, seemed satisfied to be where she was. The basket might sell for twenty dollars, or it might not. The shop never seemed busy and the things in it weren't sophisticated. The basket would never make her famous or end up in a museum. The best part of it was the making of it, sitting at the table weaving while outside the lake crashed into shore and the seagulls roosted somewhere for the night and two women stopped for a moment to watch.

Maybe Madeline hadn't missed so much, skipping art school, after all.

Lately she'd been working on a picture of Gladys and Arbutus at their morning coffee. She yearned to show their sisterness, their northernness, their old-fashionedness, the unearthly remoteness of it all. She wanted to paint Arbutus's sweetness, Gladys's resolution, their devotion to each other. Was it possible? Maybe, maybe not. Probably not, but what harm would there be (except to herself, in disappointment and frustration and the stirring up of old dreams) if she tried? How long had it been? Fifteen years at least. How was that possible?

Emmy always said she must've been born drawing. Madeline still remembered the picture she'd been coloring the day Jackie left:

Winnie the Pooh with a jar of honey. Emmy'd encouraged her right from the start: sketch pads, crayons, finger paints, watercolors. And then, on her eighth birthday, a crow-quill pen and a bottle of Higgins ink. It had made her feel so grown-up. Emmy must've gone to an art supply store and asked what to get. The crow-quill pen was great. The nib was flexible, so more pressure gave you a thicker line; less, a thin one. Madeline remembered realizing that, experimenting with it. She could see herself sprawled on her stomach on the Oriental rug in the living room, drawing thick lines and thin ones, over and over.

Emmy always took her seriously. She didn't even get mad when Madeline knocked the ink bottle over on the rug—one of the few expensive things she owned. She looked at the stain, frowning for a long moment, and then said, "You like working down there on the floor?"

Yes, Madeline said. She did. It was where she did her best thinking.

"That's where you have to be, then. The stains will wash out."

They had washed out, more or less, every time, because of course that wasn't the only ink to spill or seep through the paper. If you turned the rug over you could see the stains on the other side.

At first Madeline kept drawing when she turned down her scholarship to art school, but not for long. Emmy's cancer was slow-moving but insistent, and art didn't seem to matter anymore. Working the busiest shifts at Spinelli's to bring home as much money as possible mattered. Taking care of Emmy, going with her to all her doctor's appointments, trying to beat the monster that was living inside her—that mattered. Remembering to keep living, to let themselves forget for hours and sometimes whole days that she had a disease that was killing her. That mattered, and it took everything

Madeline had to do it. There had been nothing left for art. But now—now maybe things could be different.

Gladys shoved her hands deeper into her coat pockets and Madeline thought she looked cold. "Are you ready to go back?" she asked, and Gladys nodded.

11

The next afternoon Madeline popped the Buick's hood and wiggled the battery cable, a trick Arbutus had suggested, saying she'd never owned a car under twenty years old in her life and knew all the tricks. The engine turned over and Madeline felt a rush of satisfaction. She shut the engine off again and headed across the empty lots to see Mary.

Mary was lounging beside her display, her feet propped on a crate, carrying on a conversation with a man Madeline had waited on at lunch. He was an investment banker from Manhattan who'd come north for the trout fishing. "Pull up a stump," Mary told Madeline, pointing at a spare lawnchair. "You want a pop, there's some in with the fish. Jack, you keep away from there."

All perfectly illegal, Madeline thought contentedly. No way was it USDA approved to sell home-caught fish from an iced-down cooler you had to swat your dog away from, but one good thing about McAllaster was, nobody cared, or almost nobody. The tourists loved the local color, and the locals would live and let live, mostly. The Bensons and people like them, people who wanted things more modern, more homogenized, more like wherever it was they'd come from, well, to Hell with them. Maybe they were within their rights—and Madeline had to admit she still thought that cutting off credit on delinquent accounts was not unreasonable, no matter what Gladys said and no matter how much she herself disliked them personally—but the Bensons' influence didn't extend this far, at least. Not yet.

Maybe McAllaster could resist gentrification. The north side of Chicago hadn't, as Madeline knew from Emmy's own experiences struggling to stay in their apartment as the price of everything soared. A working-class neighborhood went upscale and pretty soon the people who'd made it what it was had to leave, unable to afford the cost of living and the homes they'd grown up in, homes where they'd raised families of their own. But here—maybe the harshness of the landscape and weather and economy would stop some of that, or slow it down. And besides, it wasn't all bad. She *liked* pesto and hummus, and if Gladys hadn't been at war with the Bensons, she'd have been in there buying those things.

Madeline shucked off her shoes. It had been busy today, challenging, and she felt pleasantly worn out. She smiled at the banker but didn't join in the conversation. Working at Garceau's, she was seeing that McAllaster was nowhere near as remote as she'd thought. There'd been a movie star out on Desolation Bay the other day, holed up on his oceangoing yacht. He hadn't gotten *off* the yacht, but still. Today alone she'd waited on a tiny indie rock band from Detroit, an elderly Japanese woman who spoke no English, and a rodeo clown from Wyoming, as well as this Manhattanite.

He and Mary were delighted with each other. Watching him lean toward Mary, his eyes bright with appreciation of the story she was telling, Madeline wished she'd brought her sketchbook. Maybe she could've shown how they were the same and different all at once. She half-drowsed while Mary talked to a couple of retired schoolteachers from Detroit who remembered her from last year.

They bought two gallons of syrup and three fillets of fish, and Mary tucked seventy dollars into the front snap pocket of her overalls. "I gave 'em a break for getting two gallons at once," she said when they'd gone. "I could've got eighty for that and the fish but it don't hurt now and then in business to give a good deal."

Madeline agreed. Their conversation wandered from there, from fishing and making maple syrup to Mary's memories of the old lumber camp days. Madeline loved hearing about that. This was turning out to be a perfect afternoon. After a while she thought about having a ginger ale. She sat up to pull one from the cooler just as Mary said, "Listen, now. I've been thinking, and I've been going to tell you—" A county sheriff's truck eased to a halt in front of them and Mary didn't finish. A tall man in a brown uniform approached with languid steps.

"What do you want?" Mary asked in her road-gravel voice.

"I'm afraid I've got to ask you to pack up and leave, ma'am."

"Is that so."

"This is Village property, Mrs. Feather, and you haven't got permission to peddle here."

"I ain't a missus as you well know," she said, looking up at him without moving. "And as far as I know, it ain't Village property, either."

"The Village is responsible for the upkeep of this parcel in the absence of the deeded owner."

"In other words, Lillian Frank ain't bothered to mow these lots in thirty years and don't give a damn what happens on 'em. Isn't that what you mean?"

"In the absence of the deed-holder, the Village may elect to perform certain upkeep."

"Running me off, that's upkeep?"

"Ma'am, regardless of ownership, the Village has an ordinance barring unlicensed peddlers."

"Oh for God's sake, Jim, stop calling me 'ma'am.' Since when do they have this so-called ordinance?"

"Since the fifteenth of May, as I believe you've already been informed by letter."

"I ain't gotten no letter."

"I've been informed that a letter was duly written and sent."

"Well I ain't duly received it, you young son of a pup—"

"Let me see that ordinance of yours in writing." Madeline felt shaky with anger. Here they were, enjoying the day, selling a little syrup, a little fish, visiting with the tourists, and along comes this jackass to ruin things.

The man barely glanced at her. "I don't need it in writing."

"You're going to have to do better than that," Madeline began.

"Ah, don't bother," Mary said.

"Mary—"

"Give me a hand packing up, Madeline."

"I appreciate your cooperation, Mary."

"I knew you when you was a snot-nosed kid couldn't balance a bike and don't you forget it, Jim Nelson. Don't you Mary me."

"Well, I'm sorry that you feel that way," he said.

He drove to the fruit man's stand, all of a hundred feet or so, to deliver the same news. Madeline stood with a gallon of maple syrup heavy in each hand, watching. Albert threw his hands up in the air and his face flowered into anger. He shook a finger in the sheriff's face, and the sheriff leaned forward and put one hand on the butt of his gun. Gus came around from the back of the van and began to shout. Madeline couldn't hear his words, just the nasal whine of his uplifted voice. She saw how ludicrous he looked—the bandy-legged old reprobate in his pointy-toed oxfords and silky windbreaker probably out on parole for some unsavory activity. The breeze lifted a plume of Gus's hair up and held it there. The sheriff advanced and suddenly, a balloon pricked with a pin, Albert subsided. His shoulders sloped and his big hands fell to his sides.

"This is terrible," Madeline said. "It's not right."

"He's just doing his job," Mary said with resignation that surprised Madeline after the way she'd argued with him. "You know his mother died when he was just a boy."

Madeline did not know what to say to this apparent non sequitur.

They were quiet after that. When Mary had driven off in a cloud of exhaust, Madeline spent a long time leaning against her car, gazing at the hotel, feeling blue. Sad, mad, lonely. She hated seeing Albert and Mary defeated, hated not being able to help or change anything. Abruptly she headed past the bank of lilacs and through the orchard to the back door. This was a bad habit, but last night she'd found no way to confess and now she couldn't make herself stop. There wasn't any harm in it. She just had to spend a little more time in there. It was a haven, a place to leave the real world behind for a little while and surround herself in dreams, like wrapping up in a blanket.

Gladys was slamming things around in the kitchen while Arbutus sat at the table worrying at a napkin with her fingers when Madeline got home. Greyson was perched atop a stack of catalogues, coloring. Randi must've dropped him off again.

"What's wrong?" Madeline asked, taking in the glum scene.

"Gladys is mad," Greyson said.

"I see that. But at what?"

Gladys had been pulling pots and pans out of the low cupboard where they were stored and piling them up on the counter, smacking each item down with force, but she stopped then. She placed both hands on the countertop and pulled herself up, and turned to look at Madeline. Madeline saw at once that something really was wrong, this wasn't just indignation. It was something worse, something deeper.

"What's happened?"

"It's Emil."

"Oh no." Madeline imagined him dead, cold in his bunk in the trailer.

"They're after him now, when will it stop?" Gladys slammed a palm on the counter, but she looked defeated.

"Who, the Bensons? After him for what?"

"Not them, but their crowd. The zoning commission and the Village board. They've condemned his trailer, they say he has to be out within the month."

"They can't do that."

"Apparently they can."

Arbutus nodded, looking woebegone. "There's a letter," she said. Greyson gave them all a serious, gauging look, then went back to his coloring.

"But that's his home."

"Tell them that. They say it doesn't meet minimum codes, it's an eyesore, it's unsafe, there's no septic, no approved water, and bingo, it's condemned, they want it hauled out of there. At his expense, mind you, or they'll do it themselves and bill him for it. *That's* a joke. Emil doesn't have a pot to pee in and come next month he won't have a window to throw it out, either. Here, read it yourself. He gave me the letter they sent."

Arbutus slid an envelope across the table toward Madeline.

"Well, he's got to protest it, that's all," Madeline said, skimming over the letter. "He's got to stand up and say no."

"Lot of good that'll do, have you ever been to one of their meetings? It's all mumbo jumbo." Gladys scraped a chair away from the table and dropped onto it. Greyson slid his picture around in front of her for her to see and she nodded absently. "That's nice, dear."

"It's an intergalactic galaxy monster. Purple Man."

"Is it?"

"Maybe he could help, he can do anything."

Gladys traced the arc of Purple Man's arm upraised in battle. "Maybe, dear."

Greyson slid the picture back around to himself and began coloring again.

"There's got to be something Emil can do. He'll have to get a lawyer."

Gladys's laugh was dismal. "On his income? He doesn't get Social Security, he never paid in. He lives off those skins he trades, and now and then his sister down in Flint sends him some money. She went down there in sixty-seven and got a job in the Buick plant, she's got a retirement. But not Emil."

Madeline rubbed her face, trying to think. "Are they going after Mary Feather's place, too? Whose idea is this, anyway?"

"That zoning committee that got put together last year, I always thought they were up to no good. And no, they won't touch Mary. They wouldn't dare. She's off their map, anyway—Emil's in just close enough to town. And he's got the view, that's what they're really thinking of. Cal Tate's got a chunk of land up there on the ridge. If he can get Emil cleared off and make his own piece that much bigger, he can sell to city folks to put up their big fancy weekend houses. A playground, that's all this is to them. Doctors and lawyers from the cities, that's who'll buy up there. Cal's probably got a whole subdivision planned."

"But that's not right. He can't use his position to line his own pockets."

Gladys and Arbutus gave Madeline ironic looks.

"Edith Baxter is the head of it, meddling old busybody," Gladys said. "I never had any use for her, she always did think she was better than six other people put together and she's got the brain of a goat. Raised here just like us, too."

Arbutus nodded at this. "Yes. And Harvey."

"That's right, Harvey Wines. He's new to town, hauled along his big ideas, wants to change everything so it's just like where he came from, I wish he would've stayed there. And Cal, of course, he put the condos in a few years back, he's worth a couple of bucks. There's a few others, too. Well, Tracy York. Her mother and me were the best of friends, she must be turning in her grave to see what Tracy's done, putting her name to that letter."

"Now, Glad," Arbutus said in a placating tone. "Tracy can't help who she is any more than any of us can."

"So you say. I'm tired of making excuses for her. She ought to be ashamed."

Arbutus sighed.

Madeline was reading the signatures on the letter. "But these people must know Emil, they must've known him since they were children, some of them."

"Yes," Arbutus said, and Gladys nodded grimly. "That's right and it makes me sick to think of it. This town is changing beyond recognition. Makes you want to throw in the towel."

"No. No way. Emil's got to fight it. That's his *home*. He *owns* that land. I think he needs a lawyer." Madeline felt fierce. Mary and Albert, and now this.

"Madeline, I would be surprised if Emil can even read beyond cat and hat and dog. He doesn't have what you'd call a job, he never really has, aside from working in the lumber camps back when he was younger. He traps some, like I said. Hunts. Does the firewood. Gets a little from his sister and a few others around. He brought the letter to me to read, they sent it to him certified at the post office and it scared him. They didn't even have the courtesy to go talk to him in person, the cowards. You know what they want, don't you?"

Madeline shook her head.

"They want to put him in the home down in Crosscut, the one for the feebleminded, the one—" Gladys cut herself off, shook her head. "It's for his own good, they say. Ha. That home is fine for those who need it, but Emil doesn't belong there, he's a whole different story." She gave a bitter laugh. "Well, that's the whole problem. Emil's different, and they just can't stand that. They can't *let* anyone be different. Now you tell me, how is Emil going to stand up for himself against them?"

"I don't know." Madeline frowned at the letter again. "But that's his home. He'll have to fight back somehow. We'll have to help him."

Gladys heard Madeline's determination when she said they'd have to help Emil. She watched her lean over Greyson's picture, giving it every bit of her attention. *Oh, Gladys,* she said to herself. *What a foolish old woman you are. What are you waiting for? There's nothing to fear in Madeline Stone. She is not Jackie. And even if she was, you'd have to tell her about Walter.*

She'd almost let the cat out of the bag this afternoon, talking about the powers that be wanting to send Emil down to Crosscut to the home for the feebleminded. The home where Walter was. That was no way to tell Madeline she had a great-uncle living.

But what *was* the way? She'd left it too long, and it would only get more awkward every minute. She should have done it right off, like Arbutus said. But she hadn't known Madeline then. She'd wanted to protect Walter in case Madeline turned out to be just like her mother. Careless of people's feelings. Cruel, when she wanted to be. Always a taker, never a giver. Walter was such a sweet soul, there was no way Gladys had intended to subject him to anything like *that* again.

Gladys sighed, caught in the web of her doubts and uncertainties and her own procrastination. Now it was going to be difficult, but she'd made this bed, so she would have to lie in it. *Show some spunk, old woman*, she told herself. *Stop dawdling*.

12

Walter Stone lived in a three-story Victorian festooned with cupolas and porches and gingerbread trim. It had been a grand house once, the home of a lumber baron who'd made his fortune off the timber surrounding Crosscut, but it had been a long time since its last coat of paint. The porch was cluttered with a sofa, rockers, an armchair, potted plants, a couple of folding tables with ashtrays and empty glasses on them. On nice days some of the residents liked to sit there, gazing out over the street.

Gladys walked up to the door, gave a knock, and stepped into a bare, sunny living room. She caught a faint whiff of urine and cleanser, and of pancakes. The walls were lined with easy chairs and rockers like those on the porch, some of them occupied. The men and women in them were old, dressed in thrift shop clothes. Some looked up when she came in; others didn't seem to notice her.

A huge television was blaring. A bomb had just exploded in the Middle East; there was the sound of mortar fire from beneath the newscaster's voice. Gladys wished Ted Braith would turn the thing off when the news came on. These poor old folks didn't need to be subjected to it, besides which it made her think of Frank Junior. She'd hated seeing all that footage on the television back then, it never should have been allowed. She'd hated it in a way Frank Senior never understood, and she'd been right, hadn't she?

Ted came toward her from the back, where the kitchen was. "Gladys! What brings you here again so soon?"

"I came to see Walter, what do you think? And why do you run that television so endlessly? No one needs to see that gore, shut it off."

Ted, bless his heart, crossed the room and changed the channel to a cooking show—which Gladys found ridiculous but at least harmless—and waved her toward the stairs. "He's in his room. Go on up."

"Thank you, Ted." Gladys touched his arm on her way past by way of apology.

Walter was lying on his bed, listening to his radio, but he sat up when Gladys knocked. "Hello. Anybody home?" she said.

Walter grinned. "Nobody but an old hound dog." This was their standard exchange and it always seemed to please him.

"How have you been?" Gladys asked, sitting in his easy chair.

"Good, good."

"Good." Walter gazed at her expectantly. Gladys cleared her throat. "Listen, Walter. You know I was just here the other day?"

"Oh, yes. It was Friday, you almost always come on Friday."

"That's right."

"You couldn't come for a while because you had to go and live in Chicago with your sister. Arbutus. Arbutus is a nice lady."

"Yes, she is."

"You don't usually come on Monday," Walter said.

"No, that's right, I don't. I came for a special reason, today. I have something to tell you. It's exciting, I think. I hope you'll think so too."

Walter sat on the edge of his bed, his hands folded in his lap. He waited for her to go on. She cleared her throat again.

"Walter, your great-niece Madeline has come back up north. Do you remember Madeline?"

"Oh, yes! She was a pretty little baby. She was Jackie's baby." His initially happy look faded and was replaced by one that was more pensive.

"That's right."

They sat in a reflective silence. "I didn't like Jackie," Walter said eventually. "Not once she got big."

Gladys sighed. "No, I know. She was never nice to you. The truth is, Walter, I never liked her, either."

Walter nodded.

"But that's neither here nor there. Madeline isn't Jackie, and she's back. Walter, I haven't told her about you yet. But I want to. I know she'd like to meet you. That is, she would if she knew. But I wanted to make sure it would be all right."

"For her to meet me?"

"Yes."

Walter nodded, smiling again. "Oh, yes. It's all right. Madeline was a pretty little baby. Joe let me hold her, I was careful. She always smiled for me. Joe said I was good with babies."

Tears brimmed in Gladys's eyes and she clamped her lips together. At last she said, "That's right. Joe always did say you were good with babies. But Madeline's grown up now."

"Yes."

"So I'll tell her about you."

"All right."

Gladys nodded. "I can't stay long. I have some other things to see to in town."

"All right."

"I'll see you soon, dear. Take care of yourself."

"Bye," Walter said, stretching back out on his bed.

The office of Henry Merrill, Esq., was in an old storefront on Crosscut's main street. The windows were perpetually dusty, and one had a long crack in the bottom corner. Henry hadn't done what a lot of men might do with a law degree, hadn't made a big financial success of it, but instead had come back up north to offer his services to whoever might need them every day of the week but Sunday. It wasn't really that he was so devoted to the law or so swamped with clients that he had to work six days out of seven. It was more that he did better keeping busy, keeping to a routine. It helped hold the black dogs of thought at bay. Also he had learned that a person could be happy with having done the best they could under the circumstances. It didn't always have to be bright and shiny and impressive to the outside observer. This shabby office in Crosscut was his life, and he didn't mind that.

"Well, if it isn't Mrs. Gladys Hansen!" Henry said when Gladys came in his door.

"Henry," Gladys answered in her schoolmarmish way.

He grinned. Gladys had been his Sunday school teacher about a hundred years ago, when he was growing up in McAllaster, and was also his buddy Frank Junior's ma. Henry'd made a point of going to see her every time he was home, after he got back from Vietnam. That was a hellish time. He was a wreck pretending to be a man, and she hadn't been much better, especially when her husband died not too long after Frank Junior.

Gladys was the one who'd hounded him to go to college. *What's the point?* he had asked her. He wasn't asking idly, or rebelliously, but just hopelessly. She punched the kitchen table so hard the kerosene lamp in the middle jumped and the chimney shattered. *What's the point of anything? You just keep going. You do things. It's*

*the only way. We're alive. Frank's dead. He doesn't get the chance ever
again.*

Henry graduated from the University of Michigan School of
Law eight years later.

Henry liked Gladys and he knew she was fond of him. Sometimes he could make her laugh, even. "What can I do for you?" he
asked now.

Gladys laid it out for him: Emil's trailer, the Village government,
the zoning board. Henry made a face. "Zoning can be tough. I'm not
saying Emil couldn't fight it and win, but it wouldn't be easy. And
it'd be costly."

Gladys made a frustrated sound.

"Can they prove the trailer's unsafe?"

"I don't know. Probably, if they want to."

"The only thing I can think of offhand is to check for a grandfather clause, something to exclude those who are preexisting from
the new ordinance. And the other thing to keep in mind is that the
Village might not have the money to enforce the order. Especially if
he put up any kind of fight."

"Well now. I hadn't thought of it that way."

"I'd be glad to draft a letter. Never hurts to have a little something arriving in the mail from an attorney. Give them something to
think about."

"Yes," Gladys said, sitting up straighter.

"If it came to an actual drawn-out fight, that'd be another thing.
He might not have a leg to stand on. But if he could scare them off
right at the outset. It's no guarantee, but—"

"Better than nothing. Thank you for seeing me, Henry. What do
I owe you?"

"Not a thing. I didn't do anything. A letter wouldn't take me ten

minutes to draft. You just give me a call if it seems like a good idea.
Talk to Emil."

"Now, Henry, I insist—"

"Not a chance," he said, holding up a hand. "I'm always glad to
see you, Gladys. Who else ever made me sit up and pay attention?"

Gladys headed next to the grocery store. As long as she'd driven
all this way she might as well make the most of her trip. Madeline
didn't leave for work until nearly noon and even if Gladys didn't get
back until a bit later than that, it would be all right. Arbutus was
doing so much better that they really were thinking that maybe she
could go back to her own house by the Fourth of July, at least for the
summer and fall, despite that little slip she'd had the other day. Butte
hadn't gotten hurt, after all. They'd even laughed about it at first.

Madeline was annoyed when Gladys left after breakfast,
backing down the drive with an impassive expression plastered on
her face. She'd thought they were united on this issue of Emil. But
Gladys had been edgy all morning, cranky and uncommunicative.

"What's *her* problem?" Madeline asked Arbutus after the car
had disappeared.

Arbutus shook her head.

"I thought we'd talk about Emil some more, come up with something."

Arbutus sighed. "I admire your spirit, dear. I just can't think
what there would be for us to do. You know this is all about money."

"Which we don't have."

Arbutus lifted a shoulder. "I hate to see Emil thrown out of his home. But I do think that if people with money want it to happen it'll be awfully hard to stop it."

Madeline frowned, then sighed, and thought, *So much for talking*. Gladys had the right attitude: just *do* something, even if it's wrong. When Arbutus was settled in the parlor with her library book, Madeline told her she had some errands to run. "I'll be back to check on you before I head off to work," she promised. "Unless you want me to wait until Gladys gets back—"

"I'm fine, dear, you go on ahead."

Emil met Madeline at his door and she made her way into the gloom. He pulled a cola from the cooler he kept on the floor and then sat with his right leg crossed over the left in the dainty way he had, nodding his foot, waiting for her to announce her purpose.

"Look, Emil. Gladys told me what they're trying to do, and we want to help."

"That ain't necessary."

"It's not right that they try and condemn your place. I think if you fought it—"

"It ain't necessary," he repeated.

"But why?"

"I give it some thought. I'm moving. Gonna take a place in the senior citizen apartments in town, gonna sell this place. It ain't even three acres but I ought to get a fair price for it. Might end up with enough to buy a new truck."

Madeline was shocked that he'd given up and made other plans almost overnight. After a startled moment she said, "Is that what you want? Really?"

He gave her an enigmatic smile, his eyes as amused as ever.

"Emil—"

"Times is changing. Gotta change with 'em. Plus I'm getting old. Be easier in town."

"But what about—" She gestured around the trailer: boxes, skins, chain saws, parts, Sal's blanket in a wad on the floor.

He looked around. "What, and leave all this, that what you're saying?"

"It's your home, isn't it?"

He shrugged. "It ain't much."

She couldn't tell if Emil meant what he said any more than she'd known if it bothered Gladys to sell her wedding silver. "Won't you hate it in the apartments? And what about Sal?"

"Beats getting stuck in the home for the retarded down in Crosscut."

Madeline blinked, surprised that he knew this part of the plan too.

"And as for Sal, I'm taking her with me. Ain't that right, Sal?" He nudged her with his boot and she looked up at him with that fond, aggravated glance. "Who'd make an old geezer give up his most faithful friend?" Emil's laugh here was delighted, a sing-songing *tee hee*, and for a moment Madeline wondered what he had up his sleeve. "I asked my pal Don about it. You can have a pet, long as it ain't too big, and Sally ain't very big at all."

"But Emil, it's so—*different* there."

"I'll probably like it all right. I got some friends there. Coupla old farts I grew up with. We'll get along."

Oh, this seemed a desolate capitulation for an independent, characterful old man. She could not picture Emil in a one-bedroom apartment with beige utility carpet and ivory-painted walls, a low-rimmed tub and toilet with handrails, a convenient, modern kitchenette. An image of a coonskin draped over the shower bar and a chain saw in parts on the rug rose in her mind and she did smile a little, but sadly. It was cold comfort to think of him that way. Tamed, reined in. And what about the board's plan to get him committed? "Please let us try to help, we can fight this."

"I'll be all right. Might be nice to turn a tap for running water, spin a dial for heat. And the rent's cheap. Based on income, how-dya like that? I oughta get a real good deal because I ain't got any. Been broke flatter than piss on a platter my whole life. They think they're gonna stick me in the home in Crosscut, they got another think coming." He gave one bark of a laugh. "I got as much right as the next fella to go live in them apartments, and I mean to do it."

Madeline nodded, not wanting to speak and expose any further her now ridiculous-seeming sense of outrage at his plight. "If you change your mind—"

"I already got a guy wants to buy the place, he's been nosing around for a while."

"All right." Madeline stood, feeling a great sense of futility. How foolish she was to feel so involved. She couldn't help and he didn't even care for her to try.

"Thank you, Madeline," Emil said as she was opening the door. She stopped short. It was the first time he'd ever said her name. "It was real decent of you to offer."

"You're welcome."

He nodded, his bright eyes seeming to gauge her. "Been mean-ing to tell ya, I always liked your grandpa. Didn't know him real good but I liked what I knew. He was good to work alongside of. Never slacked off like some fellas. And he could make that fiddle sing. Helped pass the time in camp that way."

She stared at him. "Thank you."

He nodded. She made her way down the steps and got back in her car. She felt too unsettled to head straight back to Bessel Street. She'd go see Mary. There would still be time to swing by the house and get to Garceau's on time.

———

Mary was outside, gathering kindling. It was a long winter coming up, she said. She didn't move so fast anymore and had to have the shed full by the first of October. Madeline picked up a branch and broke it into lengths. "Emil's crazy," she told Mary sadly. "He shouldn't give up."

Mary laughed. "Crazy like a fox," she said and then cried out, "Jack!" Jack came trotting back from the edge of the clearing.

"What do you mean?"

"You think they want him in them apartments in town?"

"He said he has some friends there."

"Oh yeah, sure, Donny Lunt and Bill Johnson, coupla others maybe. But I mean the bulk of them. You think those old ladies up there are going to let Emil Sainio bring his hunting dog and coonskins in to their nice new building? They gonna let him fix his chain saws in the common room in front of the flat-screen TV? Can you see him throwing his clothes in the same washer as Edith Baxter?" She gave her rasping laugh again. "Not a chance. Smartest thing he ever did."

"So you mean—"

"I mean he beat 'em at their own game. Hit 'em head-on, it's the only way. He knows they don't want him there. And legally they can't refuse him, he qualifies every which way you look at it."

"But Gladys said they want to put him down in Crosscut at some home."

Mary tapped her head. "That home's not for the likes of Emil. It's fine for some, but—well. Emil drinks but he's not feebleminded. They can't have him committed no matter how they try. That's just talk. A thing like that'd be out of their ballpark. Emil's no crazier than anyone and it'll take more than the zoning board to prove otherwise."

Madeline's hands were pleased by the heft of the next branch she picked up: dry and solid. It gave a sharp snap when she broke it over her knee. "I hope you're right."

"I am. Them old biddies'll put a stop to it all, you watch. Emil don't really believe in taking a bath much more'n once a month, if that. Heh!" Mary seemed truly delighted by the whole debacle. "They'll go petition that board to leave him alone, that's what. They'll raise all kinds of holy Hell and get that eviction stopped cold. Tracy York's Great-aunt Mirtha lives in that complex. She'll twist Tracy's arm until she says 'Uncle,' that's nothing, Tracy's got the spine of a worm when you come right down to it."

"You really think so?" Madeline was skeptical. How could a bunch of old women too poor to own their own homes stop anything?

"Them old ladies in there is powerful, you watch," Mary said, as if she could read Madeline's mind. "I know Gladys whines and cries about the good old days, everything's changing, nothing's right anymore, but this town ain't changed that much. Wasn't perfect to begin with, either. No sirree."

"You don't think Emil has any plans to move?"

"Not a one."

He'd been so straight-faced, talking about turning a tap for water. Still, Mary knew him better than she did. "I hope you're right."

"I am."

Madeline helped with kindling for half an hour more, then said she was going home. Mary nodded, her eyes intent on the ground. She picked up a branch and began to break it into pieces. "Listen, Madeline, before you go."

"Yes?" Madeline said, turning back. For the first time, she saw Mary Feather look uncertain. Maybe even sheepish.

"There's something I been meaning to tell you."

"Yes?" Madeline said expectantly.

Mary hesitated, seeming torn. Finally she said, "You remember we were talking about the lumber camp days the last time I saw you?"

"Yes, sure."

"It used to be the lumber companies would sell off their land pretty cheap once they'd cut it over. They don't do that so much anymore, but they used to."

"Uh-huh," Madeline said, shifting from foot to foot, thinking she really had to go or she'd be late for work.

"Your great-grandparents, Ada and Emmanuel, they worked for the lumber company. She was a camp cook, and he was a sawyer."

"Oh, wow. That's interesting. Nobody's told me that before."

"Yes. So." Mary cleared her throat. "They worked for the company and then when the area was cut over, they decided to stay on where they were. Bought the land, turned the cook shack into a cabin to live in."

"They must have been rugged."

"Yes. Well. What I wanted to tell you is, you got a lake named after you. I don't guess Gladys or Arbutus said anything about it?"

"A what?"

"A lake. Of sorts. Stone Lake."

Madeline had completely forgotten her earlier urgency about the time. "No way. *Where?*"

"Outside Crosscut maybe ten, fifteen miles. It's back in off the road a ways, north of town on the edge of the swamp. It's been years since I been that way, but I could tell you how to go, if you wanted."

"*Yes*, are you kidding? How amazing. I'm going to look on the map as soon as I get home, I can't believe I never noticed it. Why didn't they tell me?"

Mary grimaced and didn't answer the question. "It ain't called

Stone Lake on no map that I know of. I think they used to have it down as Cranberry. But down around Crosscut we all called it Stone Lake, because the Stones lived back in there."

"Why didn't you tell me before?"

Mary shrugged, still looking uncomfortable. "It wasn't my place. I don't like to butt in."

"Wow," Madeline said, too amazed to be angry. "A lake!"

Mary shifted from foot to foot.

"I'm glad you told me. I can't wait to track it down."

Mary chewed her bottom lip and then she said, "I don't suppose you met your Uncle Walter yet either, then?"

Mary watched Madeline tear down the narrow track with a worried expression. Probably she shouldn't have opened her mouth. Probably it *wasn't* her place. But for the love of Pete. Madeline was *here* now, after thirty years. And Walter was old. How much worse was it going to be if he up and died while Gladys was biding her time, getting up the nerve to say something? No, Madeline had a right to know.

Finally Mary turned and stumped back inside, still troubled.

13

Madeline careened down the two-track away from Mary's. Only when she hit a pothole that lurched her almost into a tree did she slow down, and even then it was difficult because her heart was pumping so hard. She could only think in choppy bursts, thoughts staccato with anger and hurt. She was going to move out. She didn't deserve to be treated this way. Gladys and Arbutus would have to look after themselves because she wasn't going to spend another night under their roof. (Even as she thought this, a calmer part of her brain was sorting through options for Arbutus. A county health nurse, maybe? A physical therapist?)

She jammed the accelerator to the floor and bulleted south down the highway, the only road that allowed her to get any momentum up. She drove blindly. She was stupid, a chump. What was she doing here? These women didn't care about her, the way she'd let herself think. They were just using her for their own ends and didn't trust her enough to tell her she had relatives living.

That bizarre fact kept banging in her head.

When the dashboard clock read eleven thirty she turned the car around. She couldn't let Paul down, none of this was his fault.

Paul asked if she was all right when she slammed the cooler

door on her hand and yelled, and then five minutes later dropped a coffeepot, splashing coffee and glass splinters everywhere. When she claimed she was, he didn't press. He did let her go almost right away, though. He said it was because it was slow. She figured it was because she was about to explode and not hiding it very well.

By the time she got to the house she had the speech laid out in her head—short, to the point, not sweet. Gladys's car was in the drive. Great. Excellent. Showtime. She marched up the walk and flung the kitchen door open.

Gladys was kneeling on the floor beside Arbutus. She raised her head and stared at Madeline, her face gray. Arbutus was moaning softly.

Arbutus had been putting the clean dishes away. Gladys and Madeline were both busy doing she didn't know what, but *some-*thing. She wanted to do something too—help out, be useful. She'd been feeling better lately, stronger. She decided to finish up in the kitchen. She reached up in the cupboard above the sink to the highest shelf to put a platter up, got up on her tiptoes to do it because she just needed that extra little inch, lost her balance, and toppled over. It was humiliating. And she hurt, worse and worse as she lay there. It was not a terribly chilly day but before long she was cold, and then colder, and then she was shivering.

It was a long time before Gladys got home. Arbutus watched the minutes creep by on the cuckoo clock, thinking that things had to change, they really did, life could not go on like this. After a while she mainly concentrated on breathing. She was so cold, and she hurt so much, especially her hip and her arm. But she was stuck for now, no use thinking about it. She talked to God a little, mentioning how nice the lilacs had been this spring. How tasty the omelet

Madeline made for breakfast was, ham and cheese and asparagus. She'd never thought of putting asparagus in an omelet, but it was good. It was wonderful having Madeline with them and she said thank you for that, too. Then she went through a long spell of shivering and hurting, then watched the minutes tick slowly by again, and then things got a little hazy and muddled.

Madeline called the ambulance. She and Gladys followed it down to the hospital in Crosscut in Gladys's car. Gladys stared out the window, chewing her bottom lip. Madeline concentrated on driving. Her earlier fury seemed far away, and tiny, like something that had happened at the opposite end of a very long tunnel.

Arbutus was carried into the emergency room. Gladys and Madeline sat. The chairs were uncomfortable—thin cushions over hard frames. This was not a prosperous, showplace facility. Madeline hoped they knew what they were doing.

The doctor came out to speak with them after half an hour. "Your sister is a tough lady," she said, smiling at Gladys. Gladys's face was pinched, pale—she looked ten years older than she had at breakfast. She didn't answer the doctor, just waited for the real information to be forthcoming.

"She's bruised up and she's going to be in considerable pain for a while. Her hip isn't broken, but the X ray shows what looks like a hairline fracture in her right femur. It should heal, but it will take some time. Her right arm is sprained—"

"When can she come home?"

The doctor held Arbutus's chart against her chest. "She'll need to stay here, Mrs. Hansen. We've got an extended-care wing—"

"No!"

"I'm afraid so. While she heals."

"Absolutely not. I won't consider it. We'll take care of her. Madeline's there, we can do it. Isn't that right, Madeline?"

Madeline said that it was.

"I'm afraid it's just not possible. She's going to need a professional facility. Despite your best intentions, you would end up injuring her further at home."

Gladys sagged.

"How long would she be here?" Madeline asked.

"I can't say. We'll have to wait and see."

Arbutus was sleeping, sedated, but only when visiting hours ended did Gladys and Madeline leave, and then Gladys dawdled, making up excuses to linger. Madeline didn't hurry her. They spoke very little, either at Butte's bedside or in the car. Madeline felt as if she'd been hit by a semi. After miles and miles had rolled by she said, "I'm sorry. I am so, so sorry. I should have been there. This is my fault."

After a long silence Gladys said, staring out the window, "No it isn't."

"I should have been there, I told her I'd be back—"

"She didn't want to be watched every minute."

"It was my job to look after her."

"Which you have been doing."

Madeline shook her head, began to argue, but Gladys cut her off.

"It's just life. Things happen, we don't always like them. It's as much my fault as yours." She said this flatly, exhaustedly. Not trying to comfort. Not trying to comfort or blame, which was very hard to take. It was as if Madeline didn't really exist.

More miles rolled past. Then Gladys said, "I have something to tell you. I should've done it sooner. I didn't know you at first, is all. But the fact is, you have a great-uncle living. He's named Walter, and he's—special. He's a very sweet man, but he's simple. He always has been that way, ever since he was born. He lives in the Adult Foster Care home there in Crosscut."

Madeline clenched the steering wheel and stared at the long road ahead.

"I should have told you right away. But I—I'm protective of Walter. I didn't want him to get hurt. Your mother, Jackie—she always teased him, plagued him. Joe told me she scared him to death one time. Shut him up in a closet. It wasn't locked, he could've got out, but he didn't know that."

Tears filled Madeline's eyes, to think of someone, especially someone helpless, being frightened that way.

"Looking back on it, I think maybe she was jealous. It was easy for Joe to dote on Walter. It wasn't so easy with her."

Gladys fell silent and more miles rolled under the wheels. Eventually she said, in that same tired voice, "So, that's why. I didn't know you. I told myself, what if she's like her mother? And you weren't. But after a while it seemed too late. Arbutus told me not to wait, and she was right."

Madeline thought of Mary Feather in her grubby sweater standing in her yard that morning—a million years ago—looking uncertain. Maybe no one ever got to a point where they really knew what they were doing. Maybe it was always a crapshoot. She sighed. "I know about Walter," she said. "Mary told me."

Madeline couldn't sleep that night. She kept seeing Arbutus helpless on the floor while she was driving around, indulging her fury like a spoiled child. She tossed and turned. She had a great-uncle living. No, couldn't think about that. The Hotel Leppinen. There was something to dwell on. That beautiful old building. It was a crime, a sacrilege to tear it down. She hated that idea.

After a while she tiptoed down the stairs with a flashlight. She crept out the back door and then went to the Buick and lifted the hotel key from the ashtray.

She just needed somewhere to go. She had to get out of 26 Bessel, away from her guilt, away from the huge emptiness Arbutus's absence left in the house.

14

One night late in June, Paul Garceau collapsed onto his bed in the back of the pizzeria. The hours were getting to him. Soon July would be here and he'd get a second wind, but not tonight. Tonight he just felt beat. He dreaded the thought of getting up in the morning and driving to Crosscut, dreaded the smell of the food and the chemicals they cleaned with, dreaded facing the lineup of guys. They were a bunch of dead-enders, waiting out their time so they could get back into trouble again. He told people the prisoners needed him, needed someone who could really cook, but that wasn't true. The food was prepackaged and portion-controlled. It came out pretty much the same no matter who heated it up, and the guys didn't give any thought to him at all.

He worked at the prison because he needed the money, it was that simple. Every year he hoped he'd turn a corner with the pizzeria and be able to quit at the prison, but every year there was something that made that guaranteed paycheck indispensable—he needed a decent truck, a new cooler or two, there was always something. On a more metaphysical level, sometimes he thought maybe he worked at the prison because it was full of guys like Manny. Society's screw-ups. Sad to say, a lot of them were not that bright. They were the ones who'd got caught. Even though a lot of them had never had a chance to do anything *but* end up in prison, on a day-to-day basis dealing with them was tedious and annoying.

When he was a kid, he'd loved his older cousin Manny. Always full of energy and bad ideas, Manny had been exciting, a nonstop adventure. As an adult, Manny would have grated on his nerves. In retrospect he'd probably been ADHD and not just the wild kid his parents despaired over. But people hadn't known about things like that back then, and if Manny'd just been full of youthful high spirits, he'd never had a chance to grow out of it. The motorcycle accident that had given Paul his limp had killed him.

Paul opened his book but couldn't attend to it. He took his glasses off and rubbed his eyes. He wished he wasn't alone. Two summers ago there had been Larissa from Kiev, and three summers before that there was Kate, a seasonal biologist with the Forest Service. With each of them he'd convinced himself it was something more than just a summer romance, but by Labor Day he'd known better, and so had they.

He thought about Madeline Stone. He'd driven past Gladys's house one day and seen her out in the side yard, swinging an ax, flailing at a chunk of wood, trying to split it. Her efforts had been clumsy and awkward and he'd wanted to jump out of the car and take over for her. But he didn't, he just watched. She bit her lip and repositioned the chunk of wood over and over, and when it finally split in two the look on her face was something to see. He wasn't sure he was attracted to her, but he found himself thinking about her sometimes when he didn't expect to, like now.

Paul sighed, tried to read again, but his thoughts nagged at him. He was nearly thirty-six years old and his life felt stale. *He* felt stale. He hadn't even picked up his guitar in how long, and playing used to be as indispensable as air. Lately—well, more than lately, for years now—he'd been in a rut that just kept getting deeper. He didn't know how to fix it, and he wouldn't have had the time or energy to fix it even if he did know. Why couldn't he be like Lily Martin at the store in Halfway and accept his life as it came? But he couldn't. He never had been able to. Or maybe he had, back when he was a kid, before the accident, but that was a long time ago.

The accident had changed everything. Before it, he was a boy who pretty much trusted in life. Afterward he knew how fast things could go wrong. Trouble could smack you down at any instant, so you'd better be on the lookout. And you'd better be careful what you asked for, too, because you just might get it. Paul had asked for—*insisted* on—a ride on Manny's motorcycle one summer afternoon. An hour later, Manny was dead.

A knock came on his outside door and Paul sat up with alacrity, glad of the distraction.

"Hey," Randi Hopkins said. She was wearing a short sky-blue dress that clung to her breasts but flared out from there, and flip-flops. She looked like summer.

"Hi. What's up?"

"Nothing. I saw your light. Wondered what you were doing."

"Reading."

Randi nodded, tipped her head a little to see past him into his room. He stepped aside and waved her in. "You want a beer, or a pop?"

She began to shake her head but then said, "Sure." She settled down into a chair, looked around. "You like to keep it pretty basic, eh?"

Paul smiled. He appreciated understatement. He'd kept two rooms for himself when he started the pizzeria. Painted them both off-white. Put a bed and a bookcase and a small table with two chairs in one, a couch and a television in the second. "Basic" was the word for it. He pulled a bottle of beer and a cola out of his mini-fridge and held them up for her consideration. She pointed at the beer. He popped off the top and handed it to her. "It's easy to take care of," he said. "Maintenance free."

Randi raised her eyebrows and gave him a very brief skeptical frown that made him laugh. He opened a beer of his own. "Just getting off work?"

She nodded and yawned hugely, covering her mouth and looking embarrassed.

"Long day?"

She yawned again, nodding. Paul found himself yawning in reaction, and they both started to laugh.

"So what are you reading?" Randi asked, reaching across to his bed and picking up his book.

"Joseph Campbell."

She shook her head, shrugged.

"Myths."

"Like Zeus and all that?" She leafed through the pages.

"Sort of. He's talking about the stories we tell ourselves to give meaning to life."

"Mmm," Randi said, nodding. After a little silence she said, "What stories do you tell yourself?" smiling at him as if she really wondered.

Paul felt his entire self lean toward her.

I'll go and get Walter," Ted Braith said to Madeline one afternoon near the first of July. He started along the hall and she followed. "He's up in his room. You can go along and sit in there."

He said the same thing every time she came. There was a small room off the hall that had perhaps once been a sunroom or a breakfast nook. A bay window bulged with houseplants. Otherwise, it held three rocking chairs, a lamp, and an end table. Madeline sat in a rocker and waited. It had been almost three weeks since she'd found out about Walter. The first time she came had been the most awkward.

She'd stood when her Uncle Walter walked in, her hands clasped in front of her, her fingers ice cold. How did you go about meeting your developmentally disabled great-uncle for the very first time?

"Walter, this is a friend of yours," Ted had said.

"Oh, yes," Walter answered, turning a worried smile on Ted.

"It's your niece. Your brother Joe's granddaughter. Do you remember her?"

"Oh yes. Madeline. She was a pretty little baby."

Madeline felt a bewildered, dizzying sense of displacement.

"All right," Ted said. "Well, she's come for a visit."

Walter wore leather house slippers, gabardine slacks, a white T-shirt with a plaid flannel shirt over top of it. His face was grizzled, with a trace of beard, and his skin was a healthy pink. He looked like a pleasant old man, and there was nothing to tell you he was different except perhaps for some lack of urgency in the tone of his waiting. She wondered if he looked like his brother, her grandfather.

"Hello, Walter. I'm Madeline," she said faintly.

"Hello." He turned to Ted with a questioning expression and Ted patted his shoulder. "Sit down, go on."

Walter perched on the edge of a rocker, both feet planted flat on the floor and his hands on his knees. Madeline pulled a rocker around and sat down across from him, then glanced at Ted for guidance.

"You'll be fine. I'll be in through the back, in the kitchen, if you need me. My wife and I are fixing lunch."

Walter and Madeline looked at each other, both she thought

with diffident, puzzled expressions. "So I'm Madeline, your niece," she said finally. "Great-niece."

"Oh, yes."

"Do you remember me?"

"Oh, yes. You were Jackie's baby."

Madeline nodded very slowly and focused on breathing. In, out. In, out. *You were Jackie's baby.* Here it was. Her past. Her time on earth before Emmy, remembered by this old man who was, as Gladys had explained, "simple."

"I don't—remember you," she apologized after a moment.

"No," Walter said. "You were a little baby. Jackie took you away." He looked off across the room, toward the plant-filled window.

Madeline got up and moved over to the window, touched the petals of a pink geranium. "It's pretty, huh?"

"Oh yes. Mama always loved posies. Animals too. We had a skunk, she called it Jim. I never was afraid of him, she got his sprayer took out." He beamed at Madeline with this remembrance.

She stroked one of the geranium's petals, inhaling its particular bitter fragrance, which she admired for its bold air of unapology. After a moment she sat down again. She rocked, and Walter did too. A clock ticked up on the wall and the rocker blades grunted on the wooden floor. She didn't want to alarm Walter (or was it herself?), and so she did not rush into questions. Plus there was something peaceful in their quiet.

She'd left when lunch was served. Walter gave her a hesitant smile and flapped one hand in a small wave, like a child. "I'll come see you again soon," she promised.

"Okay." He had hurried off to his lunch.

Now this was their routine. They visited a little, and were quiet more. Then when lunch was served, Madeline drove off to see Arbutus in the hospital.

Gladys hadn't come with her today, Madeline often traveled alone. It had been a long three weeks already, weeks in which Gladys's small house was cavernously empty and the two of them were stiff and formal with each other, polite but constrained. It was true that Madeline's fury at Gladys's keeping Walter a secret from her had faded at the instant of seeing Arbutus prone on the floor, but the hurt lingered. A trust that had been building was gone. It would take some time—some doing—to heal the wound. Madeline wasn't sure she really cared to. Gladys was very distant still. Madeline was sure she blamed her for Arbutus's fall, and wished she would just come right out and say so. Gladys wouldn't, though. She said very little. For now they were maintaining a civil relationship. Arbutus needed both of them, and so there was no option. Nowhere to go, nothing to change. But no future to it either, exactly.

There were only a few bright spots in her days, now: these visits with Walter, her times alone up in the hotel (which Gladys hadn't gotten around to selling to the Bensons yet, thank God, even though the need must be greater than ever, with Arbutus in the hospital), and the time she spent with Greyson. Randi dropped him off quite often, and with Arbutus in the hospital and Gladys in a long gray funk, it fell to Madeline to entertain him and watch over him. It turned out she didn't mind this at all. Taking care of Greyson helped her keep her mind off herself. Plus she loved him.

He was full of energy for odd projects and enthusiasms, like building his own telescope, learning the names of all the snakes that lived in Michigan, digging a squirrel tunnel in Gladys's back yard. He was convinced that if he dug it, they'd use it instead of tree branches to get around, especially if it was rainy. He was great. She was ashamed she'd resented bringing him home from Garceau's that day—a day that seemed both very long ago, and not any time at all.

Madeline pulled into the hospital parking lot and headed inside. She'd brought a map, which she unfolded onto Butte's bedside table after Butte's lunch was cleared away. She pinpointed Stone Lake. "Right there," she said, the tip of her pencil all but obscuring the spot that said "Cranberry L."

Arbutus squinted and nodded, probably not seeing but always anxious to be agreeable. "You won't get back in there with a car, I don't think. It's back off behind Crosscut Plains. Down along Wildcat Creek, beyond the old fire lookout and past Simmon's Camp. It's on Firelane Trail, and that's always been rough. You're better off to find a truck somewhere."

Madeline forced herself not to say, *Why didn't you tell me? Why didn't you tell me about Walter and this lake and a hundred other things I probably don't know? I thought you liked me. Loved me even.* She had to fight this impulse every time she was alone with Arbutus, because she couldn't help it, she loved Arbutus and the betrayal hurt. It was as if Emmy had kept something huge from her, unthinkable. But she had her pride. She wouldn't ask.

"Where would I get a truck?" she asked instead. The Buick was tough, it would make it. She'd waited long enough to see this lake. Going there would be her Fourth of July celebration, her declaration of independence. She was going to take better care of herself from now on. No one else was going to think, *What's best for Madeline?* That was her job, hers alone. The Fourth was perfect. She'd make a ceremony, an *event*, of this. She had a bad habit of never giving ceremony its due. But sometimes life demanded ceremony. Sometimes you owed that to yourself.

"Paul Garceau has a big truck. High off the ground, I've seen it."

Paul did have a truck as well as the Fairlane. It was big, almost new, and a sore spot with him she thought. She suspected it was a burden he wished he hadn't undertaken, one payment too many. He drove it as little as possible, preferring the Fairlane. He told her that the car went into storage once the snow flew, though. "I don't know if I should ask to borrow his truck. That seems like too much."

"He's a nice man. A hard worker. And nice-looking, too. You ask him." Arbutus's smile was dimply. "I'll bet he says okay."

Madeline frowned, wanting to put out the matchmaking glint in Arbutus's eye, but in the end she didn't try. Let her have this harmless, wrong idea. Maybe she was right about the truck anyway.

"My truck? Why?" Paul shoved his glasses up with the back of his wrist and gave Madeline a perplexed look across the pass-through.

"There's a place I want to go, way back in the woods. It's kind of a—quest."

"Do you think you'd be okay driving it?"

"Definitely, yes. If it's an automatic transmission. I'm a very careful driver."

He studied her somberly.

"Don't worry about it. Bad idea, forget I asked."

His face was full of misgiving. "Well—when would you want it?"

"I was thinking the Fourth of July."

"No way. You have to work. It's going to be crazy."

"I'd go in the morning, be back in plenty of time."

"If it was any other day—"

"I hear you. But it's the best day for me." She wasn't going to be swayed on this, she just wasn't. How often did she ask for anything much from the world at large? Not often, but that was going to change a little bit. She *would* have her day. Her morning anyway. "I'll take the Buick, I'm sure it'll be fine."

"God, no, you can't take that old heap, you'd never make it. Take the truck."

"Really?"

"Yeah, sure," he said, and Madeline didn't give him another chance to change his mind.

She pored over the map by candlelight up in the hotel the next few nights, memorizing the route, trying to envision the terrain. Six miles north of Crosscut she had to turn off to the east onto a dirt path. Arbutus had said it would be marked Firelane Trail on a small, hand-painted sign. The trail would wind around, following Wildcat Creek more or less, and she'd have to be careful—there'd be old logging roads, two-tracks crisscrossing it here and there.

"Just keep in mind you're following the creek," Arbutus had told her. "Keep bearing northeast, you'll be going through a big plain of stumps. Nothing ever grew back much after the first big cut. Too many fires, I guess, and the soil was too thin. Anyway, you ought to see the fire tower about five miles in, the best I can remember. It's been years. Gladys's Frank worked on a cut in there once, we took a part for the skidder out to him. Past the fire tower there's Simmon's Camp. It's an old log cabin, someone still uses it, I think. After that you're on your own, I've never gone beyond there. But you'll be close by then. Joe and Walter were both born out there as best I know. Maybe the cabin where they lived is still standing."

"Good luck with your quest," Paul said as he handed her the keys at the end of her shift on the third. "If you need the four-wheel drive, just punch the button on the dash."

The last thing Paul did every night was close out the till. If things went well this week, he'd have a few spare thousand *and* all his bills paid for the month, which would be great. He watched Randi for a moment. She was wearing the summery blue dress again, and was perched on a stool, painting her toenails pink. The tiny brush in her hand was a precision tool, and she was a master craftsman, focused and serene. Sometimes he felt a flicker of uncertainty about their relationship—she was so much younger than he, and they were so different from each other, and she was *Randi*. Flighty, restless, wild. Only now that he knew her, she didn't seem to be those things, so much.

She looked up and caught him watching. She winked. "Gonna take me out for a ride tonight, mister?"

Paul was so tired. But he was psyched, too—business was good, the Fourth was tomorrow, he had a girl. Sure he'd go out. "It's gotta be the Fairlane, Madeline's got my truck." Randi loved riding around in his truck. Once in a while he thought she liked it as much as she did him, but that wasn't fair. Randi was different than he'd always thought. Sweeter, more grown-up.

"I don't care. As long as it runs."

"It's runs great, a classic like that, what are you saying?"

"It just looks old to me," Randi said, but she was laughing. Paul went back to figuring out the till, smiling.

He'd splurged on the Fairlane two years before. He'd run across the ad in a *Hemming's Motor News* and once he called and had the owner send pictures, he couldn't resist. The car was a good deal, and practically in mint condition. Paul told himself he worked hard, he needed a treat. If he couldn't have something he wanted now and then, what was the point? It probably would have worked out except that the truck he'd been driving ever since he moved to McAllaster—nursing along, really—died exactly one week after he got the Fairlane. The Fairlane was fun; a truck was essential.

The Chevy Madeline was borrowing was overkill—bigger and newer and nicer than he'd gone out looking for. But it was solid and super-clean and the financing deal on his credit card had been great, four point nine percent for the life of the loan. He'd convinced himself he could make those payments *and* keep the car.

He did make the payments, no matter what, because if he was ever a minute late the interest rate would jump to twenty-five percent overnight. Bottom line, the car, the truck—they were both consolation prizes for the way his life felt these last few years. Dead end, frustrating, confining. (Like the lives of the prisoners he fixed food for, wasn't that ironic?) Lately Paul had been staring down some hard facts. He couldn't go on the way he had been. One thing he really should do was take the truck back to the dealer and switch it off for something more economical, something older and more basic.

"*Now* what're you frowning about?" Randi asked, coming to lean against him, twining an arm around his neck and nuzzling his ear.

"Not a thing," he said, exasperated with himself. Why'd he plague himself this way? He pulled Randi around to kiss her. She tasted good, like mint. "Ready to go?"

"I have to pick up Grey from Jo Jo's pretty soon." Jo Jo was a girlfriend of Randi's who babysat sometimes.

"So let's go get him. He can come too."

"He'll be asleep."

"He can sleep in the car."

Randi kissed his neck—a quick small dart of affection—and acquiesced, smiling. "Okay."

A wave of tenderness washed over him. Randi was happy, he was happy, his situation probably wasn't as bad as he told himself sometimes. Probably she was exactly what he needed and life was simpler than he always tried to make it.

Another wave of tenderness swamped him as he carried Greyson out of Jo Jo's and bundled him onto the backseat of the car. Paul had always liked Greyson, but now that he'd spent more time with him, he was starting to find him irresistible.

Randi had dropped Greyson off late last night, on her way to do a fill-in shift at the Tip Top. Paul had bitten back his hesitation—when the pizza place was busy, there was just no place to put somebody who wasn't a worker or a customer, especially a five-year-old somebody who needed not to get tripped over, spilt on, or burnt—because Randi said she couldn't find anyone else at such short notice.

Fortunately—sort of—there hadn't been a lot of late orders, and it had worked out all right. Greyson sat on a milk crate in the corner and played with a video game. When the batteries ran low, Paul did a quick search through his rooms for something else to entertain him with, and came up with a pair of binoculars. Greyson spent the rest of the night padding around gazing at everything through them: the customers, the pizzas, the waitress, Paul, the equipment, the toes of his shoes. Luckily half the customers were locals who knew Grey and didn't seem to mind being the subject of his scrutiny, and the other half were the nicest kind of tourists, the laid-back ones.

When the place emptied out, Greyson observed the cleanup process, his small face dwarfed by the big glasses, his mouth slightly ajar. He looked like a tiny ornithologist on the trail of some rare species.

It was at moments like those that Paul realized he was coming to love the boy. He hadn't thought about that when he and Randi hooked up. But now he was surprised to find himself missing Grey when he wasn't around, and swamped with a kind of pride when he was—as well as an urge to protect him from some of the things he knew life would throw at him, though probably that wouldn't be possible.

Paul drove down to the arm of land that encircled Desolation

Bay and parked at the pier. He turned off the engine and lights but left the radio on. The battery would last awhile. The music coming out of WFNM in Crosscut was awful—the worst of the oldies—but Paul felt loyal to the station anyway. It was part of life in the north. Randi scooted over onto the console between the seats and snuggled into him. He pointed out some stars to her. He was feeling good—a smart idea coming out here, a good night—until he heard her softly snoring.

He smiled ruefully. But this was all right too—Randi asleep beside him, Greyson asleep in the back. A little family. He felt the pull of it. What would his mother think? That it was about time, probably.

His mother had a big heart and a no-nonsense approach to life. Both his parents were that way. He knew they wondered when he'd find another wife, have a few kids like his sisters had done. They didn't harass him about it, though. The closest they came was when his mother would pull him aside for a private talk in the kitchen when he visited. She'd give him an investigative once-over, ask how he was. *Fine, great*, he always said, and that was her opening to say, *Have you met anyone?*

He'd tell her a little about his girlfriend if there was one, which there sometimes was. His mother would listen, her intelligent eyes skeptical as he gave her the pertinent details: the girlfriend's name and age and occupation, the color of her hair. Then she'd jump directly into The Talk. *You don't still blame yourself for the accident, do you? You don't let that run your life?*

No, he always said. Of course not. I was a kid, I didn't know any better.

His mother would give him a dubious, worried look, but he never had anything else to say about it.

The real answer was, *How could I not?* I was the one riding on the luggage rack. The bike just had a cop solo for a seat, putting someone on the luggage rack was a great way to throw the balance off, and I was the one who insisted that Manny take me for a ride. I plagued him about it. For once he was the one with some common sense. He took me around the block a few times but that wasn't good enough. I wanted more, I wanted speed. He didn't have an extra helmet, remember? So he gave me his. And finally he broke down and put on the speed and we went roaring down East Phillips Road to see how fast we could make the turn and it was great. It really was. But I didn't lean left because I didn't know crap about riding, and the rest is history.

So no, I don't blame myself. I was just a kid, it was an accident. You have to forgive yourself, and life goes on. But also, *how could I not?*

For a while Paul concentrated on picking out the bits of constellation he could see through the windshield: Cassiopeia, Perseus. Then he stared into M31, thinking about the Andromeda galaxy, wishing he had binoculars. Maybe he'd be able to see it. A whole other galaxy. Eventually he felt his arm begin to go numb. Randi was flat-out asleep, so he carefully maneuvered out from under her weight. As he did, he felt a light touch on his shoulder. Greyson, pointing up. "Hey, buddy," Paul whispered. "You ready to go home?"

Greyson shook his head. "I saw a shooting star. I'm waiting for another one."

The Fourth of July had turned hot by the time Madeline reached the old fire tower, though it wasn't much past seven in the morning. She'd gotten up at five to get an early start. Now she stopped, easing the shifter into "Park" with care, and got out to study the choices of two-track to follow. A chickadee called from a nearby tree, and Madeline smelled the dust of the road swirling behind her. Despite all the rain they'd had, most of the road was dry, though it was true that she might not have made it in the car. She'd crossed three flooded spots that were long and scary—where was the bottom?—the ruts leading in and out of them churned deep with muck. She'd have to wash the truck. She glanced at it, still unnerved to be piloting a late model, three-quarter-ton, four-wheel-drive truck through a vast unbroken tract of wilderness. *If Richard could see me now,* she thought fleetingly. He'd never believe it. She scrambled back up into the cab.

At last, after another half hour of driving at a snail's pace down the ever-narrowing track, she had traveled just over nine miles in from the main road and the trail petered out. With a great sense of anticipation she climbed out of the truck. Just ahead was a low, sandy hill. The brink of the lake. She hurried up it to the top.

Stone Lake lay before her, a shallow bowl that spread perhaps a mile off into the distance and half that width to the opposite shores, which were ringed all around with pines. But "shores" wasn't quite the word for it, not anymore. The lake was dry.

15

Madeline stood there for a long time, smiling she guessed. What else to do? Her namesake lake was a swale of swaying grasses. Finally she scrambled down into it. Sand and tiny pebbles crunched under her feet, sharp-edged sedges flicked against her calves.

After the first wave of disappointment, and then cynical acceptance—of course! Of course the lake was dry and empty— Madeline felt unexpectedly peaceful. She was like any other animal, or plant, or mineral. Just a soul alone in a wide, wild world.

She felt the sun on her back, smelled pine needles and hot sand, heard the breeze whispering in the trees. The rustle of grasses echoed the long-gone water. She was in this clearing deep in the woods in a forgotten place, and for at least this moment needed nothing more or less. She walked, and with each step she let another inch of the long furl of her expectations go. The place itself was like a steady hand, a low voice, a very old person who'd seen too much to get overexcited anymore. *Stop now a minute*, it said. *Stop searching.*

It was only when she heard a woodpecker—it must've been one of the huge pileateds she saw now and then, it was so loud—that she turned back and began to search the shoreline for the cabin

Arbutus said might still be standing. The woodpecker seemed to say that this was not a ghostly, forgotten place, but simply a place that had changed over time. Life was going on there still.

Madeline found the cabin, a low-slung building made of massive logs, around a curve in the shore of the vanished lake. In the years of neglect the cedar-shake roof had rotted, exposing the structure to the elements. She ran a hand over the logs and pushed open the front door, which hung by a broken hinge. The interior was nearly empty and the wide plank floor had begun to rot like the roof. All that was left of the furnishings were a couple of rusting metal bedsteads, some wooden cupboards hanging crooked off the wall, a rickety table, and a mammoth cookstove, coated with rust.

Her great-grandparents had lived here. Joe and Walter both had been born here.

She walked all around the cabin and the outbuildings—the remains of an outhouse and a few small sheds. Poked into every corner, investigated every inch of ground within strolling distance. She churned the pump handle up and down until water flowed from the rusty spout, touched the branch of a gnarled and broken old apple tree, looked off across the meadow that had once been a lake. Took her sketchbooks and pencils out of the little knapsack she'd brought and tried to draw it. With her eyes squinted, the swaying grasses looked like rippling water.

In her rambling she stumbled across a shallow pit behind the cabin. She poked through it and found a rusted metal ash bucket with the bottom missing, the spout of a thick white china pitcher, the delicate handle of a teacup, and a bunch of rusty tin cans. But better than any of this was a glass ink bottle stained indigo blue.

What words had been written with that ink? Household

accounts, tonics, a diary, letters to family?—her *own* family, she
realized with a start. If there had been letters or a diary or even
a prosaic accounting book, they were written by her own people,
by dear Walter's parents. Or by Joe. Standing beside this shell of
a cabin so deep in the woods, she was willing for the first time to
be impressed by the thought of them. What a life must have been
lived here. Not a life for the weak. A hard life that might make you
hard in return. Gladys was right, she didn't know anything about it.
How could she judge people she had never known and could hardly
imagine? They were hers, for better and worse, and they'd actually
lived and worked in this very place. She put the ink bottle in her
knapsack.

Eventually she took out the snack she'd packed, a cheese sandwich and an apple and a chocolate bar. She glanced at her watch
when she finished eating—ten thirty already. She'd better go. She'd
just take another ten minutes and soak the place in. She settled
her head against her backpack, closed her eyes, and basked in the
sun, listening to the buzzing of flies and calls of ravens and jays, the
insistent hammering of the woodpecker. Smelled the pungent wild
roses that were blooming all along the back wall of the cabin. She
felt drowsy and relaxed, as happy as she'd been in a long time.

Madeline didn't know what woke her. The shifting of the sun,
probably. A shadow fell across her, the breeze picked up a little, and
suddenly she was wide awake, shocked that she'd dozed off. How
could she have? She looked at her watch. Nearly eleven. If she hurried, she'd make it to work on time.

Things were going all right until she hit the last stretch of water
and sucking black muck. Maybe she wasn't paying close enough
attention because she was worried about being late. She knew she

was driving too fast. For whatever reason, she got stuck. Even with the four-wheel-drive button punched, she was stuck, deeper and deeper every minute, the muck swallowing the tires. Was the four-wheel drive even working? How were you supposed to know?

Madeline hit the button again and again, rocked the truck, felt it keep sinking and sinking. *No!* she yelled in frustration, but of course there was no one to hear. Finally in a great miraculous burst the truck slewed sideways and Madeline gave it a full stomp of gas, determined to get out. She did, but she had so little control in the slimy, sucking mud and was going so fast that the next thing she did was plow into a tree. The back end slid into the ruts again, and then the engine died.

Madeline dragged into Garceau's at four o'clock. She hadn't bothered to go home to clean up or change into her work shirt. She came in the kitchen door bedraggled, muddy, weary, and ill with apology and regret. Paul was swamped, chopping, tossing dough, spreading sauce, sprinkling cheese. She knew better than to interrupt him, but she couldn't wait to say what she had to.

"Paul, I am so sorry I'm late."

His face was set and pale with anger and he didn't answer. She didn't blame him. She tied her apron on. "I can't begin to say how bad I feel, and I'll work for free for however long it takes to fix everything."

His eyes flew up at that.

"I really am so, so sorry."

Paul pulled a finished pizza out of the oven and rang the bell. She was relieved he'd gotten someone to fill in—Katrina, probably, the most serious of the three Russian girls he'd hired originally. But it was Randi who appeared in the window, wearing a sky-blue

Garceau's Pizza T-shirt. Madeline stared at her, feeling a stab of betrayal, which of course she had no right to. Randi glanced at Madeline but didn't break stride. "Thank you, sir," she said in a jaunty way. She snapped another order up on the wheel and grabbed the pizza. "Looks great, keep 'em coming." She hurried away.

"Hey hey hey," Madeline heard her say in her husky, suggestive voice. "Whose pizza is this, you know it's yours, honey, and don't tell me you're not ready."

Madeline swiveled her gaze over to Paul. His look was murderous. "Randi's here, you can go."

She ignored this, because of course she would stay. "I know this is bad timing and I apologize for that too, along with everything else, but the thing is, I had an accident with the truck. I will fix it, I promise, you don't even have to think about that."

Paul stared at her for a long terrible moment and shook his head as if shaking off some thought or feeling, or *her*, and then snapped back to attention, spinning the wheel, reading the ticket, starting the next order.

"Paul?"

"Go. *Now*."

"What? Of course I'm not going, it looks crazy."

"*Now* you think of that?"

"It was an accident. I'm sorry, but I will fix it. I got here as soon as I could—"

"No."

"What do you mean, no?"

"I mean no, as in go. You're done here."

Madeline swallowed hard, staring at him. He ignored her. Finally she untied her apron and hung it back on the hook by the door and let herself out.

———

She went back late that night, after he was closed. The fireworks were starting, huge blasts of light and sound and color over Desolation Bay. It was gorgeous and exciting, or would have been. *Happy Independence Day*, Madeline said to herself with a grim set to her chin as she walked toward Garceau's.

Paul wasn't watching the fireworks, either. He was in the alley behind the shop, staring at his truck. She had been able to drive it back to town, once the engine dried out. She'd walked out to the highway, where a guy driving a Hummer had come along. He'd driven back in with her and towed Paul's truck off the tree and then given it a try and sure enough, it started right up. So that was one problem it didn't have. However. The chrome grille was crumpled and so was the hood, the air bags had gone off, the left mirror was broken, the driver's-side back end was dented. What a mess.

Madeline had showered and changed her clothes and tried to eat something but hadn't been able to. Her chest was sore where the air bag had hit her, her legs were still wobbly from having walked so far, and emotionally she was wrecked. But Paul looked even worse than she felt. He looked exhausted, *beyond* exhausted.

"I am so sorry," she began again, walking slowly up to him, one hand out at waist level, as if she was approaching an angry dog. She jammed her hands in her jeans pockets and came to a stop a few feet away. "I promise I will make this up to you."

"No," he said, not looking at her.

"Paul, please. I am so sorry, but this was an accident, and it can be fixed."

"Some things can't be fixed."

She frowned. Of course it could be. "I'll repair the truck and

I'll pay for whatever went wrong because I was late. I'm sure it was hectic, and I'm sorry. If there was a loss—"

He stared at her. "*If* there was a loss?"

"I'll make it up—"

"You can't."

"Come on. I've never been late before, I won't be again."

"No, you won't. You don't work here anymore."

"But I just said I'll pay you whatever loss—"

"No. The loss is that I can't trust you. You think I'm going to stand around wondering if you're showing?"

"I understand you're angry. I don't blame you. But I *will* make this up to you."

"You can't."

"I had no intention of—"

"No one ever does."

"Paul." Her eyes beseeched him to relent a little.

He took off his glasses and rubbed his eyes. "Just fix the truck."

"I am more than willing to work for free for however long."

"No. Fix the truck."

"I wouldn't feel right taking a paycheck—"

He erupted then. "Did you not hear me? You don't work here anymore. You have no respect for this place. I depended on you."

"But Randi was here—"

His face was full of disdain. "Oh, that's great. What if she hadn't been? What if she hadn't blown off her actual job at the bar to bail me out? You think that doesn't matter? You don't show, so then she doesn't show, and then Russel's screwed over at the Tip Top, and it's all so you can take some field trip. This isn't a holiday for us."

"I'm *sorry*. I didn't realize—"

"I don't have any margin for errors, and I can't have somebody around who doesn't respect that. And you don't. You can't. You have nothing at stake here."

"Oh," she said, feeling dizzy. Why had she assumed he'd forgive her? She recalled how immediately he'd fired Trisha for calling in sick back in June. "Okay."

He nodded.

She fought back tears with a vengeance. "You'll have to let me know whatever it is your insurance company wants. My driver's license, a report? Just, I guess, call—"

"I can't make a claim, I only carry the minimum."

Her heart plummeted further, which hadn't seemed possible. "But you're still making payments."

"On a credit card." Paul was again staring at the truck. "So it's not officially financed, so I can save on insurance."

"So—"

"So I have to pay for this out of pocket," he said with great and terrible patience.

Madeline swallowed. "Oh."

"The really great thing about this is that I was pretty much taking it back to the dealer to trade it in for something cheaper, something I can actually afford. Especially after the compressor on the pop cooler blew today."

"What?"

"The pop cooler. It died."

"Just out of nowhere?" Madeline knew it was a stupid question the moment the words were out.

"That's how things go," he half-shouted, spinning to face her. "One minute you're cruising along smooth, and the next minute all Hell's broken loose and you're screwed. You've gotten this far in life and never had to learn that? Lucky you."

"Can the cooler be fixed?" she asked timidly.

His laugh was mirthless. "Sure. For, oh, eighteen, nineteen hundred, I can probably fix it. Or for two, two and a half grand, I can get a new one."

"I'm sorry."

Paul shook his head and headed for the back door of Garceau's. "I've got to go. I promised Greyson I'd watch at least the end of the fireworks with him. I'm not letting this spoil *every*body's Fourth."

16

"Hello, Madeline," Walter said with a big smile. His acceptance of her was so unquestioning that it was easy to feel the same way toward him, and she'd been to see him often since The Day. Two weeks now since she'd smashed Paul's truck. Walter at least was always glad to see her, but then he didn't know what she'd done, and could anyone blame her if this came as a relief? They settled into their rockers in the sunroom, and after a little while she told him she'd been to Stone Lake. Finally she could bear to think about it, the adventure that had started so well and ended so badly.

"Oh, Stone Lake," he said, nodding.

"Did you grow up there?"

"Oh yes. Me and Joe and Mama and Father lived out there."

His expression was pleased and matter-of-fact and it made Madeline feel good to see it. "So it was a happy time?"

"Oh yes. Joe liked to go all over the woods, he took me with him sometimes. Mama and Father liked us to bring some game home for supper if we could get it."

"What were they like, your parents?"

"Father ran the mail to Gallion. In the winter he took a dogsled. I liked the dogs but Father said they weren't pets, I had to stay clear of them. He caught a cold and died one winter. I was ten. Mama said I was a big boy now, I would have to help her out more with the chores. And Joe had to go out to work then, he couldn't stay at home."

"Was it hard?" Madeline asked, gently. She liked it when Walter talked about the past, but she was always careful, not wanting to upset him.

"Hard?" Walter said blankly.

She let it go.

She didn't stay with Walter long. She had to get to the bank now that the quote from the repair shop was in on Paul's truck.

Madeline left the bank in shock. She'd gone in for a loan. She had the apartment for collateral, and while the mortgage wasn't completely paid off, there was a lot of equity in it, and she had good credit. The repairs to Paul's truck were going to cost almost five thousand dollars, and if she didn't get a loan she'd have to pretty much empty out her savings account, which was the money from Emmy's insurance policy, all the money she had in the world. That was a terrifying thought. She *counted* on that savings: she made the mortgage payments with it, paid the property taxes, the utilities, and insurance. She hardly made enough with Gladys to do more than put *gas* in the car; the savings account had been a big piece of embarking on this adventure.

But the bank turned her down. There was a problem with her credit.

"But there *is* no problem with my credit."

"You've been late on your payments two months in a row." The loan officer consulted her computer screen. "Last year you had some problems too."

"But I just forgot to mail the bills, that's all. And last year—Emmy died last year. It was a bad time. It wasn't that I didn't have the money. I did catch it all up."

"I understand. But that tends to make it look as if there's some ongoing issue."

"No! There's no issue. No one is more reliable than me, believe me. I mean, even when I go off the rails, I go just, like, *barely* off the tracks." Madeline made a train going barely off the tracks motion, sliding one hand just a fraction away from the other. Her hands were shaking. She clenched them in her lap. "I'm just saying, I'm so conscientious that I can't even go wrong really properly. And I *need* this money." She pressed her lips together to keep herself from saying any more.

The woman cleared her throat and looked down at a notepad she had in front of her. "It looks like there was some problem on this mortgage awhile back, too."

"*No*. When?"

"Back about five years ago?"

Madeline began shaking her head, ready to explain. "Emmy was sick. She was so sick, she'd had another remission and I couldn't take all the best shifts at my job, and there were so many expenses with the medicines and treatments, and she couldn't work. She really never could work again, those last four years, not steadily. It took us awhile to get things straightened around. But that was so long ago."

"It casts some doubt on your record."

"But Emmy is *dead*," Madeline protested, knowing that this defense made no sense, no matter how plausible it seemed to her. That glitch in her payment history was so old that Emmy had been alive then. Alive and still trying to do her home-based bookkeeping business, and still making pancakes on Saturday mornings sometimes when she felt up to it, still smiling her wonderful smile. *Oh, Emmy.*

The loan officer gave her a look of professional regret. "I am sorry. If you come back with proof of employment, something full-time, maybe then we could come to terms on some amount—maybe something less than what you're asking for here. Or if it was a capital improvement on your property."

"No, it isn't. I don't have time to wait, and I have to have the money."

"I'm sorry," the woman said again.

Madeline left the bank. She'd have to take a cash advance on her credit card, that was all. She had that much available on one of them.

Only she didn't.

"What do you mean?" she asked the associate who finally took her call, pressing the receiver to one ear and covering the other ear with her hand so she could hear above the traffic whining by on the highway through Crosscut and the clang of equipment inside the tire repair shop where the pay phone was.

"Your credit line has been adjusted to a lower level. You were sent a notice."

"I didn't get any notice." Or didn't read any notice, was maybe closer to the truth. Madeline thought of all the mail she'd been tossing in a box for the last few weeks, meaning to get to it, never quite finding the time. That wasn't like her. None of this was like her. But other people did this kind of stuff, she knew they did, she was the only person she'd ever known who even opened her junk mail and tried to read it to make sure it wasn't important, *And to Hell with that*, she'd finally decided. *Life was too short.* She had better things to do, and surely she had a couple free passes due in life. But no.

"I'm sorry, ma'am, but the screen shows you were informed by letter."

"When?"

"The letter went out over a week ago. When your payment was late again."

"But I've never been late before."

"I'm sorry, ma'am. Times are very tough, credit wise. I see here that the interest level on your existing balance was raised at the same time. Just to let you know."

"To what?" Madeline asked hopelessly.

"Twenty-nine percent."

"*What?*"

"Twenty-nine percent."

Madeline sagged against the wall, breathed in the odor of grease and gasoline and rubber. Good smells, somehow. Real smells anyway. "That's *robbery*."

The associate gave an involuntary, commiserating laugh that he quickly turned into a cough. Madeline didn't blame him. It was easy to get fired. "Is there anything else I can help you with?" he asked.

"No."

"I am sorry."

"It's not your fault," Madeline finally said, and carefully hung up the phone.

A skinny man in greasy overalls walked out of the repair bay and took a second look at her. "You all right?"

"Not really." Madeline pushed herself away from the wall and went to the car.

She sat at Gladys's desk for a long time that night, staring at the phone. The phone was ancient, squat, and black, with a cloth cord and a rotary dial. The receiver was as heavy as a brick. She glanced around the room: love seat covered in nubbly, salmon-pink fabric. End tables with curvy legs and lace doilies beneath the lamps, which had plastic-covered shades. A small, lean easy chair with wooden armrests. A Zenith television in a wood case with screwed-on legs poking out from under it. She breathed in the mothball smell she remembered from that first day. She was caught in a time warp, circa 1950.

Actually, she wished she were, because then she wouldn't have the problems she did. Problems that had piled up so fast that she could hardly keep track of how it had all happened. But it had happened, and there was only one person who might be able to help her now. She was steeling herself to make the call. She could imagine how it would go.

"Richard? It's Madeline."

"*Maddie*. Are you all right? Are you home?"

"No," she'd have to admit. "I'm not all right. I'm not home. And I'm really, really sorry to be calling because I have to ask a big favor and I don't have any right to."

Richard was the only person she knew who could afford to lend her five thousand dollars, and despite everything would just maybe do it. He wasn't truly petty and cold, as he'd acted those last days, she was sure of that. It had been anger and hurt talking, and who could blame him? Ending their engagement had been a very hard thing to do, and Madeline had been almost helpless to explain her decision. Partly it was just instinct, something saying *No* from deep inside her. It wasn't that she didn't like Richard. She liked him. But she wasn't sure she truly loved him.

She thought of their chronic petty arguments. Richard wrapped up in his research in the Nelson Algren collection, fascinated with Algren's clear, unflinching eye for Chicago's gritty underside, and

Madeline thinking that he knew nothing about the gritty underside of anything, had no clue that some people were still raw from scraping along it. Richard wanting some fancy new place on the Loop for dinner, someplace where she'd have to haul out that slinky dress and high heels when all she wanted to do was go to Gino's. Richard giving her that look that meant *Please* when she pulled on her peacoat, a coat that Emmy'd bought before they knew she wasn't going to college. Madeline loved that coat, it was warm and familiar and it wore like iron, there was not a thing wrong with it. Which she had explained to Richard once but all he'd done was come home with a new coat for her, a peacoat, yes, but pink with embroidered red piping. What could she say? He just didn't get it. And to be fair, neither did she.

The problem was that Richard came from such a comfortable background that he could afford to buy a house in Evanston, and an expensive ring, and plan a wedding that involved fancy invitations, and talk easily about paying her tuition to art school, even though he had just started teaching. Because he came from money, he could do these things. And because she didn't, it had begun to seem to her like a wedge between them that would only expand with time.

"Oh no," he would say sympathetically as she unrolled her sad story on the phone, because he did have a kind heart. Or maybe it was because he had such a good imagination. He could imagine how hard times made people feel. He could *imagine*, but he couldn't really *know*. "Oh, Maddie. That sucks. See, I told you not to go up there."

"I know," Madeline would have to answer. He would think this proved he'd been right, but the thing was, it didn't. The longer she was here, the more she knew she'd had to come, no matter how bad things were. If she hadn't, she'd never have known Walter. Never have seen Stone Lake (and never mind how badly that day turned out, it wasn't the lake's fault). Never would have fallen in love with the Hotel Leppinen (the clandestine visits to which she had become addicted). Never have tried to paint Lake Superior. Maybe never really tried to paint again at all, because unbeknownst to anyone she'd never sent in the application for art school Richard had brought home for her.

She never would've met Mary or Emil or Greyson or Paul. Never known Arbutus or Gladys. Cranky, distant, steadfast Gladys who was sitting in the kitchen right now, staring at the paper but not reading it, holding Marley on her lap, looking about twenty years older and fathoms sadder than she had a couple of months ago. Something that was mostly Madeline's fault. If only she hadn't left Arbutus alone for so long that day.

"Do you have a bank account there, you want me to wire it to you, what?" Richard would probably ask.

"You'll really do this?"

"You need the help, don't you?"

"*Yes*, but—"

"So I'll do it."

"But this doesn't mean I want to get back together, and I feel lousy for that. I know I shouldn't even ask."

There might be a long silence. Then he would say, "Give it a chance. I still think you're—"

"Going through a phase," Madeline would finish for him.

"I don't mean that to sound derogatory. I just think you're doing something you have to do, but that it's not a permanent *part* of you. When you're done, you'll come back home. This *is* your home, Madeline."

"I don't want you to count on that. You have to know that if you're going to lend me money."

"I know that," he would say. But he wouldn't really believe it.

And he might wear her down, because he was a decent person, and it would be so much easier to just give up and go back and step into the tidy, pleasant life he held out like a carrot rather than see things through here.

In the end, Madeline never picked up the receiver.

Gladys watched Madeline sit before the phone and she wondered what she was thinking, who she was considering calling. Maybe there was no one, no one at all. Gladys hated to think of that. Hated to think how close she was to having no one too. If Arbutus was gone—oh, Gladys had friends, good friends, people she'd lived amongst her whole life. But she didn't have children. Had no one to leave her meager possessions to, no one to give her memories to, and no one really to turn to if she was in trouble, no one younger and stronger who could really *do* something for her.

Gladys didn't blame Madeline for being angry with her for not telling her about Walter sooner. And she didn't blame her for Arbutus's accident, either. She was just as much at fault as Madeline, had been gone just as long. And if Arbutus had shown a little sense for once and not stood on tiptoe to stow away a platter, none of this would have happened.

Except for the accident with Paul Garceau's truck, of course. That was bad, and Gladys wished she could help, but she didn't have a red cent, so there was no use going down that road. Instead she gently pushed Marley to the floor and headed toward her bedroom. She squeezed Madeline's shoulder as she went past the desk. "Things have a way of working out," she said, because it was the kind of thing Arbutus would have said.

"Huh," Madeline said disbelievingly.

"I told Emil we'd go to the housing office with him on Monday."

"Oh?"

"He wants to put in that application for the senior apartments you helped him fill out." That was the only time Madeline had shown any spirit at all in the last two weeks, and Gladys hoped maybe Emil's predicament could rouse her again.

"He's really going for it, then."

"He hoped they'd back off if he even started talking about moving there, but they haven't. He says he's ready to move in. Sometimes I think he's serious."

"He'd hate it there. And they'd hate him."

"Hard to see those old women sharing a washing machine with Emil."

"That's what Mary said."

"So, things do work out."

"Maybe," Madeline said.

17

Money evaporated as fast as Paul could earn it. Mortgage payments, utilities, insurance, suppliers, repairs. The heating and cooling guy who'd driven up from Crosscut said he couldn't fix the pop cooler and charged him two hundred dollars for the visit. Perfect. With delivery, the new one came to two thousand seven hundred eighty-six dollars and nineteen cents. Plus a seventy-five-dollar fee at the landfill in Crosscut to dump the old one. He couldn't spare that kind of money, but he didn't have a choice.

Paul told himself to concentrate on what he was doing before he sliced a finger off. It was late and he was tired and that was a good way to have an accident, but an accident was nothing but carelessness and there was no excuse for that. *Ah, lighten up*, a voice in his head suggested, and Paul made a sound, a sort of chuff of acceptance. He was forever having these arguments with himself.

"What?" Randi said.

He looked up. "I didn't say anything."

"You laughed, kind of."

"Just thinking."

"About what?"

"Nothing," he answered reflexively. After a moment he said, "Actually, money."

"Ah."

"Yeah."

They were quiet for a while, Randi washing dishes, Paul prepping. One thing about Randi and him, they understood certain basic truths about each other's lives. Eventually she said, "I think about Grey's dad sometimes."

"Yeah?"

She splashed the dishwater with the spray hose. "I wonder who he was."

"You're not sure?"

She shook her head. "Not one hundred percent. Pretty bad."

Well, who was he to say? He'd made plenty of mistakes. Randi was doing her best, just like anyone. She was working for him and at the bar and paying Fran Kacks to look after Greyson. A few months ago—a few weeks ago, even—he wouldn't have predicted she had all that in her. "Not so bad, probably. Things happen."

"Sometimes I think I should get out of here, you know? Get a new start."

"Yeah?" They'd gotten close even faster after Randi stepped in for Madeline on the Fourth, something about being in the trenches together, and Paul thought maybe this statement of hers should give him more pause than it did.

Randi spun around and squirted the spray hose at him. "Gotcha." She was grinning. "I'm not going anywhere, where would I go?" Paul took off his glasses and dried them on his T-shirt. Her moods changed fast, sometimes.

Paul remembered another conversation he'd had in this kitchen, with Madeline, a week or so before he fired her. She'd told him that her ex-fiancé hadn't wanted her to come to McAllaster. "We were engaged," she said. "I got cold feet, I guess. Well. Gladys asked me to come up here, and I decided I would, and Richard thought it was a terrible idea. He had all kinds of opinions about it. We had a whole series of nasty arguments and in the end we called everything off."

Paul had been slicing peppers, green and red and yellow ones, admiring the look of them in their slender colorful rows. It was one of his favorite things about making pizzas, the colors and shapes of the ingredients. It wasn't the kind of thing you said to anyone, but it was one of those tiny things he loved about life. "What kind of opinions?" he asked Madeline, thinking maybe he would tell her about the peppers.

"Mainly that I was sabotaging myself. You know, destroying good chances because I didn't think I deserved them, that I was determined to keep myself down."

"Oh, so he was the one right answer on the test."

"Yes! That's how it made me feel. Nobody got that. I guess because it all seemed so nice. Well, it *was* nice. We were going to buy a little house in Evanston, it was really sweet, and he was going to help me go to school—everything lined up."

"Only it didn't?"

Madeline shook her head no. She turned to lean against the sink and face him and pulled her mouth into an upside-down smile. "Maybe it *was* crazy, but I just decided: I would come up here. And Richard took it so personally. Like he couldn't have waited a few months or whatever it turned out to be?"

Paul wasn't sure what he was supposed to do: sympathize, offer some kind of fix-it solution, just listen? "I'm sorry," he said.

Madeline shook her head, so he'd guessed wrong. "I'm glad, now. It wasn't going to work. I don't miss him as much as I should if we were going to be married. Everything with Richard was too easy. Where was the challenge? And we were from such different worlds. His family was rich. Well, not rich. But *very* comfortable. And me, well—Emmy picked me up in a church basement because my druggie runaway mother abandoned me there. I'm not complaining. Emmy was an angel in my life, she went through hell and high water to keep me."

"You were adopted, then?"

"More like signed over."

Paul made a face. "What, like a package?"

"I know. It sounds bad, but apart from the fact that I will forever think my grandfather was a rotten bastard, it was pretty great. Emmy was great."

"So how did she get you? I mean, what, she just carried you home?"

"Crazy, huh? She found me sitting there long after lunch was over, coloring in a book my mom left me with. I remember that. I remember the crayons, how they smelled, and I remember thinking if I just kept coloring, nothing bad could happen. But I was scared. I was so, so scared. I knew something was wrong. *Really* wrong."

Paul nodded, imagining it.

"Emmy always told me we took to each other right away. She was the only one I'd calm down for. She thought maybe my mother would come back a few days down the road, want me back, and somehow she convinced the pastor and the guy who ran the soup kitchen not to ship me into the system right away. And then when she got me home, she found a letter in my little parka, all folded up tiny in one of the pockets. It was from my grandfather to my mother. She must've written him for help and he wrote back and told her no. So, we always knew who I was and where I came from. And my mother never did come back."

"Wow." Paul stared at her, the peppers abandoned.

"Yeah. My grandfather didn't want me, but the State wasn't so sure about handing me over, either. Good thing possession's nine tenths of the law. Emmy had to hire attorneys which I'm sure she couldn't afford, though she never said that, and get him to sign off on it. It was forever before it was all final. Signing off was the only thing Joe Stone ever really did do for me. But anyway. Richard and I—our whole baseline outlook was different. Way different. There was going to come a day when that was a big problem, you know?"

"I can imagine."

"So what's your story?" she asked, turning back to the dishes.

His story. How did you answer a big sloppy question like that? He told her he'd grown up downstate, near Saginaw. His mom was a schoolteacher, his dad worked at Steering Gear, he had three sisters, all of them older. He'd come to McAllaster more or less by chance, and he'd been here ever since.

Madeline raised her eyebrows. "Well. Thank goodness you're not holding anything back. I mean, I just poured out my entire story and soul, so of course you're going to do the same. I'm so touched."

So he told her a little more. "I was running away, I guess. Trying to make myself feel better. Change of scenery, change of pace. I'd just gotten divorced. Her idea. She hooked up with somebody else."

"Oh. Ouch."

He shrugged. "We got married too young. My parents tried to tell us, but we wouldn't listen. The whole thing was probably doomed from the start."

"Still—ouch."

"Yeah." He told her a little more about the trip, the breakdown, the loaner car.

"Where were you going to go, before you got stranded?"

"Nova Scotia."

"*Really*. Why?"

He grinned, hoping he looked dashing. "Family history. I'm a Garceau, right? An Acadian. My great-great-grandparents came from France and settled there, at Port Royal, and then during the French and Indian wars, they got deported. They wouldn't swear an oath to the British crown. They ended up in upstate Maine. Over the years the family wandered out from there. I was going to swing through Canada on the way there, and down through all the places I could trace them on the way back."

"You're a romantic, then."

Was he a romantic? "Kind of a dumb idea," he said.

"Why? I think it sounds great. An adventure. What else is life for, anyway?" She smiled over her shoulder at him. He was going to tell her about Manny then. He suddenly wanted to. But the phone rang and she pulled her hands from the dishwater to answer it, then held it out to him.

Randi said, "Hey, Paul, are you busy? Do you think you could help me out with Greyson tonight? He'd just be sleeping, I'd have him in his pajamas."

Madeline had finished up and left while he was talking.

And now here he was, here they were, he and Randi. If you'd told him that night they'd end up together, he wouldn't have believed it. Paul felt bad now for firing Madeline so fast. The thing with the truck had been an accident. Anyone could have an accident, and the truck was just a thing. Wasn't that his goal in life, to live in the moment and not get too attached to things? But damn it, she'd done *exactly* what he asked her not to: shown up late and wrecked the truck. He had been tired and stressed to the bottom of his soul, coping with the busiest day—week, month—of the year. He hadn't had the time or energy to be understanding.

When Madeline got to Arbutus's room one afternoon there was a stout, fiftyish man with thinning hair dressed in rumpled khakis and an oxford shirt standing at her bedside. Nathan. He'd been a couple of times before but he never stayed long and Madeline had always missed him, which she didn't mind because she had a feeling he blamed her for his mother's being here, and pretty much he was right. Arbutus was beaming upon him and Gladys was scowling and he looked weary, more than anything.

"Madeline, Nathan's here!" Arbutus put a hand on his arm. "And Nathan, you remember Madeline, from Chicago. Remember she came over to the apartment?"

"Yes," Nathan said in a neutral tone. He went back to the conversation her arrival had interrupted. "Mother, you have to take this offer. Think how much easier it would make everything."

"But I don't need all that money all at once right now. I'm going to sell my house."

"Mother," Nathan said tiredly as Gladys cried, "*Butte.*"

"Well I am. And I don't think it's right, to sell the hotel to the Bensons. I don't mind selling it, but not to them. Couldn't we put something in there, a stipulation that it can't be torn down? That's our history, Glad's and mine, and yours too."

"History doesn't pay the bills, I'm sorry to say, Mother."

"I thought we had this all decided," Gladys said, irritated. "We agreed."

"Well, I've changed my mind. If the hotel is so valuable, why can't we take a loan out on it?"

"A mortgage?! At our ages?" Madeline was sure Gladys would never admit she'd already looked into this. "What has gotten into you? We *decided*. Let's just do it and get it over with. I can't stand this shilly-shallying."

"And even if you could get the loan, who would pay it back, and how? And take care of the upkeep, and the insurance, and a thousand other things?" Nathan asked.

But Arbutus seemed immovable.

"Well, we're just at a complete standstill," Nathan said finally. "I thought you wanted me to get started on the paperwork. You'll need a seller's appraisal, a disclosure statement, a purchase agreement, all kinds of things.

"And *I* can't think why you're being so stubborn," Gladys said. "We decided all this already."

"I don't want to rush into it, is all." Arbutus looked very unhappy. "Maybe there's another way. Maybe somebody else would want it. Maybe somebody would live in it and run it again, appreciate it for what it is. I don't think we've really tried, when it comes right down to it."

"No one else wants it," Gladys said. "The overhead, Butte. And the repairs. No one will take on the repairs."

"I know you said that, but you might be wrong. I don't think we've given the old place a chance. Is that really fair? What would Mother and Dad think?"

"Mother and Dad are *dead*. And we're the next to go, and Nathan here doesn't want it, he's made that clear—"

"No, I don't want it. So sue me. I live in Chicago, my life is there. Excuse me. Excuse me for living at all."

"I wish I could," Gladys said. Madeline stared at her.

"I'm sorry I lived and Frank didn't," he said in a weary voice. "We've been over that a thousand times. I know you'll never forgive me for it and it's just something I have to live with. But I still don't want the hotel."

"No, you just want the money! Made a bunch of bad invest-ments, I'll bet, and you'd hustle both of us into our graves if you could, to get the little bit we have so you can throw that away too! I may not be able to stop it, but by God I'll say it the way it is."

"Oh for God's sake, Aunt Gladys. Yes, I could use the money. It's true! You've guessed it. And what is so wrong with that? I could use the money and it might save me a lot of trouble in the long run, but that's not what I'm after. I hate to see you both struggling like this when it is so absolutely unnecessary. That old building isn't doing anything for any of us, it's a liability. Mother hobbling around the way she's been is just idiotic, she's bound to break a hip next time, and then what? Besides which, if she didn't own it she'd qualify for Medicaid."

"I don't want charity! And I'm fine. The doctor says I can go home soon."

"This time."

"This is the only time there is," she said simply.

Nathan closed his eyes. "I give up. I'm no match for either one of you, I never have been. I'll just stay out of it. I'm heading over to the motel now, Mother. I'll stop and see you tomorrow before I go back down."

"But, Nathan, you just got here—"

"I'm glad you're doing so well. I'll try to come again in the next few weeks. I'm sorry I can't stay longer, but I've got to get back for a meeting. If you really are determined to sell your house, I'll see about getting it listed."

"No," Arbutus said slowly. "No, I'll take care of that. It's too much headache for you to bother with. Such a small sale, so far from home."

"Whatever you think. I'm going now."

"Good riddance," Gladys spat.

Nathan gave a worn-out wave and left the room.

———

Madeline spent half that night gazing out the dormer windows of the Hotel Leppinen. The lake looked silvery black in the darkness. The roll of waves seemed eternal. An era of her life had ended since she left Chicago; another had begun and gotten complicated already. In the quiet dark of this attic room at the edge of the earth, Madeline was ready to admit a strange thing to herself.

She wanted this hotel. Even after everything—all that had gone wrong, everything Gladys had said about the expense and impracticality of it—she wanted it. Even if it was the worst idea she could ever have, she wanted it, if for no other reason than its beauty. But it was more than that. The hotel had a spirit and that spirit called her. It was wrong to let the Bensons tear it down. It was right that it should be open, part of the town again. If she bought it, she'd be a part of the town, too.

Despite everything, that was already happening. Mary, Albert, Emil, Greyson, Arbutus, even distant, angry Gladys—they'd become her people. They all needed each other. Or they *could* need each other, if they chose to. If she stayed. And why not stay? A person had to make a home somewhere.

At first the hotel had been a daydreamy place, an escape, a stage to play out her desire to be a painter. But lately it felt empty as much as anything. It needed people and voices, life, to fill it. It needed to be open. Of course the idea was crazy—what did she know about running a hotel?—but her conviction was like her certainty about coming north: bone-deep, undeniable.

Madeline rode to Crosscut with Gladys in the morning. They didn't talk on the way. Gladys drove. Madeline stared out the window, her stomach fluttery. She had to be sure that what she was thinking was right. When they arrived, Arbutus looked sad, but resigned.

"Nothing's worth all of us at odds like this. If you really think the Bensons are the only ones who'd want the hotel—"

"I'd be interested," Madeline said, slowly.

All eyes—Nathan's included, he hadn't left yet—turned to her.

"What on earth are you saying?" Gladys asked. "Have you gone out of your mind?"

"Maybe."

"Well this is no time for playing around. I do not appreciate practical joking."

"I'm not joking. I've been thinking about it ever since you sent me in there for the—" Gladys was giving her a venomous look and Madeline skidded to a stop on that sentence. "I've been thinking about it for a while."

"Well, it's just not possible. You have no idea what you're saying. Romantic fantasies, that's all."

"You're probably right. But nevertheless, I really am interested."

"You can't afford it! You can't even afford to fix that old wreck of a car you're driving—and last I knew, you lost your job. It's ridiculous."

"No, that's true. But I do have an apartment in Chicago."

"That is neither here not there, now don't—"

"An apartment—how many bedrooms?" Nathan asked.

"Two. It's on the North Side. An old building, but nice. It's on the third floor."

"Not bad. Property values are high up there."

"There's no elevator," Madeline said, wondering if that would make a difference.

He shrugged that off. "You have clear title?"

"I inherited it. Emmy—the woman who raised me—left it to

me, and we lived there my whole life. I've got a mortgage on it, but there's a lot of equity."

"Everybody has a mortgage, that's no problem. What's the heating system like?"

"Boiler in the basement. I think it's pretty old, but—"

"*Madeline!*" Gladys cried. "Stop it this instant. You're talking like a maniac. You *cannot* sell your home to buy the hotel!"

Madeline felt a slow smile spread across her face. "Watch me."

Nathan took Madeline's keys back to Chicago with him, as well as a contract giving him six months to sell the apartment. If she let herself think too hard about it she got panicky.

Gladys continued to maintain that the whole idea was foolish and worse, and in a way Madeline knew that everything she said was true. The hotel would cost a fortune to heat, the wiring was ancient, the roof hadn't been reshingled in fifty years, and she didn't have a clue how bad the water damage from the leak in the roof really was. There were already cabins and motels in town, maybe plenty of them, but the hotel was too big to be a house and Mc-Allaster was too small and quiet, even in the summer, to support it as a store. And how many more stores did McAllaster need, anyway? There was already a grocery and gas station, an antique shop and the craft market. The tourists weren't *that* plentiful. Or were they? Madeline didn't know. She didn't know a lot of things she should have, she understood that. Yet she would not be swayed. The hotel was going to reopen and she was going to be the one to do it.

"Oh my dear, you can't rush into this," Arbutus said, whenever Madeline and Gladys visited. "We can't let you do that. You don't realize."

"You'll lose your shirt!" Gladys said. "I don't want that on my conscience."

"Well then I'll lose it. But I'll lose it doing something I wanted to. I may go down in flames, but I'll go down trying."

"It's not that simple," Arbutus insisted. "Why, you could very well wind up with nothing. I'm sorry to be blunt but I'm afraid you don't have enough capital to start out with. It all sounds like an adventure now, but when it really happens—"

"There's no money in it," Gladys said. "There really isn't. Oh, sure, there are tourists now, right through color season, but you've got the whole rest of the year to contend with. Snowmobilers aren't going to stay in a rooming house. They don't want quaint. They want swimming pools and a bar and cable TV. And the place needs work. We haven't put anything into it in years. The wiring went in in forty-seven and none of it's been changed since. Why, McAllaster didn't even *have* full-time electricity until the sixties, the power went off with the mill at night. There's just so much that needs doing. You can't imagine how expensive it'll be."

"I want to try. I need a job. And your hotel—there's something about it. I want it. It's right. And letting the Bensons have it and tear it down—that's wrong. I don't know how else to explain." And she didn't, quite. Not without admitting to them that she'd spent hours in their hotel without their permission, wandering, daydreaming, working.

One trip at a time, she'd taken all of her art supplies up to the attic. It was a miracle that no one had noticed her comings and goings, though she always was very careful. She considered the idea that the very secrecy the spot necessitated had something to do with her painting again. If she kept it an iron-clad secret—almost even from herself—then there could be no pressure, no expectation, no disappointment or failure. There could be magic, and art could happen. The picture of the sisters at the table over their morning coffee was almost done, and she liked it. She thought it might be good, but most of all she'd liked the making of it.

Gladys and Arbutus looked at each other with worried eyes and they both said the same thing, in different words. If it was the Bensons she was worried about, she must not do this. The two of them had gotten by this long without selling to Terry and Alex, they could get by longer. She couldn't do this out of some kind of loyalty to two foolish old women who ought to have arranged their finances better decades ago.

"No, that's not how it is. I want the place. I want to make it live again. I want you to help me, Gladys." Gladys's eyes flashed with an interest that Madeline saw her immediately quell. So she'd guessed right about that, no matter what Gladys felt obliged to say about how hopeless and impossible it all was.

"I want to run it. I want to rent the rooms to people who'd love staying there. I want to shine the windows and wax the floors and polish the furniture. I want to sell antiques from behind the front counter, and serve coffee and rolls in the dining room. Cardamom rolls, I could be known for it. I want to have a big ledger for the guests to sign, and I'll hang the sheets out on the line to dry in the wind off the lake. I think I can do it. I want to try."

Neither sister said anything, but Madeline saw the skepticism on both their faces.

She flung her hands out and kept talking. "There are a hundred reasons for me to do this. I love the place. I want to stay here. I want to be part of something. I want to *do* something—to do *this*. I'm thirty-five. I'm single, I have no family and no real job. I can't stay with you forever. I have zero responsibilities, really, and it turns out I hate that. Who knew? You know, people thought it was so sad that I gave up so much to take care of Emmy, but it *wasn't* sad. It was love, it was life. And now I'm basically nothing to anyone."

Arbutus made a sound of protest but Madeline stopped her. "I'm not trying to be pitiful. Just factual. I'm on my own. And that's good in a way. No one but me gets hurt if I fail. And if I don't fail, look what I get. I get a beautiful old hotel in a beautiful spot and I get to—take care of people. It's what I'm good at, usually." When she wasn't preoccupied with figuring out what it was she wanted to be good at.

"But it's such a big risk," Arbutus argued.

"It is. That's what makes it so interesting." Madeline paused. "And after all, my roots are here."

Another look flashed in Gladys's eyes—surprise, pleasure—but nevertheless she said, "That's all daydreaming. It sounds nice but it won't pay the bills. This is my fault. I never should have sent you in there. It's a white elephant."

Arbutus shot a curious glance at Gladys: *When did you send Madeline in there, and why?* This was why Madeline didn't like secrets. You got caught. An uneasy feeling fluttered inside her about her own secret.

She didn't try to explain the rest of it to them. She understood that their arguments were valid but she wanted to do this as she'd never wanted to do anything, not even study art at the university. She was older now, and possessed of more ability to want. There was more depth to it, more poignancy. She didn't have forever anymore. No one did. She had to try for the things she wanted now.

She would make one corner of the attic a studio; she would hang her paintings downstairs, if she had the guts. If she kept doing them. She would. She had painted through everything, the mess with Paul, the disaster with Arbutus, everything. A part of her that had been dead, or sleeping, was awake again. Something about McAllaster, the lake, the people, the light—she didn't know exactly what and didn't care to know, but she was painting. Maybe the pictures would sell and maybe not, but the life she made from these ingredients would be her own.

Secretly, in some ways, Gladys was tickled about Madeline's idea. It was crazy and irrational, it wouldn't work, and there were aspects to it she'd rather not think about, but—it was exciting. And the girl was so determined that there was no sense anymore in kicking against it. Gladys had talked herself blue trying to make her see sense, but Madeline would have none of it. She *would have* the hotel, she said. Well, maybe. There were miles to go before it was anything like a done deal. The best part of it at this point was Arbutus's happiness, which was growing now that Madeline seemed so set on the idea, so sure. And the fact that the Bensons were furious. "You've got that Terry Benson spitting nails," Mabel Brink told Gladys one afternoon, and Gladys felt a surge of pure, vengeful joy.

They were more livid still when they figured out that Gladys still had no intention of paying her bill. Madeline—such a worrywart—was surprised, too.

"But you'll have the money!" she said one evening as they worked together fixing supper.

"If things work out. You haven't sold your apartment yet, the appraisals aren't done, nothing's final. I still hope you'll see sense and change your mind."

Madeline looked nonplussed. But she said, "Things will work out. It's crazy to go to court over this bill. You took the food out of the store and ate it, all except that one time. It's a simple fact."

"It's the principal."

Madeline sighed and let it go, but not for long. A few mornings later she tried again. "We should just pay and eat crow. Think of all the trouble it would save."

"Who's 'we'?" Gladys didn't bother to look up. She was standing at the woodstove waiting for the coffee to boil, reading the paper, her head tipped up to get a better view through her bifocals. Pesky things. But it beat not being able to see at all. She was reading the court news. She loved the court news.

"'We' is you and me," Madeline said, sounding far too het up for seven o'clock in the morning. So excitable. She'd taken after Jackie in that way, because Joe had never been like that. Sometimes she'd wished he would have shown his feelings more, but then, that was a man. "I'll help pay the bill," Madeline said, still yammering on over the Bensons. "God knows I've eaten enough since I got here."

Gladys gave no response.

"Gladys!"

After a deliberate moment Gladys raised her eyes.

"Would you *please* pay attention?"

"No." She folded the paper the other way, continued to read.

"No? *No?!* Gladys, look at me." She didn't, and Madeline actually growled. "Look. At. Me."

Gladys sighed, feeling very much put upon. She flicked her eyes up in an exasperated glance. "What?"

"Just please *listen* to me. It isn't worth going through with this. Think how it'll upset Arbutus. It'll be you in the court news next week."

"And so what if it is. I've got an argument, and I intend to make it." The coffee started to boil and Gladys poured herself a cup, then offered Madeline one.

"No thank you!"

Gladys shrugged and poured a dash of salt into her cup, then carried it and her paper to the table and continued with the news.

"Lou Thurston got caught driving without a license again, I see. That's the third time this year. And Amy Brighton got nabbed on a DUI. She'll lose her license altogether, see if she doesn't. It's no wonder that boy of hers is in so much trouble."

"Gladys."

"What?"

"Please. I don't want you to go through with this."

Gladys lowered her paper. "I don't see why you're so upset."

"Oh Gladys."

"'Oh Gladys' what? What is it that you're so worried about?"

"What will people say, and what about your credit?"

Gladys made a raspberry. "Credit at my age? Pish. I'm close to ninety, I am past worrying about my credit. What am I going to do, go out and buy a house? If my name isn't enough to provide me with groceries for a month or two in the town I have lived in all my life, then I don't have any credit. That's the point."

"What if you were to get sick?"

"If I get sick, either I get well or I die. That's life. And no one's going to refuse me health care because I got hauled into Crosscut over a few sacks full of groceries."

"But don't you see, that's what it is, a few sacks of groceries, it's not worth this."

"You shouldn't worry so much about what people think. You let it cripple you." Gladys turned to the next page of the paper. "I see Thelma Richter's granddaughter Nancy is having a baby down in Tennessee. I wonder if she ever married that man she was living with, the notice doesn't say a thing about it." She peered closer at the paper. "My, Nancy's gotten heavy. I suppose it's because of the baby."

"I don't worry about what other people think," Madeline said, sinking into the opposite chair.

"Mmm. Yes, you do. You give in too fast and you worry too much and you're too used to having things easy." Look how she'd gone and paid the gas bill with nobody's leave, arranged for the gas company to come and fill up the pig. Gladys had squashed that idea flat, turned them away. So much fuss over nothing. Yes, maybe it was a little too hot with the woodstove going every day, but they'd survive. They'd survived this long, hadn't they? Madeline needed a little more backbone. *Sisu.* The Finnish word for "courage in the face of trouble." Well, to give Madeline her due, she did have courage. But she cringed too much. No use in that. Gladys had learned by experience that there was no use in trying to protect yourself from the blows life was bound to rain down on you anyway. Stand up and face them.

There was—at last—silence from across the table.

"Ken Olli's youngest is getting married," Gladys said. "Seems like just yesterday he was born. And now here he is, all grown up and dressed to the nines in a black suit and tie, he looks like a crow in a pan of milk."

"I am not used to having things easy. I don't give in, not when it's important. And I'm not afraid of what everybody thinks." Madeline said each of these things as if she was thinking about them one by one. Well, she should think about them, because all Gladys had said was the plain truth. "I just want things to be peaceful. To be simple."

"Mmm, well, good luck." Gladys turned another page.

"And I do *not* let people's opinions cripple me. I don't."

"You worry too much. *Quotidie damnatur qui semper timet.*"

"*What?*"

"'The person who is always afraid is condemned every day.'" Gladys lifted her eyebrows meaningfully.

Madeline gave her a filthy look.

"I can't think why they don't teach Latin in schools anymore, I had four years of it right here in McAllaster, and let me tell you,

you'd better be ready to go through your paces or Miss Tuttle would rap your knuckles but good."

Arbutus rolled in with her walker then, with her hair in fresh curls, wearing a new pink and white checked shirt she'd ordered from a catalogue. She'd been home a week, and it was still a treat every day to see her, right there in the kitchen where she ought to be. She beamed at them and said, "Good morning!" like morning was really something, like it was Easter Sunday sunrise service and not just another muggy Tuesday in August.

She was such a pretty woman, still, plump and pink-cheeked, with those bright blue eyes ready to take pleasure in almost anything. But there was more to her than prettiness and kindness and cheer. She was Gladys's best friend, had been, all their lives. Thank goodness for a blessing like that—a soul who understood you, through and through, for better and worse, through thick and thin, who didn't plague you to be something other than you were, though she might nudge you in the direction of being a better person now and then. And she was forgiving. Too forgiving sometimes. Look at how she'd coddled Nathan his whole life long. But Butte's forgiving nature was going to be a good thing for Gladys when she found out about the kicksled, which was now in Bentley's Antiques in Sault Ste. Marie. Mr. Bentley had driven over one day last week and taken it out of Madeline's trunk, which even Madeline might not realize.

Arbutus poured herself a cup of coffee and sat down, and then, divining Madeline's cranky mood, dived right into the job of changing it. "I do wish I knew what to take to the potluck at church tomorrow night," she said, pretending a fretfulness that Gladys knew perfectly well she did not feel. "I'd like to do something different. Something—fun!" Madeline visibly set aside her pique and focused on Arbutus.

Gladys smiled to herself and went back to the paper.

18

The morning of the hearing dawned hazy and humid. "So today's the day," Madeline said glumly.

"Yes," Gladys said.

Arbutus sighed. "This is no fun. I don't think I'll go after all. I think I'll just stay here and read my book."

"I think I'll join you," Madeline said.

But of course in the end all three went, riding to Crosscut in Gladys's car. Gladys insisted on driving—determined to be the master of her own destiny from start to finish. Madeline sat in the back, her knees hunched up under her chin. The huge bright blue of Lake Superior disappeared in the rearview mirror, the acres of mossy swamp with tiny patches of water near their middles shone in the sun, the greenish-gray firs poked into the sky. Magic. But there was grimness along with the beauty, too.

It got worse as they headed inland. They passed the scattered cabins and camps that were too lonesome and poor to be quaint. There were old trailers surrounded by broken-down cars and trucks, discarded toilets and cast-off woodstoves, black plastic garbage bags stuffed with God knew what. It all sat listless in the sun, as eternal as the big lake and the pointed firs. Dogs lay panting on short chains in bare yards, and everywhere there was the barren, thin-lipped look of poverty. By the time they got to Crosscut, Madeline was in a hopeless mood.

She unfolded herself from the backseat and pulled Arbutus's walker from where it had been jammed in next to her, and lumbered after the sisters into the courthouse.

It looked like half of McAllaster was there, divided along opposite sides of the courtroom like guests at a wedding. On Gladys's side were John Fitzgerald and Mabel Brink, some women from the Lutheran church, a few others, some Madeline recognized and some she didn't. Also Randi, sitting near the back, holding Greyson, looking serious. Madeline was surprised. Impressed, really. She wouldn't have expected Randi to have the sense to take an interest. Neither Mary nor Emil was there but she hadn't expected them. Crosscut was a world away to them, only to be visited in an emergency like a hospital visit or a funeral, and then only their own funeral, and preferably not even that, probably they both envisioned themselves being buried at home in a plain pine box. Gladys had told her that, as far she knew, Emil had not gone any farther from home than he trusted his old truck to take him—*maybe* as far as Crosscut, but probably not—in the last forty years.

Besides, Mary and Emil had their pride. They were the crux of the matter. It was them Gladys was defending, really, and Randi. Madeline wondered if Randi realized it. Randi gave her a tamped-down version of her usual grin and lifted Greyson's hand to wave it at her as they made their way down the aisle. His face lit up and he cried, "Madeline! Hello!"

She gave him a wave and a big smile and continued after Gladys thinking how young Randi was. It stood out in a way it hadn't before. The majority of the people on Gladys's side of the room were old, natives of McAllaster who'd been brought up with Gladys and Arbutus and thought the same way. There weren't so many of them as there must once have been. And Randi—for one moment Madeline felt what Gladys and Arbutus must feel. For better and worse she was the next generation, one of them. The angles of her face, the brightness of her grin, the color of her hair, that husky voice even, must echo her grandmother's and great-grandmother's, women who had been their friends.

Most of the people on the Bensons' side were younger, better off. The old-timers, the old ways of looking at the world, were being pushed out. It was the end of an era, a way of life, a whole culture. But even as Madeline had these thoughts she had to admit that it wasn't just a matter of old versus new, it wasn't that simple. It was a matter of philosophy. Some people had a sense of humor and proportion and some people didn't, and this trait was scattered on both sides of the divide.

McAllaster had never noticed the Great Depression, Arbutus had told her one day, because everyone was dirt poor and half-starved, only they didn't know it. It had always been that way and everyone was the same. But it was different now. Some people had managed to make a little money, just enough for it to go to their heads. Madeline recognized Edith Baxter and Tracy York on the Bensons' side, and the county sheriff, and a few others whose names she'd never learned. And on the old-timers' side were some newcomers besides herself.

The Bensons were sitting in the front. Terry wore a flowered dress with a white lace collar, and Alex was dressed in tan pants and a polo shirt. They looked smug and self-righteous to Madeline. She supposed she looked the same to them. She'd put on her good slacks and a sleeveless white blouse with a shirred front, and had dug out her good leather sandals. Arbutus was wearing her new pink shirt again, with a pale pink skirt and white old-lady loafers. She had put two spots of rouge on her cheeks. Gladys was the most sober of them, in a navy skirt with a white blouse buttoned to the neck, and a small black hat pinned (pinned!) to her head.

She gave a nod of curt acknowledgment to the Bensons and slid into the bench opposite the aisle from theirs. The Bensons leaned together and whispered to each other, but Gladys didn't take any more notice of them. Arbutus plunked down with an *oof,* and Madeline brought up the rear. Gladys had carried her purse in—square, covered with dull black taffeta, with a silver clasp that wouldn't snap shut any longer—and held it in her lap with both hands. Madeline wished she had something to hold. She fidgeted, and coughed, and coughed again, wondering if she was getting a summer cold. Gladys gave her a quelling look and fished in her purse for something, then handed a cherry lozenge in a waxed-paper wrapper across Arbutus's lap.

There was a murmur in the room when the judge walked in. He was tall and thin with thick white hair and looked like what might have been called a ladies' man in his day. After a moment, the day's hearings began. Madeline hadn't realized there would be others ahead of them.

The first complainant was a landlord who couldn't get any money out of his renter. The man was three months behind and the landlord wanted to evict him, but the man had three kids and so he hadn't been able to do it. The man was dressed in grungy jeans and a faded Budweiser T-shirt. Yeah, he was behind, yeah, he had a job, yeah, he was getting some assistance, yeah, he'd try to do better. Things had been screwed up lately. The man half hung his head and looked off into space rather than at the judge. The judge told him to catch up the rent or he'd garnishee his wages. He slammed his gavel and held out his hand to the clerk for the paperwork in the next case.

It was a woman whose ex was behind on child support. She was a tiny person with long brown hair, wearing a dress that looked like it had come from the free box at a thrift store. She tipped her head so that her hair hid her face. The judge was gentler with her. How long since her husband had paid, how regular was he, how many children were there? She gave low, monosyllabic answers. The judge remained patient and Madeline wondered how he did it. He started asking harder questions, and it dawned on Madeline that he thought the guy was beating her up and he wanted her to bring charges. He did all this in an almost kindly way that surprised her—kindly didn't seem to be his nature, exactly—but the woman refused to say, and finally he swore out a bench warrant for nonpayment and slammed his gavel.

It went on like this. Gladys didn't belong here. Madeline wished more than ever that she'd ignored Gladys's feelings and used her hoarded money to pay off the bill.

At last the clerk announced, "Benson's SuperValu *versus* Gladys Hansen in the matter of nonpayment of accounts." Gladys took a quick deep breath. The judge read aloud from a sheet of paper he had in front of him, describing the case. In short, one Gladys Hansen had run up a bill at the grocery store that she now refused to pay. "Mr. and Mrs. Benson, is that accurate?" he asked.

Terry Benson nodded, her face already red with emotion. "Yes. She hasn't paid a cent since—" The judge made a shushing motion.

"I understand. Mrs. Hansen, do you feel this is accurate?"

Gladys rose from the bench, still clutching her purse. She stood very straight. "Almost. Not quite. May I say something?"

The judge motioned her forward. She felt very small standing on the floor below him, and he had to lean over to see her. "Come up here," he said. She climbed into the witness box. "You can sit down."

"No thank you. If it's all the same to you, I'd prefer to stand."

The judge made a face and shrugged. Gladys cleared her throat and began. "According to my figures, I owe the Bensons five hundred and thirteen dollars and seventy-two cents. They claim I owe seventy-five thirteen more than that, but I returned that last batch of groceries within two hours of getting them, and I will not agree to pay for those. There wasn't one thing missing from that bag, and not one thing opened, and not one thing harmed, I'll swear to that."

"Returned them."

"Yes."

"And why did you return them?"

"Well. I stopped at Mabel Brink's on my way home and she told me that the Bensons had cut off people's credit. They cut them off without so much as a how-do-you-do or a five-minute warning, and there was no call for it. They were brand-new to town, they hadn't even been there a year yet, and they cut off people who—" Gladys was as angry now as she'd been that afternoon, and she had to stop talking. She pressed her lips hard together and shook her head. The judge leaned toward her.

"They cut off people who have had credit at that store for as long as they've been alive," she finally went on. "And it wasn't right. I meant to let them know it wasn't. They can't just move in from away and change everything. There was just no call to cut off Randi Hopkins, with that child to take care of and she's just a child herself—"

"Randi Hopkins has got money to eat out any time she pleases," Terry Benson burst out, "but never a dime to put down on her grocery bill! I have had to hound every payment I ever got out of her, and I'm tired of it. She can drink and party and go out, but she can't pay for her milk and cereal? I do *not* feel sorry for Randi Hopkins."

Gladys saw Randi's cheeks turn red. Well, she'd made her bed, she'd have to lie in it. She would. Despite all her poor choices and flaws, Randi was one of them, a true native with that stone core that would withstand everything. She would grow up one day.

"And you're just as bad," Terry went on. "You've got assets, why should I have to carry your bill?"

Assets! Two decrepit old houses and one family heirloom hotel that they'd been pressuring her to sell. Assets. "Be that as it may. Randi is a child and she *has* a child. She was born and raised here and so were her parents and grandparents, she's not some fly-by-night passing through." *Like you*, she meant, and Terry saw that she meant it, and Gladys was glad. "We have a responsibility. I guess that makes me old-fashioned but that's what I think."

Terry snorted. "That's a bunch of—"

"Ladies."

Gladys looked over at the judge and nodded, to agree with him that things were getting out of hand. "Mabel told me they'd cut off Emil Sainio too—"

Alex Benson said, "He's an old drunk."

Gladys gazed at them with contempt and severity. "Emil Sainio's personal life is not your business."

"He buys enough liquor to pickle a horse every week!" Terry cried.

Gladys lifted her chin. "Emil is Emil. He is what he is, it's no business of yours."

"Well I don't have to pay for his habit, and I won't!"

"How much does Emil owe right now?" Gladys asked, narrowing her eyes.

"That's not the point—"

"How much?" the judge asked.

"Nothing." Terry flashed a sour look at Gladys.

"Nothing?" the judge asked with lifted brows.

"Someone sent in a payment, cleared out his bill the other day."

"And how often does that happen?" Gladys asked, forgetting for a moment that she was not in charge of these proceedings.

Terry didn't answer.

"How often?" the judge said.

"Every few months, if he hasn't paid it himself," Terry admitted, as sullen as a teenager. Which is all she was, really. An overgrown, spoiled child who never put herself in someone else's shoes, not even for a moment.

"That's right," Gladys said. "Every so often somebody pays off Emil's bill, that's just how things are done, that's how things have always been done, and there was nothing wrong with it, no need to bring it all out into the light. You can afford to wait those few months, don't tell me you can't, and if you can't it's your own fault. Overextended, that's what you are. I've seen that new truck you're driving, those fancy bikes you bought your kids, the clothes you wear. You took a vacation over Christmas to Colorado. *Ski-ing*." The Bensons' faces flushed with outrage. Well, too bad.

"My kids' bikes are none of your business," Alex said.

"And if Emil has pickled his liver, that's *his* business, not yours. He's got a lot of friends. Somebody always pays."

"That's not the point," Terry said.

Gladys ignored this piece of nonsense. "And Mary Feather. Cutting her off, I never heard the like."

"Old Mary Feather, she's still kicking?" the judge asked with a kind of wondering delight. "She's got to be older than God."

"Well, not as old as that. She's not so much older than me, really. I guess she must be ninety, maybe a little more, I recall when she moved up to McAllaster—"

The judge closed his eyes, clearly losing interest, and Gladys hurried on.

"Mary helped me out when times were hard, just like she's helped a lot of people. Lots of people found fish on their doorstep when they needed it. She never made any fuss about it. Fish, berries, syrup, whatever she had she gave it. Maybe that's why she's got almost nothing today."

"How much did Mary owe?" the judge asked Terry Benson.

"Over a thousand dollars. We let it go and go."

"It was over the winter!" Gladys cried. "You know she can't make any money in the winter, about everything she has comes in the summer, off the syrup and the berries and the fish she sells, and since you won't buy that now, she's got to try and peddle it herself, and she couldn't half of last summer. She was in the hospital with the bronchitis, you know that! And you know very well she'd have paid as soon as she could. Mary's the proudest woman ever born and she's as good as her word, and you go and make her out to be some kind of *thief*."

"Mrs. Hansen."

"It's the truth."

"This has all been most interesting. But I'm bringing this back to your bill. Am I to understand you admit to owing the Bensons over five hundred dollars?"

"Five hundred and thirteen dollars and seventy-two cents. They say I owe seventy-five thirteen more but I don't."

"Because you returned those groceries."

"That's right. And I don't feel I should have to pay for them and I *won't* pay for them, stick me in jail if you have to."

"Heh," the judge said, as if this was funny, but not very. He made a tent of his fingers. After a long pondering moment he said, "I guess I agree with you."

"Hold on a minute!" Alex Benson shot up from his pew. The judge fired him a warning look, which he ignored. "We've acted in complete accordance with every law!"

"You've acted like a couple of jackasses. Lay off the old ladies and be happy you're getting your five hundred dollars." He slammed his gavel down and wiggled his fingers to the clerk, wanting the next file.

"Thank you." Gladys couldn't help feeling smug. She set her purse up on the rail in front of her and fished out a large manila envelope. "Since I've said my piece and you've agreed about those returned groceries, I'd like to pay off my bill, right here in the presence of witnesses, because between you and me, I don't trust those people any further than I could throw a sack of cement."

"You want to pay them now, this minute?"

"If I may."

He shrugged and made a motion with his hand as if to say, *Knock yourself out.*

Gladys removed a wad of cash from the envelope and set it with care up on the podium, then dumped the envelope upside down to catch the change that clattered out: the seventy-two cents. She clutched the change in one hand, gathered the wad of bills in the other, and made her way down from the witness box and across the room to stand in front of the Bensons and pay them in front of God and everyone. She heard John Fitzgerald chuckle and Randi say, "You go, girl." Mabel Brink clapped her hands together twice and a buzzing murmur of disapproval rose from the Bensons' side of the courtroom. Arbutus and Madeline sat with their faces aglow, grinning like simpletons. Gladys gave them a little wink and then crossed the room to count five hundred and thirteen dollars and some-odd change out to the Bensons in ones and fives and tens.

19

"You think you're smart, don't you?" Terry Benson hissed at Madeline as she stepped out into the aisle. "Well I know what you really are." Tracy York, who worked in the senior apartment's housing office—she and Madeline had not hit it off when Madeline went in with Emil to get an application—pushed through the crowd to stand next to Terry. Madeline didn't answer, just aimed toward the door.

"Madeline, wait for me," Arbutus said from behind her, a little breathless. Madeline closed her eyes for an instant, and waited.

"I hope you know what you're doing, buying that building," Terry said. "Alex and I wouldn't buy it now if you put a gun to our heads, so Gladys Hansen better not ever come asking."

"I'm surprised they'll have anything to do with you anyway. Your mother was putting out for a quick buck whenever she needed one, everybody knew it," Tracy said. Everyone around them turned to look. "I guess that's how you showed up, a little surprise at the end of the deal. Do you think anybody really wants you here?"

Arbutus gasped. The people near them were murmuring and staring, or else trying hard not to. Madeline gave Tracy York just one brief look. "At least my mother isn't turning in her grave over how low I've sunk."

It was the best she could do. She checked that Arbutus was right behind her and made her way out of the courtroom. "I can't believe that just happened," she said when they got outdoors. "Those women—"

Arbutus shook her head, watching her feet as she pushed the walker across the uneven sidewalk.

"Is that how people really are? My God. How dare they?"

Arbutus grimaced, looking sorry but resigned. "It's a very small town, dear."

Gladys was at the car ahead of them, flushed with victory. Madeline stayed silent in the backseat all the way home, wishing she could go see Walter. Just sit with him and listen to a baseball game. She'd always loved baseball, had been a Cubs fan as long as she could talk, and she'd discovered that Walter was the same way. His team was the Detroit Tigers. He'd get such a happy look on his face when the games came on. He'd look at Madeline, eyes glowing, and she'd return his joyful look with one of her own and they'd settle in to listen. He had a nice radio in his room. Lately they'd been visiting there instead of the sunroom. More comfortable, more like—family.

She yearned to go see Walter, really, to soothe her wounded feelings with his company, but it wasn't going to happen. Arbutus was shifting in the front seat, sore after spending so long in the car and then in the courtroom, and Gladys was afire with her victory. She couldn't wait to get home and start reliving it with her friends. Madeline didn't blame her. She had done a beautiful thing, a wondrous, unparalleled thing. Madeline didn't begrudge her the sweetness of that triumph.

"Madeline, dear," Arbutus began later that night when they were alone. Gladys had walked over to Mabel's to continue gloating. "I wanted to say, don't pay too much mind to Tracy York. She lets her mouth run away from her, but she's not a bad person, truly she isn't. Smaller in her mind than she ought to be. But not bad."

"*Why* do you always have to defend everyone?"

Arbutus bit her lip. After a moment she said, "She's jealous, dear."

"Jealous."

"Your mother was a firecracker. Oh, how the boys liked her."

"I'll bet," Madeline said, thinking, *This does not help.*

"Tracy was always so plain. I'm afraid there was a rivalry there. Well—not a rivalry, because your mother never paid Tracy any mind at all."

"Wow. What a great reason. Now I get it."

Arbutus sighed. "She's had a lot of disappointments. She was a smart girl, you know. She had a scholarship for college, but her mother took ill. Tracy stayed back to look after her, and then one thing led to another and she never did leave."

"Yeah, well. I know how that goes, and it's not an excuse. Turning into this nasty, hateful person—that's her own choice. Some people are just plain rotten, you know. You don't have to find the good in everyone." Madeline kept washing dishes, hating how irritated she was getting with Arbutus. She wanted to destroy something. Something of Tracy's and Terry's, specifically. She'd waited on some shady people at Spinelli's over the years, even got passing friendly with some of them. People who could probably arrange—oh, arson, for example. A nice, untraceable fire. That would be beautiful.

"But, Madeline, truly, Tracy is just so *angry* about the way her life turned out. She can't help herself. She never left and your mother did—"

"She died on the streets!"

"I know that, dear. So to Tracy, your mother wasted her opportunities, an opportunity she herself would *not* have thrown away. And now here you are."

"Here I am," said Madeline flatly.

"And you're your own person, making your own way, well liked here already, successful despite everything. So Jackie *still* wins, don't you see?"

Madeline could not find it in herself to answer.

"You're very upset."

"Yeah." Madeline shot a grimace of a smile over her shoulder.

"Everyone knows she's just a terrible gossip, no one will pay two cents' attention."

"Yeah."

"I don't know what gets into her." Arbutus sounded vexed and troubled, and this only irritated Madeline more. *Bitchiness!* she wanted to yell. *That's what gets into her. It's not rocket science.* Arbutus sighed again. "You never can believe a thing she says anymore."

Madeline turned full around. "The thing is, it sounded way too much like the truth."

Arbutus's expression was tellingly unsurprised. "Oh dear."

"Yes, oh dear." Madeline spun around to lean back over the sink, hide her face, the tears that were brimming. Damn it. Of course it made sense, and of course she wasn't a child any longer, but somewhere deep inside she had still harbored a faint dream that her mother had loved her father. That they'd been foolish kids in love. That maybe—tiny, far-fetched maybe—he was around here still, and that someone—Gladys, Arbutus, Mary, Mabel, all of them—knew who he was. Maybe one day they'd even see fit to tell her.

"Jackie was a difficult girl," Arbutus said tentatively, and Madeline slammed a fistful of silverware into the sink.

"I don't want to hear it, okay? I'm sorry. I don't. I don't want to hear that she wasn't bad, or that she was just young, or any of that. I don't want any more half-stories or evasions or—or—or—*omissions*. If somebody can't just tell me the truth, flat out, I don't want to hear any of it."

"All right," Arbutus said.

Madeline bit her lips, tears leaking from her eyes. Oh God, she had yelled at dear Arbutus. But she couldn't take it back. It was the truth, she did not want to hear the filtered, censored, rewritten bits and pieces. She took a scouring pad to the bottom of a kettle and scrubbed. Oh, she missed Emmy. She was just *herself*, to Emmy. Her little scaredy-cat who needed a night-light and a story at bedtime. Her artist. Her Cubs fan, her champion spaghetti eater, her best Monopoly opponent, her dear girl. Things here would never, ever be that simple.

Madeline felt a touch on her shoulder. "I'm sorry," she said to Arbutus without looking up. "I shouldn't yell at you, none of this is your fault."

"I can take it. Talk to Gladys. I think it's time." Arbutus rolled away to her room, and Madeline followed to help her into bed.

Gladys did not come and she did not come and Madeline was more and more restless and angry. The little model world she'd built in her head, her vision of how everything would be, seemed shoddy and unreal, exposed for what it was, a silly fantasy. What was she thinking, selling the apartment to buy an old relic of a building in the middle of nowhere? She was a city girl, a waitress, an orphan, the accidental progeny of a teenaged—*hooker*. She had no place here.

After Arbutus went to bed, Madeline paced around the house. The scene in the courtroom replayed in her head. Impatient with that, impatient with being cooped up, she headed outdoors. She'd walk down to the water.

It didn't help. She tromped away from the shore after a while, back to Main Street. She stopped for a moment outside the craft shop window, thinking sourly of her too-romantic ideas about life. A decent job with benefits, that's what she needed. Sighing, she went on. There were a dozen cars and trucks outside the Tip Top, and the windows were open, letting the noise spill out into the street. The clamor sounded friendly, lively. People were having fun in there. Eating burgers, drinking beers, listening to music. She pulled open the heavy door. All this time and she'd never been inside. With any luck, Randi Hopkins wouldn't be working tonight.

The bar's high ceilings were covered in pressed tin painted dark green. High-backed wooden booths painted the same color lined the walls. Tables were wedged in close to one another, and at the far end was a pool table with a game in progress. A few people turned to look when Madeline arrived, but most went on with their dinners and drinks and conversations. She slid onto a stool and ordered a beer. The bartender was a middle-aged man in a T-shirt and jeans who served it with an automatic, uninterested smile. Thank God, a lack of curiosity. "That all?" he asked.

"For now."

He came around again half an hour later—the beer was only half gone, but he offered her another.

"How about a shot of brandy?"

He pulled down a glass and poured the shot.

Madeline swallowed it in one gulp and a wave of relaxation washed over her. "Give me another one of those," she said, and he pulled another glass down. As easily as that, she was feeling just a tiny bit better.

She didn't hurry through the second shot. She'd just sit and enjoy the novelty of it. How exciting to see unfamiliar faces that might just *stay* unfamiliar. (And wasn't *that* ridiculous? But true.) When this drink was gone, she'd go. Simple.

"Hey," a familiar voice said in her ear a few minutes later. She swiveled and slipped and found herself almost in Paul Garceau's arms. He grabbed her shoulders to steady her and then instantly let go. "Careful. What're you doing here?"

"What're you?"

"I came to see how the Tigers are doing." He lifted his chin up at the TV that hung in one corner. "My set's on the fritz."

"So you're a fan."

He said yes, he was. He wasn't overly friendly but he wasn't unfriendly either, so that was progress. She'd more than half-cleaned out her savings account to give him some of what she owed him (she didn't have any idea how was she going to keep paying her bills if the apartment didn't sell, but this was not the time to think about that), and she *would* get the rest. When the apartment sold, she would.

"Me, I'm a Cubs fan. Loyal, that's how we are. Uncle Walter is a Tigers fan like you. I respect that, I do. They're terrible. Worse than the Cubs."

Paul ordered a beer and when he asked if she wanted anything—he was so polite, even though he hated her—she ordered another brandy. It was going down so easily.

Madeline ordered a fourth brandy while Paul was still sipping his first beer. She felt nervous, sitting with him, but she wanted to sit with him. Now that she was just slightly tipsy she could admit to feeling a burn of attraction for him. *That* was inconvenient. But he was very appealing, with that little goatee and that limp. What had caused that? She wanted to ask, but she wasn't that drunk.

"So how've you been?" he asked, and without really planning

to she told him about the hearing. She grew very earnest and somber and shared with him a great deal of her sorry little story; her
fears and hopes and dreams, the scene in the courtroom, all sorts of
things. Toward the end of the last shot of brandy she began having
a little trouble getting her words to cooperate.

"How about we take a little walk?" Paul said, pushing her shot
glass away and shaking his head at the bartender when she made
motions to order another.

"I'm a grown-up! I can order my own drinks."

"Let's just take a walk anyway."

"I'm tired of walking around this stupid town," Madeline said
under her breath—she thought it was under her breath—but she
let herself be steered out the door.

"I didn't take you for much of a drinker," Paul said as they navi-
gated down the sidewalk.

"I drink alone!" This seemed witty and also quite sexy.

"Mmm. Not very often, I think."

"Hey! I'm not a nun or anything, you know." She tangled her feet
and stumbled.

"I'm thinking maybe this walk idea isn't working. How about I fix
you something to eat?"

"Oh, no way. You're *always* working. You gotta get up in a few
hours, go down to that prison. Besides, why would you want me in
the place? Nope, don't think that's a good idea."

"I don't mind," he said, his voice gruff. Angry, probably. Always
and forever angry at her. Well, so be it.

"Not hungry," Madeline declared. "Hey. We're at the hotel. Want
to come in? I want to show you something."

"Ah—"

Madeline fumbled in her pocket and brought out Gladys's key

and dangled it before him, then headed around the side to the back door.

Madeline lit some candles, put some Billie Holiday on the boom box she'd smuggled upstairs, showed him the paintings she'd been working on during her secret visits. Later she knew she'd blathered on and on about Art and Life, maybe even cried a little. Revolting. And then—then it didn't bear thinking about.

She sat Paul down on the horsehair sofa—no doubt Gladys Hansen's mother's best sofa once upon a time, before it was relegated to the attic—and flung herself at him. The moment she leaned in toward him—possibly a kiss would happen, was she crazy to think that?—he shot up off the couch and dashed down the stairs. She'd followed, suddenly quite a bit more sober. She played it cool at the door.

"Hey, no hard feelings, right? About this I mean. Because obviously you have, and have a total right to, hard feelings about the other—about the truck. Which I will fix. I'm working on getting the rest of the money."

"I'm seeing Randi, Madeline."

"What?"

He shifted uneasily. "I'm seeing Randi. I thought I should tell you."

She stepped back from him, gave him an imperious, clueless look. "Why? Why should you tell me, particularly? I don't care." She closed the door in his face and straggled back up the stairs, clinging to the banister, the brandy having quite suddenly caught up with her. *So you're with Randi, so what. I'm buying the hotel, what do you think of that?* Before she got all the way to the attic she turned around and straggled back down. She was going home. She didn't want to stay here tonight, drunk and alone.

———————

Gladys was sitting at the kitchen table with Marley, who was the very worst kind of traitor.

"What's the matter with you?" Gladys asked, and Madeline told her nothing. Or rather, *noshing*. Gladys's eyes narrowed. "Are you *drunk*?"

"Yes!" Madeline said, suddenly unrepentant. Yes she was, and she wasn't sorry, either. She was thirty-five years old, thank you very much, she guessed she had a right to go out and get sloshed every now and then if she wanted.

"Unbelievable," Gladys said, shaking her head. Madeline erupted.

"*Really?* And why is that? I mean, considering my mother, why is it so surprising, huh? And Joe? Good old Joe, was he a teetotaler? I doubt it. Emil told me they'd tipped a few back together down at the Trackside. Hard to imagine an old toughie like Joe taking it easy on the booze. Maybe that's why Jackie was such a—" Even drunk and furious, Madeline could not quite say "fuckup" in front of Gladys. "Mess," she finished lamely.

"Joe was not a drunk! That's not true! I'll not have you saying such things. Why, you're no different from her. Just say whatever you want to suit your own ends."

"How would I know what's true and what isn't? I'm not so different from her, huh? I wouldn't know, because no one's ever seen fit to tell me."

"Blood tells," Gladys spat.

"Why don't *you* tell? Just go ahead and tell me what happened. Tell me all about it. What are you afraid of anyway?"

Gladys glared at her, her mouth pulled down into a pinched and worried frown.

Something woke Gladys up, she didn't know what. Did she smell smoke? Maybe. She peered at her bedside clock. Two in the morning. She sniffed again and decided she did smell a very faint hint of smoke. Kids having a late-night bonfire on the beach, probably. She lay in bed for a while, hoping to get back to sleep, but that was impossible. She kept thinking of Madeline's accusations. Some of them were right on target. Gladys was afraid to tell the whole truth.

Finally she got up and put on her bathrobe, went into the kitchen. For lack of anything else to do she warmed up a cup of coffee from what was left in the pot on the back of the stove. She drank too much of the stuff, she knew. "Hello there, cat," she said to Marley when he jumped in her lap, and wondered how she'd ever done without him. Half an hour later she was yawning, thinking of getting back into bed, when a knock came at the kitchen door. *What on earth?*

She opened the door to find John Fitzgerald, wearing his fireman's clothes.

"Hoped you might be up," he said, his round face creased with worry. "Saw your light. Hate to be bringing bad news, but I figured you'd better know right away."

"Know what?"

"It's the hotel. There's a fire."

Gladys was dressed and out the door with John in minutes. She couldn't take in anything he was telling her. Couldn't get past those first words.

The fire was out by the time John got her there. Someone coming out of the bar had seen flames in the attic window and called the volunteer fire department. There was really, thank goodness, very little damage. A curtain had caught fire and led the flames up the wall to the ceiling. The old wallpaper was burning, and the lathe beneath the plaster was getting hot, and things were just about to explode when the fire department got there.

The damage was contained to the attic sitting room. Right now everything was dripping and smoky, but it could be fixed, John said. There was no structural damage. They hadn't even broken any windows because the front door had been open. Setting it all back to rights would be an unholy mess, but it could've been so much worse. The whole place would've gone up like a tinderbox once it really got going; the volunteer firemen with their one small pumper truck would never have been able to put it out.

Gladys felt shaky at the thought of it. It was August, hot and dry, the whole town might have caught fire. "But I don't understand," she kept saying. "How did it start? The place is empty. I haven't been in there in weeks."

"Ah, well. Someone has, though, you see. Someone had candles burning."

"That's impossible!"

"Kids broke in, maybe," John said. "Or maybe not kids. Not with the front door wide open. No booze bottles lying around, either."

"It doesn't make any sense."

John looked very troubled. "There's pictures propped against the walls. Canvases, like. Paintings. Those anything of yours?"

Gladys couldn't answer. She felt as if all the air she'd ever breathed had just been sucked out of her. *Madeline couldn't have done this, she* couldn't, *she* wouldn't. But in her heart Gladys knew that she had.

"Gladys?"

"I want to see for myself what the damage is."

"No. You are not going in there right now and that's final."

"But I am. It's my place."

"No one's going up those stairs until we know full well the fire is one hundred percent out and there's not going to be any problems with the propane or anything else. Don't argue with me about this."

"Fine. I'll wait."

"I'll take you back home," John said, gently then. "I'll come by later and let you know what the situation is."

"I'll wait here." Gladys crossed her arms over her bosom and stared up at the attic windows, and John let her be.

20

I want to go home," Madeline told Mary. They were sitting in the yard, snapping the ends off a bushel of green beans Mary'd bought from Albert, getting them ready to freeze. "Lately I just—I miss Chicago." She laughed nervously.

Mary glanced over at her. "I thought you were going to buy the hotel."

"I was. But now maybe not. The fire, you know."

"I thought it didn't do much damage."

"It didn't. Except for between Gladys and me."

"Mmm," Mary said, because she knew that was true.

"I just—I want to go to a movie."

As if that was what was really on the girl's mind. But Mary went along. "So drive over to the Soo, they got lots of movies."

"That's exactly it. I don't want to drive a hundred miles one way to see a movie. I just want to go. I want it to be easy. I want to go to a jazz club, maybe. And shopping! Wouldn't that be something? I want some bustle, some traffic. And I miss—anonymity. You know? I miss that more than anything. I would love for no one to know who I am for just, like, a *day*."

"Mmm," Mary said again.

And again Madeline skittered away from anything resembling what her real trouble was. "And bagels. God, I would kill for a real bagel with real deli cream cheese. With chives! And Ethiopian food. And *Thai*. I want to take a class, maybe. I could learn to tango. I want to go to a baseball game, and the museums, and the zoo. I want to listen to the radio, for God's sake, that's all."

Mary kept snapping the ends off beans.

"Is that so much to ask?"

"It's quite a lot."

Madeline's laugh was wavery and unconvincing. Maybe the place had just gotten to be too much for her. It was for most people. Too lonely, too remote. Not for Mary. But people got to feeling trapped, she knew. Even with all the modern things people had here nowadays—phones and computers and televisions and cars (and Mary could still remember when a lot of people traveled in wagons, it wasn't that long ago)—McAllaster was not quite in the modern world.

Madeline was rambling on again. "I just want—I don't know what. I feel like I'm in prison. My car barely runs, I'm broke, everyone hates me, I've read all the books in the library, I haven't shopped anywhere but a grocery store or a hardware or even had a *hair*cut since I left Chicago. I look like an old mop."

"Nobody hates you. And you don't look like a mop."

"Gladys hates me," Madeline said.

Mary scooped more beans from the sack at her feet. "She'll get over it."

"She kicked me out."

Mary knew that. She thought Gladys was a damned fool for it too, but you couldn't tell her. Gladys Hansen had fretted about Madeline Stone for thirty years. She'd heaped guilt on herself when it wasn't hers to heap, convinced herself that a good part of Jackie's problems, and Madeline's, had been hers to fix and prevent, plagued herself with regrets and recriminations, and then once she got the girl up here and had a chance to make things right, she threw it away. Foolish.

Madeline looked woeful. "Nothing's the way I expected, now."

"Ha," Mary said. She didn't mean to laugh at the girl but if that wasn't the story of life, nothing was.

"I thought I wanted to stay here. I did want to. But now it seems like everything is ruined and maybe I should just cut my losses, you know?"

Mary stretched her legs out and flexed her feet. Her bunions ached. Something about Madeline—she looked so much like Ada Stone—tugged at her. She tried to think of a way to explain. "It ain't everybody who can live here," she said finally. "You'll live poor. Like a farmer plowing old, stony ground. You'll never have much of nothing. Except troubles. They'll come, and they'll be hard to fix."

"Don't you like it here?" Madeline asked, looking bewildered.

Sure she liked it here, she'd been here all her life. But what choice had she had? Some ways, she'd just been stuck here and made do. "I guess I do. Can't imagine any other place. Couldn't leave if you pointed a gun at me. That don't change the facts any."

Madeline nodded. Maybe she understood, maybe she didn't. It was hard to explain. Mary gave a piercing whistle that brought Jack running and put a hand on his head. Much as she'd groused to John Fitzgerald, the truth was that a dog was a good thing to have. A dog steadied you. Just the smell of a dog, the feel of its fur, the way a dog lived, up front and simple. She stared at her feet. And then she said, "What you have to do here, you have to *accept*. You have to—lay down before the way things are."

Madeline went still, her hands at rest in the pan. "I'm not sure what you mean."

"If you want to have things your way, the way *you* want them, you don't want to stay here. That's not how it is. But if you can accept the way things are—well, then."

"That sounds harsh."

"Maybe." Mary gave herself a shake, tossing away the mood. "Don't listen to me. Probably it's not that way for most folks now, retired folks with pensions and such. They're rich, even if they don't know it. They got money. Choices."

"I'm not rich," Madeline said, morosely.

"Not even once that apartment sells? People are saying it'll bring a lot." Mary eyed Madeline with frank curiosity.

"Oh, it'll bring some money. But there's a mortgage. Once that's paid, and the hotel's bought—*if* Gladys will still sell it to me, which she says she won't now, but we did have a contract, wouldn't that be awful, if we ended up in court over it? And *if* I still want it, which I'm not sure I do—and the roof and the wiring and everything else is fixed, there won't be anything left over. There won't really be enough. She told me in the beginning that it needs a lot of work, and it does."

"So you accept that, or you don't do it."

"But I don't *know* what to do. Everything is all screwed up."

"Oh, pshaw. Everything is always all screwed up. You want me to tell you stories about what other people have done? I wouldn't worry about it."

"Right."

After a bit Mary said, "You've got the guts for it. Runs in your family."

Madeline ran a hand through her hair—it *had* gotten a little shaggy, but it didn't look bad to Mary. "Does it?"

"Sure it does. Ada, she was a character. A survivor. And Joe, too. He was a hard man, some ways, but he wasn't a bad one."

"Gladys said that."

"Because it's true. And Walter—well, he's got his own kind of courage."

Madeline smiled. "He does."

"Even your mother had nerve. You think it was easy to leave here and go to Chicago? She wasn't a good mother, I know. She made a whole lot of bad choices, I guess. But even then you have to admit, she had spirit."

"Well, that's one way to look at it." Madeline snapped the ends off a few beans. "I guess she never set fire to anything, huh?"

"It was just a fire. Not even a big one. It's not the end of the world. Look at me—I burned my own house all the way down and I survived." She gave Madeline a grin and eventually Madeline looked less glum and broody.

"You can always come stay with me if you need to," Mary said as Madeline was leaving. "I got that old camper, you're welcome to it. I spent a winter in it, it wasn't so bad. Heats up real nice." The camper wasn't much, but Madeline gave her a quick hard hug and said thank you like it was the Taj Mahal and Mary waved her away feeling unaccountably good.

Madeline drove back to Arbutus's house on Mill Street and pulled the Buick in the drive, hoping it would start again the next time she needed it. That was always a question now. The car was a dying beast with a terrible wasting disease, but she kept putting that truth out of her mind because without it she wouldn't even be able to go and see Walter, say nothing about ever getting back to Chicago.

She went in and put a pot of coffee on, then mixed up a batch of brownies. In the last two weeks she'd kept the lawn mowed and weeded the flower beds, cleaned every scant square foot of the place with a toothbrush, shined the windows, replaced the gaskets on the leaky faucets, washed the rugs, cleaned the linens and hung them out to dry, reorganized the closets and cupboards, painted the bathroom and kitchen, polished the pine paneling in the living room and bedroom, moved the furniture into an arrangement that gave the illusion of more space, and kept the little jugs of flowers she'd placed here and there changed and fresh. Now there was nothing left to do but wait.

For what she wasn't completely sure. She was here only because Arbutus had pleaded with her to be. For obvious reasons, that hadn't been her plan. She'd done enough damage. But Arbutus wore her down. It was impossible to refuse her anything after what had happened.

First Arbutus talked her out of leaving McAllaster the morning of the fire, and then talked her into staying at her house. She said she wanted Madeline there when people went through. She thought the house would sell faster if someone was living in it, making it smell good and look inviting (hence the brownies and flowers), and she couldn't stand the thought of being the one to let people in herself, nor to have them poke through her things with the realtor, who was a stranger from Crosscut. She wanted Madeline there. Would Madeline do that for her?

Madeline took the brownies out of the oven and glanced at the clock—half an hour yet before a guy was due to come look at the place. It would be a waste of time because so far, of the dozen or so people who'd trooped through, no one had any real interest. Most of them were just sightseeing, and the few that weren't, lost whatever interest they'd come with pretty fast.

The house was tiny and unassuming. It was quaint, but on all practical levels it was a mess. The plumbing and septic and wiring

were old, as were the fixtures and counters and cupboards—nothing
had been updated since the house was built back in the forties. Plus
it had a foundation of cedar posts that were rotting at different rates,
giving the floors an interesting sloping pattern that alarmed people
once they were thinking about plunking money down on it.

Madeline wished these weren't the facts because she knew
Arbutus wanted the ordeal over now that she'd made up her mind
to sell. When it did she could begin to pay off her medical bills.
And when the hotel sold—whenever that was, to whomever it
was—the burdens would really lift from her shoulders. She would
go and live in the senior apartments, she said. It would be nice.
Clean and convenient and modern, easy to get around with her
walker, and friendly, with neighbors all along the hall. She wouldn't
have to impose on Gladys every hour of the day, and they'd be able
to go back to what they'd used to be, loving sisters with homes very
near each other.

Madeline didn't know what Gladys thought of all of this because
Gladys would not speak to her and left the house each time Madeline cautiously knocked on the screen and went in to see Arbutus,
but she could imagine. Arbutus's mind was made up, however, so
that was that.

Madeline opened the newspaper she'd picked up at the gas station. Maybe she could find a job in Crosscut. An apartment too,
because the current arrangement could not go on forever. There
was a notice that the prison was looking for kitchen help. She was
thinking about that—the prison, Paul hated working at the prison,
she wondered how he was doing, how he and Randi were coping
with the summer trade, all the hours and craziness, and why did
she wonder, it was none of her business, and even if the prison was
awful it'd be good to get a job like that, it'd be year-round, with benefits, a decent paycheck—when a knock came at the door.

"Hello?" a man's voice said. "Anybody home?"

Madeline went to the door and at first she was very confused. "Hi. My gosh, what are you doing here? This is such a coincidence. Or are you looking for me?" She racked her brain trying to think of a reason why Pete Kinney should be there.

Pete looked baffled too. "*Hello.* I wasn't looking for you, no, though I planned to, later. Thought I'd see this place and maybe ask whoever was showing it if they knew you, knew how I could find you. I guess that worked out."

"But, Pete, what brought you here? Why are you looking at a house?"

He shrugged, seeming bashful. "Daydreaming, maybe. I was roaming around on the Internet, looking at properties up here—I do that sometimes—and I saw this one listed. I liked it, so I made an appointment."

"Well, this is weird but nice."

Pete nodded his agreement. He looked the same as always: a trim, slightly formal man somewhere in his seventies in a worn but clean work shirt the color of split-pea soup, with matching trousers. His hair had once been black but was now well salted with white, and his eyes were sapphire blue. He'd been so kind back in Chicago. When she took the Buick into his shop—old-fashioned, like him, the building sided in porcelain tile, the advertising sign a red-winged Pegasus, the pop machine so old that it dispensed small glass bottles from behind a narrow glass door—he'd told her she needed a new set of tires, an oil change, the points cleaned, the timing checked, the hoses replaced. She'd started to fear the car wouldn't be up to the trip but he assured her he'd get it into shape.

His eyes had twinkled when she protested that the bill was far too small. "I like the idea, you going way up there. Wish I could go with you. Eunice has been gone now close to four years and it's still hard, living in our house without her. I think of selling but my kids say no, I shouldn't."

Madeline knew how that was. So many people had ideas of what you should and shouldn't do, but in the end you had to decide for yourself. A moment of pure understanding had passed between them. And now here he was. Madeline stood in the doorway holding the screen open and could not think what to say.

"How's your car holding up?" he asked.

"It got me here." He looked dismayed and she hurried to reassure him. "You did some kind of miracle, considering how it's fallen to pieces since. If it wasn't for you I'd probably still be sitting in Milwaukee, waiting for a tow."

"So it needs some work, does it?"

"Well, in an ideal world, sure. But the way things are—" Madeline decided not to elaborate. "So you came all this way to look at this house?"

"It was just a notion I had."

She waited for him to say more, but he didn't. "Here, what am I thinking, come in. Let me get you some coffee."

"Things going all right for you, then?" he asked after she poured him a cup.

"It's been interesting." She heard how ambivalent that sounded and added, "It's beautiful."

"It seems mostly like I remember. Lots of new houses down on the water, though—mansions, aren't they? Where do people get that kind of money, I wonder."

"They bring it with them I guess. You're sure not going to make it once you get here." They smiled at each other.

"Going to stay awhile, then?"

"I—don't know. Maybe. I'm thinking of buying a place, a hotel, to run it again as a business. But there've been some—complications."

"Ah. Well. Sounds like an undertaking. Good luck to you."

"Thanks. I think I'm going to need it."

When he'd eaten a brownie and finished his coffee (he paused to inhale the aroma steaming off the surface before he took a sip, and Madeline remembered that about him, how appreciative of small things he always was), she showed him the house and yard. "Are you really thinking of buying something here?" she asked when they'd finished and were outside beside his car.

"Yes." He drew a voluminous handkerchief from his pocket and dabbed at his nose. "Life hasn't been the same without Eunice. I expect you understand."

"I think so. After Emmy died, nothing was right."

"The two of us, we always said we'd maybe retire up here one day. It was mostly a daydream. But she did love it here, we both did. Ever since I fixed up your car I've been thinking, why not come see it again? So I told my son I was taking two weeks—the shop's his now really anyway—and put my toothbrush in a bag, and here I am."

"Nice."

"Yup." Pete surveyed Arbutus's yard and house with a considering gaze. "Eunice would have loved this. I like it too. It suits me. Not too big, not too fancy, just about the right size for one."

"Are you really serious about it?"

"Maybe. It may just be that I am."

Apartments in Crosscut weren't just depressing. They were wrist-slittingly bleak, and not quite as cheap as Madeline had imagined. Three hundred a month before heat and utilities seemed like a lot once she saw how bad they were. Small, dark, and grungy, most of them haphazard collections of rooms carved out of old rickety houses that would be frigid in the winter and boiling in the summer.

"I'll let you know," she said to the landlords she'd made appointments with after Pete Kinney had left the other day, trying to keep
the dismay out of her voice. She'd take Mary up on her offer to stay
in her old camper before she'd live in any of these places. She'd give
up and go back to Chicago.

She went to the prison to fill out an application—at least that
job would let her rent a decent place—and the human resources
person told her there would be no decisions made for at least three
weeks. *Okay*, she said, feeling crestfallen.

Next she went to 512 Pine Street. She did this almost every
time she came to Crosscut. The house held a horrible fascination.
It was so grim. She could not imagine having grown up here; something about it made Jackie Stone real in a way she never had been
before. Madeline could never bring herself to knock on the door and
draw the shrieking woman from within the depths and say, *Did you
happen to know my grandfather? Do you mind if I look around?* She
came, she looked, she left.

She went and visited with Walter after that but before long she
took herself and her burgeoning headache back up the highway.

She ran into Randi hitchhiking a few miles out of Crosscut.
Randi appeared to have set out on a thirty-mile walk in her party
clothes—a gauzy top, velveteen miniskirt, strappy sandals. Madeline let off on the accelerator.

"Hey!" Randi said, trotting up to the window. "How cool,
nobody's been by at all, not going north anyway."

"You have to get in the back and climb over the seat if you want
to sit up front, the passenger-side door doesn't open."

Randi slid in and climbed over into the front. Her skirt rode up
as she swung her long legs over the seat. She tugged the skirt down,
heeled off a sandal, and propped her bare foot up on the dash, wiggling her toes. The nails were painted pink, and she wore a narrow

silver toe ring that had cut into her skin. She sighed and lifted her river of tiny braids up off the back of her neck. "It's *hot*. Am I glad you came by, I thought I was gonna be stuck walking all the way."

Madeline nodded, her mouth tight. "Where's Greyson?"

"He's in Halfway, he spent the night, we've gotta stop and pick him up."

"I see."

Randi rolled down her window and held her braids up on the top of her head with one hand, her elbow resting on the seat back, her eyes closed, the pink-nailed toes tapping on the dash. "Can we turn on the radio?" she asked after a while.

"No." Madeline was not in the mood to be more than just barely civil. But eventually she said, "It doesn't work, it quit last week, I don't know why."

"Bummer."

"Yeah."

"Paul could maybe fix it for you, he's pretty handy," Randi said.

"Is that so."

They rode on through miles of swamp and fir, tamarack and poplar and birch. An osprey flew out of a dead tree. Madeline soon heard a faint snore, which annoyed her even more. "Wake up," she said, giving Randi a jab when they neared Halfway.

Randi dropped her braids and opened her eyes. "Wow, I dozed off, sorry. I stayed up *way* too late." She stretched her arms, flexing her shoulders and twisting her wrists. She was like a cat, lithe and easy in her skin. Graceful. In fact she was beautiful. She had youth and animal magnetism and a weird kind of charm that Madeline wasn't completely able to resist, which made her feel grouchier than ever. "Grey's at the Trackside, it's up on the right—" Randi began.

"I know where it is."

Randi gave Madeline a friendly, quizzical smile. "Right. Sorry."

Madeline's silence was overpowering in the confines of the car.

"I'm always cranky when it's hot," Randi offered. "I think it gets to everybody."

Madeline clenched her teeth to stop from saying that it wasn't hot at all compared to what she knew from Chicago, and she wasn't cranky, either.

At the Trackside, Randi slid back over the seat and trotted toward the door. Madeline followed. She was in time to see Randi swing behind the bar and disappear into the back, giving a big smile and a wave to Greyson on her way past. A man and woman sat at the counter, hunched over their glasses with the focus of career drinkers. They turned when the door slammed shut, and after giving Madeline a long, flat gaze, turned away again and sat in silence except for the clunk of glass against wood each time they set their drinks down.

Greyson sat on the grimy floor, playing with a baby, a toddler wearing nothing but a diaper. The baby held a pink flyswatter in her hand and was batting at the air.

Greyson scrambled up. "Hi, Madeline. Did you bring my mom to get me?"

Madeline nodded grimly, then remembered to smile and say, "Yes."

"This's Andrea," he said, pointing at the baby, who was chewing now in a contented way on the handle of the flyswatter. "She's two. She's a baby."

"Yes, so she is."

"I stayed here last night and taked care of her."

"Did you," she said, thinking, *You probably did.*

"She hardly cried at all and she ate all her vegetables I gave her."

"That's great."

Randi reappeared. "Hey, guys!" she said to the couple at the bar.

"'Lo, Randi," the man said. The woman offered a harsh smile, ground the stub of her cigarette out in an ashtray, said nothing.

Randi swooped down to scoop up Greyson, giving him a loud smacking kiss on his neck. He giggled and wrapped fistfuls of her braids in his fingers.

"Ready, Peanut?"

"Ready!"

"Did you have fun?"

"Mmm-hmm, I got to feed Andrea. And Annie washed up that flyswatter, Andrea couldn't keep her hands off it, it was funny."

"Really?" Randi headed for the door, bouncing Greyson to make him giggle.

"What about that baby?" Madeline asked as the door clacked shut behind them.

"Oh, Roscoe's in the back. She's fine."

A wave of despair rolled through Madeline. Randi might be right. The baby might be fine, Roscoe and Annie might be fine, even the two at the bar might be fine, might be drinking water and not vodka, might actually be watching that baby to some degree, they might be her grandparents and in there for that exact purpose for all Madeline knew. She was aware that she was making judgments she didn't have the right to. Even so—but there was nothing to do.

"I thought you worked at Paul's on Thursdays," Madeline said as they pulled out on the road. Thursday used to be one of her days, and it was a delivery day too. Not a day you'd want to be on your own, especially not in the last week of August, which was busier than ever from what Madeline could see. People everywhere, grabbing their last chances at summer vacation.

"Yeah, I was supposed to be up there. But my plans got changed at the last minute. I called Kat, she's going in, Paul's covered."

Madeline frowned but she didn't say anything because it was none of her business and she had no room to talk.

There was a chirping noise and then a faint jangling melody and Randi pulled her cell phone out of her bag. "Hey," she said. "Yeah? Sure, yeah. I can do that. I got a ride, I'll meet you there." She flipped the phone shut.

Before Randi could say anything, Madeline said, "What?"

"I have to meet somebody. I was wondering, could you drop me off? It's right up here a couple of miles, it's—"

Madeline didn't want to know. "Sure," she said. They rode along in silence until Randi pointed out a trailer in a little clearing. Madeline pulled off, and Randi climbed over the seat to the rear door. Greyson was about to follow when Randi said, "Hang on a sec, Peanut."

Madeline was gazing out her side window, but her head snapped back at that. Greyson froze in mid-climb. The look on his face was wrenching. So anxious and forlorn, and so quickly erased.

"I was wondering, would you mind taking Grey home with you? This won't take long, but I don't think—well, it'd be better if you could take him."

Greyson sank back, biting his lip.

Madeline stared at Randi. She was smiling, but there was something pleading in her eyes, something sad and determined, and Madeline wondered what she was up to. It had to be nothing good. She had the impulse to try to talk Randi out of this stop, but she didn't do it. It wouldn't work, she could feel it in her bones. Instead she made herself smile in return. "Sure, no problem."

Greyson sank back into his seat.

"Scoot over and put on your seat belt," Madeline told him. "I'm staying at Arbutus's house, you know where that is?"

Greyson nodded as he worked to get his belt buckled.

"I made brownies yesterday, do you like brownies?"

He nodded again, not looking up at her. Madeline got back on the highway. "I'm glad you're coming over," she told him. "I've been kind of bored. What do you want to do? Know any good games?"

"What about hangman?" he said, tentatively. "I like hangman. Do you?"

"Love it," Madeline said.

21

Arbutus was a stickler for her exercises, she did them every day just like the physical therapist in the hospital had told her to, and she was in the parlor right now, standing at her walker, swinging her leg back and forth.

"You be careful," Gladys scolded from the kitchen. "That doesn't look safe."

"I'm fine. I have to do ten of these on each leg in sets of six, Pat said so."

Gladys made a face. She heard those words, *Pat said so*, half a dozen times a day. Not that she was complaining. But it was strange how Arbutus had changed in that month in the hospital. Gladys wasn't sure she liked it, but of course that was wrong. The people there had helped Arbutus heal up so that she could come home. And because it was a hospital stay, Medicare was covering most of the cost. Which made it even more aggravating that Arbutus had got this bee in her bonnet about selling her house.

"I promised Pat I wouldn't give up the exercises and I haven't."

Gladys grumbled as she worked at the stove. Arbutus would be in a leotard next.

"There is no point in being such a sourpuss," Arbutus said,

switching to swinging her other leg. "You brought your troubles on yourself."

This was about their only topic of conversation anymore. But Gladys was having none of it. "I did *not* try and burn the hotel down, I'll thank you to remember!"

"Madeline didn't, either. She singed one wall, and it was an accident."

"Some accident! She stole my keys! She's just like her mother. Completely irresponsible."

"That's a crock of beans. She made a mistake."

"She got drunk and deliberately set the hotel on fire!"

"She got tipsy and forgot those candles were burning. It could happen to anyone." Gladys could hear Arbutus counting beneath her breath between sentences.

"As if you ever took a drink in your life."

"You know what I mean. Things happen."

"You're too forgiving. I'm not like you."

"I know that," Arbutus said, her voice laden with meaning. "Truer words were never spoken. Imagine how it would be if you were."

Gladys glared down at the sauce she had simmering, powerless to make any retort. Arbutus's forgiveness for selling Grandmother's kicksled came with a price.

"It was a hard day for Madeline," Arbutus said. "You weren't there to hear Tracy, you were already outside. It affected her, it really did. It's not been easy for her here, not since the start. She's had a lot on her mind."

"She was here to look after you, nothing else."

Arbutus rolled her eyes, kept counting leg swings. When she'd finished she said, "I told you to tell her about Walter right away."

Gladys didn't answer. She had lunch to fix.

Arbutus started in on her arm exercises next, pumping them slowly upward, like she was lifting weights. "Would you have given her the keys if she asked?"

Gladys refused to answer that too, she knew a trick question when she heard it.

Arbutus came and sat down when she'd finished. "She's not like her mother, Gladys, and you know it. And even if she was, so what?"

Gladys rustled around in the cupboards getting dishes out.

"Look at that picture she painted of us, she wouldn't have done that if she didn't care." The picture was propped up on the bureau in Arbutus's room, and Gladys had looked at it more often than Butte was to know. Arbutus snagged a fried apple out of the dish Gladys sat on the table and Gladys swatted at her hand. "It's us but in a way it isn't us. It's more than us. Don't you think?"

Gladys finished putting lunch on the table. A piece of baked fish, broccoli with cheese sauce, a loaf of *nisu* to go with the fried apples.

"I still say you're cutting off your nose to spite your face," Arbutus said after they'd said grace.

Gladys didn't want to talk about it. "I guess Emil figures he's safe, these days," she said. "Hasn't heard any more from that zoning board."

"His plan worked, then."

Gladys speared a piece of fish off the platter and laid it on her sister's plate. "Seems to have. Though I wouldn't rest too easy if I was him. I still think Cal Tate's got plans for that land up there."

"Probably. I think I'll like the apartments, though. Unlike Emil. It'll be nice having the shoveling looked after, and people just down the hall. Less to worry about."

"You're making a mistake," Gladys warned. "Once the hotel sells, you'll wish you had your house back. I wish you'd listen to reason."

"I'll be fine. My mind's made up. I'm tired of worrying."

Gladys rolled her eyes but kept still. Arguing with Butte was a waste of breath.

Arbutus ate a little more, studying Gladys all the while, and then she said, "Nathan says Madeline's still got her apartment listed with him."

"Well, good for her."

"She hasn't withdrawn her offer on the hotel, either. It's contingent on her place selling, is all."

"La-di-da. I won't sell it to her."

"Well I will. And if you won't, you'll have to pay a big fee."

"What?"

"We drew up all those papers with Nathan, remember? Once you list with real estate you have to accept the offer if it meets your price, or else you have to pay a penalty. My realtor in Crosscut said the same thing, she said make sure you're sure, you can't just change your mind."

"Nathan wouldn't dare."

"Of course he would. I told him he should."

Gladys slammed her fork down. "Arbutus Hill, I don't believe you."

Arbutus shrugged. "Business is business."

Gladys stabbed a chunk of broccoli and ate it. Then she said, "It'll never happen anyway. She'll think better of it. It doesn't make any more sense now than it ever did. She probably just forgot to withdraw that offer. She's forgotten everything else—bills, candles, *asking* for permission to make herself at home in the hotel. You watch, next time you talk to Nathan it'll be different."

"I don't think so." Arbutus applied herself to her lunch, and gradually Gladys relaxed. Then Arbutus said, "Oh, by the way. I invited the fellow who wants to buy my house to brunch on Wednesday."

"Brunch?"

"Doesn't that sound fun? They were talking about it on the morning show the other day. It's later than breakfast and earlier than lunch—"

"I know what it is."

"I thought we could have that egg pie Verna brings to church."

"Quiche," Gladys said flatly.

"Yes, that's right, quiche. Pete's a friend of Madeline's from Chicago, did I tell you?"

"And just when did all of this come about?"

"Yesterday, when you were at Mabel's. He stopped by, and I gave him some coffee. I invited him then. I told him we'd like to have Madeline come too, it'd seem funny to him if she didn't, and besides, I'd like her to."

Gladys stared at her sister, speechless.

At nine thirty Wednesday the whole sorry lot of them—and Gladys included herself in this description—sat in the parlor making small talk about Madeline's car. "It's started making bad noises in the last few weeks," Madeline said. "A kind of knocking."

"Bad gas, maybe," Pete Kinney said.

"She fills up down in Halfway. I told her umpteen times that gas is old, you don't want it, but she won't believe me."

Madeline sighed.

"Well, I did tell you."

"Yes you did."

"As far as the knocking, it could be a number of things, I'd have to take a better look at it, give it a drive."

Gladys sniffed. Obviously it was bad gas, but it was civil of Pete not to insist.

"Would you like more coffee, or some juice?" Arbutus offered, smiling prettily.

Pete gave her a keen, pleased look. The look of a man who has taken a fancy. Gladys felt both proud and vexed. Well past seventy, crippled up, and her sister was still wrapping men around her finger quick as a wink. "I would," he said to Butte. "More of this good coffee would be just the thing." Then he recollected himself, included Gladys. "I'm pleased to meet the both of you, by the way. It's good of you to have me in to eat. It'll be a treat to have some home-cooked food, my daughter gets after me for not fixing myself better meals."

"Speaking of which." Gladys got up to check on the quiche. Leave the lovebirds alone for a minute. She didn't know whether to be glad or mad. Madeline followed to fetch Pete's coffee. They eyed each other warily and didn't speak. When they returned Pete had scooted down the couch close to Arbutus's chair and they were chatting with animation. Gladys and Madeline glanced at each other and then away, but before they could stop it there'd been a flash of understanding between them—is this what it looks like, and how nice if it is.

Pete liked the quiche, the seasoning Gladys used, what was it? (Salt and pepper and a little paprika, nothing special, she said, frowning with pleasure.) He loved Gladys's bread, and the wild blueberry jam. He remembered a neighbor lady from when he was a boy who'd made cardamom rolls at the holidays, he hadn't had anything like it since. She was Scandinavian and painted her porch roof blue like the sky and swept off her sidewalks every morning with a broom. Pete patted the Formica table in an appreciating way, admired the cookstove, complimented Gladys on her flowers and the neat shape she kept her house in. He liked McAllaster, he said, he and his wife had always told each other they'd maybe retire here one day. "It was a dream of ours. Seems wrong to me still that we never did do it. We had good times here."

Arbutus was nodding, her face sympathetic. "You miss her."

"I do. She wouldn't want me to mope, so I don't. But the world's a little lonely, on your own."

"My Harvey, my second husband, was the same way. He couldn't stand to think of me downhearted. And I haven't been. But there've been lonely times."

They smiled at each other in a way that left the rest of the world out.

"Thank you for a delicious meal and your kind hospitality," Pete said after they'd finished and he was at the door. Arbutus invited him to come to supper the next night if he was going to stay in town.

"I'd be pleased to if you're sure it's not an imposition."

Of course not, Gladys assured him stiffly. He shook all their hands, saving Arbutus for last, and held hers a little longer than he might have.

Just as he pulled out of the drive they heard a siren wailing. Gladys went to call Mabel Brink, as she did every time the ambulance went out, because Mabol had a scanner. Arbutus went in the parlor and turned on the television to catch the tail end of her favorite program. Madeline went to the kitchen sink and ran dishwater and Gladys was taken aback, but decided not to stop her. Not until after she'd made her phone call anyway.

Two minutes later Gladys set down the phone and went into the kitchen, feeling dazed. "Mabel says it's a car accident down the highway. I guess they think it's Randi, with those summer kids she's been running around with lately. It's bad, she says."

Madeline looked as shocked as Gladys felt. "What kids? The last I heard she was working for Paul *and* at the bar, how would she have time to run around? And what about Greyson, did Mabel know?"

"She didn't know. With Randi, I'd have to think. Jo Jo Finn's out of town, and Fran Kacks put her back out last week, had to tell Randi she couldn't sit anymore. Maybe he's at the Trackside, but—" Gladys shook her head, full of trepidation.

"I'm going to go see," Madeline said, wiping her hands on her jeans and heading for the door. She looked apprehensive but resolved. She was going to *do* something, and Gladys was relieved.

22

The accident happened eight miles south of town, on the sharp curve that people sometimes missed if they were going too fast.

Madeline pulled to a stop well out of the way. The wrecked car was an older sedan, and it sat sideways to the road, its hood crumpled into a power pole, the side banged and creased, skid marks making figure eights on the road. Three kids stood huddled under blankets, their faces somber and frightened. Madeline recognized them from Garceau's—summer people, college kids. *Too late, too late*, Madeline thought. *We're always too late to realize our mistakes, all of us.*

The ambulance crew was working on the front passenger's side, which was crumpled from the force of the impact. One of the crew was the basket-making woman. Madeline recognized the man from the gas station, too. He and John Fitzgerald were carrying a stretcher toward the car. John's expression was bleak. Madeline felt sick.

She heard sirens approaching from the south and within minutes, two state police cars arrived. Then Paul's car appeared on the horizon, headed north from Crosscut. He pulled over and Madeline ran toward him.

"What's going on?" he asked.

Madeline had decided as she ran just to say it, flat out. "I think Randi's in the car. I think it's bad. I'm so sorry. I'm sorry you had to find out this way."

His face went blank. "No. That can't be her, she's supposed to be at work in fifteen minutes. I don't even know whose car that is." His eyes widened with a further realization. "Greyson?"

"I don't know," Madeline said, and felt her hands begin to shake. Paul looked as if he was going to be sick. Madeline took a ragged breath. "I'm going to see if I can find out anything." She was terrified to go closer, terrified of what she'd learn, but she headed across the highway anyway.

A policeman stopped her before she got to the other side. "Ma'am," he barked. "Stay back. Get back in your vehicle and move along."

"I know. I'm sorry. But we heard it was our friend in the car, his girlfriend. I—we need to know." She looked back at Paul who stood with his arms wrapped around himself.

"I can't help you. Get back in your vehicle. You're in the way."

"I'm sorry, I am. But—is she alive? Is it Randi?"

"I don't know who it is, and I don't know their condition."

"But there's a woman in the car?"

After a moment the officer nodded, his eyes steely. "Yes, ma'am, there is."

"Is there a child, too? A little boy, about five?"

"The child is fine. He's in the ambulance. Now go."

Madeline ran back across the road. "I don't know for sure if it's Randi," she told Paul, grabbing one of his hands with both of her own. "I think so. But there was a boy who's okay. He's in the ambulance. The officer wouldn't tell me anything else."

Paul closed his eyes. When he opened them again he looked marginally less ill. "Thank you."

More emergency vehicles arrived—another ambulance, a fire truck—and the crew cut the car's dash away, then positioned a board under the woman in the car and slowly drew her out. Randi's braids dangled toward the ground, and even from across the highway Madeline thought she heard the faint clack of beads and jangle of tiny bells. She made an involuntary sound, a whimper, and Paul tightened his grip on her hand. When the second ambulance had roared away with Randi in it, John Fitzgerald headed across the highway.

"Not supposed to do this," he said, looking at Paul. "But I'm going to. She's alive, but she's all broken up. I think she'll survive. I hope to God so, but it's going to be a long haul."

Oh, Randi, Madeline thought. *Little fool. Please don't die. Please don't.*

"Greyson?" Paul asked.

"He's all right, basically, but Raylene's got her hands full with him. They don't want to give him anything, but they're afraid he's going to hyperventilate. Poor kid."

"Can I see him?" Paul asked.

Madeline felt shakier than ever—relief that Greyson was all right, and that Paul had stepped in so surely. She had to see Grey with her own eyes.

John considered. "Maybe. I'll talk to Raylene." He strode off.

Madeline kept her eyes on the broken car. She thought of Randi's husky voice that always drew her in against her will, her curvy, perfect body in snug jeans, that river of beaded braids flowing down her back, her bare feet up on the dash of the Buick, toes wiggling. There was something so human and innocent and *alive* in that.

She thought of Gladys and Arbutus's fondness for her, the grand-daughter of their old friend. They would be devastated by this. *Live*, Madeline willed.

A few minutes later a woman she'd never met strode toward her carrying Greyson, who was swaddled in a blanket. "We left it up to him," she said gruffly.

"Paul," Greyson said in a reedy voice, his fair skin paler than ever, and held his arms out. Paul scooped him up and hugged him. But then John came back with a question about Randi's insurance—or lack of—and Paul gently transferred Grey to Madeline. His legs clamped around her waist and he buried his face in her neck. She felt him trembling.

"Hush now, sweetheart," she said into his hair, which was damp with sweat, though his skin felt cold. "Everything will be all right. Don't worry." Her heart was pounding and her hands were still trembling; she had no way of knowing if things would be all right, but she had to say it. She walked a small distance off and then back again, rubbing Greyson's back. Some of the tension left his body as she paced, and the trembling had mostly stopped by the time Paul finished talking to John.

Paul reached out to touch Greyson's head as if to reassure himself that he really was all right, and Madeline felt Greyson relax a little more in her arms. "Hey, kiddo," Paul said softly, his voice cracking a little. "How are you holding up there?"

"Okay," Greyson whispered, but his chin began to tremble and his eyes filled with tears. He stretched his arms out and Paul gathered him close again. Madeline touched Raylene's arm and drew her aside.

"I'm wondering what will happen with Greyson."

Raylene made a face. "Not sure."

"Would it help if I took him home with me?" She assumed Paul would be following the ambulance wherever it took Randi, and then he'd have his job at the prison and Garceau's to deal with, whereas she had nothing but time to spare. "I take care of him sometimes, I'm Madeline Stone, I came up here to—"

"I know who you are." Raylene studied Madeline, and then she said, "Maybe so. Maybe that'd be the best thing. Hate to disrupt him any more than he already has been. Let me talk to John. Randi's conscious, just. If she gives her okay, I think we can do it."

Randi did, and John said he thought it'd be good if Madeline could take Greyson for the time being. Paul said he was going to follow the ambulance to the hospital and would let her know as soon as he found out anything.

"But Mommy's in the car!" Greyson cried when he understood everyone was leaving.

"No, she's not," Madeline reassured him. "They got her out and took her straight to the hospital, really fast. They're going to take care of her, and I'm going to take care of you." She took one of his hands but he jerked it away.

"Noooo. Mom. *Mommy!*"

Paul said soothing things and stroked Greyson's hair as he walked him toward the Buick, but Greyson continued wailing. Paul gave Madeline a lost look. She shook her head, not knowing what to suggest, and held her hands out to take him again.

"*Mommy, Mommy, Mommy,*" Greyson wailed, twisting in her arms. She swallowed hard, but kept walking.

Randi ended up in critical condition in the hospital in Sault Ste. Marie. The story of the crash had come out around town pretty fast. The three kids who'd been in the car with Randi were from out of town, staying at summer places with their families. There were drugs in the car, and a lot of cash. Someone was going to be in a lot of trouble. Probably not the summer kids, so much. Their parents could afford very good lawyers.

After two days, Madeline took Greyson to see Randi.

"*Mommy!*" he cried, breaking loose of her hold on his hand, running across the room, and clambering up the side of Randi's bed. Madeline caught him before he could fling himself on her. The emotion in him was so raw, it chastened her. Was it really she who had thought with such cold certainty that he should be taken from Randi, that she was unfit to raise a child? It was true, in a way. And in a way, he had been taken from her. So Madeline was right. But she saw now that this rightness was nothing.

"Careful." She found an edge of the bed to set him on. "Your mom's pretty sore, you can't jump on her." She could see the outline of a cast beneath the sheet. Randi's right arm was in a cast, too, and her face was badly bruised. The injuries went beyond that and Madeline wondered again about bringing Greyson so soon. But she decided it would be better to let him see her, no matter how bad it was. Better to know and see than worry and wonder.

It was huge, all this deciding on behalf of someone else. How had Emmy done it?

Sometimes Madeline wondered—had she been a burden, changed the course of Emmy's life? Was she the reason Emmy never got married; was a child—a sometimes nervous, needy child—too much for the handful of men Madeline remembered Emmy dating? Had she ever regretted her decision to take Madeline in some corner of her heart? Now she knew. You just did a thing like this, regardless of fear or doubt. Of course Madeline had changed Emmy's life. But then, everything did. A random cup of coffee, an overheard conversation, a chance meeting in a grocery store. But how, oh how, had Emmy known what to do from moment to moment?

Madeline told herself she would just take it one small step at a time, inch along from hummock to hummock, like working her way across a bog. First fix Greyson an egg and a piece of toast for breakfast, then drive him to see Randi. Then—lunch. After that, the next thing, which she would figure out when she got closer to it.

"Hey, little man," Randi said in her husky voice. She seemed groggy.

"Mom, it was so scary when the car skidded, Leon was hanging on to me and everybody was yelling and then you were the only one who couldn't get out, and then the ambulance came and you still couldn't get out and I was *scared*."

"It was pretty scary," Randi said, her eyes half closed. Probably she was full of painkillers.

"*Mom*. Wake up!"

Randi opened her eyes with some effort, smiled at Greyson. "Sorry, kiddo, I'm kinda beat."

"But when are you coming home?"

"Dunno, Grey." Her eyes were drifting shut again. "Be a little bit, I think. You staying with Madeline?"

"Uh-huh. She has a kitty, he's named Marley. He purrs a lot, he slept with me, I slept on the couch, that couch is *scratchy*. I want to get a kitty, Mom. Can we?"

"Mmm."

Madeline put a hand on his shoulder. "Your mom's pretty tired. Let's let her sleep."

"*No*. I want to talk to my mom, we just got here."

"I know, Peanut—"

"Don't call me that, you're not my mom!"

Madeline took a deep breath. "You have to let her sleep so she can get better."

"No!"

Randi's eyelids fluttered open. "Hey, Grey, you be a good boy for Madeline, okay? You do what she tells you, sweetie. Your mom kinda screwed up, so—I can't come home for a while."

"But Mom—"

She grinned. "Don't *but Mom* me, my butt's big enough already."

He giggled. A joke of theirs.

"Give me a kiss."

Madeline gave him a boost and he put a solemn smack on her cheek.

"Thanks, kiddo," she said sleepily. Greyson looked as if he would break down sobbing. Oh, the desolation in his face. Madeline really did not know if she was equal to this, but that was beside the point.

"That kiss is going to help her sleep better," she said, scooping him up. "That's the best thing you can do for her. She's got to rest, but I'll tell you what, we'll come back in a little while and say good-bye before we drive home. We'll go shopping and find a little present to give her. How about flowers, what do you think?"

He said nothing, just shifted around in her arms until he was looking over her shoulder, back at Randi.

"So we'll go get something to eat, some lunch. How about McDonald's, how would that be?" In Sault Ste. Marie, you could get fast food. There was a McDonald's, a Burger King, a Subway, a Taco Bell. Also Walmart, Kmart, gas stations with rows of pumps. It seemed so strange.

"Okay," he said listlessly.

"Okay, then!"

Greyson sighed and wrapped his legs around her waist, rested his head on her shoulder. She patted his back as she walked down the hall. Eventually—right?—he'd get used to her, and to the situation. As used to it as he could.

Madeline walked with Greyson to the little café she'd seen a few blocks away instead of driving to the McDonald's at the edge of the city. She needed somewhere quiet, serene. At the counter she ordered a double espresso for herself and a cocoa for Greyson, and got them each a tuna fish sandwich.

"I hate tuna fish," Greyson said, poking at it tearfully.

"It's good for you. Try and eat it." She closed her eyes as she sipped her coffee. It tasted good. It was wonderful to feel the thick, stubby little espresso cup with its diminutive saucer under her fingertips. Frivolous, maybe, but true. This must be where the real pleasures in life lay, in these tiny, momentary pleasures. When she opened her eyes, Greyson was sitting slumped over his sandwich, his hands limp between his legs, tears trickling down his cheeks.

"Hey, what's the matter? You're tired out, aren't you?" Of course he was, what a stupid question. Tired, desolate, terrified. And faced with tuna. His face had a pallor she should have paid attention to sooner. She hoped he wasn't getting sick in addition to everything else. "Listen, forget the tuna. How about a grilled cheese? Or some soup?"

"I'm not hungry," he whispered. She sighed, let her shoulders slump to match his. Oh, whatever were the two of them going to do? Greyson just sat, the tears trickling down, his thin shoulders shaking a little.

"Hey now," Madeline said, reaching over and pulling him off his chair and into her lap. "It's been a rotten couple of days, no doubt about that. But this silent crying thing, it really gets to me, you have to cut that out. You could yell a little maybe, huh? A little primal scream? What do you say? A little rage therapy? I don't know, I've never tried it myself, I've always been like you, pretty much, so well behaved. Too well behaved, that's what we are. But I'm thinking it's time for us to break out. It warrants a shot. Because life beats a person up sometimes, and maybe all you can do is shout back. I don't know, what do you think?"

Greyson relaxed into her like ice melting, and did not answer. She had not expected him to, had only wanted to distract him a little from his anguish. She swayed side to side, talking and talking, any nonsense she could think of, sipping the espresso, nibbling at the tuna in tiny bites.

After a time he seemed to doze off—or surrender to a sort of comatose fugue, Madeline wasn't sure which—and she fell silent. She ate both sandwiches, slowly, and had his cocoa for dessert. Read the little paper menu the café left folded on every table. Looked out the plate-glass window across the street at the Locks. A freighter was passing through—had been passing in its stately, inimitable way ever since they'd sat down. She stared at it awhile, and at the wall of the building next door, built of blocks that might have been limestone or sandstone—something native, and very old.

The menu said that Sault Ste. Marie was one of the oldest cities in the United States. It was founded by the French in 1668 and named for the rapids of the St. Mary's river, or *le Sault*, in French. So this was why everyone said "the Soo." These facts lent a dignity to the tired old city that Madeline hadn't accorded it before. She noticed two tattoo parlors, a windowless bar, and a check-cashing place on the walk to the café. But now the fact of the town's age, the way the afternoon sun shone on the old cut stones of the next building, the lingering, descriptive utility of its old name, made it seem beautiful.

She sat for a long time. Ever since she came here nothing had gone the way she'd planned or imagined or expected. It had all been a washout more or less, involving varying degrees of disaster. And yet still she did not want to leave. And now there was Greyson.

He had settled in with her at Butte's, and no one wanted to disturb that, even though other people had stepped forward to help. Roscoe and Annie wanted him to come stay with them in Halfway, but Greyson had clung to Madeline—well, to Marley—when that was suggested the first night. "I'm used to it here right now," he had said plaintively, hugging Marley close with both arms. "It's close to our house, here." Reluctantly, Roscoe and Annie had let the situation stand.

Madeline knew it bothered Paul that Grey wasn't staying with him, but it was unrealistic. Paul worked ninety hours a week and spent at least another five commuting, and he couldn't just quit, that wouldn't do anyone any good. He'd come over after he closed last night to tuck Greyson in, and they talked a little before he left. She could tell he felt guilty and frustrated, and sad, too, that he couldn't keep Greyson with him. She thought the guilt was misplaced, the frustration understandable, and the sadness endearing, but she didn't know how to say any of that. Instead she said, "I can't tell you how glad I am you're so close with him. I don't know what I'm doing, not really. And he loves you. We'll be bugging you constantly. I don't think I could do this alone." Paul had nodded and seemed marginally less anguished.

Madeline was glad Greyson was with her, and she was scared. But if the Soo could survive and have this subtle, hidden beauty, maybe so could she. She and Greyson would survive together, for whatever time he needed her.

After a time she woke Greyson enough to set him on his feet, took his hand, and walked back to where she'd left the car parked. Time to go home. Time to get on with life as it was now.

23

Madeline and Gladys packed up Randi's house. There wasn't much in it. Greyson had a lot of toys and Randi had a lot of clothes. Aside from that, her possessions were minimal: two beds, a couch, a table with two chairs, some pots and pans, a handful of silverware, a few chipped dishes. Madeline handled everything carefully, trying to be neat without looking too hard. It was such an invasion of privacy. Randi's clothes were eerie without her in them. It felt too much like packing up after a funeral.

They were quiet, methodical, glad when the job was finished. John and Paul loaded the boxes into Paul's truck and took them to John's garage. Madeline took Greyson's things to Mill Street, where they were staying until she could get the hotel ready to live in.

Someone in town (Madeline never knew who) organized a collection to help with Greyson's upkeep. It was a bundle of cash given anonymously, and Madeline was nonplussed at the trust this showed, and the easy acceptance of her as his substitute parent. Gladys brushed this off. "People're just doing what they would for anyone. You've said you'll look after him and you will. Take the money. You'll need it."

There was another collection to help with Randi's medical bills, and Madeline heard that even the Bensons sent something.

"*That's* amazing," Madeline told Gladys, but Gladys shrugged this off too. Despite everything, Gladys had accepted them at some level, that was suddenly clear to Madeline. Personal feelings didn't enter into it, not in a crisis.

And that—the bipartisan way people turned out to help—did amaze Madeline. More accurately, it took hold of her and rattled something in her. There was something to understand, here: McAllaster was a kind of tribe. This wasn't cozy, or *nice*. She sensed that it was an equation, that membership would exact a price: the loss of privacy, anonymity, certain freedoms she'd taken for granted in Chicago, maybe the loss of the right to selfishness. Everybody in this tribe didn't love each other. They disagreed and gossiped and argued; they laid traps for each other and rejoiced when the trap was sprung; they relished placing blame wherever it would stick and took pleasure in one another's mistakes. But when there was trouble, there was help.

That was sobering. At a time like this—when she needed all the help she could get—it was something to pay attention to.

Madeline's life became divided into before the accident and after, as if a cleaver had been whacked through it. Pretty soon it was hard to remember a time when she hadn't been responsible for Greyson. Her goal was to get into a routine: school, hospital visits, meals, chores, getting the hotel in order. The hardest thing was trying to keep Greyson on a reasonable emotional balance, but she just kept putting one foot in front of the other, telling herself that things would work out.

She started collecting bids for work on the hotel. The apartment hadn't sold yet but she was going forward anyway. Like Gladys said from the start, the scope of the work was huge. The roof, the wiring, the heat—all nonnegotiable, they had to be fixed. It was going to be so expensive that every time she looked at the numbers her heart seized. The cleaning she could do herself, the gutting of the charred paper and plaster and lathe in the attic, and the interior painting and papering, too—eventually—but there was no way she could tackle the outside, not physically or financially; it would have to wait. The most important thing was getting ready to open, which she wanted to do by Thanksgiving. *I need a job*, she'd told Gladys and Arbutus. *I want to take care of Greyson for as long as he needs me. I still want the hotel, and I'm sure my apartment will sell, so what do you say?*

They said all right. She could act as if she owned the hotel already. They'd pitch in any way they could. Arbutus said this with all her natural warmth and openheartedness; Gladys was a different story. She was polite now. She'd talk to Madeline almost naturally. But Madeline was sure she hadn't forgiven or forgotten. She was behaving well for Greyson's sake, and that was all that mattered.

Pete was helping too. He was buying Arbutus's house, but he'd wait to move in until Madeline moved out. He was staying in a rented cabin and helping Madeline with handyman tasks. He said it was good to have a job, even if it didn't pay. Madeline's protests, her worries that this was unfair to him, could only evaporate in the face of his good humor. "It's good to be needed," he told her one day when it was just the two of them in the hotel, looking at the boiler. "I've been bored these last few years. I don't like working on the newer cars much, they're all computer chips. I'm not a rich man but I'm comfortable. I like being here. Let me help."

Then there was Paul. Every Monday (his day "off" once he got done at the prison), he took Greyson for the afternoon. Plus he'd started opening at four instead of noon on weekdays, and when he wasn't visiting Randi he was with Greyson for whatever time he could spare. Sometimes they stayed at the hotel and played games or practiced the harmonica (a surprising talent Paul possessed and which Greyson aspired to). Sometimes they went to Garceau's, where Madeline imagined Greyson colored or played computer games while Paul paid bills. Whatever they did, Greyson always seemed steadier after spending time with him, and she was grateful.

The more Madeline saw Paul with Greyson, the more she liked him. He had a generosity of spirit that drew her, as well as a light-heartedness she might not have predicted. One day she watched him teach Greyson how to play "Yellow Submarine" on the harmonica. Paul's face was solemn as he stomped his foot in time to the beat and bellowed out the few words he could remember to keep Greyson on track, but his eyes had been shining with delight. She saw that he was perfectly aware how ridiculous he appeared, and that he was enjoying it.

It hurt a little, to think of him loving Randi. She did not admire herself for this. The good news was that he no longer seemed angry at her. She was thankful for that.

The other good news was that Pete was going to fix Paul's truck.

He thought he could get all the parts with the money Madeline'd given Paul all those weeks ago, and he didn't care if he got paid for his labor. He just shook his head in a way that allowed no conversation when she fretted about it. He liked a challenge, he said, liked the work itself. The guy who owned the tire shop down in Crosscut was a friend of Paul's, and he said Pete could work on the truck in one of his bays, after hours.

Despite all the things that were going right, sometimes Madeline was transfixed with terror at all that might go wrong. *Stop,* she told herself whenever she began to think that way. Either things would work out or they wouldn't. Sufficient unto the day was the evil thereof. The evil *and* the good.

A *month after* the accident, Randi was still at War Memorial in the Soo. She was asleep when Paul appeared at her room one day, a small bunch of flowers from the hospital gift shop clenched in his fist. He realized he was strangling them. He found a glass of water to stick them in and sat down by her bed. When she woke up and saw him, she frowned.

"You don't have to come all the time, you know. You were just here, like, day before yesterday."

"It's nice to see you, too. How are you doing?"

"I'm great."

"You look good," he said, but she just gazed at him as if he was an idiot. "I hope you can come home soon," he tried, but that was wrong too because she wasn't getting out anytime soon and they both knew it.

"Yeah, I'll bet."

"Don't be stupid, of course I do."

"Stupid, that's me."

"Randi—"

"You gonna tell me I didn't screw up?"

He didn't know what to say, and so said nothing.

Her laugh was bitter. "See? There you have it."

Paul ignored this. Maybe she'd snap out of this mood if he gave her a minute. But Randi just closed her eyes and acted like he wasn't there. Finally he said, "If there's anything you need—"

"There isn't."

"Why are you being like this?"

She looked at him hard, her eyes narrowed. "Why are you?"

"What do you mean?"

"You're mad at me."

"I am not—"

She rolled her eyes. "Don't lie. At *least* do that. I thought that was your big thing. No regrets, no lies. Don't you have some kind of quote for that?" She shifted onto her side with difficulty and stared off toward the door.

"I'm not angry," Paul said angrily. "I came to see you, not argue."

Randi sighed. Then she said, "I don't want you to come any-more."

"Oh, really." A war of feeling erupted inside Paul. Hurt, anger, confusion, and—relief. He wanted to take the relief and strangle it. Relief was not an acceptable feeling in these circumstances.

"I don't want to be a burden."

"Oh for God's sake, you sound like an old woman."

"I can sound any way I want to, I'm the one stuck in this bed feeling like crap."

"Whose fault is that?" Paul snapped.

"See? You're mad at me."

Paul groaned.

"Look," she said, after a moment. "I know you're mad. You're mad I screwed up, mad I'm in trouble, mad about the accident, all of it. I kind of don't blame you. But I'm mad, too. You're here like it's a duty. I don't want to be anybody's duty."

"You're not a duty."

Randi sighed and closed her eyes again.

Paul reached out and touched her hair—cropped short since she'd been in the hospital. It felt soft and bristly. "This is just a hard time. We'll work it out."

She shook her head. "No. We won't. You're too old for me, Paul. You're too serious. You're too—" She made a face and gave up trying to explain what was wrong with him.

"I know how you feel, you know. When I was in that accident

as a kid, I was in the hospital for weeks. I hurt, bad, and I hated everybody. I remember how it is."

Randi closed her eyes for a moment, as if to shut him off, like a TV or a radio. "Stop."

"I'm just trying to say, I get it."

"I don't *want* you to get it."

"Randi, come on." He tried to take her hand but she jerked it away.

"Look. I have all kinds of trouble to wade through. I don't want to have to go along feeling grateful to you the whole way." She shut her eyes again.

Paul waited, but she didn't open them. Finally he got up to leave. When he was at the door he stopped. "Why'd you do such a dumb thing, anyway? That's what I want to know. Things were good with us, I thought. Why get mixed up in this? Did you want the money, or what? You could've asked. I could've lent you some."

She shook her head, and tears leaked from her closed eyes.

"*Why*, Randi?"

"I don't know," she said finally. "Because it's what I do. I screw up."

"Randi, that's not—"

"I don't *know*. I didn't think I'd get caught. The money—that wasn't it. Not really. I like Leon and them. They asked me could I get them some stuff. And I did. That's all."

One afternoon Madeline put down her scrub brush and collected Greyson from where he was playing train with a row of cardboard boxes, and headed across the street. Mary was lounging in her lawnchair with Jack tied nearby. It was a bright day, mild for early October, the sunshine making everything clear-edged. Madeline thought of how to paint that—sharp outlines, primary colors. The light made the world seem unambiguous. Of course that was an illusion, but illusions had their place.

Greyson went and sat in the dirt just out of range of Jack's teeth and Madeline settled down into Mary's spare lawnchair with elaborate gestures of comfort, stretched her legs out and her arms up over her head, groaned a loud *ahhh* that made Greyson giggle.

"You're cheerful," Mary said, giving her a look that was both skeptical and indulgent. Madeline didn't mind that. Mary was older and had seen more. In a way she was Madeline's lost past. If Jackie Stone had stayed in Crosscut, local women—tough northern women like Mary and Arbutus and yes, even Gladys, women with big stoic hearts—might have looked after her when she was a child. They might have raised and taught her to some extent, kept an eye on her. Even though she'd had something else good in its place, it gave her a right feeling to be watched over by them now.

"Sheriff been here yet?" Madeline asked.

"Nope. Late today."

"What a coward."

Mary gave her a look. "Thought you didn't like con-fron-ta-tions."

Madeline had confessed that one day. "Aw, that was somebody else," she said, grinning beneath the brim of her hat. The hat was white with lime polka dots and had a huge floppy brim. She'd found it in the hotel, still in a crinkled, yellowed cellophane wrapper—an old piece of inventory, circa 1970 probably. It had made Greyson laugh when she put it on so she wore it whenever she could. She shoved it back on her head, slumped in her chair, tucked her thumbs in her belt loops, and said, "Let's give 'em Hell," drawling like a gunslinger on one of the old Westerns Greyson and Arbutus liked to watch together. He giggled.

"You're not supposed to say Hell."

"Oh, you hush. Go make yourself useful, why don't you, go over to Albert and get us some peaches."

He scrambled up and came to Madeline for money. She gave him a ten-dollar bill—cautiously, though she tried not to let him see that, because she had so few of them left. He trotted away and Madeline sighed. "What'll his life be like, I wonder."

"Just like it is, I guess."

"Mmm."

"Could be a whole lot worse."

"Seems like it would be nice if it was a whole lot better."

"Randi ain't a bad girl, but she doesn't know which end is up, really."

Madeline didn't respond to that. Randi was going to be released from the hospital later in the week and moved to the AFC home in Crosscut where Walter lived, courtesy of the State. She didn't belong in a home for the mentally impaired, but if she didn't go there she'd have to stay in the Soo, so much farther away from McAllaster and Greyson. Randi had been assigned a social worker, who went through a great deal of effort to arrange this. Randi seemed indifferent, but Madeline was grateful. It would simplify her schedule and cut down on the gas and mileage. Of course Greyson would want to see his mother more than ever, which was maybe not so good for him, but Madeline couldn't tell him no. She thought that he saw Randi both too much and too little. Just enough to upset him and knock him—and Madeline—constantly off balance. And as for Randi, she almost seemed not to care what they did.

Her court date was months off still. Madeline thought she'd end up doing time at the county jail in Crosscut, or if her luck was really bad, the women's prison downstate. Mabel Brink said that her great-nephew, who was a police officer, claimed that the district attorney was making a name for herself as being tough on drugs. As little as Madeline liked the things Randi'd done, she feared for her. She found herself hoping the court would go easy on her, and not only for Greyson's sake.

"Some folks are just born to suck hind teat in life," Mary said.

Madeline could have been one of those people if not for Emmy. And now she was following in Emmy's footsteps, something she would never have predicted. She'd never imagined raising a child. It was always something she thought she'd think about later, and never got to. Too scared, maybe. Guilty of what Richard had accused her of, back in April when she gave his ring back: holding herself apart, never trusting anyone but Emmy, never giving herself over to anything. Well, maybe he'd been right. But now here she was, the same person, but different. She felt herself smiling as Greyson headed back toward them, the bag of peaches clutched to his chest. He arrived puffing, with red circles on his cheeks.

"You're the little engine that could, aren't you?"

"Huh?"

"It's a story. I'll tell it to you sometime. Here, wash off three peaches."

"Can Jack have one?"

"No, Jack can't have one," Mary growled. Greyson shrugged and took the jug of water Madeline held out to him and poured it over three peaches, one at a time, causing a small river of mud to form at the toes of his ripped-out sneakers. She would have to look for a new pair for him next time she went out of town. She took the peach he held out and closed her eyes as she bit into it: the last taste of summer, juicy and sweet. Greyson leaned on her knees and when Madeline opened her eyes he held out his arms to be picked up. She bundled him onto her lap.

They ate their peaches, juice dripping everywhere. Greyson hummed a song to himself. Mary stared off across the horizon.

Madeline studied her from beneath the brim of her hat, wondering what her thoughts were. Mary and Albert had kept showing up at the empty lots, selling what they could before the sheriff ran them off. Mary argued every time, telling the sheriff to go to Hell before she shoved her syrup and fish and lawnchairs in her truck and roared away. Albert argued too, waving a license in the sheriff's face, showing him it said he could peddle his fruit anywhere in the state, shouting that he was a disabled veteran and his license superseded any local municipality's ordinances, stumbling a little over the officious words but dogged in his surety. He'd shown Madeline the piece of paper, and it did say exactly that, but it made no difference to the sheriff.

She wondered how they could face the conflict over and over. She thought she would have folded up her tables and gone away with much less fight. But she was learning. She'd have to, if she was going to stay, because it appeared that a great part of victory—or at least survival—was simply a dogged hanging on.

Madeline sighed, content for the moment to do nothing at all. The lake rolled into shore, the sun shone hot on the top of her head, and Greyson lounged heavy in her lap, a small parcel of person with whom she was inexorably connected. The flies buzzed, lazy and indolent, and time seemed suspended. McAllaster seemed ageless, infinite, eternal. It was a hard feeling to pin down with words, but it was a good feeling, a big feeling.

Then the sheriff arrived and the small battle waged itself again and Madeline thought how paradoxical this place was: the best place, the worst place, all at once.

Pete was puttering under the hood of the Buick when Madeline and Greyson got to Bessel Street that evening. (Pete was invited to dinner often, and Gladys made a point of inviting Madeline and Greyson too. It was all part of making Grey feel secure, that his entire world hadn't evaporated with Randi's accident, nothing to do with Gladys forgiving Madeline, sadly.) Arbutus sat in a lawnchair on the sidewalk, her ankles crossed, a sun hat with a wide ribbon tipped back on her head, the walker nearby. She was wearing a flow-ered dress and had her book in her lap, but Madeline didn't think she'd been reading. *Smitten*, she thought. It was sweet. Also inspi-rational. Maybe someday, some far-off day, she might have this too, for as much as she liked to deny it, at heart she was a romantic. And what was *this*, after all, but hope, a declaration that life did not end at seventy or eighty, that anything could happen.

Greyson ran up the walk into the house and Madeline followed. She smiled at Arbutus, who gave her a merry look in return. Pete didn't have a chance, he was snagged. Lucky Pete.

"You know that hotel is one in a million," he said after dinner.

"It is," Madeline said. She was tired and felt less certain than she did sometimes, but grateful for the encouragement.

"You're a big help," Gladys said. "I keep telling her to give up before she's put anything more than elbow grease into it."

"Ah, now, don't say that. A certain kind of person's going to flock to it. People will come. They'll pay more than you think, too."

"But it's just a few months of the year that people like that come here," Arbutus said, and Madeline heard in her voice that she found them well-meaning but naïve. "Those busy months have to stretch out over the quiet ones, and they stretch thin. You can't imagine how thin."

"She doesn't want a big living. Do you, Madeline?"

"No."

Gladys leaned forward. "Do you have any idea what it'll take to get open? Really? To keep it all going? I still say the place'll do you in."

Madeline wondered if that was what Gladys hoped for.

"I'm pretty handy," Pete said. "And that building looks sound, it's standing straight. Wouldn't do that if it had been built shoddy. Might not be so bad as you think."

"Oh, *fizzle*. You two are not listening."

"Learned it from you," Madeline said, hoping to make her smile, but Gladys frowned instead.

"I thought maybe you'd come to your senses once you'd spent a little time in there. But it doesn't look like that's going to happen. I've said it all before, but I don't want you to waltz into this without warning you. Do you know how long it will take to make your first dollar? I mean, make it over and above the cost of keeping it all going, if you can even manage that?"

"Oh, fifteen or twenty years, probably. Maybe longer, maybe never."

Arbutus was studying Madeline, her expression solemn and anxious.

"Do you know you're not kidding?" Gladys asked.

Madeline shrugged. "As much as you can know anything before you really do it."

Greyson wandered in from the parlor where he'd been watching television. He came to Madeline and with a deep sigh leaned into her legs. He always seemed at his most vulnerable in the evening. "Can't I stay at the hotel with you tomorrow?" he asked. "I hate school." She said no, he couldn't, but that she'd pick him up after and they'd fix lunch in the hotel's old kitchen. It'd be like camping out, sort of. "Sound like fun?"

He considered this, his narrow face so serious that Madeline wanted to hug him. "Can we have hamburgers? With potato chips?"

She smoothed his hair. "Sure thing."

"Are you sure about this?" Gladys asked.

"About the hotel?" Madeline felt Greyson's weight against her. "Yes."

"Well, then." Gladys nodded once. "I'm sure you'll be fine."

Madeline smiled at this sudden capitulation. "You think?"

"Look at me and Butte. We've managed. We're still getting up in the morning, anyway; they can't take that away."

Madeline smiled at her gratefully and Gladys's expression seemed less remote than usual.

A week later there was an offer on the apartment. "It's fair," Nathan said over the phone. "I think you should take it."

"All right," Madeline said, and felt dizzy.

Pete offered to follow Madeline down to Chicago and take the Buick into the garage for an overhaul and it seemed natural to accept. He was so much like family now. They left a few days after Nathan's call. She kept him in sight in her rearview mirror as she drove south along the same route she'd traveled in April. They stopped at gas stations and fast-food places together, his sedan easing off the highway right behind her every time she pulled in somewhere. Madeline loved it. She'd accidentally acquired something like a father.

It was evening when she pulled across the hose that made a bell clang at the service station. She climbed out, gazed at the redwinged Pegasus, the old Coke machine. Funny to think that in a way her journey had started here, with Pete fixing up her car.

Pete pulled in after her. "What a change," he said. She nodded. Bumper-to-bumper traffic on a maze of streets and highways, the noise and smell and sound of it, houses and offices and apartments and stores on every inch of ground, people everywhere, so much of everything. It seemed outlandish.

"Won't take me but a few days to get her shipshape." Pete patted the Buick in that fond way he had. "I expect you've got plenty to do in the next while."

"Yes. I don't know how I'll get to everything."

"You'll manage. We'll be headed back north in no time, you'll see. I have to remember that portable air tank I've got, I want to blow those lines out in your plumbing, and see what I can do about the radiators, too."

"You're too good to me."

He grinned. "Keeps me out of the tavern."

"Keeps you close to a certain lady I know," Madeline said and his blue eyes sparked brighter.

She spent a harried week emptying out the apartment, shipping what she wanted north, setting aside some things for friends, donating the rest to Salvation Army. She was going through the drawers of her nightstand when she found the scrap of paper her friend Ramona had written the lost word on at Emmy's funeral. There it sat, scrawled in black ink in Ramon's strong hand: *tzadik*. Madeline sat looking at it for a long time. The word that had launched this whole fleet of events, in a way. The trait that made Arbutus so compelling and inspired Madeline to leap into the unknown. She taped the piece of paper into her sketchbook, finally, and went on with her packing and cleaning. She'd emptied out the kitchen before she left, and barely restocked it now, so she ate at Spinelli's half a dozen times, sitting in the back at the break table to talk to her friends when they had time, especially Dwayne, who'd been there when Madeline started.

"You met some man up there or something?" he asked one afternoon when it was just the two of them. He pulled his cook's cap off and rubbed at his scalp.

"No. A boy, though." She told him about Greyson and he listened as closely as ever. She wondered if Dwayne and his wife, Estelle, and daughter Candice might ever come see her. Wouldn't that be something. There weren't many black people up north. A few, in the cities. A worry pulled at her. How would it really be, living in such an insular world?

"You excited about staying?"

"Mostly. Scared sometimes in the middle of the night. But yeah—I want to do this. I have to, somehow."

Dwayne gave her a broad smile. "You'll be all right. Don't doubt it."

It wasn't a platitude. He was the kind of person who somehow always seemed to know more about you than you knew of yourself.

"You should see the sky up there. Out over the lake—it's so beautiful."

"Worse reasons to move to a place. You gonna paint it?"

"I'm going to try."

"Well, then. Sounds like you hit the jackpot."

Gladys put Greyson on the phone one day and he told Madeline he'd colored a picture for her, Purple Man on a mission in the city, flying over skyscrapers. It occurred to Madeline that he'd never seen a skyscraper except for on television, that the Hotel Leppinen was the tall building in his world, the tallest he'd ever seen besides the old brick six-story Ojibway Hotel in the Soo.

"I can't wait to see it."

"I miss you, and Mr. Pete. I was going to help him fix your car, he said I could. He said he'd show me how the engine works, but now he's doing it all himself."

"Oh, I wouldn't worry about that. That car will always need fixing."

"But you've been gone for*ever*."

"We'll be back before you know it."

"I miss my mom, Gladys only took me to see her once so far."

Madeline's heart sank as it did sometimes with the renewed realization that she was setting herself up for heartbreak with this child, but what else could she do? In looking after him she was bound to love him. For his part, he was bound to love his mother, and she would not have had it otherwise. "I'll be back soon," she promised.

24

Madeline loved her attic rooms. There was a small old-fashioned bath with a claw-foot tub, the big sitting room with its windows looking out over the water (this was where the fire had done all its damage), and two bedrooms, one empty except for a small bed and dresser, the other furnished with a spindle bed, an armoire, an oak highboy, and a rocker with no arms. A sewing chair, Gladys called it. It had been her grandmother's, like the old couch, which Madeline had to have hauled away to the landfill in Crosscut after the fire.

The attic was shabby, really, except for the new wall (Paul had hung drywall on it while she was gone), and Emmy's Oriental rug in the center of the sitting room floor, but the romance of it made up for everything. The sitting-room windows had the view of the bay and the lake, and the bedroom windows looked down—far down—on what Gladys said had once been the kitchen garden. It would be again, Madeline decided. Once there was a kitchen.

The kitchen was a world unto itself. The burners on the mammoth stove worked, but the oven didn't, and for now it was going to stay that way. It was the same with everything: a refrigerator circa 1950 or so that didn't keep cold, the dangling lightbulbs in the ceiling that didn't cast any really useful light, one electrical plug down near the floor that didn't provide enough juice to run anything more than a toaster. There was an enormous oaken icebox with double doors that smelled of must but did, Madeline discovered, hold the cold if provided every other day with a new block of ice in its tray. She was surprised to realize she could buy these blocks at the gas station for two dollars each. The icebox was too big for the few things she'd keep on hand for Greyson and herself, but for now, like everything else, it would work well enough to get by.

The hotel was heated with radiators and potbelly woodstoves scattered here and there, one in the lobby, one at the end of the second- and third-floor halls, and one in the corner of the attic. Madeline was pleased by this, and imagined she wouldn't mind the chore of hauling wood up the stairs if she could sit close by the stove on a cold winter night, absorbing that bone-deep heat. Emil was working on getting wood around, and Madeline was excited at the thought of buying an ax. She'd checked them out at the hardware. The one she wanted had a hickory handle and a serious-looking blade.

Gladys and Arbutus took an interest in everything. They came every day to inspect her progress. Arbutus couldn't climb the steps so stayed in the lobby—looking happiest when Pete was nearby tinkering—but Gladys liked to come upstairs. Madeline wondered if she had happy memories of her early married days with Frank here. Even with things less fraught between them, it couldn't be Madeline's company she was after. No, she was excited about the hotel, that was all.

She'd tell stories while Madeline scrubbed away at walls and floors and furniture. "Are you writing some of this down?" Madeline asked now and then. She'd picked up a journal for Gladys while she was in Chicago, one with hard black covers and creamy pages and a spiral binding that made it easy to flip open on itself, buying it with the five-dollar bills Gladys had sent over the years. She'd meant it as a sort of peace offering and because she really did think Gladys should write her stories down, but it had gone over like a lead balloon.

"Who'd want to read anything I put down?" Gladys always said.

The sisters' friends began to stop in, the spryest ones climbing the stairs and drinking cup after cup of the coffee Madeline kept brewed in an electric drip pot she bought at the hardware, eating Gladys's cardamom rolls, or Finn buns as all of them called them. Madeline had splurged in Chicago on coffee beans that she ground fresh for every pot. The ladies—and once in a while a husband— liked this. "Good coffee," they'd say, nodding their approval, and Madeline would feel a splash of pride, as if she'd really done something. She added coffee beans to her mental list of things she might sell in the shop she was imagining downstairs.

Gladys mentioned one day while Madeline was cleaning the floors that Mabel had been a lumber camp cook over by Gallion. Mabel sat in the sewing chair, knitting.

"Oh, pshaw, Glad, that was a million years ago."

"You were a good cook, everybody said so."

"Only because I replaced Toivo Ylimaki. That man couldn't parboil shit for a tramp."

"Frank claimed Toivo put mice in the stew to stretch it. Why, they ran him right out of camp one spring. Chased him out and threw his pots and pans after him."

"Wouldn't surprise me if he did put mice in. There were enough of them."

"Frank's sandwiches used to freeze solid before he got to them on the cold days."

"Yes, I remember. They'd build a fire at lunchtime to thaw them out."

Madeline unbent from her hands-and-knees stance down on the floor to listen. "How many did you cook for?"

"Oh, twenty or thirty, most times, it was a small outfit."

"Was it hard?"

Mabel didn't look up from her knitting. "It was what it was, it was work. I didn't think anything of it. I got up at four a.m. and was in bed by ten at night if I was lucky. I did it all. Split the wood, hauled the water, fixed the food, cleaned up after."

"That's amazing!"

"Times were different. Life was plain."

Madeline knew that Mabel did not consider it extraordinary that at ninety she still lived in her own house and walked a mile or two every day and organized all the church potlucks. It seemed not to faze her to have lived so long that she had cooked for thirty lumberjacks on a wood-fired stove and also had driven to the Soo and bought a computer and learned to surf the Internet and sell things on eBay. Her expression said Madeline was peculiar and naïve but harmless. At least she made decent coffee.

"The *food* was plain," Gladys said. "That's a big difference."

Mabel grinned. "Potatoes and meat one night, milk potatoes the next. All kinds of variety."

"Potatoes, bread, venison, fish, milk. That's what I remember."

"Oatmeal," Mabel said.

Gladys nodded, a nod that said oatmeal was a given. "Remember Fred Ooman?"

Mabel snorted. "Who could forget him? When he was drinking—"

"*Always*—"

"He almost froze to death out back of our place one night. He fell down in the alley going home from the bar and would've lain there all night and froze if Tom hadn't gone out back for more stove wood. I was always nagging him to keep the woodbox filled and he never did. Fred was just about a goner when Tom found him."

"He was a sweet man when he was sober."

"Remember that elixir he used to make and peddle around to the taverns—"

"Sweet White Birch Vitamins and Minerals!"

"Yes. Lord. I wonder what was in it."

"Birch ashes, I know that. I don't know what else. He used to go around and get the empty wine bottles to put it in, big green bottles with the raised design—"

"They'd never let you do that today."

"He wouldn't let it freeze, remember?"

"Yes! He had that old Chevy, put a little stove in the backseat where he carried the stuff, ran a stovepipe out the window."

"I can see it now, that stovepipe puffing smoke out the car window and Fred inside the tavern, drunker than a skunk."

"He had a good time."

"I guess he was happy."

"I don't know how Celia put up with him."

"She was a saint—"

Madeline let their stories wash over her as she worked. And then Mabel said, "Well, your great-grandma was a camp cook too, didn't you tell her, Gladys?"

There was an awkward silence. Gladys cleared her throat. "I guess I never did."

"Mary told me," Madeline said.

Mabel nodded, intent on finding a stitch she'd dropped. She seemed oblivious to the tension in the room.

"Did you know her?" Madeline asked. "Did you know Ada?"

"Not really. She kept to herself pretty much back there on Stone

Lake, and when they left there, they went to Crosscut. I never had much cause to know her."

Madeline nodded.

"I didn't know her, either," Gladys said abruptly. "If I had, I'd tell you. Joe never talked about her much. Well, Joe. He just plain never talked about *anything* much. What he had to say, he said it with the fiddle."

Madeline and Gladys gazed at each other. "I would tell you," Gladys said softly.

After a moment Madeline said, "I believe you."

In the wink of an eye it was the middle of October. Gladys still had her Rolodex filled with the phone numbers of customers who used to stay, and she was calling. Madeline had better be ready by the middle of November like she'd planned because Gladys had already lined up three deer hunters who were delighted to hear the old place was reopening.

Gladys leafed through the Rolodex again to see if she'd missed anyone. She lingered at the card with the number of the antiques man over in the Soo. She wondered how much he'd want for Grandmother's kicksled. It went against her grain to even think of such a thing, it showed a lack of backbone. But she wanted it back. And now, more or less, she could afford it. Maybe best to let sleeping dogs lie, however. She sighed and flipped to the next card.

She knew Madeline felt a great sense of urgency to have things perfect even though Gladys had told her the hunters wouldn't mind a little clutter. But Madeline worked every possible minute. She could hardly be bothered to quit for dinner; only Greyson tempered her burning fire to work, work, work every moment.

Gladys hoped she would not burn herself out. As angry—or

perhaps not angry, but cautious and hurt—as she still was, she did hope that. And she hoped Madeline wouldn't get her heart broken over Greyson, either, because the lay of *that* land was treacherous, looking after another woman's child. She admired Madeline for having the guts to do it. She couldn't say it to Madeline, but she did feel it. She could want the best for her without quite being able to forgive her, couldn't she?

Madeline kept taking Greyson to see Randi three times a week, somewhat against her judgment. Randi'd grown morose. Her braids had been cut in the hospital and she dwelt on this endlessly. It wasn't fair, nobody'd asked her, she hated her hair this way, she was going to make a complaint, it was an infringement of her rights. In the meantime she resisted having it washed. She also refused to do her exercises. "I hate trying to work with patients like her," the physical therapist—the same one who had helped Arbutus—confided to Madeline one day on her way out the door. "They won't do anything for themselves. Not like Arbutus. She is such a trouper."

Maybe Randi was feeling just well enough to realize how bad things were. Her injuries were slow to heal and the doctor said she'd be lame for the rest of her life. Her court date had been postponed, which prolonged the agony of waiting, and it was very likely things would not turn out well when it did happen. Sometimes her mood was so bad that Madeline thought it would be better not to take Greyson to see her so often, but the visits seemed crucial to him.

"Mom, look what I did in school," he told her one day, a big sheet of green construction paper cradled in both hands. He had carried it on his lap in the car, declining Madeline's offer to set it on the backseat because if they had to stop fast it might slide and get bumped. "I love you MOM," was spelled out, the "MOM" done in elbow macaroni. Thick gobs of glue had oozed from beneath the crooked pasta pieces, drying in translucent bumps on the fuzzy paper, and a red crayon heart encircled all of it. In one corner Purple Man brandished his sword. Greyson said the teacher had helped them to write whatever they wanted on their papers, but he'd done everything else himself. Madeline had told him truthfully that it was beautiful.

Now he struggled to clamber up into Randi's lap without crumpling the paper. She was sitting in a wheelchair in the front room facing the enormous television.

"You're hurting, Grey, get down." She didn't take her eyes from the TV.

Greyson's face crumpled.

"Randi," Madeline said. After a few stubborn moments Randi raised her eyes and they glared at each other. "Greyson, go and find my Uncle Walter."

"No, I don't want to, we just got here, I want to show my mom what I made her."

"You can show her in a few minutes. Go find Walter. He likes to see you."

Greyson trudged away.

Randi was staring at the television again. Madeline went and switched it off, to the disgust of an old man parked in a recliner who shouted, "Hey!"

"Sorry." She switched it back on. Randi looked pleased and Madeline grabbed the handles of her chair and pushed her out onto the porch.

"It's cold out here, take me back in."

"I'll take you back after you listen. You have royally screwed up, Randi, you're going to jail unless some miracle happens. Did you ever stop and think how that's going to be for Greyson?"

"He's fine. He's got you."

"He's not fine. He does have me—and Paul and Gladys and Arbutus and a dozen other people—but the one he wants is you. Don't make it worse than it is. Get yourself together. Pay attention to him."

"You have no idea what this is like."

"I don't care what this is like. You created the problem, you fix it. Greyson looks forward to seeing you like crazy, and you act like he doesn't even exist anymore."

"I'll just screw up his life anyway, he's better off without me. Everybody is."

"That's a cop-out. People care about you."

"Like who?"

Madeline stared at Randi in disbelief. "Half the town's pitched in to help."

"People just do that here, they'd do it for anybody, they have to. They don't care about *me*."

"Nobody *has* to do anything. And what about Gladys and Arbutus? And Paul? And me?"

Randi bit her lip, shaking her head, and stared into the distance.

"Look. The worst thing you can do to Greyson is to just disappear."

"I'm right here," she said dully.

Despite herself Madeline felt a flash of sympathy. How hopeless it must all look from the vantage point of this chair. But Randi couldn't give in to that. "Ignoring him is like disappearing. You're not yourself anymore."

"No shit."

"Things will get better," Madeline said, thinking that they would. Better, and worse, and better again, that constant ebb and flow that life was.

"Nothing's ever gonna be the same," Randi said, and for the first time her tone was devoid of attitude. "I can't even walk."

"I know."

"I didn't do anything different than anyone else." The whining note was back in her voice. "I just can't handle Greyson right now."

"You have to. He thinks all this is his fault somehow, you can't do that to him."

"He's better off without me, I'm just a fuckup, it's all I ever have been."

Madeline flinched. It was less gratifying than she might have imagined, hearing her own old opinions voiced by Randi. "Everybody screws up. The important thing is what you do after, maybe."

"Well, me, I'm sitting in a wheelchair and headed to jail, so I don't see where I'm going to do Grey much good."

"He doesn't care what you've done. He just wants his mom. And if you think you're such a mess, well then, change. It's up to you. Isn't he worth it? Isn't Paul?"

Randi stared stubbornly out across the street.

"Any of that mean anything to you?"

"Go to Hell, Madeline," Randi said with a surprising lack of venom. "You don't know anything."

Madeline sighed and pushed Randi's chair back inside, then went to find Greyson. He lay on Walter's bed staring up at the ceiling and Walter sat in the easy chair by the window. A rehash of last night's ball game was on. "Hello, Walter," Madeline said. Walter smiled and nodded. "Ready to go see your mom, Grey?"

He rolled his head toward her. "I don't wanna bug her, I can just stay here if she's tired. Walter doesn't mind."

"You're not bugging her, come on."

When they came back in the front room, Randi gave Greyson a

smile that was, to Madeline, obviously manufactured. But at least she tried. "Hey, Peanut," she said, with little energy. "Did you have something you wanted to show me? I'm sorry I snapped at you before, I hurt all over and I'm crabby."

"That's okay," he said, and brought her his paper.

Madeline climbed the stairs back to Walter's room. She knocked. "Hey, Walter. Mind if come in? Listening to the game talk?"

"Yes."

"Too bad about the Tigers, huh?"

"Yes." He nodded, his face grave. "They made the Series in sixty-eight. Joe took me to see them. In Detroit, it was."

"Wow. Long trip."

"Yes."

Walter's room was nicer than any of the others she'd seen. He had an easy chair and a small sofa and a deep-pile rug on the floor, plus a big radio with a tape and CD player built in (and a satellite antenna and subscription so he wasn't limited to the same two lousy stations Madeline was), a small television, a thick comforter on his bed. His clothes were a little nicer than anyone else's too, and Ted had said that Walter had a little spending money, enough to buy small treats now and then.

Madeline took Greyson's spot on the bed, tucked her hands beneath her head, and listened to the clips of the Boston Red Sox beating the Chicago White Sox seven to two.

Walter turned the radio off when the program ended. Madeline remained where she was, staring up at his ceiling. After a while she said, "What was your mother like, Walter?"

"My mother?"

"Yes. Ada. Mary Feather told me she was a lumber camp cook."

"Yes, she was. And Father was a sawyer."

"That's what they said."

"Father ran the mail to Gallion, too. He had a team of dogs. He told me I had to stay clear of them, they weren't pets."

"I know. You said, before. But what were they like?"

Walter looked confused. "They were my folks. My mama and father. And Joe was my brother. My big brother. He took me out hunting with him sometimes."

"I know. But were they—I don't know. Where they nice? Did you have fun together?"

Walter's look of confusion deepened. "They were my folks. Father died when I was ten, of a fever. Mama said I'd have to help with the chores more, and I did. Joe had to go out to work, he couldn't stay home anymore."

"I know," Madeline said.

"He always took good care of me, Joe did."

"I know," Madeline said softly. "I'm glad."

Walter nodded and sat with his hands folded in his lap, waiting with absolutely no impatience for Ted to come say it was time for supper.

On the way home Madeline thought about what was left to do before she could let even three people stay at the hotel. She had to have the heat and plumbing operational on the second floor, which Pete was still working on. Most of the lines and fixtures had to be replaced, which was messy and expensive—but not anywhere near as expensive as hiring a plumber. Thank God for Pete. All the rooms on the second floor were clean now, every inch of wall, floor, and furniture. It had taken much longer than she'd expected, and many more buckets of hot soapy water. But it was done, even the bedding, which she'd washed at the laundromat in Crosscut and dried outside on the clothesline in a brisk October sun. There was still the third floor to tackle, but not as much hurry.

Her next undertaking was the lobby, though Gladys assured her the hunters were only looking for a bed, nothing fancy, that they would just troop through on their way upstairs and she shouldn't drive herself crazy worrying. Still, she couldn't have it dusty and dirty and didn't want them to see it as it was now—a jumble of boxes and furniture.

She wanted the hotel to be a landmark, charming and warm, historic, the kind of place people fell in love with. She couldn't let it be forgettable, didn't want it to be just a cheap room for the night. (And it wasn't going to be cheap like it had been in Gladys's day, it couldn't be. She wondered how that would go over with the old customers. She was giving the hunters an opening-week, returning-customers break, but after that, things had to change.) She planned to fill the lobby with comfortable furniture, good rugs, a brand-new airtight woodstove with a glass door to watch the fire through. She'd ordered the stove and the men were coming next week to install it. She'd already sent the check: four thousand thirty-seven dollars and sixteen cents.

Gladys had declared she was out of her mind, spending that kind of money when there was a potbelly there already. But Pete and Madeline had played with the pretty little parlor stove and discovered that not only did it smoke—a long crack ran up one side of it—but even when it did get burning hot it didn't throw out much heat, though it sucked wood like a freight train.

She reassured herself it was the right decision. The fire would make people feel they were really in the north; the new stove—a powerhouse of heat—would be the centerpiece of the room. She could use it most of the year because even in May and September the weather was often cold enough for a fire. It would be cozy, irresistible. And once she'd made people comfortable, she was going to provide tempting things for them to buy, everything from candles to comforters. She'd use the parlor stove as a prop, stack something for sale on it: pints of Mary's syrup, maybe.

The whole project was going to cost so much that frequently she couldn't sleep at night. Sometimes she wished she had a partner to hash things out with. But she had only herself, and had to hope her choices would work. The truth was, they had to work, there was no margin for error. The hotel had to make her a living or she wouldn't have one.

"Madeline, I'm hungry, can we stop at the Trackside?" Greyson asked. He sounded bored and cranky. It was usually this way after a visit to Randi.

"I don't think so, kiddo. Not this trip."

"But I want to see Andrea, I haven't seen her in forever."

Madeline was tempted to give in, but she couldn't always be feeling sorry for him and getting guilted into things. "Not today. We've got chicken soup to eat, Gladys and Arbutus will be waiting."

"I hate chicken soup."

Yesterday he had loved chicken soup. "Poor you."

He slumped into a sullen slouch.

"I'm thinking we can move into the hotel this weekend, what do you think about that?" Madeline said after a few moments.

He stared out the window.

"Won't that be fun?"

More silence.

"Well, I know I for one am excited. It's going to be neat, you'll see."

"I want to go home," he said in a tiny voice. "I don't want to live at the hotel. I want to live with my mom in our house."

They passed a stretch of pointed fir trees mixed with birch, a stand of feathery tamaracks that had turned golden with autumn, a bog with a tiny glint of water at its middle. A raven flew over the road, low, the sun reflecting off his wings. The day was cool and bright, and had seemed so promising. Finally Madeline said, "I know you do. But you can't. I'm sorry."

"How long before my mom gets back?"

So far she'd evaded the whole truth, everyone had. But looking at his small unhappy form, she thought that this was useless. They weren't protecting him, they were just giving him false hope. "It might be a long time. Maybe a year or more. Nobody knows right now. I'm sorry."

"Couldn't you and me go and live in my mom's house?"

They couldn't, even if she didn't hate the idea and didn't have the hotel to think of. "Your mom rented the house, sweetie. That means she had to pay a certain amount every month to stay there, but somebody else owns it. You know that, right?"

He nodded, but his eyes were beseeching. Her heart ached for him. "You've just got to make the best of a bad situation, I'm afraid. You're kind of stuck with me for the time being."

He nodded again, looked down at his hands, which were folded in his lap. "I wish I had a dad," he whispered. "If I had a dad then he could live with me in my house until Mommy gets better. That's what Eddie Tibbett's dad did when his mom went away to live downstate."

Oh boy. Madeline drove on without responding at first. After a while she said, "I never had a dad around."

Greyson looked over at her. "You didn't?"

"No. I never knew who he was. I never will."

"Really?"

"Really. It didn't bother me too much. I was used to it. Sometimes other kids asked me about it, and that was when it bothered me."

He was nodding. "I know. Like in school one day Amanda Walker said she was going to beat me up if I didn't tell who my dad was."

Madeline made a mental note to watch out for Amanda Walker. "I know you miss your mom and want her to come home, and I'm sorry. All I can say is, I'm glad I get to be the one who hangs out with you in the meantime."

He looked at Madeline with a funny expression, something between a smile and a frown, and scooted closer on the seat. "I like you, Madeline," he said.

"I like you too."

"Could I have a grilled cheese with my soup?"

"I think that could be arranged."

"Can we go to Garceau's after school tomorrow? I haven't seen Paul—Mr. Garceau—hardly at all this week."

"I guess we could do that," Madeline said, smiling across at him.

25

Hello, Mr. Garceau!" Greyson called out as he and Madeline came through the door of the pizzeria.

"Afternoon, Mr. Hopkins." They'd been doing this, calling each other Mr. Garceau and Mr. Hopkins, for a while now. Paul didn't remember exactly how it started. He was glad to see Greyson looking so cheerful. Madeline was doing a good job. Well, everyone was—half the town was helping out in one way or another. But Madeline was the main deal, and as far as he could see she never looked back once she took Greyson on. He liked her for that. He wished he could do more than he did, but there was never as much time as he needed.

Greyson ran into the kitchen. "What're you doing?"

"Chopping."

"Chopping what?"

"Chopping stuff up for pizzas, whaddya think, I'm making pressed duck?" Paul ruffled Greyson's hair. The worst part about the split with Randi was that he would lose his direct ties to Grey too. He hadn't told him about the breakup yet, hadn't mentioned it to anyone. It was awkward. He wasn't the kind of person to talk about his personal life in the best of times, and what incentive was there to tell people that Randi didn't want him around?

Paul wished he could ditch Garceau's, drop everything right where it was, and take Greyson on some kind of adventure. They could go fishing. When had Paul last been fishing? Four or five years ago? Grey would love it, he thought, and so would Paul, the time spent, just the two of them, sharing the quiet, Paul teaching Grey about a part of the world he probably hadn't yet discovered. He wanted desperately to give the boy more than scraps of time wedged between his work. It'd be great to make a grand gesture—go to Detroit for a ball game, say. Or even just to the Soo for a hamburger. Anything, really.

He went right back to slicing mushrooms. Every day was hard to get through now. Every year by this time he toyed with the idea of closing and going back downstate, and every year he got a second wind and soldiered through. But maybe there was no sense in that. Maybe he was missing too much that mattered. All of his sisters had children, kids he barely knew. He had a nephew in Iraq, which felt strange and impossible. Tommy had been a skinny ten-year-old when Paul left, and now he was a soldier? He probably went by Tom and not Tommy now, and it was a sure bet he no longer messed around in the kitchen making weird snacks the way he used to. There was a bad and very real chance he'd get killed over there and the next time Paul would see him would be at his funeral. This idea was so wrong that Paul couldn't think about it.

"Earth to Paul," Madeline said. She cut her eyes toward Greyson.

Paul forced himself to smile, to put the knife down, to crouch down to Greyson's level and give him a hug. Greyson returned the hug in spades, and Paul stood up with Grey dangling from his neck and laughing with a glee that made Paul's heart swell.

But then Madeline and Greyson had finished their pizza and

gone home, and Paul's spirits sank once again. Not long after they left he turned the sign to "Closed." It was hours early, but for once he was doing himself this favor. He turned off the coffeepot, shut down the lights, shoved the components of his unfinished sauce into the cooler. He slid into a booth and leaned against the wall, closed his eyes, and rehashed it all in his head again. The season was over and he had just managed to break even. Every time he thought he might make an extra dollar, something went wrong—the coolers, the truck, always something.

Yesterday he got a notice saying the water bill was going to be four times higher starting in January. The Village hadn't put any money into the system in years and now they were going to make up for it. He wondered if Madeline realized. Everybody who was commercial was going to pay a steep price, motels and hotels in particular. Well, she must've gotten the same notice he did, so good luck to her.

There'd been a note from the bank, too. His mortgage rate was going up and there was nothing he could do about it. It'd be expensive to refinance and with the shape things were in, he might not even get approved. Also there was a notice from the Feds claiming he hadn't paid his taxes on time and they were going to penalize him for it. He *had* paid the taxes, but someone had gotten something screwed up. Paul had no idea how to fix it, but he'd have to figure it out because he was the person in charge here.

How great to be your own boss. He was working a hundred hours a week and only halfway making it because of the paycheck from the prison. Without that he'd be in a bad way. *With* it he was in a bad way. He was running like a rat on a wheel, and for what? He couldn't even tell anyone any of this.

He'd felt for Madeline, that night she was tipsy and spilled out all those miserable little truths you really had to keep to yourself in a place like this. Paul knew how he would've felt after—like a fool. She'd pretended ever since that it never happened and he did too. It was exactly the way he would have played it in her shoes.

Now there was a job offer back downstate, and he couldn't talk to anyone about that, either. He was on his own to decide, take it or don't. His high school buddy Jim had a construction business and had won a bid on building a school. He wanted Paul to come work with him. The money would be decent, it'd beat working in the prison (wouldn't it?), and Paul thought he could do it. It wouldn't be easy, the way his leg was, but running this place was hard too. Between Garceau's and the prison, he was on his feet fifteen hours a day, and it wasn't like he was going back to school to learn how to do some desk job. It was a little late for that, and he wouldn't want to anyway. No, if he worked for Jimmy he'd just soldier through the pain, figure out a different way to do things when the bad leg said he had to, the same way he did here. Construction would be something different, anyway, and the hours would be shorter, and it'd be back home.

The last time he was there and had run into Leanne, it was fine. They'd said hello, how are you doing, all the banal things people who were mostly strangers did say to one another. It was hard to believe they'd been married for six years. It was ancient history. The best part of the offer was that he'd be close to his folks again. He was worried about his dad, who was tired every time Paul talked to him anymore. What was that about? As things were, he couldn't even take the time to run downstate and check on him.

Paul rubbed a hand over his face. He was sick of thinking about it. It made sense to take the job. The problem was that despite his chronic internal grumbling, he didn't want to leave. Less than ever now. He loved helping with Greyson. He didn't want to leave him, and really, how could he? Especially now. He hadn't bargained for all this—*involvement*. But he didn't regret it, either. It just left him unsure how to proceed.

As the October days passed, Madeline watched Arbutus and Pete with something like envy. Mild and wistful, but envy nonetheless.

Pete's eyes lit up every time he saw Arbutus; his smile for her was jaunty, a little amazed, very proud. Hers for him was merry, adoring, kind. They held hands every time they could. Arbutus sat right next to Pete whenever they rode in his car, her hand on his knee, and his face above the wheel always had a look of barely suppressed joy. There was so much tenderness and pleasure and devotion between them. Was this, after all, what life was about? Love? Could it be that simple?

For some people, apparently. Pete and Arbutus made an announcement at the supper table one night. They were getting married.

Gladys blinked and something raced across her face. Desolation? Of course. She had lived for her sister, done everything in her power to bring her home and take care of her. She had sold her possessions, made herself sleepless with worry, pushed herself too hard physically, braved the wilds of Chicago, laid aside pride and fear to ask Madeline to come stay with them, taken all kinds of chances. And now she was being deserted. How lonesome this house would be, with Arbutus gone—and who knew where. To Chicago? Wouldn't that be ironic. But the shock and sorrow were instantly buried. Gladys clapped her hands together and said, "Married! Well, I'll be. Congratulations."

Arbutus was sparkly with happiness. "We want to do it right away. It's too late in life to waste any time. We're going to elope."

"Elope!" Madeline was stunned.

"What does that mean?" Greyson held a drumstick in one hand and looked around at all of them with a baffled expression.

"It means they're going to try and sneak off to a justice of the peace instead of having a proper church wedding, and I won't have it," Gladys declared.

Arbutus and Pete smiled at each other. "No, we've decided. We're getting married in Crosscut at the courthouse. It's what we want. Something quiet. We want all of you to come. Pete's daughter Marion is coming, too, she's the only one who could get away on such short notice. She said she wouldn't miss it. We called her this afternoon."

"You're serious?" Gladys asked, dismayed. "What will Pastor Alton think?"

"Oh, never mind Pastor Alton. I want something simple, and quick."

"But what about a reception, then?" Gladys asked, somewhat desperately. "Why, the whole town will want to come. You can't deny them."

"Oh, I don't know," Arbutus began, but Pete broke in.

"That might be a fine idea. It'd give me a chance to meet people I haven't yet." He turned to Arbutus as he said this and Madeline watched a look of understanding pass between them. "I wouldn't know how to organize something like that—" Pete trailed off, sounding regretful and helpless.

"And I'm afraid I'm not up to it," Arbutus added. "All that running around—"

"I'll organize it, of course." Gladys was brisk and frowning and the smile that lit Pete's eyes was quickly hidden. Gladys went for a pad and pen and began rounding up punch bowls and planning how many pounds of ham and scalloped potatoes would be needed.

"That Naomi who makes the baskets makes a nice wedding cake, I'll talk to her. I'll have to stop at the Village office, make sure the hall's free. What date have you set? We'll have the party that same night if it's a Saturday."

Madeline was impressed. That look of desolation had come and gone fast, but it had been there, and here Gladys was planning the party.

They finished dinner and Madeline cleared the table. Greyson wanted to paint pictures (Like her? Maybe. She felt a flash of terrible, vulnerable tenderness at this.) and brought the sketch pad and set of watercolors she'd given him to the table and set to work. Pete headed back to the hotel to check the radiators. "Don't want you two to freeze in your beds tonight," he said as he left. The night before, Madeline had woken up at three shivering, and padded around the cavernous building with a flashlight to find all the radiators cold. Pete thought he had fixed the problem that afternoon. Gladys and Arbutus retired to the front room. Madeline could hear the low murmur of voices.

She carried the platter on which the chicken had been served over to the hutch near the parlor to put it away, and heard Gladys say, hesitantly, "Where will you live, then? After you're married?" Madeline stayed to hear the answer.

"Live? Why, in my house, my house that Pete just bought of all things." She laughed at the strangeness of the way things worked out, and then she said, puzzled, "What did you think?"

"I—didn't know. I thought maybe Pete would want you to move down there to Chicago. Thought maybe you'd want to go. Be closer to Nathan and all. You can, you know. I'm fine here. It'd all be different this time, I don't blame you if you want to go."

Arbutus laughed. "We'll live right here, McAllaster is my home. Why, how could I ever leave you? Pete knows that. And he loves it here. I'm sure we'll go down to visit, but I am too old and set in my ways to move to the city."

"Oh," Gladys said, brusque. Madeline felt as relieved as she had to be. "Have you told Nathan yet?"

Arbutus hesitated before she admitted, "No. I'm afraid he's not going to like it. You know how he is, so conventional. I guess I can't blame him, I'm sure it will come as a shock."

"What if he tries to stop you? Tries to get you declared incompetent? I wouldn't put it past him."

"Oh, no, he won't do that." Arbutus sounded very certain.

"How can you be so sure? If I know Nathan that'll be the first thing on his mind, now that there is some actual money involved."

"No, you see, I already gave it to him. I knew it would prey on his mind as long as I had it. Now that our bills are caught up and I've put a little aside, I didn't see where I needed it. I'm glad not to have the worry of it."

If Madeline hadn't already set the platter down, she might have dropped it.

"Arbutus! You didn't! That's your *security*."

"Of course it isn't. I have my house, and you, and Pete now too. And Madeline will be right up the street in the hotel. If that's not a miracle I don't know what is. And I have Nathan. He'll take care of me, if need be."

"He'll put you in a home, is what he'll do, we've already seen that."

"Well, so be it. People do end up in homes, that's the way of life. It's no tragedy. I've had a good life. I'm getting *married*, Glad, think of that."

"But, Butte, to just give him all your money, I can't believe—"

"He's my boy, my only child. I didn't need the money."

"But the future, you don't know what might happen."

"The Lord will provide. He always has. You know it as well as I do."

Gladys was silenced by this. Madeline wondered if she agreed or didn't. She picked the platter up and fitted it into its place in the stack on the shelf, then bent over Greyson on her way back to the sink to see what he was painting.

"It's the hotel," he said, chewing a little on the end of his brush. "Can you tell?"

"I sure can. Is that a garden down there?"

"Yep. Those are tomato plants. I put them in 'cause there's orange in them and I thought it needed some orange."

"Good call."

"I still have to put a car in it. That's what I'm doing next."

"Sounds good. I've got to finish these dishes, and then we'll go, okay?"

"Okay," he said, outlining a car in green paint.

Madeline finished the dishes feeling a strange mixture of things: joy, peace, a wistful lonesomeness for which there might not be a cure.

Halloween day was chill and blustery, drizzling an icy rain. Madeline worked all day on the lobby, cleaning and dragging furniture around. Now she was stocking a small expanse of shelves behind the registration desk with a mini-inventory—some of Mary's syrup, coffee beans from a company in Chicago, a tiny fleet of woven baskets. Madeline had worked up the courage to approach Naomi in the shop one day, and she'd agreed to let her carry some of her things. It'd be good to have some merchandise out in time for the wedding reception—which was only a week away. Not in order to sell, but just to show that she *would* be selling.

She hummed along with the radio as she set out bags of coffee. It was the public station out of Sault Ste. Marie, and the reception faded in and out with the wind. They were playing a recording of Vivaldi's *Four Seasons* that Madeline had always loved, done by the Academy of St. Martin's in the Fields, and even though the signal was weak it made her happy.

"You going to play this elevator music all the time in here?" Gladys asked.

"Leave her be, Glad," Arbutus said without looking up from her novel.

"The next fine day, I'll get up on the roof and set up a better antenna for you," Pete promised from where he lay on the floor, peering at the underside of a radiator. Gladys had charged him with getting the heat pouring out in time for the reception. "You might even pull in something out of Canada then, when the weather's good."

Gladys sighed from where she sat at the registration desk over a spiral-bound notebook where she was keeping track of her party organizing: how many tables and chairs and coffee urns and punch bowls borrowed from which churches, how many pounds of meat and rolls and salads ordered from the big grocery store in the Soo, announcements sent to which papers, flyers put up when and where, individual invitations sent and answered. It appeared that not only all of McAllaster but most of Ojibwa County and the eastern U.P. was invited. *What if they all come?* Madeline asked her that morning, looking dubiously around the lobby, which was roomy but not *that* big. *They won't*, Gladys said. *But they'll like being asked, and those that do won't all stay long.* Still, the list of things Madeline was not to forget to bring back from the Soo the coming Friday was staggering. Gladys added to it all the time until Madeline was sure there wouldn't be room in the car, especially given the wedding present she was bringing back with her, a secret no one but Pete knew.

"Just what I need," Gladys said now. "Canuck elevator music. Give me some of that Big Band like we used to dance to over at the VFW Hall, remember, Butte?"

Arbutus smiled, but she didn't answer. She was sitting in an armchair by the window reading with Marley on her lap. She seemed serene at the prospect of being married and feted in just a few days. Of course, Gladys was doing all the planning. Arbutus was to be decorative and Pete and Madeline were the mules. Willing mules.

Madeline glanced at the clock. Greyson was due home from kindergarten any minute. Home, well. This was only temporary, Madeline had to remind herself of that, but for now, yes, home. She set a pint of Mary's maple syrup on the shelf thinking that it was a kind of elixir, a cordial for the sustenance of life itself.

At dusk she lit the jack-o'-lanterns they'd carved with Paul Monday night. They'd carved the pumpkins and then made macaroni and cheese from scratch and put it in the oven (which Pete had repaired), and all evening long it sent out a smell that said *Home*. Once it was baking, Paul sat down at the piano in the dining room and started playing. Greyson climbed up on the bench beside him.

"What's that called?" he asked.

Paul smiled down at him. "'Maple Leaf Rag.' I learned this one to impress girls, back in junior high."

"Did it work?"

Paul grinned. "It wasn't the worst idea I ever had."

"Harmonica, piano, what else do you play?" Madeline asked, and he looked up at her while his hands kept moving.

"Guitar. That's my real love. Used to play all the time, it's all I ever did."

"How can you stand *not* playing now, then?"

"I don't know." The thoughtful look settled on his face as his hands went still. "There aren't enough hours in the day anymore, I guess." He shoved his glasses up with his wrist and then sat with his hands dangling between his legs. Thinking. But Greyson poked him and said, "Don't stop," and Paul started playing the melody of "Yellow Submarine," very slowly, saying, "Come on, you know this one," giving Greyson one note to play in the bass.

For that night they'd been a family. She wished Paul could go trick-or-treating with them now, but he was working. Always working.

The trick-or-treaters began to arrive, the little ones brought to the door by their parents, the older ones covering the streets with their friends, the girls and adults sheltering themselves beneath umbrellas, the boys getting drenched beneath ball caps and sweat-shirt hoods. There were ghosts and witches and ballerinas, monsters and psycho killers and cowboys and Indians. A steady stream of children came to the door and Madeline hoped she wouldn't run out of candy.

She was going to take Greyson out as soon as Gladys and Pete and Arbutus arrived to man the door. He was impatient, running to the hall every time someone knocked, sighing in exasperation when it was only another batch of children. He'd been dressed since four, as a clown in huge shoes of Paul's and a polka-dot jumper Arbutus had sewn, with circles of rouge from Randi's makeup case on his cheeks.

At last Pete and Arbutus came; Gladys had stayed home to hand out candy on her own porch. Wanting to practice being on her own again a little, maybe. "Let me get your coat," Madeline said, and Greyson said, "No! It'll ruin my costume."

"Yes. It's cold out there."

"Madeline!"

"Greyson!" She rummaged in the closet for something she remembered, a big old suit jacket with a patched elbow. She held it up. "A clown coat, just like at the circus."

"Excellent choice," Pete said. "It makes the costume."

Greyson flicked a mistrusting look at them but then sighed and said, "All right."

Madeline put the jacket on him and adjusted the ruffed collar of his costume and dropped a candy bar into his bag. "Seed candy," she said solemnly.

"Thank you, Madeline."

"You're welcome. Ready, then?"

"Ready!"

Madeline pulled her lime green polka-dotted hat on, and a rain coat, and they ventured out. She felt so tender. Even if things went terribly wrong, he'd still have this. He'd have these happy times when he dressed up as a clown on Halloween and got given a Snickers bar at the Hotel Leppinen. For now his world was small and as safe as it could be, all things considered. It wasn't perfect, but it was what they had, and it was good.

26

The judge was senatorial and yet twinkly in his office the morning of the wedding, and did not rush through his speech about how moving it was to see two people vow to love and care for each other at any age. Arbutus wore a new suit in soft pink wool with a frilly ivory blouse beneath, and sensible shoes in a darker shade of pink. Pete stood nearly strangulated with feeling beside her in a trim blue suit. His voice caught as he said, "I do," while Arbutus's rang out clear.

"He's a wonderful man, your dad," Madeline whispered to Pete's daughter.

"He is," Marion agreed. She was slight and unremarkable-looking except for the startling sapphire eyes she'd inherited from him. She had a wonderful laugh.

"She's just like my Eunice," Madeline heard Pete tell Arbutus after the ceremony was over, gazing on his daughter, and Arbutus nodded, smiling her understanding. She did not seem upset that Nathan hadn't come. Madeline had to give him credit, there'd been a gigantic display of flowers delivered by FedEx with a card that said "Best Wishes from Nathan." It must have cost the earth. But then, considering that he already had his inheritance, he ought to be able to afford it.

According to the satin-covered guest register, more than three hundred people drifted in and out of the reception through the long afternoon and evening. Not Paul, sadly. He was working. Gladys presided over everything with tranquil confidence, her planning-stage brusqueness gone. Madeline, on the other hand, lapsed into scattered moments of panic—*More coffee! More punch! We're out of 7-Up! Where's the mustard?!* Greyson ran around in a steadily more rumpled suit and tie, and John Fitzgerald and his wife served punch and refilled bowls of potato salad and cole slaw with unflagging enthusiasm, promising not to abandon Madeline for the cleanup.

Pete and Arbutus opened their gifts late in the evening—Arbutus and Gladys both getting teary-eyed over the kicksled that Madeline had bought back from the antiques man over in the Soo—and then drove off in Pete's sedan, a string of streamers and tin cans tied to the bumper fluttering and bouncing down the street after them. They were going home to Mill Street, and then in two days to Chicago for another party and a visit to Pete's friends and family. They'd be gone two weeks—time to make the trip in stages so that Arbutus wouldn't get too tired and uncomfortable. Madeline wondered how she and Gladys would manage without them.

Sunday was devoted to cleaning up, Monday to recovering, Tuesday to running the errands she'd let go the week before. Madeline took Greyson to see Randi on Tuesday afternoon, leaving him with her in the main room and climbing the stairs to Walter's room. He was dozing and didn't wake up when she came in, so she sat in his armchair and looked out the window. After a while, looking

for something to read, she opened his desk drawer. Maybe there'd
be a magazine in it—he had a subscription to *Sports Illustrated* he
must've paid for with his spending money. She didn't care much
about any sports but baseball, or any teams but the Cubs, but it'd
be something to look at.

There were a few magazines in the drawer, and also a thick
notebook with tattered cardboard covers held together by a piece
of string. It was worn and very old. Glancing at Walter—was this a
terrible thing to do?—Madeline slipped the book out of the drawer
and onto the desktop.

It was a journal, a notion book, really. The name inscribed in
old-fashioned script in the front cover was Ada Stone. Madeline
stared at it, her heart beating faster, and gingerly turned the first
few pages. Ada seemed to have put down whatever she wanted in
it: recipes, quotes, thoughts, the weather. How to get an ink stain
out of cloth, what to give a baby for croup. Madeline turned more
pages and stopped to study a drawing: Ada had planned out how
she'd set her furniture in the cabin. Madeline leaned over to gaze at
the penciled diagram on the yellowing paper that had suffered many
erasures: here the settee, there the coal stove, over on the other wall
a sideboard and rocker and table.

Walter stirred and her head snapped up. He swung his feet over
the edge of the bed and sat rubbing at his eyes. "Hello, Madeline,"
he said.

"Hi, Walter. You were sleeping, I didn't want to wake you."

"Okay," he said.

"I was looking for something to read and went into your desk.
I'm sorry."

"That's okay."

"I found this." She pointed at the journal. "I know I shouldn't have taken it out, but I couldn't resist." Walter scratched the back of his head and yawned. "I'm sorry," she said again.

"That's okay. That's Mama's book. Joe had it after she died, he gave it to me. She liked to write things in it."

"I see that," Madeline said gently. "She says that on June sixth, 1932, it was cool and rainy and you helped her clean up the cabin."

"Oh, yes. I always liked to help Mama."

Madeline read the rest of the entry. *A mouse in my drawer of stockings. I caught it and put it outside. It will be back in tomorrow but it looked at me so pleading I couldn't kill it.* She turned a few more pages and then became very still. She'd come to a sketch, a drawing. It was a picture done in ink of a skunk with a sweet and mischievous expression on its face. "Oh," she breathed.

Walter walked to the desk and leaned over her. "That's Jim."

"It's wonderful." She thought of the ink bottle she'd found, imagined Ada Stone dipping her pen into it, sketching, Jim emerging from thin air on the paper.

Walter sat back down on the bed and yawned again. "I'm hungry."

"It's almost suppertime, probably."

"We're having spaghetti, Ted said."

"I love spaghetti."

Walter nodded. "It's messy." He smiled at her then and said, "You can have Mama's book if you want it."

"Oh Walter, no. No, I can't take it from you."

"It's okay," he said, looking shy and pleased. "I want you to. There's no one left but you and me."

She stared at him, tears pooling in her eyes. He did know, more than she thought sometimes. "I'll take it someday, then. Not now. I'll just look at it when I come to see you, if that's okay."

"Okay." Walter sat swinging his legs, his hands folded in his lap. "Joe always took good care of me, and Mama too."

"I know. You've said."

"When Mama got older we came to live with him in the winter. It was on Pine Street. Number Five One Two, Mama made me memorize it. It was a nice house, there was a bathroom inside."

Ted tapped at the door and said that dinner was almost ready, and Madeline went to get Greyson. He and Randi were watching TV, Randi in her wheelchair and Greyson on the floor at her feet.

Greyson and Madeline ate supper with Gladys. After the roast and potatoes were gone, Greyson went to watch television, taking a slab of apple pie with him and promising not to spill it on the sofa. Madeline stayed in the kitchen. A fire was burning and the room smelled of pie and meat. It seemed timeless, a world apart. She poured coffee, cut slices of pie and slid them onto plates. How familiar she'd become here. Had it really been more than six months since she left Chicago? Even with their problems, she and Gladys kept dealing with each other. They had become, however wary, family. She told Gladys about Ada's journal.

"Is that right? I never knew he had such a thing."

"It was in his desk drawer. It's fascinating—like I get to meet her, in a way."

"I expect it is like that."

"She had a sense of humor. She seems smart."

"I'm sure she was. Joe was a very smart man. Not educated but smart."

"Walter said Joe had them come spend winters with him when she got older, at the place on Pine Street."

"It was awfully harsh for them back on Stone Lake in the winter,

I think. They would've had to get all their supplies in before the snow got deep, or else snowshoe out. That was all before I knew Joe."

"Did my mother grow up there, on Pine Street?"

"Yes. Mostly. Joe never lived up here until he moved in with me."

Madeline paused in forking up a bite of pie. "Moved in with you?"

"Yes."

Madeline narrowed her eyes. "You weren't—Were the two of you married and you never told me?"

"No, we weren't. I hope that doesn't shock you. But I didn't care to marry again. There came a time when it made sense for us to share a house, and I wanted to stay here." Gladys cut a precise triangle of pie and ate it.

Madeline was about to take a bite of pie herself, but she paused. "You and Joe got together *after* I was born, you said. And I was born here, my birth certificate says so. It doesn't add up."

Gladys shifted in her chair and made as if to get up, but Madeline leaned closer and said, "What, Gladys? What aren't you telling me?

Gladys sighed. "Jackie got expelled from Crosscut in the tenth grade, so she came up here to school. There was nowhere else. We still had a high school here in those days. She didn't want to go to school at all but Joe insisted. He drove her back and forth every day, and then—well."

"What?"

"You're not going to like this."

"*What?*" Madeline leaned toward Gladys, wishing the story was a fish she could yank up out of her on a line.

Gladys traced patterns on the oilcloth with one finger. Then she said, "The driving back and forth got to be too much, come winter. He needed a place for her to stay, to board."

Madeline stared at Gladys. "And?"

"I still had the hotel open in those days and I—Joe—well. Jackie stayed with me during the week, went home on the weekends. Sometimes." Gladys made a face. "That girl went her own way, there just was not a thing you could do when she got her mind set. Anyway. Joe paid a little, and I gave Jackie her meals as well as a place to sleep. That's when Joe and I first got acquainted, though that's all it was then, just being acquainted."

Madeline was speechless. She took a gulp of coffee, wanting the jolt of it, the hot scald down her throat.

Gladys looked defensive. "You needn't look at me like that. Boarding wasn't all that uncommon. Two other students did it too, they lived too far out in the woods to go back and forth every day."

Madeline nodded, and resisted shouting, *That is not the point and you know it.*

Gladys hurried on. "Joe was just determined that Jackie would graduate. But of course she didn't. Back in those days a pregnant girl didn't go to school the way they do now. So that was that. I've often wondered if that wasn't why she did it. To get the best of Joe. And to get out of going to school. She was no scholar, I have to say. She was bright, don't get me wrong. Smart as a whip, just no good at schooling. It didn't make any sense. I don't know if she was just stubborn or if she really could not read, the way it seemed."

"Couldn't read."

Gladys shrugged. "That's how it seemed. Or could barely read. I always tried to make sure the boarders were doing their schoolwork. And for such a bright girl it just didn't make any sense."

"Didn't they do any testing?"

"Testing?"

"For a learning disability."

"There was nothing wrong with Jackie, not like that. She was wild, that was all. And no one would want to get stuck with a label like that anyway. Why, the kids would have called her a retard, the way they did Walter. They probably did anyway, just because he was her uncle."

"Probably," Madeline said, feeling faint. She was dizzy, and she put her head down on the table.

"Madeline?"

Madeline didn't lift her head. Jackie Stone came walking toward her, a tiny figure from out of a far distance. Maybe she'd been dyslexic. Madeline knew a little about that. Dwayne's daughter Candice was dyslexic, and the struggles they went through had been awful. Smart as a whip, like Gladys just said, but virtually unable to read. It had taken batteries of tests to figure it out, and now a very sophisticated teaching system to help her. Before she got diagnosed she'd been on a constant roller coaster of emotion: furious, demanding, rebellious, unpredictable. The whole family had been at the mercy of the problem. It was a nightmare until they figured it out.

Maybe it had been like that for Joe and Jackie. Something was wrong, they didn't know what. It would have seemed to Joe like good old-fashioned *bad*ness on Jackie's part. And Jackie—maybe she never knew why she did the things she did, felt the way she felt. It was all speculation now, no one would ever know. It was a sad little tragedy. How to come to terms with *that*?

"I *tried* to keep an eye her," Gladys was saying, her voice querulous. "But you can't watch people all the time, you can't control a girl who's just intent on trouble."

"You blame yourself," Madeline said, lifting her head.

"She was staying with me! She was my responsibility. I ran a tight ship with my boarders, I paid attention."

"I'm sure you did."

"And still somehow she managed—"

"Who was the father? My father?" Maybe after all someone did know. But Gladys was shaking her head.

"Jackie just would not say a thing about it and I think—I'm afraid—" She faltered to a stop.

"Say it, Gladys."

Gladys did, after a moment. "Well, I wouldn't be surprised if it was someone passing through. Someone she met up at the tavern. She was always slipping in there to play pool, and *I* couldn't stop her. No one could."

Madeline told herself that this was not news, there was no use dwelling on it. "So why was I born here and not in Crosscut?"

"She wouldn't go home, at first. She just wouldn't. She moved in with a girlfriend of hers, Cindy Tate. Cindy and her mother lived here just for a short time. Her mother worked at the tavern. She was a sloppy kind of woman, she never cared what Cindy did. Anyway. You were born while Jackie was staying with them. Then Cindy's mother quit the tavern and they moved and I suppose Jackie didn't have anywhere to go but home."

Madeline nodded.

"She left when you weren't very old—only two, I think. I suppose she just couldn't stick it any longer—living at home, having to go by Joe's rules, having a little one—" Gladys shook her head. "I never liked Jackie, Madeline. I hate to say it so plain, but it's the truth. I didn't like her and I hated what she did to you. But she was young, and she was full of life, and—well, I can feel for her, in a way."

Madeline nodded. So could she. She didn't want to, she never had wanted to, but—maybe a little, now, she could. Maybe she didn't have any choice.

Gladys took a swallow of coffee. "I ran into Joe at the fiddle jamboree that summer, and I suppose he was lonely. I was too. I always felt for him, trying to raise a girl alone." She looked lost in memory. "My land, he could play that fiddle."

"Where was Walter all this time?"

Gladys came out of her reverie. "He moved into the AFC when his mother died. That was a year or so before you were born. Joe was off working too much to take care of him the way she had, and it would have been just awfully lonely for Walter."

"So what happened to everything? The place out on Stone Lake, the house on Pine Street?"

"Joe sold it all, every last bit of it, when he moved in with me. He didn't need the house anymore, and then too I think there were so many memories there. I think he wanted a clean slate." Gladys swallowed more coffee, cut off another bite of pie and ate it. As if the story was told, and that was the end, and a pretty satisfying end at that.

"A clean slate."

"A person can want that anytime in life, you know." Gladys frowned and got up from the table. She began rinsing the plates in the sink.

The dark feeling she'd been pushing away overtook Madeline. "So what happened to the money? Did he ever think how hard it was for Emmy to make ends meet with me to take care of? She never had anything. She could only afford our apartment because she'd been there forever and it was in such bad shape when she got it, and it was *hard*. And he was what—living off his girlfriend? That's not right."

Gladys spun around. "He put everything in a trust for Walter. Walter didn't have *any*one else. Who on earth was going to look after him when Joe was gone? That worried him more than anything. And he was proud. He didn't want Walter dependent on the State for everything."

Gladys's fists were clenched and her eyes were bright and Madeline was sorry in a distant way to have caused this upset, but more than that she felt a stubborn mutiny. Gladys shook a crooked finger at Madeline. "Joe took care of Walter. That's what he did with the money. From the house and the land and everything else he could set aside! He *never* lived off me, and it's a lucky thing he's not around to hear you say that. He worked hard all his life, Madeline Stone, harder than most people ever will. He had less than most people today can even imagine, and he still took care of Walter."

Madeline said nothing. There had been a surge of rage in her gut, in her *soul*, it seemed, to hear those words, *Joe took care of Walter*. None of the Stones had ever looked after her. At last she said, with tears that she resented brimming in her eyes, "Walter's a really special person. I'm glad he was taken care of. And I'm glad I get to know him." It was the truth, and it was the best she could do.

Gladys gradually relaxed, but she didn't look happy. Eventually she went back to rinsing the dishes and Madeline got ready to leave. It seemed as if they'd lost the little bit of ground they'd gained between them.

Back at the hotel, Madeline put Greyson to bed and then wished she had his company. She stood in the sitting room studying a painting she'd been working on, the lake framed in the attic window. She'd been trying to show just enough of the room to give its flavor, plain and austere, then outside that vast expanse of water. That was life, right? That juxtaposition of in and out, home and nature, tame and wild. She had no idea whether it was good or not. She was sick of questioning it. It was what it was. Paint on canvas.

She stretched out on the sofa and pulled an afghan (a housewarming gift from Arbutus) over her legs. Moonlight fell through the window, and she watched it as if it were a visitor, a companion. She remembered something Mary Feather had said one day. *What you have to do here, is accept.* She thought of Stone Lake. Dried up, the long grasses waving in the wind. She had wanted water there. But she'd accepted no water, and felt the beauty of it.

She thought of Jackie Stone, a wild, troubled girl who threw herself out upon the world and was devoured by it. She'd died in Denver, Colorado, when Madeline was seven. The police said it was heart failure, probably brought on by drugs and hard living. Emmy didn't tell her until she was older.

After a long time, Madeline closed her eyes. Eventually she slept.

A few hours later she woke up to a presence beside her—who? Oh, Gladys. Perched on the edge of the couch. Madeline rubbed her face, scooted into a sitting position. "What's wrong?"

"I couldn't sleep."

"Oh." Madeline rubbed her eyes, still confused. "Are you okay?"

"I'm fine." Gladys patted her hand, and then held it. "I came to say I'm sorry."

"Oh."

"I don't know what to tell you about Joe, or Jackie. I don't like to bring up a lot of bad old history, I guess."

Madeline listened as Gladys talked. Joe Stone had a lot of responsibility young. That wasn't unusual, in this place, in that time. Maybe it made him a little hard, but it also enabled him to survive. He worked in the woods, helped look after his mother and Walter, got married, had a child. His wife ran off when the child was young, and Joe did the best he could to look after her, but the girl grew up wild.

Maybe it was in her genes, maybe it was because her father didn't know what to do with her, maybe it was the times, but either way, Jackie was out of control. She did all kinds of things Joe didn't want her to do. Worst of all, she was horrible to Walter. Also, she ran around with men. The two of them fought morning, noon, and night. Even so, when Jackie got pregnant it wasn't the last straw. "I think he was delighted with you. It was before my day, but I got that feeling, the little we talked about it."

"Why did she leave?"

"He never said. It could have been anything. But it *was* the last straw. It may not seem so to you, but he tried in his own way to do the right thing by her, over and over. And that last time, he just said no. It wasn't something he talked about. But I knew Joe. She broke his heart. That last time he closed the door."

"But I was a *child*. It could've been horrible. It's a miracle it wasn't."

"I know. He should have tried to take you. I always thought he should. It bothered me so—but he would not budge. A man like Joe doesn't change his mind. And I wasn't family. There wasn't a single thing I could do about it." Gladys's voice had turned fretful, defensive. Uncertain. That was so unexpected that Madeline couldn't think how to respond.

"You sent all those cards," she said after a moment.

"That was nothing."

"It was decent of you."

"It only seemed right. But it seemed like nothing too. Ridiculous. A Band-Aid on a severed limb."

"I wonder why he was so afraid of me. A little kid."

Gladys worked her fingers in the crochet-work of the blanket Arbutus had made. "I think he was terrified of having it happen all over again. And a man like Joe doesn't admit being scared of anything. Not even to himself."

"Scared of getting his heart broken?"

"Scared of failing. That's how he saw it. He'd failed with Jackie. Didn't bring her up right. Didn't know how. Couldn't go through it all again."

It seemed a poor excuse to Madeline. But maybe she could understand, just a little. She stared off into space. Overall the story was not surprising. Just one with an overabundance of human frailty. No heroes or villains, exactly. Just people who'd done what they'd done, too late to change any of it, and in the end that wasn't the worst news in the world.

27

On a very windy night soon after, after a long sprint of cleaning and errand-running and taking Greyson to see Randi (and feeling exasperated with Randi, Madeline's good intentions of seeing her good side, sympathizing with her pain and depression, flown out the window in the face of Randi's ill humor), Madeline fixed the easiest thing she could think of for supper, hamburgers, and made Greyson succumb to a bath. When he was shiny with cleanliness and in bed, she snuggled the comforter under his chin with a sense of relief. One step at a time, they had survived another day. He gave her a peaked smile. He was worn out by the visit to Randi and so was she.

"You want me to read you a story?"

"Okay." He sighed and she smoothed a flop of bangs away from his forehead.

"What'll it be tonight?"

"I don't care. Whatever you pick."

Madeline read from the *Song of Hiawatha*, whose rhythms had been so entrancing to her at his age. Outside the wind had picked up another notch and was howling around the building with an insistence that was a little alarming. Thrilling too, though. "*'By the shore of Gitche Gumee, by the shining Big-Sea-Water,'"* Madeline recited, the roar of the lake and the moan of the wind seeming a fitting backdrop to Longfellow's poem.

After Greyson dropped off to sleep she curled up on the couch with a sketchbook and found herself drawing Ada's cabin. She frowned at the picture, but how unsurprising that this is what her hand would choose. In quiet moments her thoughts lit on her family, on Jackie and Joe and Walter and Ada. She thought of the little skunk in Ada's journal, so alive and mischievous. No matter what else had happened, this was something they had in common, Ada and Madeline. And Joe.

Maybe she would find one of Joe's caricatures somewhere, someday.

This unexpected thought—startling in its arrival, its matter-of-factness, in the forgiveness it implied—brought with it a sudden, unlooked-for sense of peace.

Maybe it would not be impossible after all to keep her word to Emmy. *Promise me you'll try and forgive the man.*

She headed downstairs after a while, thinking of cocoa, but stopped on the way at Room Five. Jackie's room, according to Gladys. It was the same as all the others. Floral wallpaper, a light dangling from a cloth cord, a bed and dresser and chair, a rope fire escape coiled on the floor beneath the window. Had Jackie ever used it to sneak out? Probably. Madeline went and grabbed the rope—thick scratchy hemp anchored to the floor by a massive bolt, with knots tied in it every few feet—and tugged. Still solid. Every room had one. Maybe this was the only one that had ever been used.

She could, if she squinted, see a girl flinging her books on the bureau, scrambling out of her school clothes and into something more fun. How prisonlike this room must've seemed in 1973, when Jackie was burning with energy and youth and frustration. When the world outside was happening, and nothing at all was going on in McAllaster, never had been and never would be, in the mind of a sixteen-year-old girl. Or maybe instead it had been a release from the tensions at 512 Pine Street.

Something was banging against the building. She went to the window to see if she could tell what it was, but it was too dark to be sure. Maybe a tree branch. After a moment the banging stopped, though the wind howled on. Madeline closed the door and continued toward the kitchen.

While she was putting the kettle on, the phone on the registration desk rang. "Madeline?" Gladys's voice came tetchy over the wire. "Is that you?"

"Yes." Who else?

"Are you all right?"

"Yes, why?"

"Oh, this wind. My power's gone out."

"Mine's on."

Gladys grunted. "I wondered about those old apple trees in the yard. They're so close to the dining room windows."

"I think they're okay. I didn't hear anything. You want me to go check?"

"My dad planted those."

"I'll go take a look."

"No, don't. You'd have heard if a limb cracked off, I'd think. And what would you do about it, anyway? No, stay inside."

"All right."

Gladys was quiet then. Madeline tried to figure out what it was she really wanted. Maybe she was just unnerved by the wind and the loss of her electricity. "Do you—"

"It's just wind," Gladys broke in, as if Madeline had been the one to call her. "A November gale. It was like this the night the *Fitzgerald* sank. I'm going to bed, goodnight."

Do you want me to come up there? was what Madeline had been going to ask, but Gladys had already hung up.

In the tiny hours of the morning, Paul stood in the street staring at a mishmash of shingles and rafters and two-by-fours and clapboard and tree limbs and branches. His pizzeria, his loved and hated pizzeria, smashed. He couldn't get his mind around it.

"You okay?" John Fitzgerald asked. His face and gear were littered with sawdust. He'd been sawing up maple limbs and branches for the better part of two hours, ever since Paul'd called the volunteer fire department in to help him make sure the tree that had come down wasn't going to bring any other surprises, like a fire from downed wires. So far, so good, on that score. But as for Garceau's—the kitchen, anyway, where the damage was the worst—it was a disaster.

Paul nodded, although he was not okay, not at all.

"You want to come stay with the wife and me for the rest of the night?"

Paul shook his head.

John considered this, and then he said, "I think you better."

Two days later Paul called Jim and told him he'd be ready to start in a week. He gave his notice at the prison, put in a forwarding order for his mail, told his suppliers he'd pay them off as he could, put the Fairlane in storage, and notified the water company and the phone and electric and gas companies that Garceau's was history. He hauled truckloads of debris and ruined equipment to the landfill in Crosscut, got a couple of guys to help him patch up the roof and wall as best he could with plywood and tarpaper and tarps, and barred the doors and windows so no one could sneak in and get hurt. He was operating in a haze, but a methodical haze.

He avoided everyone while he made his arrangements, especially Greyson and Madeline. They tracked him down a couple of times, but he pleaded busyness, something pressing he had to do, somewhere he had to be, and shuffled them away before anything of consequence could be said, or asked.

It was a lousy way to act, but necessary. He was a turtle drawing into his shell. He knew it, he knew it wasn't fair, but he had to do it. Turtles had shells for a reason. He saw himself now as a man who had been drowning gradually, sinking under an ever-increasing weight. The mammoth old maple cracking through the kitchen roof and wall was the last stone on the pile; it put him under.

He walked from John's to the hotel on the day he was leaving, a sunny November afternoon, unseasonably mild. It was hard to believe that just a week ago a gale had been blowing. Hard to believe that in a few minutes he'd be headed down the highway. He switched the thought off. Madeline and Greyson were sitting in rockers on the porch.

"Hello, Mr. Garceau," Greyson said.

"Afternoon, Mr. Hopkins." Paul tried a smile out on Greyson, but it fell flat. He couldn't manage to make it real, and Greyson didn't even pretend he was interested in joking around.

His expression was very serious. "I'm sorry about the wind blowing the tree down and wrecking your kitchen."

"Me too, buddy. Me too."

"What will you do?" Madeline asked. She had a shirt that must be Greyson's in her lap, and it looked like she was trying to mend it.

"I'm going downstate. I came to say goodbye."

"Oh," Madeline said, looking dismayed.

Paul transferred his attention to Greyson. "I'll miss you, kid."

Greyson nodded, biting his lip.

"I'll write to you. You write back, tell me how you're doing. I'll call, too."

"But you aren't moving away for good, right? It's just for the winter?" Greyson looked at him anxiously, and Paul didn't know what to say. A lot of people went away for the winter, for work or warmer weather, it wasn't unusual. It'd be easier for Greyson to think that. And by the time spring came—maybe he'd have forgotten Paul, more or less. Didn't kids do that? Bounce back, adjust?

"Yeah, I might be back in the spring."

Madeline was frowning, and he knew what she was thinking. *Don't get his hopes up if that isn't true, he's had enough disappointments. Just be honest.* That was fair, but Paul couldn't do it. Faced with leaving the boy, the lie made Paul feel better too, was the truth of it.

Greyson scrambled from his rocker. "I'm going to get you something to take with you. Wait, I'll be right back."

Paul nodded.

"I'm sorry too," Madeline said quietly. "Gladys told me she heard you were moving, but I guess I didn't believe it. You know how rumors are."

"The damage is bad. You can see."

"I know. But—don't you have insurance?"

Paul didn't want to talk about what insurance might or might not pay out, or how he might be able to rebuild. He was leaving, period. Part of him yelled *No, stop,* at every turn, but it was the only thing left to do.

"What happened?" Madeline asked when he didn't answer her first question.

"The wind brought that old maple on the west side down. It's my own fault. I should have had it taken down years ago. It was rotten at the core and I knew it. But I loved it. I loved the shade. And then there was a leak in the roof I never got around to fixing. The wall was pretty rotten, worse than I realized, and it just gave."

Madeline grimaced in sympathy. "You were there, right?"

"Sleeping. The first crack of it breaking woke me up."

"Scary."

Paul shrugged. "Yeah, well. It's my own fault."

"It was a wind," Madeline protested. "A wind like the wind that sank the *Fitzgerald*, is what Gladys said."

"I knew that tree was rotten. I knew the roof was leaking. I just didn't do anything about it. I deserve whatever I get for being so stupid."

"You can't blame yourself, it doesn't do any good," Madeline said. She knew this from experience.

"It's a miracle it didn't happen a long time ago. This was just so damned unnecessary."

Madeline saw that he was not going to be talked out of his guilt and regret. She reached up and took his hand. "I'm really sorry."

He'd heard this so many times that he couldn't respond to it again.

"Hey," she said, shaking his hand to get his attention. "I mean it."

"I know," he said, staring off across the water.

"Do you really think you'll be back in the spring?"

He looked at her then. Her eyes seemed full of sympathy, a willingness to understand. "I don't know. The truth is, I was thinking about going anyway."

Madeline took her hand back and poked her needle in and out of the fabric of Greyson's shirt a few times. Without looking up she said, "Greyson's going to hate this."

"Me too." Paul rubbed the back of his hand against his face, then took off his glasses and scrubbed at his eyes. He thought about taking off, avoiding this. But no, he had to wait for Greyson.

"You've been so much help."

"No big deal." He could hardly get the words out.

"Ha. All that drywall! And the time you spend with Grey. This will be hard."

"I know. I'm sorry. I'm going to miss him like crazy."

"Randi was in such a bad mood the other day. I guess this is why."

Paul looked at the top of Madeline's head, her short dark hair, the curve of her neck. He swallowed back a feeling that wanted to burst out of him, an emotion that would interfere with the course he'd laid out for himself in the last few days. "Randi got rid of me awhile back."

Madeline's head shot up then, and her expression was gratifyingly baffled. "What? *Why?* You have to be the best thing that's ever happened to her."

He couldn't help but laugh, a real laugh. Something inside him felt less weighted down for an instant. "She didn't see it that way."

"Well, then she's blind. Anyway, I'm sorry."

"Don't be."

"You're too old for her anyway."

"Thanks!"

"I didn't mean—I meant she's too young for you."

"Great." Paul made it sound sour, but he was smiling. He was going to miss Madeline. Greyson, Madeline, the smell of the water always in the air, the outlines of this town that had become so familiar, everything. He couldn't think about it.

The door of the hotel opened and Greyson came out holding something in his hand. A kaleidoscope. He held it out to Paul. "This is like looking at the stars," he said. "Only you can look anytime, even when it's light. It's really cool, you want me to show you how it works?"

A *great quietness* descended over Madeline after Paul left.

"I'm going upstairs," Greyson said, sounding flattened. Madeline nodded, but pretty soon she decided this was no good. She trotted up the stairs and banged on his door and flung it open. He was lying on his bed, staring up at the ceiling, tossing a rubber ball in the air. "Come on, get up." She grabbed his ankle and shook it.

"I don't want to."

"Too bad. There's someplace we have to go."

"Where?" he said, without interest.

"It's a secret. Put on your shoes."

"Don't want to."

"Too bad," she said again. She went to her own room to get a knapsack, and after a moment heard his feet hit the floor.

It was dark before they got back. Madeline fixed grilled cheese sandwiches with the last of her energy, and watched Greyson nearly nod off over his plate. "Go on, get ready for bed," she told him when he'd finished eating. "I'll be up in a few minutes."

He nodded, yawning. When she checked on him ten minutes later he was already asleep, one arm flung over his head, the other curled around Marley, who gazed at Madeline with a satisfied expression. Greyson was still in his clothes and wearing a sneaker. He'd probably crashed before he ever got his teeth brushed. Good. He was worn out from their excursion.

He'd perked up a little when they turned off the highway onto the two-track that led to Stone Lake, and by the time they climbed up the small rise to the shore of the vanished water, he'd shed several layers of sadness. So had she, at least temporarily.

It didn't change the fact that they would miss Paul. They would. But they'd have to go on. They'd survive this. Madeline felt as though a hole had opened in the fabric of her fledgling life here; it must've felt the same way to Greyson. But it was a hole she'd just have to figure out how to mend, or jump over, or live with. They both would.

28

Suddenly it was the twelfth of November. In two days the hunters would arrive. Madeline was almost ready to pull the little chain to light up Gladys's sign that said "Rooms to Let."

She quit at eleven o'clock that night. The sofa and easy chairs she'd had delivered looked plump and inviting; the antiques that had been in the lobby—two plant stands with marble tops (now topped with Boston ferns she hoped wouldn't freeze when winter came), a curio cabinet, a library table, a china cupboard—shone with polish. A fire flickered in the woodstove, casting a soft light on the modestly stocked shelves. She'd found a dozen rugs rolled up under the eaves in a corner of the attic early in the fall, runners woven on Gladys's grandmother's rug loom, and cleaned them with a scrub brush and hot water and hung them outside to dry. Now they lay on the wooden floors as if they'd never been taken up and stashed away.

The rug loom itself sat in a corner, reassembled by Madeline with the help of Gladys. It wasn't strung yet, but she thought visitors would like to see it. Someday she'd learn to use it. She had vague ideas of selling rugs, eventually. It was a four-harness loom, Gladys had told her. A good one, you could make patterns instead of just stripes if you knew what you were doing. Which she did not,

Madeline pointed out. Gladys had better remember how it all went. In fact, she'd better write down everything she remembered about the loom and the grandmother who'd brought it from Finland before it was too late and the story was gone.

As far as Madeline knew, Gladys hadn't written so much as her name in the journal she'd given her, but she kept prodding anyway.

She sank down onto the sofa. Done. The registration desk gleamed and the guest register—a massive book—lay open on top of it, the hunters' names penciled in.

There were probably a thousand things she'd missed. She sprawled out, exhausted but still thinking, ticking things off in her head. Clean towels—thick and plush, in eggplant and sage and peri- winkle and rose—hung from the bars in the rooms. The sheets and blankets smelled of fresh air, and the iron bedsteads shone with new black paint. Extra blankets were folded at the foot of each bed, crisp paper lined the dresser drawers, and a balsam sachet lay in each. She had coffee beans in the hopper, cocoa mix and tea bags in tins on the kitchen counter, fresh cardamom cake in the cupboard. The issue of what to do with the impossible old kitchen and how to serve breakfast—Madeline thought she wanted to do this—were yet to be dealt with, but for this winter she wouldn't worry about it.

Madeline pushed herself up from the couch and headed toward the stairs. All kinds of things would have to be enough to start: the little bit of money she had left, her patchy knowledge of what she was getting into, the time and energy she was splitting in so many different directions. But there was time. She told herself not to panic. On her way out of the lobby she straightened the picture she'd hung near the front door. The study of the lake out the attic window. She'd framed it and hung it with a discreet tag advertising that it was for sale. She bit her bottom lip, studying it for the thou- sandth time. Good, bad? She wasn't sure, but she left it hanging.

The hunters came, and were both a delight and a letdown. For the duration of their stay Madeline felt like a real innkeeper, smiling her welcome, handing out keys, changing sheets. The men were affable, but Gladys was right, they were only looking for a room. They weren't interested in the ambiance of the hotel, or traditional Potawatomi baskets woven by Naomi, or woolen Hudson's Bay blankets. She did sell one of them half a gallon of Mary's syrup. She let them hang the deer they shot from the limbs of the maple in the side lot, as they always had when Gladys was the owner, and told herself she would get used to the sight.

Only a few scattered visitors, walk-ins, stayed in December. Madeline tried not to worry about that. She was just getting started. There was time to figure things out. The entire winter. She felt a rush of glee each time this thought came. It was as if she was embarking on an epic adventure, a trek to the Arctic by dogsled. And at the same time, a voice inside her nagged: *Look at the money the place is already eating. How're you ever going to keep up? Gladys was right.*

She couldn't worry about it. Not yet. Not until she'd had her winter.

Madeline went to 26 Bessel one morning, a week before Christmas, to return a casserole dish. She tapped at the door but when there was no answer she went in. Banging came from the direction of Arbutus's old room, and Madeline headed that way. Gladys was just coming down the hall, her hair covered with a printed scarf, an apron over her slacks and sweater. "Oh, Madeline, it's you. I was up on a ladder—"

"A *ladder*? Are you nuts, you could fall and break your neck."

"Oh, fizzle. I'm not falling anywhere. Come in the kitchen, I'll put coffee on."

Just then a small form darted down the hall, skidded on the linoleum, circled the kitchen at high speed, and slammed into Gladys's ankles.

"Don't be a pest, Edmund."

"Edmund?"

Edmund had a tan body and chocolate ears, feet, and tail. He gazed at Madeline with slightly crossed blue eyes. Madeline squatted down and held a finger out toward him, and he trotted over and rubbed his face along it. Madeline looked up at Gladys. "Where on earth did you get a Siamese kitten?"

Gladys went to the sink, Edmund tagging behind, and ran water in the kettle. "John Fitzgerald found him down in Crosscut at the pound. He brought him home but Ruth claims she's allergic. So John brought him over and asked if I could take him in, though what he thinks I want with a cat I don't know." Gladys sat down and Edmund leapt into her lap. She began petting him and Madeline could hear his purr from across the room. Madeline tried—not very hard—to hide a grin.

"Gosh, I don't know either, everybody knows how you feel about cats."

"I couldn't tell John no, he's always been good to us." Gladys turned Edmund belly-up to cradle him in the crook of one arm and he continued to purr. She stroked his throat with a bony finger before setting him back down. "So now I have a cat."

"So you do." Madeline pulled mugs down from the cupboard. She got milk from the icebox and adjusted the flame under the kettle. Gladys still did all her baking with the woodstove, claiming everything turned out better in it, but she would use the gas stove for simple things like boiling water now. "What are you up to on a ladder, anyway?" she asked when the coffee was perking.

"Making Butte's room over. John had a table he didn't want any longer, so he brought it over and moved the bed for me. I'm just putting shelves up."

"Really. What're you going to do in there?"

Gladys blushed, to Madeline's astonishment. Then she cleared her throat and said, "I'm going to write down my memories. My life story, I guess you'd say."

"You're kidding, that's great."

"Do you think so?"

"It's a great idea, haven't I been telling you that for months? I can't wait to read it. I mean, if you'll let me."

"We'll see." Then Gladys made another admission. "I've bought a computer. One like Mabel's."

"A computer! Gladys, you're amazing."

"I went ahead and got that high-speed Internet connection, I thought I might go on eBay. I'm looking for alarm clocks for you, if you want to know the truth. I wish I never would have sold them. You wouldn't believe the price I'm going to have to pay."

Madeline laughed and then—probably to Gladys's astonishment, and to her own as well—she got up and gave Gladys a hug.

Gladys went back to work when Madeline left. There was the still the closet to go through. Arbutus had insisted she didn't need more than a few inches of space while she was there, and shame on herself, Gladys had acquiesced. She was going to have a devil of a time now.

First there were the hangers to empty, clothes of Frank's she hadn't been able to part with when he died. Now was the time. That red-and-black plaid hunting jacket might fit Madeline. She tsked at herself over the shirts and pants. Frank had been buried in his one good suit, no one was going to use what was left here unless Madeline ever got around to getting that old rug loom up and running. She came to Frank Junior's dress uniform and gazed at it for a long time. She left it hanging.

She began pulling boxes from the recesses of the deep closet: old receipts, letters, bills, photograph albums. She leafed through one. There was Frank Junior with Henry out on the docks with a big steelhead they'd caught, grinning to beat the band. Oh, it was too much. Gladys closed the album and reached for the next box.

More photos, she wasn't going to look at those, and more odds and ends. She lifted up a pair of suspenders and then she knew— these were Joe's things. Oh, dear heavens. She did not know that she was up to this. But well started was half done. They were modest things—the suspenders, some tarnished cuff links, a pipe, a shaving mug, some road maps, a few photographs. Gladys stopped short at the photos. She should have remembered these long ago. What had she been thinking?

She hadn't been thinking, that was the truth. She didn't like to think of any of it. She'd loved Joe, more than she ever would've wanted anyone to know, and she still missed him. At the same time she hated how obstinate he was over Madeline, a little child left to be brought up by strangers. It wasn't right. Gladys always thought it wasn't right, and she found it galling and insufferable how little there was for her to do about it. All her life, Gladys had been doing things. It was the only way she knew. But this—there had been nothing to do about this, or if there had been she hadn't discovered it. It was all water under the bridge.

Only it wasn't. Madeline was here, and little by little Gladys had been trying to admit that the past wasn't all done and gone after all.

It was late when she left the room Arbutus had stayed in. She was grubby and tired and sore, but she was victorious, too. The closet was clean. She should have done it years ago. She had a pile of things for Emil, and one for the thrift shop, a big bag of garbage, and a few things Madeline might want. There were only two things she kept back, and only until Christmas.

29

The countryside near Saginaw where Paul grew up was flat, cut into big squares by country roads that bordered fields of corn and wheat and sugar beets. It had seemed beautiful to him once, and it was still pretty in a way, but it felt oppressive, too. Where was the water? At least in the winter the air was not as heavy as it was in the summer.

When he was growing up, his parents had an old farmhouse on an acre of land at the edge of Edwardsville, but a few years ago they'd moved into a subdivision. Paul had always hated subdivisions—their sameness and banality—but it wasn't bad. The house was cheerful and bright, comfortable. It was nice, in a way, that his mom had gotten rid of most of the old furniture when they moved; everything didn't remind him of the past.

Paul had a routine. Get up in time to go to the gym, get a shower, change into work clothes, stop by the Speedway for coffee, then head to the office. Mostly he was on the phone and the computer, ordering materials, looking for deals, doing paperwork. He took a bag lunch and ate at his desk around noon, and then worked until five.

At home he fixed dinner if he could talk his mother into letting him, washed the dishes, ditto if his mother would let him, then strong-armed his dad into taking a walk because his doctor said it was important to do that. Then they'd watch a little television and go to sleep. Weekends he got together with his sisters and their husbands and kids. The job was okayish (although more deskwork than he'd expected), and it was good to be around his family, but after a month Paul started to think, *This is it?*

From Christmas to the third week of January the construction office was closed. Jim did that every year, laid everybody off and took a couple of weeks himself. Paul had known it was coming up, but when it happened it threw him. He couldn't stop prowling around the house, looking for things to do. There wasn't much, barely even a lightbulb to be changed.

"You're making me nervous," his mother told him one morning, a week into his mandatory vacation. His dad had gone to drink coffee at Hardee's with his buddies. He'd invited Paul to come along but Paul didn't want to. "Why don't you relax?"

"I am relaxed," Paul said, drumming his fingers on the table, then jumping up to fiddle with the doohickey that controlled the blinds. It seemed sticky to him, maybe he could fix that.

"Paul. Sit down."

Paul frowned but he did sit because even all these years later he was conditioned to obey when his mother spoke in a certain tone of voice.

"What are your plans?"

"What do you mean?"

"You're welcome here anytime, but—"

"You're not throwing me out, are you?"

She put her hand over his to stop the tapping. "You can't go on like this."

"Like what?"

"You're just marking time. There's more to life."

Paul had tried for that brass ring, the elusive "more to life" people talked about, and he'd failed. Marriage, Garceau's, Randi—nothing worked. He never said that, it sounded like whining. But his mother was looking at him with such a serious expression that he decided to tell her the truth. "I don't think there is, though. I really don't."

His mother was a lanky woman with a strong, angular face, a face that was plain in one light and beautiful in another. Right now her expression was grave. "Listen to me, Paul. I know you think you've failed at things, but you've lived, that's all. You've tried. That's life. It's messy."

"Mine is anyway."

"Will you go back up north in the spring?"

"You know I took this job for the long term."

She shook her head. "Your heart is not in the back office of Jimmy's company."

"Yeah, well, it wasn't in pizzas, either."

"Are you sure?"

Paul wasn't sure. Now that Garceau's had caved in, he wasn't sure he hadn't loved the place. And after six weeks of managing Jim's paperwork, he wasn't sure his own business had been so bad. Maybe he'd paid too much attention to the downside, never gave the positives their due. He'd broken even, eaten well, been warm, had a car *and* a truck. What else had he needed? He shrugged in answer to his mother's question. "I was killing myself trying to do two jobs. The show must go on, that's what I thought. And you know what? The show doesn't have to go on. The place fell down and the world hasn't stopped."

His mother was giving him the same look she always did when he said he didn't blame himself for the accident. Her silence made him feel defensive.

"I thought you liked having me back."

She grinned. "Yes and no. It's a little like living with a caged bear."

He stared at her, speechless at the injustice of this.

She came around the table and gave him a quick hug. "Paul, Paul. What am I going to do with you?" She went into the kitchen and he heard her clanking dishes in the sink. "What about that boy you told me about whose mother's in so much trouble, and the woman who's looking after him?" she asked. "Seems to me like there are some people who need you."

Paul fiddled with the place mat. It was woven in stripes of bright pink and orange, sky blue and lime. It was cheerful, not garish. His mother had an eye for things like that. "And you don't?"

"We're fine, Paul."

"I can't go back to the prison," he said, loud enough to be sure she could hear him over the dishwater. "I can't do that."

"Of course not. But you have to do something."

He stared at the place mat. "Do I? I was thinking it's pretty easy just to float."

"You'll soon get tired of that," she called back to him cheerfully.

He raised his eyebrows at the place mat, which stared back at him blankly. *Right again, Ma.* The phone rang and his mother picked it up, and he could hear by her side of the conversation that it was good news, great news. He went in the kitchen and she grabbed him.

"Tom's coming home!" she cried, her face shining.

In McAllaster, the winter was like living in a painting. Starting at Christmas the snow poured down, and the wind blew, and the cold got deeper. By the middle of January, icebergs were building up along the shore. Madeline went to her attic windows every morning to look out over the rooftops of the tiny town huddled beside the immense lake. To the north was water for almost two hundred miles. To the south and west and east, thousands of acres of swamp and forest blanketed in snow in almost unbroken expanses.

On clear nights, she went out to see the stars, and she really could *see* them, even from her own porch in town. That never happened in Chicago. Sometimes she'd leave Greyson asleep upstairs and walk the few blocks to the beach to get an even better view. It still amazed her that all of this was safe: leaving him asleep, walking alone in the dark, wandering the beach. She was learning a few constellations: Orion and the Pleiades, Cassiopeia and the Big Dipper, which was really just part of the great bear. Often when she stepped outside she'd hear coyotes howling from a few blocks away, where town ended and the woods began. Their eerie, thrilling voices always made her shiver.

It had been exactly like this when Ada Stone lived on Stone Lake. The photos Gladys gave Madeline for Christmas, two sepia-toned prints taken at the Stone Lake lumber camp in 1933, sat in a place of honor on a bureau in the sitting room. She gazed at them again one morning after getting Greyson off to school.

How had people done it, back then? She was finding it hard going in town, with a phone and radiators and neighbors and stores. How had it been in a lumber camp? In one of the pictures, a woman, two boys, and two men stood outside a building of massive logs that was banked with snow and hung with icicles as long as a man's leg. The cabin at Stone Lake. Ada and her husband—named Emmanuel, Gladys had told her—and Joe and Walter, and another man, the cook's helper posing with a dinner horn.

Ada wore a long striped dress with an apron over it, a knit cap on her head. Her sleeves were shoved up to her elbows, and sturdy shoes peeped out from underneath her skirts. She had her arms cocked at her hips and she was grinning, her eyes bright with smartness and cheer. She leaped out of the picture like she was ready to wrestle a bear. Oh, the look of *life* in her, flashing out after all these years. Ada Stone stood out in the snow like she'd never heard the need of a coat. Madeline's great-grandmother. It was a good feeling, a *strong* feeling.

The cook's helper was slight and dark. His mouth curved up in a mischievous grin beneath a long handlebar mustache. He held the dinner horn in one hand and a great long carving knife in the other. Emmanuel was taller, broader, in a striped Mackinaw jacket belted at the waist. He stood off to the side, smiling shyly, leaning on an ax. The smaller boy sat on a wooden sled with a tin milk can on it, the other, a little older, stood beside him, his hand on the brother's shoulder. Joe and Walter. Both were bundled up in hats, scarves, thick woolen jackets, boots. Impossible to really see them, under all the layers. Where had they all gone right after the shutter had flashed? The boys down to the lake to fill the can with water? The cook's helper back inside to chop something up with that big knife? Ada off to tend the fire, roll biscuits, set places out for the crew?

The other picture was taken inside. The room was filled with benches built of planks and long tables laid with tin plates and mugs. The tables were covered with checkered oilcloths, tan and gray in the photo, but they would've been red and white in life. Madeline closed her eyes to picture the scene full of color. A moment in time when the people living it didn't think of themselves as history, antiquated and done with. They were just about to sit down and eat, that was all.

Ada was a blur, her back to the photographer as she worked at a cookstove. Emmanuel wore a battered felt hat in this picture, a ragged long-john shirt, wide-legged trousers held up by suspenders.

He held a cat up against his chest, black with white paws, and wore the same shy smile. Madeline thought, *He loves that cat.* She laid a finger on the photo, over the cat's nose. "See Marley, a cat," she said. Marley looked interestedly at her. She picked him up and went to the windows.

The skies were so beautiful, some days iron-gray and stolid, others bright, others yet celestial with pinks and lavenders and blues. The clouds were enormous. She loved to watch the weather move in from out over the lake, weather that had come from the Arctic, down through Canada, skimming across Ontario before it reached them. The break between sun and cloud was sharp and exact. She'd tried to paint it a dozen different ways and had yet to find the right one.

Most days the lake pounded in the wind, crashed up over the icebergs in plumes of freezing spray, clawed at the shore. On rare calm days it would settle to a slushy rocking. She had a map of it pinned on her bedroom wall: 350 miles long, 160 miles wide, a surface area of 31,700 square miles. The largest freshwater lake in the world, ten percent of the whole world's fresh water. Only Lake Baikal in Russia compared to it.

She was entranced by it, this inland ocean. The lake was so deep and cold and large that it created its own weather, and made a kind of weather inside Madeline, as well. A stark, beautiful weather that was unlike anything else. Intoxicating and grounding both. Just like life.

There was virtually no money coming in and she was already dipping into what she'd slated for the roof. There wasn't much in that fund. The sale of the apartment had paid for the hotel outright, with only a little left over for repairs. And now she was cold all the time and pouring heat through the building at such a rate that she was afraid her wood would run out and she wouldn't be able to pay the gas bill to run the radiators. How quickly she'd come to the same impasse as Gladys. And how swiftly her devotion had grown to match Gladys's too.

She closed the bedroom and bathroom doors to make the attic as small as possible and fed the stove logs and stared at the lake and painted through the hours Greyson was at school. When he got home, he helped refill the woodboxes and shovel paths to the doors at the hotel, and at 26 Bessel and then Mill Street, if Pete hadn't beaten them to it.

The winter seemed infinite. It was possessed of a kind of quiet Madeline had never known before. It was a quiet that gave her time to paint, and to think. Sometimes instead of drawing she'd write in her sketchbook, nothing she'd ever want anyone to see. Sometimes she wrote letters to people who could never read them—Emmy, and Joe Stone, and Jackie. One night she wrote to Paul. She wouldn't send it; it was just a way of setting down her thoughts, hopefully leaving them where they'd bother her less.

Often Greyson drew while she fixed supper in the evenings. Every time he filled up a sketchbook, she would pick up a new one for him at the variety store. Sometimes he was so compelled to keep drawing, in between pads, that she had to let him tear pages out of hers. It flattered her that he seemed to have copied this interest from her. Beyond that, she loved that he had this outlet for his thoughts and ideas and feelings. She knew how important that could be.

Jim stopped by to see Paul in the middle of January, just before the office was scheduled to reopen. He knocked on the back door and Paul let him into the kitchen and offered him a cup of coffee. Jim said no, and then yes, and bounced on the balls of his feet, and wouldn't sit down, but then did.

Paul eyed him suspiciously. "Spit it out."

"We lost the school contract."

"What do you mean, lost it? I thought it was final."

"They're canceling the job. Budget cuts."

"Hell. That's bad news."

"Real bad." Jim's leg was still jumping up and down.

"What else?" Paul said, his eyes narrowed.

Jim said that business was not so good. Way down from last year. Not as many houses going up. He'd been hoping it would turn around, expecting people to plan their new homes in the winter and line up a builder for spring. It wasn't working out, and without the school job he couldn't keep Paul on.

"You're joking. You just hired me, and now you don't have enough work?"

"It's the economy, I can't change that."

"Screw the economy. You don't have any better grip on your business than that?"

"It's nothing I have any control over. The school—"

Paul hit the table with his fist. "Screw the school. You shouldn't have brought me all the way down here based on one job. I treated part-time seasonals better than this." Jim's face turned red, and he seemed about to launch into a defense that Paul knew he couldn't stand to hear. "Forget it," he said.

"I can give you another two weeks."

"I don't want another two weeks."

"Really. That's some attitude."

"You're going to talk to me about attitude?"

"I thought I was doing you a favor with this job, man. Putting you in the office, giving you a good wage."

"A *favor*."

"Well, there was no way you were going to climb around on roofs with that leg of yours, and I always felt bad for you about that. I figured I could give you a better chance than you had anywhere else."

"A better chance."

"You can't tell me you were doing any good way up there with that pizza place. And the prison, come on. You hated that. Listen. You'll get another job. I'll give you a good recommendation. Don't be like this."

Paul stood up and opened the door. "Get out of here, Jim. And don't ever do me any favors again, you got that?"

After Jim left, Paul got in his truck and drove. He roamed all over the back roads surrounding Edwardsville, up and down the streets of the town itself, around the old two-story brick high school, through the parking lot of the A&W. He ended up finally at the curve on East Phillips Road. He coasted to a stop on the shoulder, then got out of the truck and stood on the crunchy, sun-sparkled snow.

It had been hot and muggy the day of the accident. The cicadas were rasping in the trees, and the world had seemed slow, so slow. It was summer vacation, Paul was twelve, and he was bored. He was sitting on the porch drinking Tang with ice cubes in it, reading a *Popular Mechanics*. He was supposed to be mowing the lawn, but he figured he'd do that later, when it was cooler. Suddenly there was a roar in the driveway. Manny, on his new bike. Paul dropped the magazine and ran down the steps, thinking, *Thank God, something to do, I'm saved*. The slow, dull world had burst into life.

Manny took him for a ride around the block, and then another one, and another. At first this was great, but pretty soon it was boring. "Come on, let's go somewhere," Paul had said. "Show me what this thing can do."

"Can't do it. You don't have a helmet, and this thing's not built for two."

It didn't take Paul all that long to wear him down.

They headed out into the country, going slow at first but then faster and faster, and then they came up on this curve and everything after that was a blur. Paul knew he hadn't leaned the way he should have. He knew Manny was going way too fast. God, it had been fun before it was all disaster.

He walked slowly along the curve, more aware of his limp than ever. He knew from having been told—here was where he'd been thrown, clear of the bike and clear of the trees that lined the road. Here was where Manny had landed. Hit his head, died instantly. The bike had scattered into a hundred pieces from the force of the crash. If he looked, he could probably still find a chunk of something, hidden in the gravel and weeds, twenty-four years later.

Twenty-four years he'd been limping along on his bad leg, telling himself he was a philosopher, a thinker, a student of life. What bullshit. Really he was just a man who always expected the worst.

Paul stared into the winter sun for a moment, giving himself an excuse for his watering eyes. *You're an idiot*, he said to himself, but not unkindly. He tried, but he couldn't keep tears from brimming in his eyes.

"Manny, I am sorry," he said out loud. The words vanished into the clear winter air. But it was true. Manny shouldn't have died that day. Paul shouldn't have ended up in the hospital and come out six weeks later with three pins in his leg and a burden of guilt so big he could barely drag it, and could never set it down. He was sorry, but he couldn't change the past. *We were dumb, both of us*, he thought to his cousin now. *It was an accident. A stupid, useless, unnecessary, preventable accident. It was both our faults, it was nobody's fault, it doesn't matter whose fault it was. I'm alive and you're not, and I have to accept that. It's done.*

Back at the house that night Paul sat on the couch beside his dad, turning Greyson's kaleidoscope in his hands, putting it up to his eye now and then. He pretended to watch the news. There was a letter written on a heavy piece of drawing paper in his pocket that had come in the mail that day. The address was in Greyson's hand-writing, but Madeline wrote the letter. He knew she didn't know it had been sent. He knew her. No way would she have put this in the mail.

Dear Paul, the letter said. *We miss you. That's all I'm writing to say. We're okay, but—*

> *Remember the night we carved the pumpkins? Remember how good it smelled and how you played the piano? I didn't know you could play the piano.*
>
> > *I don't know what I'm trying to say. Greyson's good, but not as good as with you here. I wish—*

The letter broke off there. There was a sketch of Paul playing the piano, Greyson beside him with a harmonica, a line of pump-kins carved with different funny faces. It made him smile.

Paul heard a vehicle pull in the drive, heard the kitchen door open and close, heard his mom talking to someone. He got up to see who it was. His nephew Tom, improbably grown into a man, a man who'd been to and returned from a war. He was thin but strong-looking, and quieter than ever. He'd been home a week now.

"Hey, Uncle Paul," Tom said.

It was always a strange feeling when his sisters' kids called him "Uncle," especially this weary soldier. "Hey. What're you up to?"

"Just came to say hi to Grandma." Tom's eyes met Paul's briefly and traveled on. He looked pale, drawn. "Guess I'll get going now."

"Don't take off," Paul said. "The last time I saw you, you were perfecting some God-awful thing you thought up, popcorn shrimp and peanut butter on a Ritz cracker, I think."

Tom's grin seemed inadvertent. "Yeah, that was pretty bad."

"I've had crazier ideas." Paul put Greyson's kaleidoscope on the counter and grabbed two beers from the fridge. "Would you believe bleu cheese is great on a pizza?"

Tom picked the kaleidoscope up and looked through it, turning the base slowly. "I ate some pretty strange stuff in Baghdad. A lot of the guys wouldn't try anything, but I figured, Hell, I was there. Might as well make some kind of sense out of it. I liked the kabobs. Good spices."

Paul's mother squeezed Tom's shoulder on her way toward the living room. "You two catch up. We'll be in watching *Jeopardy!* if you get bored."

"*What do you think* of winter now?" Mary Feather asked one morning. Madeline was in Mary's woods trying out the snowshoes she'd found in the hotel.

The sun was shining after endless days of wind and snow. The winds had blown without pause, gusting sixty miles an hour, howling around the attic and sucking the warmth out of everything. Madeline had never been so cold. For the duration of the storm she never took off her hat, indoors or out. It was a watch cap of black wool, a gift from Mabel. ("Knitted you a chook," she said at Christmas, handing the hat to Madeline without ceremony.) She stayed bundled up in long johns and the insulated Carhartt pants she'd found at the thrift shop in Crosscut, and two wool sweaters over layers of shirts. A pair of fleece-lined slippers that Arbutus and Pete gave her for Christmas had become her most prized possession, as well as her goose-down comforter. She thanked Emmy nightly for having gotten them each one, years ago.

Madeline put Emmy's blanket on Greyson's bed and he pronounced it snuggly but really he seemed unfazed by the fact that as long as the winds blew she could not get the temperature in their attic rooms much above fifty. He had grown up in this wind-battered town, and took it for granted. The fuel she burned keeping the hotel just bearable made her cringe even as she turned her hands over and over above the potbelly stoves and radiators. But even cold and worried, she could not resist the storms. She always hovered at the windows to gaze out at them, or bundled up to go out into them.

But now the most recent storm was over. She'd jumped that morning when the county truck roared by: enormous and orange, with a plow big enough to scoop up a small house. Sparks flew from the blade as it rumbled down the street. A few minutes later a deer wandered past, its delicate black hooves click-clacking on the newly scraped pavement like high heels. Now the sky was a bright, clear blue, and the wind for once was still. The temperature was only ten degrees below freezing.

"I love winter," Madeline told Mary, bending to buckle a snowshoe.

"You still think so this far in, then you'll make it," Mary said.

"Emil wants to take Greyson out rabbit hunting. I don't know if I want him to."

Mary raised her brows. "Why not? You can trust Emil with a gun, he likes to drink but he's no fool. He's hunted his whole life, made his living off it you might say, he'd never mix business with pleasure."

"It's not that so much. It's just—the idea of it. Rabbits make me think of the Easter bunny."

Mary made a dismissive noise. "Rabbits make a good stew, is what rabbits do. Here, I'll send one home for you, got it froze out here in the woodshed. You'll see."

"Oh, I don't think—"

"Try it," Mary growled. "I'll give you some venison, too. You're going to live in this country, you should eat of this country. That's what's wrong with the world today. People want to eat lettuce and tomatoes in January, I never heard of anything so foolish, the stuff's got as much taste as an old shoe."

This was true. "All right. I'll try it."

"You ever hear from that young man of yours?" Mary asked just as Madeline was about to trek away across the clearing.

"What?"

Mary made a look of impatience. "Paul Garceau."

"Ah—he's hardly mine."

"He used to come now and again, to visit. I got the idea he thought a lot of you."

Madeline felt herself flush. "I liked him too. He was good to Greyson."

"That ain't what I meant," Mary said, sounding put out.

Madeline ignored this. "He writes to Greyson, short things—cards, a note—and Grey writes back. He's so independent about it. Has to have his own envelopes and paper and stamps. I can't believe how much he's grown up just since I moved here. Paul calls every week, Greyson loves that. And Paul did send me a postcard too, I got it the other day. He's somewhere down south right now, working for the Red Cross. He and his nephew are there for a month. A hurricane ripped through someplace and they decided to go help rebuild." She shrugged at how unpredictable people's lives were.

"Bah. Don't you know life is short?"

"What?"

"Life can get lonesome on your own," Mary said in a warning way.

Madeline decided to ask a really honest question, which in her experience people usually did not do. "Has it been, for you?"

Mary looked off across the horizon. With the trees bare of leaves you could see the lake clearly. She squinted, her eyes watering a little in the cold. "Naw. I wasn't never lonely."

Madeline nodded, not believing this at all. She shifted on her snowshoes, suddenly anxious to get moving.

Gladys was behind the registration desk when Madeline got back. Greyson was on the lobby couch playing with his handheld computer, Marley tucked into his hip.

"How's it going?" Madeline plucked off her hat and ran her fingers across her scalp. She was drenched in sweat and thought of a shower pounding down on her back. But such things did not exist in the Hotel Leppinen and she'd have to be content with a soak in the tub. Maybe Pete would have time to help her install the fixtures she'd ordered to convert the taps to include a showerhead tomorrow. Maybe not, too. He and Arbutus were heading to Chicago again in a few days and were busy getting ready to go. Madeline had gotten so dependent on his help, it made her nervous to think of his being gone for that long, two weeks. She wondered how Gladys was handling it. It had to be at least twenty years since she and Arbutus had been apart as much as they had been in the last few months.

"Things are fine," Gladys answered. "Greyson got home from school about twenty minutes ago."

"Earth to Greyson," Madeline called and he nodded without

looking up from his game. Madeline sighed. "I hate that thing. He disappears into it."

"He's all right, he doesn't do it every minute. It's probably relaxing."

"Relaxing! Jabbing away at those buttons, trying to blow up something?"

Gladys shrugged. "He's good at it."

Madeline studied him. Probably Gladys was right. The toy let off a series of beeps and whirs and squeals and Greyson said, *"Yes!"*

"Any phone calls?" Madeline asked idly, not expecting any. Gladys glanced up, then looked down again to make a notation in the guest register, which was lying open before her. The journal Madeline gave her was open on the desk too, and Madeline tried to decipher a few words of upside-down writing. Gladys flicked the cover closed. "Pretty quiet," she said. "I did rent a room for tonight and tomorrow. A couple coming up to cross-country ski from downstate, I put them in Two, it's warmest, backing up to the chimneys like it does. The woman said she read your ad in the Crosscut paper, some friends had brought a copy back with them, so that wasn't a total waste of money."

"A room! You sneak! That's great."

Gladys grinned. "Guess what else I heard today?"

"What?"

"The Bensons have put the grocery up for sale. They're moving back down below. Mabel told me."

"What? Like, ten minutes ago they were buying the hotel and tearing it down for more parking."

"Mmm-hmm," Gladys said. "Isn't that the way. They come with their fancy ideas, and then pretty soon, they go."

"But why would they sell? They've only been here—what? Two

years? And they've put so much into it. And you have to admit, they've done a nice job with it."

"I imagine they figured out they're not going to make any money. No *real* money, that is." Gladys was smiling, not bothering to hide that she took pleasure in the Bensons' demise. "That's all it really took to get rid of them. The facts of life. Life here anyway."

"Huh," Madeline said. She couldn't help it, part of her felt as smug as Gladys. But another part was unexpectedly sad for the Bensons. The news that they were selling suddenly humanized them. They were just people. Sure, they were very conventional, not extra-nice people, but they'd tried to do something and found they couldn't. They'd had hopes and expectations that had been disappointed. It wasn't very hard at all to imagine herself in the same boat.

30

Valentine's Day dawned sunny in McAllaster. Greyson was at his friend Ben's, a decision Madeline agonized over a little. Ben's parents were schoolteachers. Gladys had told Madeline they'd grown up in McAllaster, been high school sweethearts, gone off to college together and got married, and returned together. It was very sweet, and Madeline found herself fascinated by such an old-fashioned love story. She was curious to meet them, and when she did, at the school Christmas pageant, she liked them. They were completely down-to-earth, vaguely hippie-ish, very friendly.

So when Greyson asked to spend the night, she knew there was no reason to say no, but she was so aware of being *responsible* for him. It was important not to be wrong. "We'll take good care of him," Ben's mother, Allison, had assured her the afternoon before, bouncing another, smaller child in a woven sling on her hip, patting her very pregnant belly, and casting a fond glance at the boys, who were sitting in front of the woodstove playing a game.

"He just seems young for a sleepover," Madeline said, trying not to sound fretful.

Allison smiled, shrugged one shoulder. "It's up to you. I promise I'll try not to go into labor."

"When are you due?"

"Two weeks. I'm set to go to the Soo two days before, but we're ready if it doesn't work out. I swear the whole ambulance corps has been boning up on how to deliver a baby."

"Aren't you scared? I mean—it's a long way to the Soo."

Allison shrugged. "I made it with these two. And like I said, we're ready. We've read everything we can. I think Kurt kind of *wants* me to deliver at home."

"Oh my God."

Allison laughed. "Well, it would be kind of fitting. *I* was born at home. My birthday's in March. I came a little early, in the middle of a blizzard. It worked out. I'm the last baby born in town, a local celebrity, didn't you know?" She grinned widely, and made a face that said *Ta-da*. Madeline liked her even more.

Greyson looked up then. "*Please*, Madeline. I promise I'll clean my room when I get home. But me and Ben want to do stuff in the morning. We're going to help feed the dogs, and go for a ride on the sled, and everything."

Well. No way could she refuse him this. Allison and Kurt kept a small team of huskies trained to pull a dogsled. So, she'd spent her first night at the hotel without him and now had the first half of the day to herself. It was odd but intoxicating. She felt giddy and gleeful from the sun as much as from the unexpected time alone. Plus she had rented four rooms—four!—over the weekend. The guests seemed happy. Charmed, even. They were a group of eight snowmobilers, four couples from Green Bay who were following the shore of Lake Superior from Big Bay to Sault Ste. Marie.

"We do it every year," one of the women told Madeline. "We make a week of it—start out at Big Bay and end up at Sugar Island. We always stop in McAllaster and this is perfect. We will definitely be back, your place is darling."

Madeline glowed. Now they'd checked out and she had the rooms to clean. She also had enough cash to pay most of the month's bills without dipping into the roof fund.

When she was done with the rooms she'd spend the rest of the morning painting. She'd finished a picture of the hotel the week before, framed it, and hung it. She didn't know if it was good or not, she couldn't decide, but one of the women in the group of eight had looked at it for a long time that morning. Then she said, "Do you ever do house portraits?"

"Ah—no. But I'll bet I could." Madeline smiled in what she hoped was a confident way.

"I'd like a picture of our cottage, it's down on Lake Michigan but I could give you photos of it. Do you work from photos?"

"I never have. But I think I could." Madeline was scrambling inside herself. Did she mean this? Did she want to do something as confining as this? Well, yes, maybe. It'd be a job. It'd be income from painting.

"What would you charge?"

"I'd have to think about that," Madeline admitted.

"Do that," the woman said. "I'll leave you my phone number."

So here was a whole new world of possibility. Ideas crowded into her head. House portraits, dog portraits, advertisements, menus, note cards—maybe there were a hundred things she could do art-work for. Maybe—maybe—this was a way to have everything: the hotel, and painting, and a living too. It was a possibility anyway.

Madeline plugged a radio into the socket in Room One and turned on a rock station out of the Soo, cranked the volume up to match her mood. She began stripping the blankets and sheets, pol-ishing the furniture and windows, rolling up the rugs to take outside and shake. She finished up that room and moved on to the next, bringing her radio and hamper and carryall of cleaning things along.

She'd just gotten started when Grand Funk Railroad came on, doing "The Loco-Motion." One of her favorite songs from childhood, a song to make you feel good. She could see Emmy and herself singing along whenever it came on, doing the Loco-Motion all over the apartment. She turned the sound up as high as it would go—she was alone, wasn't she? Who was to see or know?—and sashayed around the room feeling ridiculously happy. She polished the nightstand and sang along with energy, did the *chug-a chug-a* motion, feeling about ten. What fun they'd had. She could not have had a better mother.

Madeline sang and danced, using the dust rag as a microphone, safe in the knowledge that she was alone. No one was going to stop by looking for a room on a February Sunday at midmorning (and if they did, they weren't likely to come upstairs). Gladys and Arbutus were at church, Greyson was at Ben's, Pete was probably tinkering away at some project at Mill Street. She belted out the lyrics, pulling the sheets off the bed and bundling them into a wad. She turned to throw them into the hamper that was sitting just inside the door to find a man leaning against the doorframe. She shrieked. "Paul. My God. You scared me."

A slow smile spread over his face. His dear, dear face. Oh, Paul. He was really there. Madeline stared at him, still clutching the sheets.

"I gotta tell you, I would love to do the Loco-Motion with you," he said, his brown eyes squinted a little, gleaming with something between merriment and lecherousness.

"Paul." She felt struck dumb, unable to come up with anything beyond this.

"You looked so happy, I didn't want to stop you. Don't think I ever saw somebody look so happy over changing sheets."

"I rented out four rooms this weekend. *Four.*"

"That's great."

"What are you doing here? I can't believe you *are* here. How are you, is everything all right?"

"I'm okay. How's Greyson?"

"He's okay. He misses you."

"He always sounds good on the phone. You're good for him."

Then they were silent, studying each other.

"I liked that little dance move you were doing, that little thing with your hands," Paul said after a moment.

Madeline felt foolish and embarrassed.

"Hey," he said, seeming to see her discomfort. "I really did like it. You looked so happy. Like everything in the world was going your way."

She gave him a tentative smile. "It's a sunny day. I've got enough money to pay the bills this month, as long as nothing breaks down. And I love that song."

"Me too. Always did. It's a feel-good song." He pushed himself off the doorframe and shoved his hands in his pockets. He looked around the room, and Madeline felt awkwardness growing up between them like a tangle of brush.

"So what are you doing here?" she asked again, softly.

He looked down at his battered leather work boots. They were so familiar—she'd never thought of knowing his shoes when she worked with him, but she did. The Loco-Motion had ended and an advertisement came on the radio. Roof rakes were on sale at the Soo Lock Hardware, thirty-four ninety-nine, get yours today, pull that snow off before it builds up and caves your roof in. Madeline crossed the room and switched the power off. She and Paul stared at each other in the sudden quiet.

To Madeline he looked wonderful. He looked dear. She wanted to wrap her arms around him and hold him tight. She wanted to dispense with this absurd awkward pretense of talking and just absorb him through her skin. She could admit this now, at least to herself.

"Did you get the card I sent?" he asked.

"I did. Thank you."

Silence fell again. Paul was looking at her so oddly. Intense, hopeful, sad—she wasn't sure what the expression on his face meant.

"Why are you here?" she asked again, just as Paul said, "Listen—"

They both stopped talking, began again. "I'm just so surprised to see you," she said, as he said, "I didn't know how else to do this—"

"Do what?" she asked while he said, "Except to just show up."

She took a quick breath, let it out again. "Do what?"

Paul nodded once, as if deciding finally on some course of action. "I'm back to open up again. I got a little money from the insurance. Not enough, but we'll figure it out. Being down there, working for Jim—getting laid *off* by Jim about ten minutes after I started and him thinking he was doing me some favor—it all made me realize, this is where I want to be. This is what I want to be doing. Sure, it's never perfect, but it's mine, you know? *My* life, *my* business. And my nephew Tom's coming with me. He's going to help me put it all back together and then run the place with me. At least for a while. He was over in Iraq and he's kind of at loose ends now. Turns out he was an army cook. Can you believe I didn't even know?"

"It's easy to lose track of people." This was probably the longest speech she'd ever heard Paul make, and Madeline was startled by it. She didn't understand all of it, but that didn't matter. She was startled, and incredibly happy that he'd said, *I'm back.*

"I had some time to think. And to grow up a little, I guess—"

"You're grown up," Madeline protested, but Paul rolled on as if he didn't hear.

"The thing is—the thing is, that I—oh, hell." He crossed the few steps between them and suddenly was very near. He smelled good, of some kind of spice, or soap. His eyes were so brown, big and serious. He took her shoulders, drew her closer. He kissed her. Madeline didn't think her response through; she put her arms around him.

"I missed you," he said when they broke apart.

"I missed you too."

"All the way up, I was thinking maybe could we try—"

"Try what?" she said softly. He was only a little taller than her; their eyes were almost level.

A looked flashed across his face, a look that had hope and daring in it, but shyness too. "Being together."

"Oh." She had a sudden vision of them together in this hotel years from now. How far off that seemed, and how unlikely. But she loved his eyes, his merry smile, his way of standing. It felt that simple. Maybe it really was that simple. A smile spread across her face. "Okay."

Paul drew her close and she buried her face in his neck. "Don't go away again," he whispered.

"I didn't go, you did," she whispered back.

"But still, just don't."

Just then footsteps came pounding up the stairs and Greyson burst into the room, saying, "Madeline, guess what, me and Ben— *Paul*. Mr. Garceau! It isn't even spring yet. Cool. What time did you get here, can you eat supper with us?"

After Greyson was in bed, Paul and Madeline sat as close together as possible on the couch in her attic sitting room while he told her about his plans. He was looking forward to having Tom around; he'd be coming north in a few days. "It'll be good to have the help, good to have family here. I like him; we get along. And he needs this, I think. Needs something to do, a purpose."

"That's good."

"It is, I think. For both of us."

"You won't go back to the prison?"

"I won't live like that anymore."

"Won't it be hard without that paycheck, though? I mean, it is for me here—"

"It'll work out. I have to believe things will work out. Not always the way you think, but somehow. Like now I'm glad I have the Fairlane, because it'll just about cover the cost of a new oven."

"You're selling it?"

"Yep. Don't need it; need the oven."

Madeline nodded.

"I've been thinking maybe I'd give guitar lessons. It'd be a little extra, and I'd love doing it. Garceau's Pizzeria and Music Studio, how's that sound?"

"A little goofy. But good."

"So how about you?" he asked, taking her hand and entwining their fingers. "How's it been, your first winter?"

"Good. Pretty good."

He raised his eyebrows, and she confided the truth in a rush. "I'm scared. There's so much I have no clue about. This hotel is—" She stopped, wooshed out a huge sigh, shook her head. "It might be a pipe dream. Gladys tried to tell me, but I wouldn't listen. And so far it's been great. I mean, really amazing. I've done the work, I'm here, I'm opened up, I haven't run through all my money yet. It's winter, it's beautiful, all that's true. But at the same time, it's all a crapshoot. What will happen, will I make it?"

Paul was smiling. "Welcome to my world."

"It's terrifying."

"But you're really doing something. You're trying anyway."

"Yes, but—what if I fail?"

"You can't fail."

"That's not true!"

"You've already not failed," he said, his eyes very serious behind his glasses. Madeline wanted to kiss him for that.

"But what if I can't do it alone? This place, Greyson, everything."

"You don't have to."

Madeline stood at her windows watching the water after Paul had gone downstairs to sleep. She thought she'd make silver dollar pancakes for breakfast, with eggs and bacon. Emmy had always made silver dollar pancakes on the weekends, and Madeline would eat as many as she could hold and then one more.

She closed her eyes and was in the kitchen of the apartment in Chicago. Some nameless windy winter day, somewhere around 1984. She had feathered bangs and was wearing leg warmers and hoping against hope that Tina Petry would invite her to her birthday party. Emmy flipped the tiny pancakes and the aroma of them rose up, and she turned to smile at Madeline—

Madeline drifted in and out of time. The wind howled and the waves chopped at the shore. How she loved the lake, that strength no one could tame. The sky was somber, forbidding. It would take a lifetime to try to paint it.

She wondered if Walter was awake down in Crosscut, listening to the snow on his window. Mary would be sitting by her stove, warm as toast, and Emil would be hunkered on his bunk, drinking whiskey, Sal on her blanket on the floor beside him. Arbutus and

Pete were probably asleep by now, like Greyson, or maybe watching the eleven o'clock news on television. And Gladys—she was looking out a window at the storm, like Madeline. How like they were in some ways. Madeline took a long breath in and let it out slowly. *Emmy, Emmy,* she thought, as she so often did. A kind of peacefulness filled her.

Epilogue

One Year Later

The bay began to freeze over in the end of February, and by the first week of March there were shanties on the ice. Paul looked out the attic windows as he sipped his coffee one morning. "We should go fishing. Tom won't need me today and I don't have any lessons scheduled."

Madeline carried Marley from where he'd been napping on the rocker. Two shanties sat near shore, one bright blue, the other unpainted plywood. "Scary. Is it safe?"

Paul drew her close. "As long as you stay in the bay. You want to be careful. But yeah, those guys know what they're doing. There's probably eight, ten inches of ice. That's plenty to hold you."

Madeline started to feel excited about the idea. There were a few more people staying this year than last, but it was slow enough that she could go.

"Buddy, you want to go fishing with us? Maybe we could steal you out of school for an afternoon," Paul said when Greyson came out of his room.

Greyson shook his head. "Mrs. Callihan comes for arts and crafts today. And it's pizza at lunch."

"Oh well, then." Paul gave him a skeptical look.

"Mrs. Callihan always brings treats. Last week she brang candy bars."

"Brought," Madeline said.

Greyson shrugged. "We're making pot holders. I'll make you one, Madeline. I'm making Mom one too."

Madeline called Gladys and asked if she could come down and babysit the hotel in case someone wanted to check in or call with a reservation.

"I'll be there in fifteen minutes. Just have to get my coat on."

"You're sure? I don't want to be a bother."

"No bother," she snapped. "I ran that hotel before you were a glimmer in your mother's eye, I guess I can handle it for a few hours, and Greyson too."

"I only meant—"

"It's nothing."

"There's no hurry, I can get Grey off to school."

"That child is absolutely no trouble, we'll be fine. Maybe Butte will come down, too, I'll ask her. Either way, I'll see you in a jiffy." She slammed down the phone.

Paul was watching. "She can come, I take it?"

"Yep. Glad to. Annoyed I suggested it might be a bother."

"You've given her a new lease on life."

"She didn't need one. She *owns* life."

They loaded snowshoes into the back end of Paul's truck, as well a sled, an ice spud to chisel the hole open with, a bucket stocked with ice-fishing poles and bobbers and sinkers, and a kerosene lantern. They bought minnows and fishing licenses at the hardware, then drove to the marina.

Paul lit the lantern in the shelter of the cab, and they trekked along the shore and out across the ice. He strode along, testing the ice with the spud, and Madeline followed. Looking out toward the open water she thought they could have floated in time, landed anywhere in the last thousand years. Abruptly, Paul stopped. "Here's as good as anywhere, I guess."

He spudded the first hole in the ice and let her try the second one. It was harder than he'd made it look, but after twenty minutes of pounding she broke through, and the icy water burbled up. Paul scooped it clear with a sieve on a long handle, then tested the depth of the water with a weight on the line. He baited a hook with a minnow and squeezed a weight on the line with pliers and dropped it down the hole, then attached a bobber. "You do the other one." Madeline did, balking a little at stabbing the minnow onto the hook.

"Now what?"

"Now we wait."

The bobbers floated in the holes. Water froze on the lines, which made a tiny scritchling noise as they fluttered in the breeze. Madeline's face got cold, and she turned her back to the wind. Now and then they warmed their hands around the glass globe of the hissing lantern.

"So, how's married life treating you?" he asked at one point.

Madeline grinned. "Not bad. Survived the first year, almost."

They'd gotten married in April at the courthouse in Crosscut. They had a reception at the hotel and invited everyone: Paul's family, everyone they knew in McAllaster and Crosscut, all their friends from everywhere. Madeline started crying when Dwayne and Estelle and Candice walked in. Dwayne grinned and picked her up for a hug and told her to stop bawling or they'd turn right back around for Chicago. Ted and Lisa Braith brought Walter, who sat tapping his foot to the music and smiling at everyone all afternoon.

Time had flown by since then. The summer and fall had disappeared in a haze of work, but the winter was theirs.

Paul trained his gaze on the bobbers again. Madeline squatted down and warmed her hands around the lantern.

"Randi's coming up for a parole review, eh?"

Madeline nodded, but she didn't want to think about it. The trial had happened in June and Randi'd gotten a year in the county jail. Maybe she'd only serve part of that before they let her come home.

"She'll want Grey back when she gets out."

Madeline squinted off across the lake. The wind made snow dervishes rise in swirls up off the ice. "I know."

"She's better with him lately."

"Yeah. Better." Randi wrote Greyson letters, made him things in the craft shop. She was allowed to go out in the yard with him—she was using a walker now—to play games and visit in an open room, and she was more herself again, tickling and hugging him to make him giggle, calling him her little man.

"Maybe she'll let him stay with us some. Or even, I don't know, a lot. I mean, if that's what you want."

"You know it is. But it might not be what he wants. I mean, it probably isn't. And that's—" Madeline couldn't bring herself to say, *That's okay.* She loved Greyson. And he loved them, but when Randi was back, he would want to go home. It was inevitable, it was probably—maybe—even right, but the thought broke her heart.

"It'll work out," he said. Madeline wished she could share his certainty. The fishing lines fluttered in the breeze, the bobbers bobbed. She hunkered down, stared across the horizon. Felt the vast cold world spread out all around her and was reassured by the impersonality of it. This land—wild and serene, huge, ruthless and gentle by turns, was always unconcerned with her, small Madeline who was a tiny dot on its landscape for a moment in time. It reminded her over and over that there was only now. The future would come, unfolding itself as it did.

"It will," he said, giving her a funny little smile. "Things do. Not the way you expect, but still all right."

"Yeah. Maybe."

Paul studied her a moment and then shuffled through his layers of clothes for a pocket, fished around for something, and came up with a folded piece of paper. He handed it to her. She unfolded it and frowned, not remembering at first, and then remembering and being baffled. It was a letter. *Dear Paul*, it said. *We miss you. That's all I'm writing to say. We're okay, but—*

"Where'd you get this?"

"Greyson sent it to me. Last year before I came back."

"How did he get it?"

Paul shrugged. "Don't know. But things do work out."

Madeline decided it would be silly to be embarrassed by this revealing letter now. After all, things had worked out. And Greyson—what nerve. She smiled to herself. She read the letter, studied the little drawings. They were pretty good, she could see from this remove of a little more than a year. They had charm. They gave her an idea for the book she was going to illustrate. It was a self-published thing a woman in town had done, nothing big, but she liked the story and it would pay a little.

An hour passed. Her feet began to get very cold. She wondered when they would eat the sack lunch they'd packed.

"*Hey,*" Paul hissed. "Look."

The bobber quivered, then dipped down into the water. Paul grabbed the pole from where he propped it in the snow, fed out a little line. The bobber rose and dipped again, faster and deeper. Madeline stared at it, transfixed. The possibility that they might catch their dinner galvanized her. She glanced up at Paul and saw a look of concentrated glee on his face. She watched in anticipation for what would happen next.

ACKNOWLEDGMENTS

McAllaster is a fictional town, but it's like the one I live in—a small village in an isolated spot along Lake Superior—so I'd first like to thank Grand Marais, just for being itself. Also my thanks to the Gitche Gumee, the Big Water that makes life so special here.

Midway through writing this book, I started doing interviews with some of the elderly people in town and writing their stories for the local newspaper. I want to thank those people for sharing their lives and outlooks with me. This novel became something I was doing for them, in many ways. If I could create a character or two who hinted at their great reserves of strength, acceptance, and humor, I would have done something worthwhile. They inspired me to keep working.

Yale Bailey, b. January 1, 1918, Manistique, Michigan.

Isabella "Bess" Capogrossa, b. June 19, 1911, London, England.

Bruce Erickson, b. January 25, 1932, Grand Marais, Michigan.

Nelmi Hermanson, b. May 25, 1910, Grand Marais, Michigan, d. June 6, 2008.

Bill LaCombe, b. August 7, 1917, Grand Marais, Michigan, d. February 18, 2009.

Aino Schultz, b. October 10, 1913, Grand Marais, Michigan, d. June 20, 2009.

Ted Soldenski, b. December 29, 1912, Grand Marais, Michigan, d. February 22, 2008.

Evelyn "Tudy" Tornovish, b. June 1, 1916, Grand Marais, Michigan, d. March 3, 2010.

Evelyn Wood, b. September 1939, Petersburg, Michigan.

Many people have shared their stories and memories with me over the years (mostly over coffee), and I thank all of them. But also particular thanks to:

Bill Bailey and Al Tornovish, for many memorable phrases, including "Always been broke flatter than piss on a platter."

Jack and Mary Alice Johnson, for telling me about Sweet White Birch Vitamins and Minerals, and for letting me consult on all things Finnish. Also thanks to Jack for keeping the whole show running by fixing everything from Jeeps to espresso machines.

Also special thanks to:

Rich Anderson, for a tour through the Hotel Nettleton.

Stan Bontrager, for miraculous technical support.

Ilsa Brink, for a lovely website.

Rebecca Fuge, for photographs that I love.

Kristen Hurlin, for insight into an artist's life.

Steve O'Connell, for building the office.

George VanderHaag, for decades of hard work and fine produce, plus permission to put a produce man much like him in the book.

The West Bay Diner crew of 2010, for going the extra mile on top of all the normal extra miles, so that I could take care of not only the diner but also the book: Laura Bontrager, Amelia Brubaker, Rebecca Fuge, Jamie Hersman, Jenna Hoop, Meghan Malone, Patience Neville-Neil, and Terri Poliuto.

Our friends and customers at the West Bay Diner, for their enormous enthusiasm and support.

A number of friends read this book in manuscript form and gave me valuable insights and encouragement. Thanks to Jean Battle, John Battle, Karen Cody, Tom and Debbie Darling, and Sarah Miller. Jean in particular read this story more times than any civilian should have to, and read like a professional editor—her contribution was significant. I'd also like to thank Lisa Snapp for her years of friendship and reading.

Peta Nightingale's interest in the manuscript from afar—London, England—was heartening at a crucial time, and her input was invaluable to the story's development.

I want to thank Caroline Upcher for her editorial work with me, for her admiration of Gladys, and for going beyond the call of duty on my behalf.

My undying affection goes to Joy Harris and all at the Joy Harris Literary Agency. Special thanks to Sarah Twombly for the title.

Similar affection and regard to Sarah McGrath and Sarah Stein at Riverhead, and to everyone at Penguin who had a hand in building this book.

And now for the family . . .

My mother encouraged me as she always has in every endeavor.

My father held an unshakeable conviction that I was a writer from the get-go.

Mark was one of the earliest readers of this novel, and he understood what I was getting at right away—he always does—which was heartening through the years of work that followed.

Mariann has always been a tireless listener and reader, and her ways of helping are too various to list. On top of this she sends packages full of things I need.

Matt takes a serious interest in my work and offers comments that get right to the heart of the matter.

Peg has been a great listener and friend, happy for me in whatever makes me happy.

And finally my love and gratitude to my husband, Eric, who has always understood my hunger to write.

Airgood, Ellen.
South of superior.

$25.95

DATE	
JUL 07 2011	JAN 03 2012
JUL 15 2011	JAN 26 2012
JUL 29 2011	FEB 03 2012
AUG 23 2011	MAR 09 2012
SEP 16 2011	APR 27 2012
OCT 07 2011	JUL 20 2012
OCT 18 2011	